The bronze giant, who with his five aides became world famous, whose name was as well known in the far regions of China and the jungles of Africa as in the skyscrapers of New York.

There were stories of Doc Savage's almost incredible strength; of his amazing scientific discoveries of strange weapons and dangerous exploits.

Doc had dedicated his life to aiding those faced by dangers with which they could not cope.

His name brought fear to those who sought to prey upon the unsuspecting. His name was praised by thousands he had saved.

DOC SAVAGE'S AMAZING CREW

"Ham," Brigadier General Theodore Marley Brooks, was never without his ominous, black sword cane.

"Monk," Lieutenant Colonel Andrew Blodgett Mayfair, just over five feet tall, yet over 260 pounds. His brutish exterior concealed the mind of a great scientist.

"Renny," Colonel John Renwick, his favorite sport was pounding his massive fists through heavy, paneled doors.

"Long Tom," Major Thomas J. Roberts, was the physical weakling of the crowd, but a genius at electricity.

"Johnny," William Harper Littlejohn, the scientist and greatest living expert on geology and archaeology.

**WITH THEIR LEADER, THEY WOULD
GO ANYWHERE, FIGHT ANYONE,
DARE EVERYTHING—SEEKING EXCITEMENT
AND PERIOLOUS ADVENTURE!**

Five Complete Adventures in One Volume

No Light to Die By

The Monkey Suit

Let's Kill Ames

Once Over Lightly

I Died Yesterday

Kenneth Robeson

BANTAM BOOKS
TORONTO · NEW YORK · LONDON · SYDNEY · AUCKLAND

NO LIGHT TO DIE BY, THE MONKEY SUIT, LET'S KILL AMES, ONCE OVER LIGHTLY, I DIED YESTERDAY

A Bantam Book / published by arrangement with Condé Nast Publications, Inc.

PRINTING HISTORY

No Light to Die By *was originally published in* Doc Savage *magazine, May-June 1947. Copyright 1947 by Street and Smith Publications, Inc. Copyright © renewed 1975 by The Condé Nast Publications, Inc.*

The Monkey Suit *was originally published in* Doc Savage *magazine, July-August 1947. Copyright 1947 by Street and Smith Publications, Inc. Copyright © renewed 1975 by The Condé Nast Publications, Inc.*

Let's Kill Ames *was originally published in* Doc Savage *magazine, September-October 1947. Copyright 1947 by Street and Smith Publications, Inc. Copyright © renewed 1975 by The Condé Nast Publications, Inc.*

Once Over Lightly *was originally published in* Doc Savage *magazine, November-December 1947. Copyright 1947 by Street and Smith Publications, Inc. Copyright © renewed 1975 by The Condé Nast Publications, Inc.*

I Died Yesterday *was originally published in* Doc Savage *magazine, January-February 1948. Copyright 1948 by Street and Smith Publications, Inc. Copyright © renewed 1976 by The Condé Nast Publications, Inc.*

Bantam edition / February 1988

Bantam Books are published by Bantam Books, a division of Bantam Doubleday Dell Publishing Group, Inc. Its trademark, consisting of the words "Bantam Books" and the portrayal of a rooster, is Registered in U.S. Patent and Trademark Office and in other countries. Marca Registrada. Bantam Books, 666 Fifth Avenue, New York, New York 10103.

Contents

NO LIGHT TO DIE BY

FOREWORD

By chance just now I found in an old notebook an entry that reads: *This thing started Nov. 12, 1932*, This brusque notation, it so happens, was made the day the writing of the first Doc Savage novel began. . . . If you'll notice the year—1932—you will see that it was fourteen years ago. Fourteen years is a long time, and from it we get, by multiplying, one hundred and sixty-eight months, which is about the number of book-length Doc Savage novels that have come from this typewriter. One hundred and sixty-eight.

Now, these novels were author-told. They were written as authors tell a story. They were narratives by Kenneth Robeson about an extraordinary character named Doc Savage and a few of his friends.

If this is boring you already, I'll get to the point, and say that in a hundred and sixty-eight stories Doc Savage has been presented as Kenneth Robeson saw him. . . . Now we're going to have a look at Doc Savage as a young fellow named Sammy Wales sees him.

I'm not sure you're going to like Sammy Wales. Sammy may shock you. Sammy doesn't always see Doc Savage the way Kenneth Robeson saw him, for Sammy is an individual with notions of his own. Sammy's not an outstanding guy, and in some ways he is a bit of a heel. He's no hero, but your sister would be safe with him unless he out-talked her. Sammy would return your lost pocketbook if he found it, but brother, how he'd hate to. A dollar an hour looks like darn good wages to Sammy, and a hundred bucks is a lot of dough. Sammy could be the guy you buy your gasoline from, or the fellow who sells you your shirts. But you'll meet Sammy Wales in a moment. . . .

Incidentally, Sammy Wales can put words together, even if he isn't too literary, I think you'll discover.

—KENNETH ROBESON

3

ROBESON, NEW YORK
DISAPPROVE OF THE IDEA. SORRY.

SAVAGE

SAVAGE, LONDON
SAMMY IS BULLHEADED ABOUT THIS. HE IS GOING TO
PUBLISH MANUSCRIPT. WON'T LISTEN TO ME. SAYS HE
NEEDS THE MONEY.

ROBESON.

ROBESON, NEW YORK
BUY THE MANUSCRIPT OFF HIM. BURN IT.

SAVAGE.

SAVAGE, LONDON
SAMMY WON'T SELL. SAYS THE PUBLIC SHOULD KNOW
THE TRUTH ABOUT DOC SAVAGE.

ROBESON.

ROBESON, NEW YORK
THAT'S WHAT I WAS AFRAID OF. I'LL WRITE SAMMY.

SAVAGE.

MEMO FROM THE DESK
OF DOC SAVAGE:
To: Sammy Wales.

Mr. Kenneth Robeson, the author, advises me that
you have written a first-person account of a recent
adventure which brought you in contact with myself
and my group of aides. He states that you intend
seeking a publisher for this manuscript, and that
you have refused to sell it to him. I disapprove of
this. It is true that Kenneth Robeson has written a
hundred and sixty-eight novels around the adventures of our group, but these were fictionized ver-
sions and in no way hampered our work. It is not
satisfactory to me to permit publication of an ac-

count written by an unskilled outsider. I hope you will drop the matter.

SAVAGE.

RADIOGRAM

SAVAGE, PARIS

WHO'S UNSKILLED? AND WHO IS AN OUTSIDER? I WAS THERE WASN'T I? THIS GUY ROBESON IS A FICTION WRITER ALL RIGHT. I HAVE READ SOME OF HIS STUFF AND HE SOFT-PEDALS TOO MANY FACTS. I THINK WHAT I'VE WRITTEN SHOULD BE PRINTED.

SAMMY WALES.

RADIOGRAM

WALES, NEW YORK

HOW DID YOU KNOW I WAS IN PARIS?

SAVAGE.

SAVAGE, CAIRO

A LITTLE BIRD TOLD ME.

SAMMY WALES.

MONK MAYFAIR, NEW YORK

IF YOU ARE THE BIRD TELLING SAMMY WALES THINGS, CUT IT OUT.

SAVAGE.

SAVAGE, BOMBAY

SO THAT'S WHY THAT PRETTY FIANCÉE OF HIS GAVE ME A DATE.

MONK MAYFAIR.

CABLEGRAM

ROBESON, NEW YORK

DO NOT UNDERSTAND SAMMY WALES ATTITUDE. WILL YOU ASCERTAIN HIS TRUE REASONS FOR WISHING MATERIAL PUBLISHED. CABLE ME SHANGHAI.

SAVAGE.

RADIOGRAM

SAVAGE, SHANGHAI

SAMMY FEELS TRUTH ABOUT YOU SHOULD BE KNOWN. SEEMS SINCERE. SAYS IT WILL SCARE SOME PEOPLE WHO NEED SCARING.

ROBESON.

RADIOGRAM

ROBESON, NEW YORK
IT SCARES ME ANYWAY. WHAT IS YOUR OPINION OF
SAMMY'S MANUSCRIPT?

SAVAGE.

SAVAGE, SHANGHAI
I THINK SAMMY AS A WRITER IS NO SHAKESPEARE. BUT
HIS INTENTIONS GOOD. CAN MAKE DEAL TO PUBLISH
MANUSCRIPT IN MAGAZINE. SUGGEST DO SO. SUGGEST
YOU BREAK ALL PRECEDENT AND GIVE PERSONAL
STATEMENT TO BE PUBLISHED. THIS IS ONLY OUT I SEE.

ROBESON.

CABLEGRAM

ROBESON, NEW YORK
HAVE READ SAMMY WALES MANUSCRIPT. SHAKESPEARE
WILL SPIN IN GRAVE. SO WILL I IF I EVER REMEMBER
THIS. STATEMENT FOR PUBLICATION FOLLOWS AIRMAIL.

SAVAGE.

STATEMENT BY DOC SAVAGE

You are about to read a manuscript written by a young
man named Sammy Wales. Quite probably you have never
heard of Mr. Wales. I certainly had not heard of him until
quite recently when the incidents described in his writings
occurred. Sammy seems to feel what happened was extremely fantastic and exciting. It was.

But Sammy Wales has made a mistake—he has told about
what happened, and neglected *why* it happened. Perhaps that is
not Sammy's fault. He knows me only from what he saw me do.
He knows the whole world, really, only from what he has seen it
do to him and to others. You'll have to look deep into Sammy to
see it, but I think Sammy has a universal fear.

Who can blame Sammy Wales for being afraid? These
are the days when all brave men tremble a little for the future
of humanity. And no wonder! There has just swept over the
world an epidemic of unworkable schemes derived from

Hitler, Mussolini, a poison gas thrown into our minds by theorists and demagogues, by tyrants and rascals. Wasn't it Doctor Johnson who wrote, "Patriotism is the last refuge of a scoundrel." Thirty years ago they were beginning a great war to save liberty. We have just finished another. And yet I dare you to show me a square foot on the earth's surface where liberty is safe today.

Don't misunderstand me! I have faith. I think I know why we are afraid, too. I think it is change that has terrified us. Changes always breed fear, and that is good, because a change is a dangerous thing, not to be avoided, but to be approached warily. And any kind of changing that destroys is particularly vicious. Destruction, like death, is so permanent. And the professional wreckers of houses are almost never the men who build homes.

Have you heard anybody, when speaking of crime, of deplorable government, say: *But what can just one guy do?* Certainly you've heard that. You've heard it many times. And each time it was the voice of cowardice that spoke. Speak out, my friend, and speak out firmly, and you will find that you are the multitude. When you let a bad thing happen to you, you have it coming to you.

One thing I can say for Sammy Wales—he speaks and acts with the courage of his convictions. I admire that in him, although Sammy has certain other deplorable traits.

Sammy Wales, as you will see, is perfectly willing to fight single-handed against anything he dislikes, or for anything he likes.

That has been my creed, too. I had the fortune, or misfortune, to receive an odd training as a youth. My father, victimized by criminals, imagined that he could turn me into a sort of modern Galahad who would sally out against all wrongdoers who were outside the law, and who would aid the oppressed. My father, before his death, outlined a stringent course of training in which I was placed in the hands of a series of scientists, criminologists, physical culture experts, psychiatrists—I won't bore you with an endless list of these experts, but they had me in their hands from the time I was fourteen months old until I was twenty years old—so that I might be fitted for this career of righting wrongs and punishing evildoers. I chose medicine and surgery for specializing, largely because the understanding of human beings that a doctor has fitted in with the other, and because I liked it.

This training, foresight of my father's imagination, equipped me with many skills, mental, physical and scientific. There is no point in being modest about that. If you study and practice many things, you become adept at many things. The only remarkable thing about me is that I have worked like the dickens to master some skills. You'll be surprised at what patient and continual trying can accomplish.

You see, I believe in trying.

There is where Sammy Wales missed the boat in this account he has written. He has not painted me as an individual who has earned whatever abilities he has the hard way—and there is no other way—by repeatedly trying. Sammy seems to frankly believe that the strong things in life are passed out ready-made, instead of being created by the individual within himself.

Sammy should have told more about *why* things happened. Sammy himself is a changed man—not yet changed as much as might be desirable, however. He hardly mentions this change in himself, possibly because he does not fully grasp it—yet surely he could understand such an important thing as a man acquiring a purpose in life, when the man is himself. But Sammy glides over this; he is too much interested in the action of events, rather than their causes.

He should at least have stated the philosophy that society prepares the crime and the criminals only commit it, and that each individual is a part of society, and indeed he is that society. . . .

CLARK SAVAGE, JR.

THE SAMMY WALES MANUSCRIPT

I

The telephone had a voice like a truckload of coal banging down a tin chute, straight into my ear. My head felt just about big enough to hold a truckload of coal, too.

It was probably a beautiful morning outdoors, for the sunlight stood through the hotel room window in bright hard bars and dust mice rode up and down them. I rolled over and took hold of the telephone very gently, before it killed me, and answered. The voice that came out of the receiver was as sweet as honey on ice cream. It said: "I want the moonlight man."

"Who?"

There was some kind of a conference at the other end of the wire. I thought that a male voice addressed lovely-voice sharply. Then lovely-voice said, "Hello?"

"Yeah?"

"Is this Mr. Samuel Wales speaking?"

"Who wants to know?"

She did not have to confer about that, but it stopped her short for a moment and put a bit of vinegar in her honey voice. About a drop of vinegar to a barrelful of nectar. She said: "This is Miss Fenisong speaking. Is Mr. Wales there?"

"Partly so, I would say," I said.

I didn't know any Miss Fenisongs yet.

"May I speak to Mr. Wales?" she said.

"You are."

"Oh," she said. "Oh, indeed! ... You are Mr. Wales, the expert on moonlight?"

"Expert on what?"

"Moonlight."

That sort of had me going. It couldn't be a gag because I wasn't aware that I knew anyone in New York City. To a lovely voice like that and to such a question, what was there to say?

"It could be, Miss Fenisong. It could be."

"Are you free this afternoon, Mr. Wales?"

"Is there a moon in the afternoon?"

She laughed heh-heh to show that she didn't think I was very funny, but she was willing to be agreeable. "Say about three, then. Is that satisfactory?"

"Why not lunch? Why wait?"

"Well..."

While she was considering, I saw my pants hanging over the back of a chair, the right hip pocket weighted down by a big fat billfold that was stuffed, as my billfolds usually are, with everything but money. There were nine one-dollar bills in it, and there weren't any more in the world, I was beginning to figure.

"Maybe we'd better skip the lunch," I said.

"Very well," she said. "Three o'clock, then."

"What address?"

"The *Parkside-Regent*," she said. "Goodbye."

I put the telephone on its cradle and laid my headache back on the pillow as gently as possible. The headache was a dog. It was one of those things where your temples bulge out about a foot each time your heart beats. But it wasn't an entirely unforseen headache, because missing three meals in a row invariably produces such an effect on me. The trouble was, the cheapest meal I had seen on a menu last night was a dollar forty. With only nine paper dollars between me and poverty, I wasn't shooting any dollar forty on dinner.

So now I was an expert on moonlight. . . . This very unusual fact wouldn't let me sleep again. I tried going into the bathroom and getting a drink of water that tasted from standing in pipes, then sitting on the edge of the bed and holding my face with both hands. It didn't help. No good. I would have to eat.

The telephone operator was cooperative when I got hold of her a minute later. She said: "Mr. Samuel Wales is in four-twelve. Oh! . . . Oh, that's you, isn't it?"

"What about another Mr. Samuel Wales? Have you got another one of us?"

After she had probably consulted whatever it is that operators in big hotels use to keep track of the guests, she said, "A Mr. Samuel Wickert Wales is registered in sixteen-forty."

"Will you ring him?"

"Yes, Mr. Wales. I'll ring the other Mr. Wales."

He didn't answer.

So that was that. There had been an error. The expert on moonlight wasn't the Sammy Wales who had a headache from hunger. I would have called lovely-voice and told her about it, but that would have cost a nickel. A dime, probably.

I should have let it go at that. I thought I had.

Putting on two suits of clothes, I went out to look for a cheap breakfast. Wearing the two suits was a precaution, because it looked as if I was going to have to beat that hotel bill.

In Grand Central Station, in the men's room, I took off both suits, put the one that was not wrinkled back on, and made a bundle of the other one and gave it to one of those locker contraptions that keep your stuff twenty-four hours for a dime. I had an old slot-machine slug that would exactly fit.

A cheap breakfast in New York wasn't easy to find. I didn't know the town, and must have walked the wrong directions, because I did not come upon any part of the town that looked cheap. I finally compromised on an Automat. There at least you get a preview of the size of the portions your money is going to buy. The girl who skillfully slung out nickels and dimes for one of my dollars said, "Thank you," in a voice that reminded me of Miss Fenisong, who wanted a man who knew about moonlight.

I sat there at the little marble-topped table with its puddle of coffee that another diner's cup had left and its bread-crust crumbs and ate my thirty cents worth with great care. Then I sat there some more. I hadn't had spaghetti, but there was a spaghetti worm about an inch long lying on the table. I didn't know why I was sitting there until it dawned on me that I was listening to the voices from the other tables, just to see whether there was another voice that sounded as nice as lovely-voice.

Three employment agencies took my name, two employers expressed no interest in hiring me, and at three o'clock I turned up at the *Parkside-Regent* to find out what went with that voice.

It was easy to see what went with the *Parkside-Regent Hotel*. Probably a minimum bill of fifteen bucks a day.

She invited me into her sitting-room. She said: "Come in, Mr. Wales. I'm awfully glad you're here."

So was I glad. This might be a very temporary visit, but already it was definitely a pay-off. I had known there were people like her, because I go to the movies. I had supposed there might be hotel suites as fancy as this one was, for the same reason.

"You don't need a moon," I said.

She didn't warm up very well to that. I was sorry about this, because I was doing my awed best to pay tribute to a masterpiece. It wasn't just that she was tall, blonde, peach-colored, although even that was a little like describing a mansion by saying it was a house. It was the plus details that were important; an air of quietly drawn reserve, for example, that probably indicated no great emotional need of being surrounded by others, which might mean a little inhibition. But who wanted to be psychological about Miss Fenisong. With that figure!

A trim, dark-haired man sat in a chair holding a cigarette in a holder that was long and as white as a tooth. He looked a little too wide for his suit.

"Mr. Albert Gross," she said.

We didn't shake hands. I wondered if we took such a sudden dislike to each other for the same reason.

"So you're Samuel Wales, the moon expert," he said.

"My name is Wales," I said. "But it so happens—"

"Make it snappy, will you," he said sharply. "We haven't got much time."

Miss Fenisong said, "Mr. Wales, would twenty dollars be a satisfactory fee?"

"Twenty dollars would satisfy me plenty," I said. "But I'm afraid—"

"Give him fifty bucks, baby," Albert Gross said. "We haven't got time to fool around."

"Look," I said. "It so happens that—"

"What the hell's the matter with you?" he complained. "Do you want fifty bucks or don't you?"

"Albert!" the girl said. She seemed to think he was making an ape of himself, which he was.

I didn't like him well enough to let him keep his money.

"Sure I want fifty bucks," I said, and went over and shoved my hand out to him, and added, "As long as it comes from you, and not her."

"What's the damned difference—"

"From you and not her," I said.

He counted out five tens and I took it. I might give it back to him after letting him know he had paid out to the wrong Samuel Wales. But again, if I got to disliking him much worse, I might not.

That seemed to settle things down temporarily.

For about forty-five seconds, that is. Long enough for Miss Fenisong to take my hat and place it on a table, and seat me in an overstuffed chair and ask, "Shall we start at once?"

"Why not?"

She seated herself on a straighter chair, and she became a fairy princess on a fairy throne. She had a notebook and pencil in her hands. She was going to take notes on my words.

She said, "I have backgrounded myself fairly completely."

That was good to know. Such a lovely one should have a nice background. I said it was good.

"Good," I said.

She said, "What I want to ask you about is the Eber idea of starting with a preliminary lunar theory solution in which the orbit is supposed to lie in the ecliptic and to have no eccentricity, then finding the additional terms which depend on the first power of the eccentricities and of the inclination."

"What?" I said.

"Do you agree with Eber?" she asked.

"Who is he?" I asked.

Her smile was strictly not from the heart. "You have a sense of humor, Mr. Wales," she said. "But, really, we are pressed for time. So if you will kindly coach me on the matters I wish to know, I'd appreciate it."

Apparently it was coaching she wanted, but she was out of my pond. I would have loved to explain to her about moonlight, as who wouldn't, but it seemed that it was lunar theory she was interested in. Lunar theory probably had to do with the moon. More than that about lunar theory, I didn't know.

"I'm sorry I haven't met this Eber," I said. "I'm sorry about that, indeed I am."

The pencil stood up straight and astonished in her fingers. "What do you mean?"

"I'm afraid I'm just plain Sammy Wales. Lunar theories are out of my line."

"You're not Samuel Wickert Wales, astrophysicist at the Compton Observatory?"

"I came here to tell you I'm not."

Trim-and-dark-haired put down his cigarette holder that was the color of a hound tooth. He came over and hit me on the head.

He used an ash-tray. It was a sort of surprise; he did not look like that kind of a fellow, although in looking back I can see that he had talked like that kind of a fellow. He came at me silently; he was there before anything could be done about it.

The ash-tray was a heavy thing of crockery, about a foot across, an inch thick, glazed and almost like glass. It broke. He picked up one of the larger broken pieces, and prepared to cut my throat with it. Possibly he was not in earnest about the throat-cutting, and only wanted to distract my attention enough that he could kick me in the stomach, which was what happened.

The carpet nap against my face was thick and soft and did not smell of dust. It was the first carpet my face had been on that did not smell of dust. I lay still, but watched him with my one eye that had him in range. He was as disgusted as a dowager who had cracked her lorgnette.

He told Miss Fenisong: "You've made some kind of a stupid mistake."

She didn't say anything. She looked scared.

He added: "This bum isn't your moon man. I wonder what happened?" He scowled, didn't wait for her to answer, and continued, "Well, there's no time left to fix it up. The reception begins at five, so you'll have to go on and do your best. Do you think you can get by with what you already know?"

Her voice was high and scared, like a cat on a tall pole. "Why did you hit him?" she asked.

He yelled: "Do you think you can get by?" He sounded like the dog that had chased the cat.

She was silent. She was looking at me and anxiety was taking her lips away from her nice teeth.

"Answer me!" he bellowed.

She didn't.

He got even with her by moving over and aiming a kick at my face. But I'd had time to rest and organize. I got his foot, gathered it in my arms like a football, and tried to turn a cartwheel, but his leg was rubbery and wouldn't break. He made, in pain, a large hissing noise, and I climbed up the front of him, trying to take an arm off him, or at least a nose or an ear. All I got was the front of his coat. It tore off. He had paid his tailor probably two hundred dollars for the coat, and I took the front of it off him like stripping one peel off a banana. He didn't like that.

"You dirty thug!" he said.

I whipped him in the face with the coat rag, the way you would use a dishrag on a naughty dog. He went back a few paces on his heels. There was a large cut-glass vase on a gilded wood French side table, and he took the vase, rapped it on the table to break it and get a cutting edge of glass, and made for me. I made for the door and got through it into the hall and got the door closed.

He didn't come out into the hall. Presently the key turned in the door lock.

"Come out and fight like a man, you dirty-so-and-so," I said.

"Beat it, bum," his voice said.

"Miss Fenisong," I said.

She didn't answer.

I said: "I'm sorry about the mix-up, Miss Fenisong. There were two Wales registered at the hotel and you got the wrong one this morning, which was me. I was groggy with sleep and didn't get it straightened out at that time. I really came around just now to square it."

"Scram," he said.

On the way to the elevator. I threw the part of his coat I had taken into a corner. . . . But I went back and picked it up and examined the pockets. There were three engraved invitations that read:

> *You are cordially invited to a Reception honoring the esteemed Isotopist, Professor Enri Baedeker, at the Parkside-Regent Friday, 5 p.m.*
> *Doctor Morand Funk Hodges, Chairman.*

Scripted in ink at the foot of the invitation was this additional information:

> *The celebrities present will include Clark Savage, Jr. (Doc Savage).*

I didn't know what an isotopist was, and had never heard of Professor Baedeker or Doctor Hodges. . . . It seemed to me that the other name, Doc Savage, should be vaguely familiar, perhaps mean something, but I couldn't quite place it.

The shindig was this afternoon.

II

I had his fifty dollars, anyway.

Even the washrooms in the *Parkside-Regent* were as regal as such a place could conveniently be, and apparently it was not unusual for a guest to come in and repair minor physical damages. I was treated very discreetly by the attendant; he pretended he could see no evidence whatever that I had been in a fight. I was tempted to hand him one of Mr. Albert Gross' ten-dollar bills, an impulse that was overcome easily.

Repaired and enraged, I sat in the lobby. There is nothing quite as full-blown as the kind of anger that you have righteously after you have come out of a mess second-best. Particularly if it follows something that swatted you without just cause. Admittedly I wasn't the moon expert, but that didn't seem to me like a good reason to be hit over the head and kicked in the middle.

After sitting in the elegant hotel lobby for a while, I began to get the feel of the place enough to see that something out of the ordinary was happening. Men were arriving, were getting a lot of attention, getting ohs and ahs of wonder, were being put in a private elevator and whisked aloft somewhere.

Presently there was a particularly violent spell of gasping and eye-popping. A very large man who had just entered was the cause of this. I stood up to look. He was large, all right, but not in the sense that you mean fat when you say large.

This was a giant bronze man, so excellently proportioned that his size wouldn't have been jarring if he hadn't been near other men. He was good-looking, not pretty-handsome in any sense, but really something to look at and impress. He seemed a little embarrassed by the twittering and finger-pointing. Moving as easily as if he was on oiled bearings, he went to the special elevator and was taken up.

"Who's that?" I asked a fat man.

"That," said the man pompously, "is Doc Savage."

"And who is Doc Savage?" I inquired.

The fat man stared at me as if I had not heard of Christopher Columbus, the New Deal, and night and day.

"A poor joke, sir!" he said, and walked off.

I asked a bellhop, and he said, "Doc Savage? He's the big shot they're all coming to see. I wish to God I could get an autograph off him."

"What does he do?"

"Savage? He rights wrongs and punishes evildoers."

I looked to see if the lad was ribbing me. The expression on his face was as serious and admiring as that of a pickaninny who had just touched Joe Louis.

"He shouldn't lack for business in this world," I said.

The bellhop sighed loudly.

I asked: "Are you serious?"

He just looked me up and down and walked off, the way you would leave a stray dog after you found fleas on it.

I thought I would sit in on this Reception upstairs, whatever it was.

Now, I always have a reason for everything I do. Sometimes the reasons don't satisfy anyone but me, but that's all right with me. In this case, I felt a little guilty about embarrassing lovely-voice, and about taking fifty dollars of her friend's money, if he was her friend, and I wanted to clear the slate of that. I might even offer to give him back his dough. But not if I saw him again. In that case, I intended to take a stroll across his face.

The man who hired the waiters was a slick-mannered white-haired old gentleman who was a little distracted by the moment of the occasion.

"From the union?" he asked.

"From the union," I said. "I'm an extra they sent over in case you need more help for this shindig upstairs."

He said: "We always need help. Where's your working paper?"

"I lost that, but I can run back to union headquarters and get a new one signed," I said. "It won't take long."

He shrugged and said, "Never mind. What is your name?"

"Samuel Wales."

"Sam, can you bus?"

I did not have much of an idea what he meant by bus.

"If I can't, I won't expect any pay," I said, trying to sound as if I didn't think much of being a bus, and was half-way insulted.

It was an insult, all right. The job was that of bus-boy; they handed me a big bowl with ice in it, a pair of tongs, and it was my job to go around and chuck ice in the glasses. It was a good thing they didn't start me laying out the silverware. There were enough tools around each plate to look as if a mechanic had laid out his kit.

"What are these guys?" I asked a waiter.

"Scientists," he said.

If scientists are supposed to be bald men in shaggy suits and with no hair, only about half of those present qualified. Many of them were young, and there was a woman here and there.

The big bronze fellow, Doc Savage, was getting a lot of play. He was being talked to more than he was talking. The bellhop downstairs had said he righted wrongs and punished evildoers, which sounded like something you hear in Sunday

School, and didn't go with this fellow's appearance. Savage looked as if he was a man who knew where all the marbles were. Galahad went out of fashion a long time ago, and this man didn't seem back-dated. He puzzled me.

"Who's the big copper-colored guy?" I asked another waiter.

"That's Doc Savage."

"I know, but what makes him rate?"

"Boy, you're kind of ignorant, aren't you?" the waiter said, and walked off.

Miss Fenisong—lovely-voice—came in presently, but her entrance was ruined for my money by Albert Gross being with her. He was slick in tails and white tie, and he looked too wide for that outfit too.

Two other men were with Miss Fenisong and Gross. One of these was somewhat taller than the other, and the taller one had the redder face. There was an air about them that spoke of something in common, although it probably wasn't a family tie. It was hard to say what they shared, but it was probably something in their minds, a common interest or purpose.

The four didn't have but one engraved invitation between them—the other three had been in Albert Gross' coat and I had them—but they got in all right. A fine-looking old fellow at the door was checking names off a list, and he had their names on the list. I went over, asked him who they were, and he showed me.

Miss Paula Fenisong.

Mr. Albert Gross.

Mr. Alec McGraff.

Mr. J. B. C. McCutcheon.

"Fellow, aren't you one of the waiters?" The fine-looking old gentleman was scowling at me. He must have noticed my bowl of ice cubes and tongs.

"Waiter!" I sneered at the idea. "I'm the bus." I went back to my work.

The words that came out of the little groups that had gathered to talk were long on syllables and, as far as I was concerned, short on meaning. They talked isotopes and alpha particles; the arrangement of carbides and ferrite in relation to martensite. Not all of it was that dry though, and a few of the good scientists were conducting mild experiments with their own bodily tolerance to alcohol.

The doings of Miss Fenisong's little party were more interesting. Miss Fenisong began by waving her eyelashes at

Doc Savage. She could have only one idea there; but the pickup didn't work—the big one either wasn't interested, or wasn't showing it.

Albert Gross gave a little cooperation. He moved a place-card from the dais at the head of the room, where the great ones were to sit, to another position at a side table that was more secluded. It was Doc Savage's place-card he moved, and he put it next to Miss Fenisong's.

The ice-man job afforded an opportunity to circulate and watch the conniving progress. I was nicely disguised—the management had fitted me out with cadet-striped oversized black trousers, a brick red mess jacket and white gloves. I combed a lick of hair down over my forehead like the late Adolf Hitler, and hardly knew myself.

Presently they began introducing each other to Doc Savage. Mr. Alfred Gross introduced Mr. McCutcheon to Doc Savage. Then Mr. McCutcheon introduced Mr. McGraff, and McGraff introduced Miss Fenisong, who introduced Mr. Gross who had started the whole thing. They had it straightened out now; between the four of them, they had introduced each other to the bronze man.

The girl remarked that it was a wonderful affair, wasn't it?

"Yes, isn't it. Quite nice," he said, with something less than enthusiasm.

"So many eminent people here," she added.

"Indeed?"

I wondered if Savage was married, had a jealous girlfriend, or was just cautious. Probably by the time you have become as important as he seemed to be, you have learned to be cautious. If Miss Fenisong had been giving me the kind of office he was getting, they would have had to sandbag my feet to keep me on the ground.

They were working on him like a basketball team in slow-motion. They were using signals—one eyebrow higher than the other, a small smile, a head gesture—to keep in touch with each other. They probably had other signals I didn't catch.

But I got it when one of the Macs came in from the terrace and ran his hand through his hair. I didn't know which Mac was which, but he was the taller one with the redder face. He could be McGraff or he could be McCutcheon.

Miss Fenisong took the signal with a widening of the

eyes. She said: "Mr. Savage, will you look at the moon with me?"

Would he look at the moon with her! Would the mouse like some cheese! Only he didn't take her up very happily.

Mostly she had to drag him toward the terrace, and from the others present she got the kind of looks that a beautiful babe always gets when she drags the lion away from the party.

So they wanted him on the terrace, and were going to a lot of trouble to get him there. . . . I moved that way myself.

The *Parkside-Regent* probably had its own yardstick of snobbery. A gathering of mere artists and writers would no doubt rate no better than the basement banquet room, while diplomats might rank the Imperial Room that opened off the mezzanine. The doings tonight, obviously extraordinary, rated the Starlight Room on the roof. It was only a few steps outside to the terrace, a wondrous place well-equipped with potted greenery.

There was some kind of a hitch. The Mac suddenly reappeared with another kind of signal, a go-back one made with down-hooked mouth corners and a head-shake. Something that was supposed to come off on the terrace wasn't going to come off, his high-sign said.

It seemed to be too late for Miss Fenisong to stop the trip to the terrace with Doc Savage, so she went through with it. She did and said things that weren't what she had planned to do and say was my guess.

She said: "I wanted to ask you about the Eber idea of starting with a preliminary lunar theory solution in which the orbit is supposed to lie in the ecliptic and to have no eccentricity, then finding the additional terms which depend on the first power of the eccentricities and of the inclination."

That sounded familiar. . . . Why, sure. She had used the same words on me. Hearing it twice made it sound as if it was something she had memorized out of the encyclopedia.

Doc Savage looked mildly surprised. I didn't know whether she had fooled him or not. The surprised look didn't mean a thing. Words like that from such a beautiful girl would surprise anybody, like hearing a canary sing bass.

"Quite logical," he said vaguely.

"Then you agree?"

"With what?"

"With Eber's hypothesis."

"I—ah—wouldn't quarrel with Eber," he said.

"Oh, I'm glad," she said.

She didn't seem very glad to me. It was hard for me to distinguish fright amid such beauty, but I thought I could see it. They always have one of those phony palms on a hotel roof terrace, and I and the ice bucket were behind it. . . . Yeah, she was scared.

She added, "Look, they're starting to take seats for the banquet. I'd love to get more of your thought about Eber, but we'd better go in, hadn't we?"

He bowed politely, took her arm, and they went back inside.

There were plenty of stars overhead. There wasn't any moon.

Alfred Gross strode out of the darkness. He said, "McGraff!" sharply. The tall red-faced Mac appeared. Alfred Gross called him a long breathful of names, none complimentary, and finished with: "Why did you give a false alarm, you dumb boob?"

McGraff made a sickly upward gesture with his thumb. "I thought I saw it begin."

Gross threw a glance at the sky. "There's no sign of it," he said. "And it isn't time yet by twenty minutes or so."

"I can't help it," McGraff said.

A waiter captain came up to me and said, "Get to work, bud!" I had to go back to the tables, where service was beginning.

She had done a fairly smooth job of handling Doc Savage on the terrace mix-up, and it had not entered my mind that the big bronze man suspected anything. He looked dignified, bored, and harassed by being stared at by so many people, the way a convention of misers would look at the stuff in the Fort Knox vaults. Obviously he was aware of Miss Fenisong, but he seemed to be in the indecisive stage about her, like a fox eyeing a bait of a sort that had poisoned him previously.

Suddenly Doc Savage arose, excused himself to lovely-voice, and moved around the table to where Albert Gross sat. He laid a hand on Gross's shoulder, said something, and Gross was dumfounded.

Gross, besides being too wide for his suits, had a jaw like a mule's hoof. The jaw fell.

"Nice work with the place-cards," Doc Savage said.

"I beg your pardon!"

"I don't mind." Doc Savage patted the man's thick-looking shoulder. "The scenery at the new location is quite interesting."

Gross registered the expressions of a man who had unexpectedly found a hundred and ten volts of electricity in the seat of his chair, but he didn't say anything.

Doc Savage rejoined Miss Fenisong.

He hadn't missed anything, it appeared.

That was the end of the genteel jockeying for the evening. The stage was all cleared for the fireworks.

III

A short bald man who seemed to be a sub-chairman stood up and introduced the Chairman, a Doctor Morand Funk Hodges, president of the Welland Institute of Physical Sciences, distinguished in the field of the strontium isotope, and Albert Gross left while the words were being said.

Gross left unobtrusively, like a polecat leaving the vicinity of a chicken-coop at dawn.

Doc Savage smoothed down his left eyebrow with a fingertip. I'll swear that was all he did. But a very wide apish looking man, homelier than a frog, got up from one of the tables and sauntered out after Gross.

We had about three minutes and forty seconds of uninterrupted dish-clattering and lip-smacking. Doctor Morand Funk Hodges had stood up long enough to say we would have music by the stringed ensemble. The music seemed to be slow getting started.

Mac—the shorter one this time—dashed in from the terrace.

"For God's sake, come out here!" he said in a loud attention-getting voice. "Come, quickly! Look at what is happening to the sky!"

He was stared at, but nobody did or said anything. They probably thought it was a gag, part of the entertainment of the evening.

"Gentlemen!" he screamed. "Please! Please, for God's sake, come and look at this!" He sounded about as unconcerned as a cat with its tail freshly stepped on.

Finally one of the scientists did get up somewhat sheepishly—you could see he believed he was biting on something—and go outside. He was back with his coattail stretched behind him. He yelled: "Come out here!"

Curiosity had bitten every man and woman in the room, and now they had the excuse they wanted. Within a couple of minutes, the terrace was packed. I was late getting out there, and I wanted to laugh when I saw that every head was thrown back, every eye fixed on the sky, as if they had been ordered to take that position and hold it. The heads were held a little to one side or the other, or straight back, but the attention was undividedly straight up.

A light was up there. It could have been moonlight, except that there was no moon, and that much of a glow couldn't have come from it if it had been there. There was, also, no evidence of a single brightly lighted object such as the moon. . . . No sign at all of the source of the brilliance.

"Aurora borealis," someone said.

I thought so too. My education had gone that far. The aurora borealis was the two-dollar word for the Northern Lights.

A gentleman with a trimmed white beard, standing at my left, snorted forcibly.

"Borealis!" he said. "Ridiculous!"

He had expressed the general opinion, it seemed. Nobody who knew anything about the Northern Lights would admit the manifestation above us bore any resemblance to Northern Lights. But no one had another idea to offer.

Doc Savage, his voice plainly identifiable in the stillness, requested, "Will someone switch off the terrace lights."

The electric lights were doused in a moment. The glow from above was then more impressive. It had the shape of a circular patch, fuzzy around the edges, and was a rather poisonous looking purplish grey in color. It didn't cover the whole sky. I held both hands above my head, the palms about two feet apart, and that about spanned the glow area.

I noticed the thing, whatever it was, shed enough light that we could see each other distinctly.

"Savage," a voice called. "What do you say it is?"

There was no answer. While I was listening for one, a couple of pairs of hands laid hold of me, a pair on each arm, and I was told, "We would like to speak with you, son."

* * *

It is unlikely that every individual hair stood erect on my head, but the one or two that failed to do so didn't detract from the effect. Looking up at that spook light had done more to me than I had been aware of. I think my body became as stiff as a post also, and the two Macs moved me off the terrace by sort of lifting me and skidding me along like a pieace of statuary. By the time the kinks began to return to my hair, they had me in a niche just off the banquet room.

"Son," said the shorter Mac, "aren't you the phony Mr. Wales?"

"Wales is my name," I said. "I'm not phony."

"Indeed?"

"That's right," I said.

"When," asked the taller Mac, "did you become a waiter?"

"Tonight. But you mean a bus, not a waiter," I said.

"Are you being humorous?"

We had the niche to ourselves, and it was a little dark there, but a lot more lonely than dark.

"No," I said. "I'm not being humorous. Leggo my arms, do you mind?"

"We're intrigued," the short Mac said, "by the oddity of your presence, and the way you have been fanning out your large ears. We're rather puzzled, as a fact. Could we ask you a question?"

"I'm good on questions," I said.

"How is Mr. Spatny?"

"Who?" I asked.

"Spatny."

"Don't know him."

Short Mac looked past my chest at tall Mac and said: "He states he isn't acquainted with Spatny."

"That speaks well for his character," tall Mac said.

"Son, we'd like to have a long talk with you."

"Let's not," I said.

"Walk between us," the short one said. "And wipe that my-pants-are-on-fire look off your puss."

"The hell I will," I said.

They did a quicker job on me than Alberto Gross had done earlier with the ash-tray. The speed they got into it and the thoroughness was proof that it pays to organize, to have a plan. Tall Mac jabbed two fingers into my eyes, and then I couldn't tell who was doing what as they kneed me, slammed my jaw, banged my nose, kicked my feet from under me and stamped on my face. I fought them like a bundle of wildcats. I swung blows that would have wrecked a house if they had hit a house. They didn't hit anything. But I did considerably better with my howling for help.

Quite likely it wasn't the hour or more that it seemed before the Macs ran away from me.

The room, a small one, not ten feet on a side, ornate, completely without furniture but with numerous mirrors, fooled me for a while. It turned out to be the elevator, and it and not my head was doing the moving.

"I haven't any eyeballs left," I said, when my teeth would stop gritting long enough to let words out.

"Pepper."

"Huh?"

"One of them had the foresight to have pepper under his fingernails," Doc Savage said. "A bit painful, I imagine."

"You cover a lot of ground with that word bit," I said. "You mean I've got eyes after all?"

The elevator stopped. I was not yet feeling well enough to know, or care about knowing, which way the cage had been traveling, but presumably it had gone down, because I could hear muffled through the door the low cave-like sound that is in hotel lobbies.

I was sitting on the elevator floor. Then suddenly Doc Savage had a fistful of my coat front, and I was no longer sitting on the floor. I was on my feet, or rather up in the air.

He said: "Now would be a good time for you to do a quick job with the truth."

The way he said it made me glad that I couldn't see his face very well. I'm no Jack Dempsey or Charlie Atlas, but neither do I have to be helped across streets, yet he was holding me up there against the elevator sidewall, and I was completely helpless. I felt like an insect that a kid had just fastened to a plank with a pin.

"What do you want to know?" I gasped.

"Use your judgment," he said. "As long as it's the truth."

I didn't stop to figure out why I suddenly wanted to talk—it obviously wasn't a time for pausing to figure out reasons. Not that he was exactly threatening me. He didn't sound like one guy laying it down to another on a street corner, not a lawyer bulldozing the opposition witness, and least of all did he sound like a ballplayer mistreating the ump.

He'd merely said I'd better talk, and I knew that was what I'd better do, if I didn't want them collecting me off the sides of the elevator with a putty scraper. I'd never had anybody scare me so much so quick.

Doc Savage listened while I packed a couple of minutes full of words. . . . If I told him any lies, it was an accident due to excitement.

He said: "So you don't know what it's all about?"

"That's right."

"You have nothing on me," he said. "I don't know either."

He opened the elevator door, and we stepped out into the lobby. He laid a hand on my elbow, about as gently as a blacksmith's vise, and guided me across the lobby. Then we stopped.

"Monk!" he said.

The fellow who had followed Albert Gross out of the banquet room upstairs, the short and wide man who looked like an ape, was sitting in a lobby chair. He seemed a little battered. He had a thumb stuck in his mouth, feeling to learn how many teeth he had left.

"Doc," he said. "I must be losing my manhood."

The bronze man said nothing.

"Or that Gross guy is specially tough," Monk added.

"I could have told you that," I said.

Doc Savage introduced me to the baboon. "This is Monk Mayfair, a friend and associate of mine."

Monk pointed a finger at me. "The waiter!" He had a big finger, attached to a hand that was also large and covered with almost as many bristles as a toothbrush. "The nosey waiter. What does he know about this?"

"He has a funny story," Doc Savage said.

"It better not be too funny."

"What happened to you?"

"Gross somehow got the idea I was following him, which I was," Monk explained. "I got in the elevator with him. I acted as innocent as anything, and while I was doing that, he hit me between the eyes. It felt like he used an anvil. I guess it was a blackjack. Did you know a man could be knocked sillier than a coon by getting hit between the eyes with a blackjack?"

"Where did Gross go?"

Monk said bitterly, "The guy had his nerve. He told the elevator operator, who hadn't seen me get hit, that I just gave a jump and keeled over. When I woke up, I was in a nice comfortable chair on the mezzanine with an assistant hotel manager throwing ice-water in my face."

"And you do not know where Gross went?"

"Nobody seems to know."

Doc Savage asked, "Did you see what happened in the sky?"

"Sky?" Monk shook his head carefully. "All I saw was stars—from the blackjack."

"Did you ever hear of a Mr. Spatny?" Doc Savage inquired.

"Who?"

"Never mind," Doc Savage said.

The assistant hotel managers were fluttering around us now, looking as if they would have liked to wring their hands, and introducing a Mr. Casey, the house detective. Casey fitted the picture of a house man, five feet seven and tapered at both ends like a seal. He was no help.

Doc Savage spoke briefly to Monk Mayfair in a language I did not understand. Evidently the bronze man had suggested that it would be more private in his car parked in the street, because that was where we went.

The automobile, a large sedan and not a new model, had an unusually solid quality that I noticed when I was boosted in. I looked at one of the windows where it came up through the body, and it was more than an inch thick.

"Is this thing armored?" I asked.

"That's one of your lesser worries, bud," Monk Mayfair said.

They got in, one on either side of me, and the car door sounded like the door of a bank vault when it closed. Doc Savage flicked a switch, presently a radio speaker was hissing, and Savage said into a microphone: "Police radio from Special 243." They answered him. He gave the police a specific description of Miss Fenisong, Albert Gross, Alec McGraff and J. B. C. McCutcheon. It was a wonderful description; I could almost see them from his words. He said: "I dislike making extra work for somebody, but I would certainly appreciate a rundown on the name of Spatny. Probably a man. I have nothing but the name, but I'd like it checked against anything you might have."

"Don't worry about making extra work, Mr. Savage," the cop's voice said. "We'll get the stuff for you. What do we do with the other four if we pick them up?"

"I'd like to question them," Doc said. "If you need a charge, one of them committed an assault on my aide, Monk Mayfair."

"And lived through it!" The cop sounded surprised. "Very well, Mr. Savage. You can expect the fullest cooperation."

I said: "I didn't know a cop could be that polite to a citizen."

Savage took another look at the sky to learn whether the odd light was still up there. It wasn't.

I said: "That was a nice description. I could almost feel the two Macs kicking me in the slats again."

"You say they were going to take you out of the hotel with them?" Savage asked.

"That was the idea they expressed. By the way, why didn't they?"

"They made quite a bit of noise working on you, enough to get my attention. They saw me and ran. Unfortunately, they had an escape route all planned, with doors they could lock behind them. They got away."

I said: "That's the way I figured."

Monk Mayfair showed some life. "What about gorgeous?" he wanted to know. "Miss Fenisong, if that was her name? What became of her?" He sat up straight, adjusted his necktie, and added, "You know, I think we should question that babe."

"I saw her first," I said.

Monk gave me a look that would have cracked a rock. "Yeah?" he said. "Well, maybe I'll hand you something else to think about."

"Easy on that," Doc Savage told him. "Sammy has been rather cooperative so far."

"Who's Sammy?"

"Me," I said. "What *did* become of the girl?"

Doc Savage said: "I have an associate following her."

"By God, have you got that shyster lawyer trailing her!" Monk yelled. "Having Ham Brooks shadow that girl is about as practical as posting a hound dog to watch a beefsteak."

I gathered that Monk Mayfair and Ham Brooks had

opinions about each other, and Doc Savage was accustomed to it.

"Sammy," Doc Savage said. "Tell Monk how you got into it. And if you think of anything you forgot to tell me, toss it in."

"You mean I gotta go through that again?"

"Probably several times," Savage told me. "You see, we probably know less than you about the affair."

"In that case," I said, "you're probably without any information at all."

The way they let me recite my tale again—without a single interruption—wasn't too reassuring. I would have liked them to indicate whether they did or didn't believe me. All that came out of them was attentive silence.

"If you're a liar," Monk said when I finished, "you're pretty fluent."

Savage said: "His story has the ring of truth, Monk. And it's logical except on one point—his reasons for going to the hotel to see Miss Fenisong after she phoned him by mistake, and then going to the trouble he did to be present at the banquet."

"Shucks, that's the only part I believed," Monk said.

"You think his actions were reasonable, then?"

"You saw the babe, didn't you?"

"Well . . ."

"Take it from me, Miss Fenisong was the bait that got him into it," Monk said. "That part I believe." He shoved his face at me and added, "But you'd better get over the yen, bum."

"I don't think I can lick you," I told him. "But you call me a bum again, and I'll test it out."

"Aren't you a bum?"

"Only to my friends."

He grinned, and I was glad he did. I was going to hit him, and he would have ruined me.

I asked: "How come you fellows took hold of the thing the way you did, if you didn't know something was coming off? It looked to me like you were cocked and primed."

"How do you mean?" Monk asked.

"Well, you followed Gross when he left. This Ham Brooks, whoever he is, is tailing the girl. And Doc Savage didn't exactly sleep through it. All of that seems to require advance arrangements to me. How come?"

Monk shrugged. "We've developed a technique."

"Huh?"

"When you've been in trouble as many times as we have," he explained, "you just function automatically when something doesn't look right."

Doc Savage said: "There was no magic about it. I saw Gross change the place-cards, and Miss Fenisong was fairly transparent—she claimed to be a lunar expert, but what she didn't know about it was considerable. I saw McGraff signal her to bring me out on the terrace. That was fairly obvious. I had the four of them spotted—I'd noticed that they went through a mumbo-jumbo introducing each other to me—and so, without attracting any more attention than necessary, I asked Monk to trail Gross, and Ham the girl. I was going to do my best with the other two. As it turned out, my best wasn't good."

"Whooeeee!" I said. "You had your eyes open."

"I think the whole arrangement was designed to get me out on the terrace when the chromospheric eruption occurred," Savage added.

"The chromo—the what?"

He hesitated. "There was a rather unique luminance in the sky—"

"I saw that," I said. "You mean you've got a name for what we saw?"

He shook his head. "I wouldn't want to be quoted, but it seemed to be in the nature of what scientists call chromospheric eruptions, although certainly I know of no recorded instance of such magnitude and purely localized nature. Apparently, too, it occurred far short of the Appleton stratum, but without the aid of an electronic multiplier, it's hard to say—"

"You've gone off and left me in the bushes already," I said. "Negative and positive electricity is as far as I go, and all I know about them is that they're marked plus and minus on a battery. . . . Tell me this—is it bad?"

He hesitated over that one, too.

"It might not be good," he said.

"How do you figure that?"

"I haven't figured it. If what happened up there in the sky tonight is what I think it was, it stepped off into the field of advanced science, and when you do that these days, it's not safe to predict what might be done. Let me put it this way—if that manifestation in the sky we saw tonight was man-made, and there are indications it was, we're up against knowledge reaching beyond that necessary to create the atom bomb."

I was impressed enough to hang my mouth open and not say anything. He had an effective way of saying what he said, and I didn't doubt for a minute that he knew what he was talking about, my thought being that all those scientists tonight wouldn't have all but fallen on their knees if he was an ordinary guy.

He gave us a piece of his philosophy. "It's unfortunate that the moral enlightenment of the human race isn't keeping pace with its scientific discoveries. It's frightening to think that a crook might someday get hold of something as effective as the gadget they dropped on Hiroshima."

"What makes you think that thing in the sky was man-made?"

"They had it timed. . . . Miss Fenisong seemed to know to within a few minutes of the time it was going to come," he said.

He was right. And he had me scared. He had the little cold-footed things scuttling up and down my spine. If anybody had said boo! right then. I would have made a good try at jumping right through the side of that armored car. They had me frightened stiff of something I didn't know what was, and they didn't know what was.

IV

He was dying when he came down the street. Not yet dead of course, but well on his way to it—enough of his life had leaked out of him that he probably had no very clear idea where he was going or what he would do if he got there.

Savage saw him first and pointed, said, "Look at that!" Then, when Monk started to get out, he added, "Could be a trap. Stay in the car. We'll drive up beside him."

This was a fine street of tall modern buildings with no basement entryways and no iron picket fences to give a staggering man trouble. That was probably why he had gotten this far. Maybe he had not come a great distance, but even a few feet would be a great distance for him. He kept against the buildings, kept his feet under him somehow, and moved by skidding a shoulder against the buildings.

Our car came up with him as warily as a kitten stalking a cricket. We sat there a moment. "It looks clear," Doc Savage said.

Savage got out, stood before the man, stood in the man's path, and the man came sliding along the slick granite side of the building until he was against Savage, and even then he kept pushing with rubbery legs.

"Gross," Savage said to the man. "Gross, do you know me?"

Gross' knees kept bending forward, then back, a little more each time, and he seemed to grow shorter and settle into the pavement. He moaned—a hurt-sheep sound—as Savage took hold of him and lowered him to the pavement.

Doc Savage leaned down and wrenched open the man's vest and shirt. An ice pick had done it, it seemed to me. I counted seven little pits with scarlet yarns coming out of them, and it was dark and I could only see a part of his torso.

"Holy smoke, why didn't somebody help him?" I said.

Monk Mayfair said: "This is New York. Nobody bothers with anybody else. It's the damndest town that way. . . . They probably thought he was drunk."

Albert Gross spoke, and I jumped a foot. I had supposed his voice would be made of thin gasps and gurgles, but it was strong and bell-clear.

He said: "I was trying to get to you. Did you see the sky?"

"I saw it," Doc Savage told him.

"We wanted you to."

"Why?"

"Listen to me," Gross said. "It was black, but it wasn't big. Black, see—maybe fifteen feet long and not quite as high nor that wide. The outside looked sort of fuzzy. It seemed to keep that shape. It came out, or seemed to come out of a doorway, a kind of an arcade into a building. There was no appearance of it flowing out. It just came out, full-blown. It came to me, or toward me, and I ducked into a niche between two buildings. It came right in after me. It was black as hell inside the thing. Then I felt sharp things sticking into me, and it didn't hurt too bad, and then it hurt like hell."

"More than one sharp thing?" Doc Savage asked.

"One thing, sticking into me many times. I could be wrong, though."

"Then what?"

"I don't know. I passed out."

Doc Savage asked: "Who is Spatny?"

"A great one," Gross said.

I wondered why Savage had changed the subject to Spatny, and then I knew. It was because Albert Gross was dead. He was spread out there on the sidewalk, and his life was all gone. His last words had been clear, fine and clear as a politician telling a constituent the high taxes aren't his fault.

"Go through his pockets, Monk," Doc Savage said.

I didn't believe it, and I still didn't believe it even after we dug up three different people who had seen the black object. One of them had seen Gross run into the niche between the buildings—we looked at the niche and it was there, all right, a kind of service alley about five feet wide— and the same spectator had seen the black object go in after Gross. It hadn't come out. The police dug up some more witnesses with the same yarn, except that one of them had the black thing a hundred feet high. The cops weren't any more willing to believe it than I was.

"Nothing in his pockets," Monk reported.

"Nothing?"

"He's been gone over with a vacuum cleaner."

Doc Savage made me a proposition. "Do you want to go to jail, or do you want to go with us?"

That had been on my mind. I could see I wasn't going to just walk out of this.

"Your company satisfies me," I said.

We went back to the *Parkside-Regent* and paid a visit to Miss Fenisong's room. She was not inhabiting it. Nobody was surprised.

"We'll go down to headquarters, and see what we can work out," Savage said.

He didn't mean police headquarters, which is what I supposed. We rode downtown in silence. They didn't mention what they were thinking about, but I was thinking of Albert Gross, too wide for his suits, too quick to hit people on the head, and now too full of little holes. We got out in front of a building, and when I looked up I realized that I'd seen plenty of picture postcards of the place. I gathered it was a private elevator we used; there was no one else in it, and no operator. You pushed a button. It went up as softly as a whisper in a girl's throat, and let us out into a hall. We walked into a reception room, on to carpet that felt like a fall of snow underfoot.

There was an enormous ancient safe, a table of inlaid woods that was the most beautiful thing I'd seen in the way of tables, and no furniture that you needed to look at twice before you sat on it.

Through a door, there was a library which seemed to have about as many books as I imagine the Library of Congress has. Beyond that, past another door, there seemed to be near an acre of floorspace cluttered with the sort of stuff—enameled tables, glass tables, chromium thingajigs and thingajigs of glass, trays, retorts, filters, pumps, bottles, phials, coils, tubes, wire—that you see in moving picture scenes of laboratories.

"Well?" Monk Mayfair asked. He was watching me.

I pulled my jaw and asked, "Whose diggings?"

"Doc's."

"You mean one guy, all of this?"

"That's right."

They fixed a comfortable chair for me, and Monk brought out a piece of apparatus that could have been a radio but wasn't. They put the gimmick beside my chair. "Take off your coat and roll up your sleeve and sit down," Monk ordered. I did, and they put attachments on my hand, around my chest and one, the only one I recognized, on my arm above the elbow. The latter closely resembled, or was one of those things the doctors wrap around your arm to get blood pressure.

"What's this?" I asked.

"Lie detector," Monk said. "Are you worried?"

"Okay," I said. "Okay, but stick to what's your business, or I'll stuff the thing down your throat."

Monk grinned. "I wouldn't want one of the things on me, either," he said. "Not all the time."

You had to like the homely baboon. He was uglier than a mud fence. A mud fence would have looked like a piece of silk ribbon beside him. But it was an amiable kind of homeliness—you felt the same way toward him that you feel toward St. Bernard dogs, who also have faces which don't take beauty prizes.

"Let's have your story," Doc Savage said.

"Heck—again?" I complained.

This time they didn't sit back and let me recite. They had questions, a hundred questions about details. I had always supposed my memory was pretty good, and that I had an eye for details. I was wrong. Five minutes of this, and I felt like a blind cow.

Doc Savage asked: "What did you do with the part you tore off Gross' coat?"

I told him what trash-can I had stuffed it in.

"Get it," he directed Monk, and Monk left.

He threw a question at me every other word, and we covered the rest of it. The machine was making a zig-zag mess of lines on a roll of moving graph paper, and he had watched it closely.

"Do I pass?" I asked.

"Ever been in New York before, Sammy?"

"No. I mean, I went through it when I was in the army, which I don't call being here," I said.

"Where are you from?"

"Kansas City."

"Why did you leave Kansas City, Sammy?"

"I was getting fired off too many jobs," I told him. "I wanted to see if a change of scenery would change my luck."

"What seemed to be the trouble?"

"Not enough money, too much work, and bosses looking down my collar," I said.

"Everyone has that kind of a problem."

"Yeah? Well maybe it's none of your business," I said.

He said: "Maybe you didn't put it out. Maybe you felt the world owed you a plush living."

"Why not?" I said. "I spent a lot of time in foxholes, and while I'm lying in mud and being shot at, guys not as good as me drew their hundred bucks a week and saw their babes every night. Okay, now I want some of that."

"Oh, a professional hero."

"I resent that."

"Look," he said. "There were ten million men more or less in service, just about all the able-bodied men in one generation, just about all the men who are going to be capable of being successful for the next few years. That would have been true if there hadn't been a war. What would happen if all ten million stood around holding their hands out and yelling for a hundred dollars a week and no work?"

"You mean I'm a bum?"

"I mean you are making noises like one."

"I don't know what the hell started this," I yelled. "But I got a couple of medals that says I did this nation a service. Now it owes me service, what I mean."

"Who is the nation?"

"Huh?"

"Think it over," he said. "If you and the other ten million aren't the nation, you might tell me who is."

That was all of that—except that I happened to wander into the big room where the books were, and while I was looking to see whether there were any at all with titles I could understand—it was entirely scientific stuff—I came across a little display case. It wasn't conspicuous, back in a corner. It was full of medals. I got a funny feeling. There was everything from that little blue ribbon with the stars on it on down, and I mean it made me feel down, to the couple I had. I thought maybe, at first, he'd warmed a swivel chair for them. The trouble with that idea was, you didn't get purple hearts for a swivel chair pinching your bottom. And he had four! There was a little leather folio containing some of the citations, and I read a couple. He hadn't been in any swivel chair. I didn't have much to say for a while.

Monk Mayfair came back. He had the part of Albert Gross' coat I'd torn off, and a question. "Any word from the shyster lawyer?" he wanted to know, and looked worried—while trying not to look worried—when told there had been no news from Ham Brooks.

For my money, the piece of coat wasn't going to do them any good. I'd looked it over, and all it had given me was three invitations to the Reception. I figured it was a dopey waste of time, going back uptown for it.

Monk said: "I checked with old Doc Hodges, the chairman, about how the four of them got invited to the Reception. He'd wondered himself, and he's finding out. He'll call."

Doc Savage went over the coat fragment. He became interested in the inside of the coat pocket, and cut the pocket out with a razor blade.

"Laundry marks," I said. "That won't help you."

Not discouraged, he got on the telephone, talked to some expert in the police department, and made a liar out of me.

"The suit was cleaned the last five times by a shop in the eleven hundred block on Lexington Avenue," Savage said.

He telephoned the cleaning shop proprietor at home, but the fellow was out on a party. He called the police, and got them looking for the man.

He handed the coat fragment and pocket to Monk, and said, "Run a chemical and microscope test on the cloth and the pocket scrapings. It might give us something."

Monk Mayfair didn't look to me as if he had brains enough to run a test on anything, unless it was to run his eye up and down a pretty leg. There was less than an inch between his eyebrows and his hairline.

We had a visitor then. Doctor Morand Funk Hodges, chairman of the doings at the *Parkside-Regent* tonight. He had a thin young man in tow, and was acting as if he intended wringing the latter's neck a bit later. The thin young man had wet lips, a pimple on his neck, and was wearing a large scare.

"Tell them, Wilfred," Doctor Hodges said ominously.

Wilfred had more trouble with his words than a guy juggling a lighted match in a powder factory. He, it seemed, was the banquet secretary, the one who sent out the invitations.

A man had paid him a hundred dollars to mail four invitations to Miss Paula Fenisong, Mr. Albert Gross, Mr. Alec McGraff and Mr. J. B. C. McCutcheon. And, of course put their names on the guest-list. The man who had spent the hundred was Mr. McCutcheon. The taller and redder-faced Mac.

"Wilfred, you're fired!" said the good Doctor Hodges. "And I am going to kick you a good one in the pants."

He sounded funny, the dignified way he said it, but at the same time as if his mouth was full of knives. He was an eminent-seeming old codger, quite likeable. And so help me if he didn't lead Wilfred out in the hall, and we could hear him put his foot against Wilfred's seat. It sounded like a good one.

Doctor Hodges came back in, sat down and took off his shoe and examined his foot for damage. He said, "A hundred dollars—they wanted to meet you badly, Savage. Nobody ever pays a hundred bucks to meet me. Fools if they did. You know, that business really livened up the banquet, didn't it?

Good thing. We had a lousy program. You should have heard Baedeker's speech. It put half of them to sleep—those who didn't know enough about what they saw in the sky tonight to have their hair scared up on end."

Doc Savage said: "Doctor, do you think what we saw was a chromospheric eruption of terrestrial origin?"

"Sure. So do you." Doctor Hodges had chin whiskers of the nanny goat variety, and he gave them a worried yank. "Drat it, man, who could have developed a means of creating molecular collision with free electrons in one of the perturbing strata? I thought I knew all the atmospheric physicists doing work along that line. But I know of no one who is near achieving the sort of success we saw demonstrated over that hotel tonight."

"It's a puzzle," Doc Savage admitted.

"Dammit, doesn't it scare you?"

"Somewhat."

Doctor Hodges did some shuddering and whisker-yanking, and pondered, "How do you suppose it was achieved? To drive electrons against molecules and obtain optical wave emission, in the visible spectrum—for at least part of it was in the visible spectrum, since we could see a round luminous patch in the sky—they either had a terrific transmitter for microwave-lengths, or they had stumbled on a short-cut. God, I wish I'd had an electronic multiplier there while it was going on, with enough other apparatus to get a test."

The next five minutes of discussion was over my head. Probably I recognized two words. My minus and plus electricity didn't get me far.

The eminent doctor could have talked about it all night, but Savage threw him out in a polite way, promising to let him have a peep at the gimmick that had made the light if we found it.

"Nice old guy with a lot of big words," I said.

"And big deeds," Doc Savage said sharply. "Doctor Hodges is the man who—"

He didn't finish that. But whatever Doctor Hodges had contributed to science, I gathered it was plenty.

I said: "The old gaffer didn't seem to have heard of the black it-can't-be that was crawling around in the street and did in Gross."

"That reminds me," Doc Savage said, and he telephoned the police medical examiner, asking if the exact cause of the death of Albert Gross had been ascertained. Evidently it had, because he listened intently to the news.

"Well, what did Gross die of?" I demanded.

"Of little holes in him," Savage said briefly.

This hardly came under the heading of fresh news. I gathered that he thought I couldn't do much with the details if I had them. It could be.

Doc Savage made telephone calls. He got hold of Samuel Wickert Wales, the astrophysicist of the Compton Observatory, the guy whose phone call I'd accidentally received that morning—and how I was wishing I hadn't!—and learned that Wales had made a deal to coach Miss Fenisong on the lunar theory. The deal had been made by telephone; Wales had never met Miss Fenisong. In other words, he had nothing to contribute. Savage thanked him as gently as a chorine stroking her new mink coat.

"If it was me," I said, "I'd throw a little scare around."

"If it was you," he replied, "you'd probably get hit on the head again."

"Touché," I said. "Only there's been murder done."

"Probably worse," he said, and went into the laboratory, leaving me to discover that I had a first-rate case of the creeping jeebies. I didn't know exactly what there was to be afraid of—I wasn't that scientific—but I knew alarm in other people when I saw it. Savage was alarmed. Doctor Hodges had been alarmed. The only emotion that would show on a face like Monk Mayfair had was dumbness, but he was probably alarmed too.

I wasn't kidding myself—mostly I was afraid of what I didn't know. As a kid, I always ran like blazes past graveyards at night, for the reason that I didn't know what might come out of a graveyard. Only a few months ago, I was one of those who figured those tinkering scientists would probably blow the world to dust with their atom bomb tests. Ignorance isn't bliss sometimes—it can be stark terror.

Anyway, I was in such a tizzy that I was forgetting lovely-voice and how swell she looked and how nice a dish she would make across the breakfast table of mornings. That, for me, was quite a tizzy.

V

It was a surprise for a rough crummy-looking package done up in burlap and tough cord to contain a fistful of polished diamonds—but that was what Monk Mayfair turned out to be. He finished with his microscope and some mixtures of stinking chemicals which he had been using on Albert Gross' coat fragment.

Monk said: "Well, here's the story on Gross."

"Let's have it," Savage told him.

"You want me to interpret?"

"Sure."

"Albert Gross," Monk said, "lived on the north shore of Long Island, in a large house that is part of an estate having a greenhouse and stables. The house is new, been built within the last year, and the outside is white-painted brick, which should make it easier to find. The room in the house that Gross liked best is furnished in green velvet and the furniture is overstuffed. . . . Take a look and see how far you think I missed it. Here's my notes." I said: "Nice guessing."

"What guessing?" Monk asked.

"That stuff you just spouted."

"Don't be a dope."

"I'm not," I said. "That's why I don't swallow that line of Sherlock Holmes guff you just put out."

"No?"

"No," I said.

Monk gave me that baboon grin. "There were traces of salt on the coat fabric, and that—and the distribution of the traces—meant exposure to sea breezes. Ergo, he had been around the sea or seashore. I didn't find any salt-water spots, so it was probably the seashore. There was pollen from nine different flowers, including orchids of three varieties, on the cloth, or in it. That meant either a flower shop or greenhouse. There were several horse hairs on the lapels, from at least two different horses, both greys. He didn't get them petting horses ridden by New York cops, because the mounted police don't use grey horses. That meant country, an estate, a greenhouse. Get it?"

"Is this a rib?"

He shrugged. "There was a flake or so of white brick paint—a new type the Nazis developed during the war, and never on sale in America until the last year. It doesn't work on old brick that has been painted, only on new brick. Hence a new white house—and probably quite new, because he's been fooling around the outside of it to get the paint traces on him. There were plenty of green velvet hairs from upholstery fabric. . . . So, we get an estate in the country—where but in the country do you find estates?—with a greenhouse, near the north shore of Long Island. The last is a guess—the North Shore is where you find most of the estates near a seashore around New York City. And the house is white brick. Now do you catch on? See how simple."

"It sounds like moon-jumping to me," I said.

Doc Savage said, "Gross probably owns the estate."

"Huh?"

"Expensive suit. Three hundred dollars, probably. A man with that money for his clothes could own an estate."

"You too!" I said. "You mean to tell me you look at a piece off a guy's coat and tell where he went to school?"

"He went to school in Vienna, Austria," Doc Savage said.

"Yeah?" I said. "Now I know it's a rib."

Presently the telephone rang, and it was the police. They said they'd found the proprietor of the cleaning shop on Lexington Avenue, and were rushing him down to look at his records and see if Albert Gross had left an address when he left his suits to be cleaned.

"Ain't Lexington Avenue right here in downtown New York?" I asked. "Down the spout goes your wild-and-woolies about Gross having a Long Island estate."

They didn't seem discouraged. It appeared they were going to look on the north shore of Long Island for the place.

"You've laid out a month's job there," I said.

The police called again. They were at the cleaning fellow's shop, had found out all the man knew about Albert Gross, and it wasn't much. He remembered Gross. But it wasn't Gross who had brought in the stuff to be cleaned; it was the chauffeur. The chauffeur had brought in a half dozen of his boss' suits at a time, explaining the boss had a mad on at the cleaner out on Long Island where he lived. The man didn't know Gross' address, nor did he know the chauffeur's name and address. The chauffeur didn't answer the description of anybody we knew.

"What do we do now?" I asked. "Spend thirty days combing Long Island?"

Monk dug me. He said: "Oh, you admit Gross lived on Long Island, now?"

"Just because one pin fell down don't mean you got a strike," I said.

Doc Savage telephoned somebody named Edsing. He didn't get much satisfaction. He called somebody in Albany, the state capitol, and the somebody said he would phone Edsing right now and see that Edsing delivered satisfaction.

Monk Mayfair had me puzzled. When he went in the other room, I asked Doc Savage: "This guy Mayfair's got me guessing. He looks like an empty box. He looks like something grass wouldn't grow on. Maybe his looks are deceiving—eh?"

"Maybe," Savage said.

"Who is he?"

"Monk? His full name is Lieutenant Colonel Andrew Blodgett Mayfair. He has a lot of letters after his name meaning degrees and fellowships, but if you used them he'd hit you in the eye. He's one of the world's leading research chemists."

"I guess I'll overhaul my human-nature yardstick," I said.

The fellow Edsing, the one who hadn't given Savage satisfaction on the phone, arrived. He was weighted down with satisfaction and anxious to deliver it. The somebody in Albany had certainly built a fire on his coattail.

Edsing was with the New York State Highway, Department of Planning—a job he obviously feared might terminate as of tonight—and he had a suitcase full of aerial photographs. It seemed that, last fall, his department had made the pictures as a part of the planning for future highway development. He sweat a couple of pints while he was showing Doc Savage which photographs were the north shore of Long Island.

Doc Savage thanked him mildly, and asked me to show him out.

In the hall, Edsing grabbed me by the necktie and blurted, "Do you think I'll be fired?"

I asked him: "What's the matter, did a taxpayer bite you back?"

"Good God, I didn't realize who he was," Edsing gasped. "The Commissioner in Albany was mad as a hornet. Man, he ate me out up to here." He looked as if he was going to spray me with tears. "And me with a home I just paid two prices for, and a pregnant wife. Could you smooth it out for me with Savage?"

"I'm having trouble smoothing it out for myself," I said. "But I'll try."

Edsing filled my ear full of grateful words, and I got rid of him.

Savage and Monk Mayfair were going over the aerial photographs.

I said: "That guy thinks he's going to lose his job. His wife is in a family way, and it might go hard on him."

Savage was concerned. He told Monk Mayfair to send Edsing a note of thanks, and say that if Edsing would call so-and-so hospital, Mrs. Edsing would find her hospital services wouldn't cost her anything.

I asked: "Ain't that a kind of expensive tip for the reluctant favor the guy done?"

Monk said: "Doc owns the hospital. So what?"

They finished up by marking rings around three houses, or estates, which had greenhouses or stables and where construction of one or more buildings had been recent, as evidenced by fresh grading work around the buildings.

"We'll try those," Savage said.

"Damn it!" Monk said suddenly. "I'm worried about Ham Brooks! Why hasn't he reported in? Something has happened to him."

I said: "The way you've been talking about this lawyer Brooks, I figure you rated him about the same as a bad smell in your socks."

"Shut up!" Monk said.

They left a message for Ham Brooks in case he called. They told him the places they were going in Long Island, and why. Savage spoke this information into a gimmick that recorded it, and Monk told me the machine would put the words into the telephone when Ham Brooks called, if he called the unlisted phone number the contraption was hooked up to. I took his word for it.

"Sammy, you go along with us," Doc Savage said.

"Why?"

He didn't give me much satisfaction. Monk was more explicit, if less reassuring. He told me, "Doc probably thinks it a little odd that you got yourself in all this by chasing a sweet voice you heard over the telephone."

"You saw sweet-voice, didn't you?" I asked him.

"Sure. But Doc is more babe-resistant than you and me. and he probably overestimates our strength where one like Miss Fenisong is concerned."

"I don't think I got much strength where she's concerned," I said.

"You better get strong," he advised me. "Because I liked her looks, and I'll walk right over you, you get in my way."

"That face of yours will scare her to death," I said. "And if you fool with me, the face will look worse."

He wasn't much impressed.

I looked at the clock as we left. Only two hours! In two hours they had taken a piece torn off a man's coat and made it read like a book. I didn't know much about scientific detecting, but I was impressed.

I said: "There's one crack been made that I don't get."

"Only one?" Monk said, meaning that he was thinking about Miss Fenisong and didn't like me.

"Somebody said Gross went to school in Vienna, Austria," I explained. "That one I can't see through."

Savage said: "Gross attended *Osterreich Zoologische* University, or at least he had a tattoo mark in his armpit which was affected by the *Zoologische* students during the early twenties. The idea of armpit tattooing, instead of a class-ring, was a general practice, and preceded the Nazi practice of armpit tattoos to identify SS men, of which you may have heard.... Incidentally, you didn't see the armpit mark on Gross, nor have I but the police medical examiner described it accurately over the telephone."

"From Austria, huh?" I said. "That could mean something, couldn't it?"

He glanced at me as if I had pulled the rabbit out of the hat.

"It could be," he said.

Anyway they were some detectives. They had just about made a believer out of me.

VI

It was the third house. At the first place we tried, an aged butler in a nightshirt was polite to us, and at the second place two Great Dane dogs offered to eat us alive, if one was to believe their uproar. I was about to drop the needle on a recording of I-told-you-so, but something restrained me—probably common sense was getting a toehold on me.

The night was still with us, and would be for another two hours, since this was February and the nights were long. But there was a scattering of snow out here in the country that made the night seem less dark. Old snow, scabs too tough for the sun to melt, now hard-frozen, crusty, shiny. The driveway where it turned off had a thin glaze of ice, and we skidded across that and up to a stone gate-house and a pair of iron gates formidable enough for a penitentiary.

Nothing more than our headlights brought an old man out of the gate-house. An old man who was as big as a buffalo, taller than a buffalo and nearly as wide, but as thin and bony, and perhaps as tough, as he would be if constructed of oak sticks. He was wearing an enormous black overcoat. It looked like a shroud on a dead tree. He had a voice as deep, as amiable, as a skull rolling down a roof.

"Good morning," he said. "Can I be of some service?"

Savage asked him who lived here.

"The owner of the establishment, sir," said the old giant.

"Would his name be Albert Gross?" Savage asked.

He buttoned the black overcoat, doing it slowly, taking time to measure us with a micrometer and do a little thinking. His hair was as grey as an old seagull, nearly a foot long and seemed to stick out straight from his head everywhere. All he needed was a scythe, and he could play Death.

"This is indeed the residence of Mr. Albert Gross," he finally admitted.

He put one word after another like a mason fitting a row of stones in a wall. Each word was finely chiseled. English wasn't the language he'd heard in the cradle; I had been introduced to the detective business tonight, so I deduced this with confidence.

45

"We'd like to see Mr. Gross," Savage said.

It would be quite something if we did, I thought.

"I'm sorry. Mr. Gross is not here," said the old tower of bones.

"Mr. McGraff?"

"I'm sorry."

"Mr. McCutcheon?"

"Indeed I'm sorry," said the old man. "Mr. Gross, Mr. McGraff and Mr. McCutcheon left for the city early this morning—yesterday morning, I mean—and have not returned."

Doc Savage asked. "And Miss Fenisong?"

"Again I'm sorry. Miss Fenisong, I know, is an acquaintance of Mr. Gross—perhaps his niece, although I am not sure—but she does not live here, and is rather seldom a visitor. I regret being so disappointing."

Monk took it up. "We'd compromise for Mr. Spatny," he said.

"Who?"

"Don't you know Spatny?"

"I'm afraid I can't help you, sir." Old rack-of-bones shrugged. There was a gun in his hand, a gun that was big the way he was big. "Unless, of course, you prove to be friends of mine," he added.

He put the cavernous mouth of his firearm into the car window and let it look at us. Savage had rolled down the window in order to talk with him.

I don't know what got into me. Maybe I had just seen too much preposterous magic for one night, and this was the last straw. It wasn't heroism. I was scared cold as a kid who'd broke his first window. The first thing I knew, I had hold of the gun with both hands.

The second I matched strength with the old man, I knew I was going to need my rabbit-foot. He was tough like a thirty-cent steak. Trying to twist his arm was like trying to do the same thing to the leg of a mule. He used his free hand on me and gave me a worse headache than I'd had that morning.

Suddenly there was more noise in the car than anybody wanted. The old man's gun was speaking. It spoke twice. Both bullets hit the left-hand window, flattened and fell away, and so help me the window merely had two small splattered places where a couple of hard-flying and well-fed bugs might have hit.

Then old hard-as-nails no longer had the mortar, and I didn't have it either. Savage had taken it away from both of us.

The old man drew back. He didn't run, but merely waited.

Monk Mayfair spoke to me. He spoke fluently for more than a minute, giving his opinion of my impulsiveness, not one word fit to print.

"You're a fool," Doc Savage told me.

"Listen, guns make me jumpy," I said. "Where'd the old boy get it from, anyway? One moment he was bare-handed, and the next one he was loaded for bear."

"The car," Doc Savage told me, "is equipped with a device which discharges an odorless, colorless anaesthetic gas. He could have been overcome without all the wild-west."

"The gas would have got us, too," I said.

"No. We merely hold our breath, and in about forty seconds the gas undergoes a chemical reaction with the air and becomes ineffective."

"You couldn't have told me to hold my breath without him hearing," I said. "You'd have gassed me, too, I suppose."

Monk Mayfair said: "I'm in favor of doing that anyway! It would be a good idea. I vote for it."

We got out of the car. It was cold here in the country. The old man's breath came from his leathery lips as if he was blowing cotton. He said: "It's warmer in the gate-house, if you would care to converse there."

"We prefer the car," Savage said. "Climb in."

The old man limped slightly in his left leg as he moved. He got in the back seat with me, and I would have as soon welcomed a man-eating tiger. Monk Mayfair came around and got in with us, searched the old giant, and looked over what he had found—a wallet, a dun from the light company, a crested gold cigarette lighter, and more than a dozen big fat walnut-colored cigars.

"Fifty-centers," Monk said of the cigars. "And his name seems to be J. Heron Spatny, of 1880 Vista Road. His January light bill was eight dollars seventy. He has slightly over seven hundred dollars in cash."

Monk made a second search. He didn't find a holster. "Where were you carrying the gun?"

"Why, it was reposing in my sleeve," Spatny said.

Monk got out and looked in the gate-house, came back and reported, "There's a repeating shotgun standing inside the door, where he might have grabbed it if we had accepted his invitation for a conference in there."

The old man stirred uncomfortably. "Really, you're attributing me with excessive bloodthirstiness," he complained.

"Would you care to correct any other wrong ideas we might have?" Savage inquired.

Spatny sat with back bent, head bowed. But the top of his head was nearly against the top of the car anyway. He was taller than Savage. He said: "First, would you mind telling me who you are?"

Savage introduced himself, Monk Mayfair and me. The names seemed to mean nothing to the old Alp.

"I don't know you," Spatny said gloomily. "That's my trouble—I don't know enough about anything. If Albert had just told me more . . . But he didn't. Albert was so afraid, too."

"Albert Gross?" Savage said.

The old man lifted his head; it whacked the top of the car, and he lowered it again. "You know Albert Gross?"

Savage said: "Sammy, here, got better acquainted with him than the rest of us."

"A wonderful chap, Albert, don't you think?" Spatny said to me.

"Great," I agreed. "Very quick with a rap on the head, that Albert."

"I wish we could get hold of Albert and have him vouch for you gentlemen," Spatny said thoughtfully.

I said: "He ought to be easy to get hold of. But he's a little dead for vouching."

The old man jumped with every muscle. He rocked the car like a rowboat. Thinking he was starting a go-around, I ducked. But he gave only the one jump, sank back in the seat, and laid off breathing for a while. It was quiet enough to hear our breath condense in the cold. Then Spatny moaned like a hound that had ground glass with his dinner.

"Alfred is dead! *Das ist zu arg!* Oh my God!" He brought his hands to his face, and long as his face was, his hands would span it. The yellow skin showed between the fingers. "Is this true?" he blurted. Without waiting for an answer, he added, "Alfred—I was waiting here for him—he is my friend. He is in danger. He told me so this morning, and asked me for help. He made an appointment to meet me here, secretly, at midnight—after I agreed to help him."

Savage said: "Midnight? A meeting here?"

The words came out of the mountainous old man like rain out of a cloud. His name was J. Heron Spatny—the J. was for Jemnost—and he was a Czech, a refugee, five years in this wonderful United States of America. He had refugeed via Vienna, Austria, where he had met Albert Gross—then wearing the name of Albert Grossberger—under awfully nice circumstances. Albert had helped him lam from the Nazis, I gathered. Here in America. Spatny had spent four years in the traveling salesman business in Florida, and one year here in New York in the flower business. He had a shop on Madison Avenue near Thirty-fourth Street, he said. He was happy, getting rich, and Alfred Gross had turned up a few months ago, and they'd had a delightful reunion.

Alfred Gross didn't seem to have any business, and he had for partners in it Mr. McGraff and Mr. McCutcheon. Spatny intimated he didn't like McGraff and McCutcheon, didn't think highly of them either. But they, and Albert Gross, lived well at this estate, which Gross professed to own. Spatny thought the Macs were refugees too. Three idle refugees rolling in wealth, apparently.

"Truthfully, I imagined they had profited well in the business of getting refugees out of Europe, and had settled down to enjoy the fruits of their labors," said the old man.

Yesterday his friend Albert Gross had called on Spatny; they'd lunched, discussed old times, and Gross was noticeably jerky. But they hadn't done business yesterday—he kept referring to day before yesterday as yesterday—and the next day Gross had called on him again. Gross had intimated he was in a predicament, his life was in danger, and there was great devilment afoot. Would Spatny help him? In memory of old time spent dodging Nazis. Spatny would. The midnight appointment was made, Spatny had kept it, and here he was—Gross naturally hadn't shown.

That was what he had to tell us.

Doc Savage chiseled on him for more details. Savage asked: "What about Miss Fenisong? You said she was related to Gross—his niece? Was that straight?"

He confessed he'd made that up. He didn't have the speck of an idea who Miss Fenisong was. "I didn't know who you were, and I was pretending to be the gatekeeper," he explained.

"What about that chromospheric eruption tonight?" Savage demanded.

The old giant merely hung his mouth open.

I said: "And a black scare-baby in the street. Don't forget that one."

No pay.

Savage asked him how he'd like to help us pay a visit to the estate. He said he'd like it fine, and wanted to know exactly how Albert Gross had died. Savage told him about it without really telling him anything—just that Gross had been found dead of little holes following some strange doings at a banquet for scientists. Meantime, Monk got out and found the large iron gates were locked.

The gate-lock didn't stump Savage long. He picked it. He also found an alarm on it, and short-circuited the wiring so the thing wouldn't do us any dirt. We drove up a lane that could have been the Pennsylvania Turnpike, and came to the mansion, the greenhouse, the stables, a garage, servants' quarters, tool houses, guest cottage and a few other buildings. It was still dark night; if anything, it was darker than it had been. Clouds like soot rolls had moved in overhead.

Savage radioed the police. He asked them to check up on Mr. J. Heron Spatny, Madison Avenue florist.

At that, the old man hissed once like a viper.

"I'm relieved to find you are affiliated with the police," he said, which didn't fit with the hiss.

We got out of the car. The snow grunted under our feet, or squeaked like nails being pulled. It was cold, and the cold took hold of my nose and cheeks like somebody's fingers. I thought that an estate like this should have servants enough around to keep the sidewalks shoveled of snow.

Savage said: "Here, Sammy. Better put this on." He was offering me a kind of a jacket; I took it and it was a lot heavier than a jacket should be, but not as heavy as I thought it should be when I found out what it was.

"What's this?" I asked.

"Bulletproof vest."

"Wait a minute," I said. "Does anybody mind if I just start back to Kansas City?"

"Put it on," Savage said, and leaned a finger against a button. We could hear a set of chimes clanging, and no other sound for a while, and then a voice said loudly—and too friendly—a greeting.

"Come in, fellows," the voice said. "I'm glad you got here."

Savage looked at Monk. Monk looked at Savage. There was a certain amount of cooperation in the way their eyebrows went up, then down, questioningly.

"Ham Brooks?" I asked.

"His voice, anyway," Monk said.

"What's the matter?"

"Too friendly," Monk said. "Watch." He lifted his voice and called, "Ham, this is Monk."

"Well, come in, old pal, old pal," said the deep oratorical voice. "Don't stand out there in the cold, old friend."

Monk shook his head. "Something's wrong. Normally he'd invite me to freeze to death."

We went in anyway.

He was a man I had seen at the banquet, and not remembered as well as I should have. He had wide shoulders, a trim waist; a good-looking man except for an over-wide mouth and hair that was a little slick, too wonderfully barbered for my taste. He wore full dress—tails, white tie—and I had supposed one monkey suit was about like another, but this one had class and snap. I found out later Ham Brooks was reputed one of the best-dressed men in New York, but I think I knew it then.

He sat in one of the parlors—there would be several parlors in a house like this—on a gold-brocaded, purple velvet, fringe-edged divan that was large enough to hold half a dozen other occupants. He didn't get up and the great pleasure in his voice was not matched by the expression on his face as he said, "Come in, come in. How many of you are there? Just four of you? Is that all?"

Monk said: "We left the others outside holding the reindeer. . . . What are you pulling off, Ham?"

Ham Brooks said too loudly, "Nothing at all—unless I want to learn whether or not I'm bulletproof. I'm quite sure I'm not, so the test doesn't appeal."

"Huh?"

"I have great faith in my judgment of human nature," Ham Brooks added. "I hope it isn't misplaced. Otherwise I'd have a rather sad opinion of myself for inviting you in."

Monk got it. He said: "Male or female?"

"Who?"

"Behind the pretty divan," Monk said.

Ham Brooks sighed like the fellow who had decided he would have to swim the creek where the alligator was. He said: "It's Miss Fenisong."

"Ah!"

"Indignant and well-armed," Ham added.

In the silence that followed, if frowns had had magnetic properties, the divan would have been lifted and suspended. Monk Mayfair said: "Sammy, would you care to try out the properties of your new bulletproof vest by being first to look behind the divan?"

"Miss Fenisong wouldn't shoot nice people like us," I said. "But no thanks, anyway."

Doc Savage said: "A tense situation like this makes one hold one's breath, doesn't it?"

I missed the cue. The floor rocked a little, steadied, came up and rested against my face, gently enough. I slept, but I didn't dream of a thing.

VII

Awakening was just as pleasant—I swam up out of nothing that was soft and not at all bad, and there I was, on a nice tiled floor, with ice-water flying into my face. No headache. Not much dizziness. Just a feeling of having been a fool.

My head came clear quickly, too; because at once I knew that Savage must have used some of that gas they had talked about, the stuff that you couldn't see nor smell, that would knock you, but not if you held your breath for as long as forty seconds. I hadn't held my breath. Savage had hit me with a hint that was as big as a scoop-shovel, but my latch string hadn't been out.

"Never a dull moment. Oh, boy!" I said.

Monk Mayfair said: "You should have let me put him in the bathtub." He was talking to Ham Brooks, who was looking pleased with the world, and with as much of Miss Fenisong's leg as he could see.

Miss Fenisong still slept. Whoever had picked her up and arranged her in the chair should have been a window-dresser in one of those Broadway shops I'd noticed that day, the places where sexy black underthings seemed to be the principal article of trade. Asleep, she was nice. I was wide awake in no time.

"We ought to get together on these things," I said. "If you've got any more trick gadgets, how about letting me know?"

Ham Brooks examined me. He didn't exactly fall on his face with approval. "Who is this chap?" he asked. "A taxi driver?"

"What's the matter with taxi drivers?" I demanded.

Savage told the dapper lawyer who I was. He could have made my character stand out a little more in the telling.

"Miss Fenisong is reviving," Monk remarked, and that put a stop to my history. We gathered around and waited admiringly. Even the old giant, Spatny, had his shoulders back.

She awakened the way I had. Quick. Clear-headed. She arranged her skirt more decorously, disappointing Monk. She had a natural question. "What happened?" she wanted to know.

Doc Savage said: "Mr. Brooks advises me that you took him unawares, menaced him with a gun"—he nodded briefly at a .25-caliber automatic, blue, lady-size, on the table—"and were holding him here, apparently pending the arrival of friends."

"Unawares—nothing!" she said. "He had been trailing me. He had his eyes open wide enough, particularly when I was getting out of a cab and the wind blew my skirt. I may have outsmarted him, but he was clearly aware I was in existence."

She saw me, and said, "Oh, hello, Mr. Wales. I'm glad Mr. Gross didn't do much harm to you."

"It's all right with me now," I said. "I should have made it more clear that I wasn't Mr. Wales the moon expert when I came to see you at your hotel."

"I'm sorry Mr. Gross was nasty," she said. "It was uncalled for. I'm going to tell him so, too."

"That will be a hard—"

Doc Savage, cutting ahead of me before I could give anything away, said, "Did you leave the banquet with Mr. Gross, Miss Fenisong?"

She shook her head. "No. Mr. Brooks can tell you that."

"And you haven't seen or heard of Mr. Gross since?"

"No."

"And Mr. McGraff and Mr. McCutcheon—what about them?"

She hesitated. We could see she had decided not to tell us anything.

Ham Brooks said: "I think she was waiting here for Gross, McGraff and McCutcheon."

They were building Miss Fenisong up to a shock when she found out Gross was dead. It was all right with me; I didn't think she would feel too badly; it was my idea that she hadn't thought too much of Gross. Still, the guy had been at home in her room at the hotel, and he'd ordered her around as if he had certain rights. . . .

When Savage had her set up, and had given her a chance to be cooperative and she wouldn't, he gave her the Gross death.

She fooled me and probably all of us. She fainted.

I was trying to think of one single nice thing to think about what had probably been her relationship with Gross when Ham Brooks looked at the window, and said, "Say, it's getting daylight in a hurry, isn't it?"

Savage went to the window, went fast, and said, "It's not dawn—unless the sun is coming up straight overhead." He sounded shocked.

It was that light again. Not quite the way it had been earlier that night, when we saw it from the hotel terrace, thirty or so stories above the street, and with no clouds above that. The clouds didn't seem to cut it down in brilliance, exactly, but they changed the effect, gave it a different coloring, a kind of bluish quality that seemed to get in your eyes and stay there, as if you'd been looking too long and too close at a cop's uniform.

Spatny came over, stood beside me. He seemed to be twice as tall as I was.

Spatny said: "What is this?"

"You tell me," I said, and put my face close to the window glass in order to see how it looked coming through the clouds.

"Better not look directly at it. There might be emanations harmful to the eyes." This was Savage. There was plenty of alarm, of the kind you feel when you're lying in a shellhole and know a tank is going to run over it, back of his calmness.

I didn't want to look at it any longer anyway. There was something coming across the lawn that I wanted to look at a lot more. It was thirty or forty feet in diameter and as black as the original bad luck cat.

Monk Mayfair, probably intrigued by our petrified stances, came over and took a look.

"A visitor," he said.

He sounded as if his head had moved about six feet from his body to make the statement.

Savage said: "Get to the car! Everybody! Quick!"

I picked up Miss Fenisong. I was thinking about Gross in her hotel room, but I picked her up anyway. I beat Monk Mayfair to it by a yard.

Monk said: "Let a strong man carry her, panty-waist."

"If you're so strong," I said, "go out and fight that thing in the yard!"

Monk showed how upset he was by bellowing at me, "What is that thing?"

I didn't take the trouble to tell him I didn't know. I started walking out of the room with the girl. She didn't weigh a thing in my arms. I didn't weigh an ounce myself. I was so scared I floated in the air.

Spatny went with us. The old giant was active, or he couldn't have managed that—we passed through the rooms like antelope. The old man's right foot made a little more noise than his left foot hitting the floor, because of his limp; I remember thinking it must be a genuine limp, or he would have forgotten about it now. Awfully genuine.

There was another one in the front yard.

Two black scare-babies.

This second one was poppa. About sixty feet across and nearly as high. There was a tall Australian pine tree out there that I'd noticed when we arrived that was all of fifty feet, and it was hidden behind this thing.

"Perhaps," Savage said, "we best not go outside."

It was all right with me. They couldn't have shot me out into the yard if they had stuffed me in a cannon. I still wasn't weighing a thing, and neither was my lovely burden, and if I still had a heart I couldn't find it.

Savage said: "Has anyone got a gun?"

No one had a gun.

He went back after the little pea-shooter they had taken from the girl. I don't think anyone liked his going; we didn't want to be left alone with the goblins.

Old man Spatny made us a bitter speech. "No guns!" he said. "*Das ist zu arg!* No guns! Of all the unequipped fools! When there is such danger, not to have armed yourselves— you are imbeciles! I was beginning to admire your methods, but you have disappointed me grievously. No guns! Disgusting! Surely it should have occurred to you to—"

He stopped expressing my opinions and his, and took off. He just seemed to split at the seams, and what came out was action. He wanted to get away from there, and he did. I was under the impression he went through doors without troubling to open them, but that must have been an illusion, because there were no splinters in the air after he had gone.

"Catch him!" Monk yelled.

"Catch him yourself," Ham said. "I may follow his example."

We heard the little gun go *pip!* in another part of the house. Savage had started shooting. It was an utterly inadequate little noise, it struck me.

The old giant was crashing and banging doors in the back of the mansion somewhere. His flight had the sedateness of a bull in a crockery shop. The terminus of the uproar was a particularly loud jangling crash of glass—and I happened to be standing where I could see what Spatny had done. The mansion was T-shaped, and we were in the stem of the T; the old man had come into the left arm of the T, where there were large French doors of glass. He had gone through one of these French doors, or windows—just simply passed through it.

I wished I had been with him.

And then I didn't—for the it-couldn't-be in the yard began chasing him. The *it* didn't move rapidly, not as fast as the old man was moving—possibly nothing could have traveled quite that fast—and it took a rather erratic S-shaped route across the grounds. The serpentine path was puzzling. . . . It was following a sidewalk! That was the reason! It seemed to have no liking for the grass, which was a white carpet of frost where it was not glazed over with snow. It kept on the paved walks which snaked across the grounds in almost any direction one cared to take.

Monk said: "I'm going to try something." He began working at a window, and got it open. There was a storm sash and he threw that upward—he had one leg over the sill when Savage came in, demanding, "What are you doing?"

"The old guy ran—"

"Stay in here," Savage said. He seemed confident his instructions would be followed, because he went back to the other part of the house, the part where he had been, and his little gun went *pip!* again. This time there was a deep bass rejoinder—a rifle had been fired at him, a rifle that was plenty of gun because we could hear plaster falling off at least three walls that the bullet had gone through.

The old giant screamed. Off there in the garish phony moonlight somewhere, he cried out. . . . I went big-game hunting in Wyoming one time—well, at least I was there; I was the big-shot's chauffeur—and the coyotes occasionally howled around the camp in the night, and I think that coyote howling is the most ghastly sound there is. This sound old Spatny made was something similar. It made my teeth feel as if they were on a grindstone.

Five seconds, ten, after the old man kiyoodled, the black business was gone. It was out there in the trees and shrubbery; it got smaller. It was like a black balloon with the air going out, except there was no noise. In a trifle of time, it was smaller than the trees and we couldn't see it at all.

Monk said hoarsely, "The poor old devil!" He wheeled and ran through rooms. He was looking for Doc Savage to tell him what had happened.

Savage was in a large room, an enormous room that was a state dining room or a ballroom or possibly both. He was throwing small stuff—vases, statuettes, light chairs—at the ceiling fixture trying to put out the illumination in the room.

Savage said: "Watch out! Keep away from the windows!"

Ham Brooks said: "Why—"

Three bullets came in, giving him an answer. They dug holes in a picture, walls, and in our peace of mind. There was very little of the latter left. I listened closely to the sound of the weapon outdoors, and I figured about three years spent during the water listening to guns whack made me an authority, so I said: "A rifle, a .30-06 caliber and probably a model M1."

Monk Mayfair said, "Shorter barrel, I think from the

sharper sound. More likely a carbine. Those short guns always talk like a short man, too big for their britches."

He was probably right at that.

The phony moonlight went away. It just died out. Not instantly—the process of going took a second or two; it was like when you throw a bucket of water in the air; a few drops are always late reaching the ground. Then it was dark.

It seemed to be over for the time being. We picked out different windows and did plenty of cautious looking and listening, but outdoors it had become a normal night again.

Miss Fenisong awakened. She didn't have much to say— we had doused all the lights in the house in order to see into the night better, and apparently she thought at first that she was alone in the mansion, because she began trying to stumble around. Savage told her, "Better sit and rest, Miss Fenisong."

She did that.

I broke out into cool sweat and had a couple of chills, a reaction from what had happened. It was the worst when I thought of how the old giant had yelled out there in the night when that impossible patch of blackness had overtaken him. I said: "Nobody is going to tell me that was straight stuff, not anything that fantastic. It's a gag of some sort. It's got to be."

Nobody agreed with me, but Monk said, "It's good to be ignorant, because ignorance is bliss."

Presently it began to get a little lighter outside, but this light didn't scare anyone. It was the dawn. It came to us quite slowly and normally, as daylight should come. The clouds weren't as thick in the sky as I had thought. They were cumulous, a thin layer of cotton-ball clouds.

Savage said: "I guess it's safe to look for tracks."

If he meant footprints, there weren't any. At least none I could see, and I heard Monk and Ham telling each other there didn't seem to be a trace—other than the widely spaced prints, a little like those of a hard-pushed jackrabbit, that old Spatny had made leaving the house. We trailed him through a neatly trimmed woods to a black-topped road, and that was the end of his trail. There were no signs of a struggle. The black-top hadn't retained a trail—the sun of the last few days had melted the snow off the road, as it had off the sidewalks that turkey-tracked the estate.

Miss Fenisong had missed out on our visitation from the

queer light and the black no-such-things. I told her about it. She was so beautiful that I got to thinking about her and Gross, and I said most of the last part of it through my teeth.

She listened without a word, then asked, "How did Albert die?"

I told her that. Maybe my tone partly conveyed that it was going to be hard for me to shed tears about Gross not being one of us any longer.

"Albert was my half-brother," she said.

"Huh?"

"My mother was first married in Czechoslovakia, and separated from her husband, leaving her baby—Albert—with her husband when he got custody of the child in court. She came to the United States, married again to a man named Fenisong, and I was her child by the second marriage."

I was so pleased I couldn't have hit the floor with my hat. I wasn't even able to keep my feet on the floor; it was almost the same thing as a while ago, when I had been so scared.

"Savage!" I yelled. "Come here!"

Her parents—mother and second husband named Fenisong—had died natural deaths two and seven years ago. Fenisong, an art gallery operator, had been well-to-do, and Paula Fenisong had inherited his money, which explained how she was able to live in a place like the *Parkside-Regent*. She had only lived there a couple of weeks, having moved from an even more expensive place, which accounted for her not being well known to the management.

The half-brother, Albert Gross, had looked her up more than a year ago. He had changed his name from Grossberger to Gross, migrated from Austria—he said he had been living in Austria for several years, having left Czechoslovakia to escape the domination of his father, who was a tyrant and a Nazi to boot—and had a nice stamp business in New York. He dealt in rare stamps, finding and buying them on order for wealthy collectors. There had been no special closeness between brother and sister—or half-brother and half-sister—which was natural since they had never seen each other before, but they'd had dinner together a few times, and the relationship had been all right. Not close, but friendly.

She had not, at this time, met McGraff or McCutcheon.

That had come a few days ago when Gross came to her and said that he needed her help. He wanted her to get

acquainted with Doc Savage, and see that he took a look at
the moon from the terrace of the *Parkside-Regent* at precisely
fifteen minutes past seven o'clock. Miss Fenisong had—or
she said she had, and I for one believed her—been under-
standably reluctant and curious. Her hesitancy had been
overcome by Albert Gross's protestations that this was a
tremendous thing, vitally important to a great many people—
and finally, when he broke down and told her there was a
devilish plot afoot and that he couldn't go to the authorities
about it because he, Albert Gross, was an alien illegally
resident in the United States, she had agreed to decoy Doc
Savage, see that he was on the terrace and looking at the
moon at seven fifteen.

Gross had impressed her with the fact that Doc Savage
was an extraordinary sort, wary of feminine traps, and that
the best way of getting his interest was to be very erudite and
scientific. Considering the circumstances, the moon seemed a
logical subject to be scientific about, and so she had read up
on lunar theory, and, finding it was quite involved and
mathematical, they had negotiated for a coach named Wales.
That was how I got into it.

She told all of it without coaching, said that was all she
knew, and answered Savage's questions. He wanted to know
what the strange light was, what the black things were, who
Spatny was, and where the two Macs could be found, and
who the two Macs were. Negative answers to all this. She'd
told us all she had.

"Mind re-telling it to a lie detector?" Savage asked.

"Now wait a minute!" I said. "It's not any fun to have
that gadget strapped to you and—"

The too-sweet ding-dong-bong of the door chimes
interrupted me. Monk went to the door. We heard him swear
a mighty oath. He sounded like a pirate who had sighted two
treasure-laden galleons.

Monk, wearing a grin that pushed his ears together at
the back of his head, brought the company inside and introduced them as: "Our two lost sheep!"

The two Macs were ready and willing to tell us plenty of
nothing. McGraff—the shorter one with the lesser red face—
made most of the speech. McCutcheon confined himself to
head-nodding, or saying, "That is correct!" in a fine baritone
voice.

Albert Gross had been their pal. He had asked them to help him get Savage to look at the moon at 7:15 p.m.

Gross hadn't said why.

They had picked on me because they felt I was no friend of Albert Gross—that much of what they said was certainly true.

They had come out here to see Albert. They didn't know he was dead. . . . Dead! Albert dead? How awful! They blew their noses into handkerchiefs. They wouldn't rest until their friend's murderer was found. Never! McGraff said this first, then McCutcheon said it.

Savage asked: "We can depend on your help?"

"Emphatically!"

I opened my mouth to say let's try the lie detector on them. But I didn't, because Monk Mayfair kicked me on the shin. Just before that I had been smiling at Miss Fenisong, and Monk kicked a lot harder than neccessary.

VIII

The next five hours were productive of nothing. The police came to the Long Island estate, listened to the facts, which they naturally didn't believe, and were polite about it all.

McGraff and McCutcheon seemed surprisingly willing to be locked up if the police wanted it that way. When Doc Savage said that he would like to have them along so they could be asked more questions, they were agreeable to that also. But no more agreeable than they were to being in jail.

I said: "I don't make them two guys out."

"They're scared stiff, you dope," Monk said. "They want protectors. Either us or the police will do."

This did seem logical.

We all went—excepting the police, of course—to Doc Savage's headquarters on the eighty-sixth floor of that midtown building. While they had Miss Fenisong in the library, fitting the lie detector to her, I got myself alone in the reception room with tall Mac. I hit him. I began with a light chair, figuring it would soften him up.

Maybe a heavier chair would have been a better idea. Perhaps not. From the unhampered quality of his reactions, a sixteen pound sledge would hardly have been adequate. He was all over me. I was on the floor. The best I could do was keep him on the floor with me.

Monk Mayfair came in. All he did was watch admiringly. All he said was: "I've paid ten bucks ringside, and seen less."

Ham Brooks came in too, and his attitude was about the same. A bit more clinical, perhaps, because he remarked: "The technique is certainly original Bushido judo."

I was too busy to even ask for help, although I outweighed the tall Mac at least thirty pounds. Most of what he was doing to me he did with the tips of his fingers, the edge of his hand, and a lot of the time he handled me so that I seemed to be doing it to myself.

It was certainly a relief to have Savage come in and detach my intended victim from me.

My excuse was: "That guy started the beating I got at the hotel by sticking his fingers in my eyes. He had pepper on his fingers, remember?"

Savage had no comment. Miss Fenisong had entered, a part of the lie-detector hanging to her arm, to watch. I felt about as heroic as some of those guys we saw after we got into Germany.

"You two had better shake hands," Ham Brooks suggested.

"And get my arm torn off?" I said. "Not me."

That happened about nine o'clock, and by ten I wouldn't have bid high on the chances of finding any more answers than we already had. The latter, everyone seemed to feel, were negligible.

Miss Fenisong came through the lie-detector with flying colors. She was most cooperative, even letting Monk Mayfair ask her a few personal questions which had no bearing on the mystery, but were questions I wanted answered too.

"Okay," I said, getting Monk into a corner afterward. "Is she fancy free?"

He said: "You're out of luck. She's married to a guy named Culpepper, an engineer who is in South America building a banana plantation."

"That's oil from some of his bananas you're giving me," I said. I had seen him looking at the wiggly mark the lie detector had made, and grinning.

Doc Savage had been tinkering with the lie detector. He was frowning. "Ham," he called, "have we an extra third stage bypass electronic tube? This one has been getting weaker and weaker, and seems to have given out."

Ham Brooks said: "I don't know of a way of getting one of that special type short of Pittsburgh, where they're made."

Savage got on the telephone and ordered one from Pittsburgh, directing it be air-mailed.

"They can't get it here before late afternoon," he reported. Turning to the Macs, he added, "We intend, of course, to give you two gentlemen a lie-detector test. I gather you have no objections. Unfortunately, our apparatus is out of commission, and we'll have to postpone it until this evening."

The Macs didn't seem at all unhappy.

"The police use them things, don't they?" I demanded. "Why not borrow one?"

Savage shook his head. "I'm inclined to distrust the accuracy of the type they have."

Ham Brooks got me aside and said: "Keep your smart suggestions to yourself, pumpkin-seed."

"Oh!" I said.

If they were fixing something for the Macs, Sherlock Holmes and his magnifying glass couldn't have seen what it was. Relations were most amiable.

It was one of the Macs—McCutcheon—who suggested that we all stay together, which possibly saved Doc Savage from making the same motion. McCutcheon used too many words to say that, although he realized the facts did not substantiate the belief fully, it was conceivable that we might all be in danger, not so much because of what we knew, but because our antagonist—man, machine, or man-from-Mars, whichever it was—might feel that we knew more than we did. In view of such hypothetical danger, perhaps we should stick together for mutual protection. Savage agreed it was a sound idea, so we stuck together.

We had breakfast—discovering that Savage had his own food privately prepared—and some of us tried to sleep. I hadn't had a wink last night, my eyes felt like golf balls and my tongue tasted like last week's cigar stub, but I was able to get just as much sleep as everyone else—none at all.

"Do you mind not hanging around in here?" Savage asked when I tried standing around in the laboratory.

The big bronze man had dropped everything to work on

some kind of a contraption, and I was curious about what it was.

"Go keep Miss Fenisong company," he added.

I liked the advice, but the Macs were moving in on that territory. They had smooth manners, voices as confidence-building as insurance salesmen, they didn't find their work unpleasant, and they had an additional advantage in having known the deceased half-brother. They did plenty with the last, building Gross up as a great guy, their pal, a fellow who had been kind to dumb animals.

It is not supposed to be cricket to speak ill of the dead, but Albert Gross was down in my book as a large stinker. Right alongside him were the Macs. I did not participate in the conversation, not trusting myself to show either respect for the departed or politeness to the living.

Around eleven o'clock I accidentally happened to over-hear a conversation between the Macs and Miss Fenisong. This accidental bit of news was interesting, even if the only accident about it was that they didn't happen to hear me ease along behind a row of bookcases in the library until I was in earshot. For once I was light-footed as a leaf.

Short Mac—McGraff—was saying, "—not deny for a moment your contention that the man has personality, a presence, and surroundings." He gestured at the surroundings, added, "This layout, as you can see, cost a fortune. How does Savage explain it? Why, on the basis that he needs such laboratory and research facilities for his profession, which is righting wrongs and punishing evildoers—to use the words I heard somebody speak. Now I ask you—what do you think of that for a profession?"

"I—well—it seems unusual," Miss Fenisong said.

They already had her doubtful.

McGraff closed with her, selling his proposition at full speed. He said: "Look, how old are you, Paula? Twenty-three? Let's say you're twenty-three, that you've been around this world that many years. Then I want to ask you how many knights in shining armor, good fairies, or just plain Good Samaritans you've met in that time."

"I've met some Samaritans," she said, not entirely with him yet.

"Well, it's ridiculous! A grown man, righting wrongs for a career! Even with salt. I can't take that," McGraff said.

Miss Fenisong frowned. "What are you getting at?"

"Something pretty serious," he told her. "It's this: Why do you suppose Albert was interested in Doc Savage—and so secretive about it? Doesn't that strike you as peculiar?"

"It certainly did." She was emphatic about that.

"Maybe," said McGraff, "Albert knew what he was doing in being secretive."

"Oh!"

"Yeah—maybe it was Savage whom Albert was afraid of," said McGraff grimly. "McCutcheon and I know Albert—and we know he was as honest as a July day is long. Albert was no crook; I don't care what happens, Paula, you can bet on Albert. Now, Albert was afraid of someone, and the person he was investigating was Doc Savage. That must have been what Albert was doing—investigating Doc Savage. That's probably why he wanted Savage on the terrace of the hotel at 7:15. He wanted to watch Savage's reaction. Albert probably felt that, by observing Savage, he could see whether the man was guilty."

Miss Fenisong was silent. A shocked silence, I gathered. Like my own.

"Because of what he had done, Albert got killed," said McGraff. "Albert was investigating Savage, and he got killed. Now, who would be likely to kill him? Let's be practical. Let's not dream. Let's say the logical one to knock him off was Savage."

She must have looked pretty upset at that, because the long Monk jumped into the selling job. His voice sounded as if he had been oiling and preening it while he waited.

McCutcheon said: "Mr. McGraff and I have discussed this Spatny chap, and we've concluded he must be what he said he was—another good friend of Albert's. And he, too, met foul play."

"But Mr. Savage didn't have anything to do with what happened to Spatny!" she objected.

I knew what the Macs were doing with the silence— sneering.

"How do *you* know, my dear?" McCutcheon asked. "You were unconscious, were you not? You had fainted from the shock of learning Albert was dead."

Her indrawn breath was like fear going into a cold room.

"Uh-huh," said McGraff. "That's it. That's the point we're making. . . . We, the three of us, may be in just as much danger as Albert was—and not from some mysterious mumbo-jumbo. From Savage!"

McCutcheon laughed about as ugly a laugh as you could take out of a coffin. He said: "You don't for a moment believe this mumbo-jumbo about black things fifty feet high, do you?"

That was something Miss Fenisong hadn't thought of. It was a good argument, a fine clincher, too. The best argument is one you can't answer without seeming a fool, and this one was that. Who was willing to believe there were black spooks fifty feet high? They were hard to believe when you had seen them, and Miss Fenisong hadn't seen them. . . .

Monk Mayfair, the big chew, came into the library yelling, "Sammy! Hey, Sammy! Where are you, shining-eyes?" And I had a busy three seconds moving down to the other end of the library where I could call, "I was just coming in here to get a book. What do you want?" As innocent as anything.

"You couldn't understand any of these books," Monk said. "Doc says you can beat it if you want to. He's decided you're innocent enough."

"On what theory does he figure I'm honest?"

"Search me. On the theory no evil can grow in an ivory ball, I guess."

From the other end of the library, behind the big bookcases where the Macs had been doing that selling job on Miss Fenisong, there wasn't a sound. They were as quiet as the mouse after the cat ate it.

"No, thanks," I told Monk. "I'll stick around."

"No need to trouble yourself," he said.

"Oh, you're real educational, and I like it," I said, and leered, meaning to let him know that I knew the main idea with him was to get me out of competition for lovely-voice.

Savage listened to me patiently—but without, I had a feeling, removing more than two per cent of his attention from something purplish that was happening to something liquid yellowish in a glass thing I had heard called a wash bottle.

I said: "You're being sold down the river by two ter-mites. The Macs are boring from within."

He asked what I meant, and I told him.

"Indeed?" he said.

"The rats," I said.

"Oh, they were only doing some natural conjecturing," he said.

"They were conjecturing a coat of tar on to you, as far as the girl is concerned," I said. "If you've got a baseball bat around here I can borrow, I'll do a little missionary work on the Macs."

Savage said: "The technique of Bushido judo which McGraff demonstrated includes quite a repertory of moves for disarming an opponent armed with a club, in case you are interested."

"Yeah, but the alley will be dark next time," I said. "Thanks for the note, though."

"I appreciate your interest."

"Aren't you gonna take steps about this?"

He said: "If you don't happen to notice any counter-moves don't feel unduly alarmed."

I felt better. "This guy Monk is trying to chase me. What about that?"

"Want to pull out?"

"Well, no. I haven't got a home, but that's not why I don't want to go to it." My ears got red and I had trouble with my words like the tough kid standing in front of the class while teacher made him admit he pulled Mary's pigtail because he liked Mary. "Miss Fenisong has happened to say a couple of nice words to me. That's the rock Monk is chewing on."

"Stick around, then," he said, and I walked out of there with the little wings on my feet helping me along. He was on my side. The Monk must have given trouble before with his chasing.

Six hours passed and it was five o'clock, a long time later. It probably seemed longer than it was. The telephone had done plenty of ringing, but it was either the police or Doctor Hodges, the scientist, and they had no developments to report. They only wanted to know if there had been any. They seemed to feel that Doc Savage was taking, for him, an unusually long time to show results.

"Come into the laboratory," Savage said.

He looked hard-used. His fingers were stained from chemicals, his shirt was wrinkled, and sheets of notes were sticking out of his pockets where he had absently stuffed them.

The laboratory was too full of complicated gadgets—I didn't notice that anything new had been added, not until he pointed out two clusters of apparatus—wires, tubes, things that looked like a composition of all the radar transmitters I had ever seen in the army—at the other end of the laboratory. There was a cleared space there. Nearer at hand was a smaller portable gadget in a box hastily improvised from a big suitcase.

Savage distributed eye-protectors, saying, "Better put them on, in case there should be flying glass." There was nothing unusual about the shields; they were of plexiglass shaped like welder's masks. The grinder operators in the bomber plant in Kansas City, Kansas, where I worked before the army got me had worn similar transparent masks.

Savage said: "We won't be technical. . . . At the other end of the room is a transmitter of microwavelengths, built on laboratory scale—which, incidentally, is as far as we have been able to progress in the research field—probably similar to the one being used to cause the effect we refer to as chromospheric eruptions. It has to be similar, in fact. The other transmitter is enormously more powerful, however."

He showed us a large glass bottle—about five-gallon size—surrounded by magnets and stuff.

"Air has been pumped out of the bottle, and certain elements introduced, and magnetic effects applied, so that we have here what amounts to a bottled bit of the stratosphere layer where the effects we saw last night were produced."

He said he would demonstrate. He turned on the machine. The result was not anything to stand my hair on end; the transmitter contraption just lit up like a radio. There was no particular sound.

"Notice the interior of the bottle," Savage said.

The bottle was glowing with approximately the same quality of ghost-light that had appeared in the sky last night.

"Now," he added, "we will recreate the field of neutralization."

He threw a switch, and the second piece of apparatus proceeded to give me a mild case of cold tracks up and down the back. . . . A noticeable darkness had appeared around the thing.

Savage said: "Turn out the lights, draw the curtains, and

the impression one would get is of a fuzzy black area completely enveloping the neutralizing transmitter. Simply stated—the visible wave-lengths of light are no longer present, having been broken up around a short area, and what we have left is a patch of the normal darkness of the night."

"Hey!" I said. "You mean there wasn't any black can't-believe-its?"

"Exactly. What we saw was merely a small area of normal night. It looked spectacular because it was something we were not accustomed to. We are perfectly familiar with making a light in the night. But making night in the light is something different."

I think I admitted it was different, all right.

Savage was speaking naturally and even using a tone that implied there was still a great deal he didn't know about the thing, but he was becoming impressive as anything. The Macs did not like that; both of them were glancing at Miss Fenisong dubiously, and the admiration on her face did not cheer them. The long Mac began tearing it down. He said: "Mr. Savage, you admit being present when Albert Gross died last night"—he gave that some extra meaning—"and you said, I believe, that it was a city street where it happened. The street near the hotel. Now, you're not telling us there would be the darkness of night in a city street, with lighted windows and streetlamps, are you? After all, witnesses say a black thing pursued poor Albert. By your own words, there couldn't be a black thing unless there was night. How do you account for that?"

Savage turned to me. "Sammy, what did I do with you after I took you out of the hotel?"

"After these two lugs were scared off before they could knock me off, you took me downstairs and we talked in your car," I said.

McCutcheon yelled: "You silly fool! Do you imply your life was in danger from us last night?"

"I know damn well it was!" I yelled back at him.

Savage made smoothing-down motions with his hands and said: "Let's skip personalities—we can gain nothing by becoming a house divided. . . . The point is that Sammy sat in the car on the street and talked to me. Isn't that right, Sammy?"

"That's right. But I don't like this guy calling me a fool—"

"Did you see Albert Gross immediately?" Savage asked.

"See him? No, not right away."

"Why not?"

"It was a side street, kind of dark. Pretty darn dark, in fact."

"You're sure it was rather dark?"

"I ought to know," I said. "I could hardly make Gross out even after you pointed at him, and I didn't recognize him until we were right beside him."

"That should answer the question of whether the street was dimly lighted enough for the black 'thing' effect to be achieved," Savage said.

The Macs subsided. They didn't want to, but they saw they were getting nowhere, and probably felt that they had made their point for Miss Fenisong—that Savage *could* be lying.

"Now," Savage continued, "we have produced the chromospheric eruption on a laboratory scale, proving we have the fundamentals of the system used. And we have a demonstration of the neutralization of the visible spectrum of the emanations to indicate how the effect of black shapeless objects was produced. If you'll step to the other end of the room . . ."

He had the other piece of apparatus, the stuff in the suitcase, for our attention.

He said: "This is also a neutralizer, but of a different type—I won't become technical about this one either. Let's say that it merely creates a high-frequency field which blocks certain cathode functions in the other transmitter, with violent results. Any questions?"

McGraff put out his jaw and said: "You say you're not being technical, but it sounds damned complicated to me. If you turn on this contraption here—what will happen exactly?"

"I could demonstrate," Savage said.

"Do that."

"Hold your hat," Savage said. He closed a switch and nothing much happened except some tubes lighted up; then closed a second switch, and the other end of the room came apart in flash and noise.

*   *   *

It was a little too late to hit the floor, but I hit it anyway. The Macs were there ahead of me. Their speed in getting there gave me a fact from their past history—they had once been in a war somewhere. A one hundred per cent civilian background wouldn't produce that kind of reaction.

The plastic shields came in handy, because a little glass reached us, fragments that buzzed like mosquitoes as they traveled. And the room suddenly had the smell of an electrical power-house in a thunderstorm.

"Jove! The transmitter blew up," Ham Brooks said, sounding about as startled as a senator who had dropped his briefcase.

Monk gave it more. He yelled: "Hey, you gotta gadget that'll destroy the transmitter!"

The Macs got up from the floor with sheepish looks and—but this went away quickly—about the same surprise they would have had if they had been shot at. When the surprise left, cupidity took its place. They looked at the gimmick in the suitcase. Loving looks. I didn't understand why they should be so affectionate.

Savage switched the device off.

McGraff said, "You mean that thing will blow up his transmitter?"

I waited for things to pick up. McGraff had said *his*. He had professed not to know anything like that. . . . But Savage said nothing, and there was a weight on my toe, about half a ton, as Monk Mayfair put his foot there. Apparently I was supposed to be silent.

Savage, replying to McGraff, said, "You saw what happened."

"You knew it would?"

"Certainly."

"How far will the thing do that? I mean—how close to the other gadget would you have to be?"

"Possibly a greater range than two hundred feet would not be effective," Savage said. "By the way, I demonstrated the thing so you will understand that we now have a weapon. In case any of you should need to use the thing, I'll show you how to turn it on."

Turning it on was as difficult as winding your watch.

IX

By six o'clock the police hadn't found Spatny. The old giant had disappeared—personally I had been thinking maybe the black scare-baby had carried him away or digested him or disintegrated him or something, but if there was any fact in Savage's show with the contraption, Spatny's fate had probably been more normal. I didn't know how much fact there had been in Savage's show. Possibly not too much.

Nor had the police dug up anything on McGraff and McCutcheon—anything the Macs liked, at least. The cops had learned so remarkably little that they were beginning to wonder; they wanted a detailed account of the lives of both Macs for the last five years. Savage said he would get it for them.

McGraff said he had been, beginning five years ago, a truck driver for six months, a door-to-door salesman for two years, foreman in a chemical plant until the plant went bust—two years and one month, that was—and for the remaining five months, the most recent, he had played the stock market at a profit.

McCutcheon's life had been simpler. He'd made a living off the stock market all five years.

The two Macs had met in a broker's office one day when they both had a stock that shot up ten points, and having this in common had led to friendship.

Savage made no comment about these professions being hard ones to check on. But he did pass the information along to the police, and let the Macs hear him doing it.

He could be scaring them.

Miss Fenisong's attitude had undergone a change I didn't like. She had grown cold toward us, and friendly in a we-know-something-that-you-don't way with the Macs. I was not allowed much time to worry about this, however. Things, which had been slow, began picking up.

Monk and Ham left to learn whether there was a delicatessen in the neighborhood that would provide enough for our dinners.

Five minutes later, the telephone rang, Savage answered it, and said, "Yes, I suppose I can come down." He hung up and told Miss Fenisong, the Macs and myself: "The police have something they want to discuss. . . . Sammy, will you take any phone calls and look after things. I'll be back, probably, in half an hour or a trifle over.

"Sure," I agreed. "You think we're in any danger?"

"It's quite possible," he said. "That is why I have insisted on sticking around here all day." He frowned at the Macs and added, "You two will stay here, you understand. I believe this matter the police wish to discuss concerns you—possibly the fact they can't seem to corroborate your version of your whereabouts for the past five years."

"I'll hold the fort," I said.

Savage went out, got in the elevator, and I returned to the reception room—which lived up to its name. They had the reception all ready for me.

It was short, but not sweet. The room—everything— turned the color of nothing at all. I read somewhere once that an astronomer said that if you could get to a place where there was nothing—no matter, life nor soul—what you would see would be blackness blacker than a charcoal factory. Here was such. Maybe there were accompanying phenomena, but I wasn't aware of them.

In a voice much too unconcerned, Savage was saying, "You obviously have no cardiac decomposition, so an extra heavy dose of aspirin won't hurt you. And the head will appreciate it."

I heard myself asking something. It was: "Where am I?" Presently it seemed an extraordinarily stupid remark, even for me.

He said: "Alive. Fortunately."

"Want to bet on it?" My eyes were old rocks, my skin was used sandpaper and my tongue was a tired gopher. I moved my head a trifle, enough to cause it to come loose and roll across the floor and I up the wall. There was a picture of Doc Savage's father—he didn't look too much like Doc—on the wall, and my head circled that a couple of times before it came back. I didn't like the returned head; it surely couldn't be mine.

"Notice which one hit you?"

"Was I hit?"

"Apparently."

"What with? A truck?"

"Dictionary. Hold still." He did something to my skull with his fingers, asked, "Does that hurt?"

"Damn! Yes!" I yelled.

"You're in fine shape," he said. "One of the Macs struck you down—I doubt that it was Miss Fenisong—and they have gone. They took the gadget I demonstrated earlier—the thing I called a neutralizer, the one in the suitcase. You get that? McGraff, McCutcheon and Miss Fenisong have departed, taking the device. This happened all of forty minutes ago, probably. So we'd better be following them. Come on."

"I can't walk," I said, stating what seemed to be a conclusive fact. "I'll come to pieces. I won't be able to get within fifty feet of my head."

He shrugged, began putting some gadgets in a ditty bag, and preparing to leave. It came to me that things were moving, that this might be the home stretch, and it was not too hard for me to stand up and move after all—as long as there was something for both hands to hang to.

The dictionary they had used on me lay there on the floor, as thick as a concrete building block. I kicked the thing automatically, so probably I wasn't going to die after all.

Presently we were going someplace in the car with the thick glass. Savage and myself.

"Where are Ham Brooks and Monk Mayfair—not that I can't do without the latter."

"Trailing the Macs and Miss Fenisong."

"Yeah, but where?"

"We'll know soon."

He turned on the radio in the car, said into the microphone: "Monk?"

"Yeah?" was the homely chemist's response from the loudspeaker. "You want to know where they are? Take the Tri-Borough Bridge, then keep on the parkway. I'm about half a mile behind them, I'd judge."

"Don't get any closer than that."

"Roger."

Savage said: "Ham?"

Ham's voice said: "I'm on the parkway about the middle of the island, in case they turn south. This way, I'm able to get a crossbearing. Okay?"

"Okay," Savage said.

* * *

The night had settled down darkly, and there was some rain, thin stuff that fell through the headlight beams like dying gnats. There were no pools of water on the pavement yet, only a continuous wet steaming sound from the microphone—it was attached to a reel that withdrew the cord from sight. He glanced at the speedometer needle. It was swaying around sixty, as troubled as a politician's conscience.

I said: "So you set a basket for them, and they fell into it."

"Something like that," Savage admitted.

"You sent Monk and Ham out—but not to scare up some food. You got yourself out—the phone call was from Monk or Ham instead of a cop. Is that good guessing?"

He nodded. "It goes back farther than that."

"How far?"

"This morning," he said. "Why do you think we stayed in one spot all day? It was to get McGraff and McCutcheon impatient. If anything would make them nervous, being exposed to us all day would do it."

"That's true. I could see their hair get gray."

He nodded again. "It was encouraging to watch them grow a crop of nerves. Anyway, we decided to try this."

"We?"

"Monk, Ham and myself."

"So I'm an orphan?"

He didn't say what I was, because a police prowl came up beside us as slyly as a schoolgirl, and cut loose a howl from its siren. A red-faced cop stuck out his mouth and demanded where in hell and three blanks did we imagine the conflagration was? Savage rolled down the inch-thick window and said: "Good evening, Morneci—those new sergeant's stripes look nice on you."

Officer Morneci said: "The hell!" Then he asked: "Do you want us to run ahead of you, Mr. Savage?"

"Thanks, no, Morneci. And don't say anything on the radio about seeing me. The people we're having some trouble with are a scientific sort—they just might keep a radio tuned in on the police frequency."

The prowl car let itself get swallowed in the night behind.

I thought about the thing. I picked out the points that puzzled me. There were enough of these to make them easy to find, but I fished out one that was particularly baffling.

"Mind telling me how you knew the Macs and Miss Fenisong would make a break if given the chance?"

"Didn't you think they were scared?" Savage asked.

"Sure, but what made that a novelty? I was scared too, and so were Monk and Ham—even old Doctor Hodges, the strontium isotopist. I think you were, too."

"I still am," he said.

That called for at least an inner shudder, and no words. Of course the only man who is never afraid is the one without enough sense for it. But it wasn't comforting to hear a man like Savage say he was afraid.

He added: "I'm not a mind-reader. I didn't know they would make a break. I merely tried out the chance that they would—and it seems they have."

"Where are they going?"

"To get rid of the people they're afraid of. . . . That is a guess, mind you."

"How do you reason that way?"

"They took the gadget in the suitcase."

"They took—that's right, you said they did. . . . But I don't see—or maybe I do. You mean that they figure that with the gadget to use, they can clean up on the fellow who makes moonlight?"

"Yes," he said. "But there's more than one fellow, I suspect."

"Did you show them the gadget so they would get the notion of borrowing it?"

"Yes."

"For crying out loud!"

We had crossed a long bridge now, and were running through heavier rain past naked trees and wet shiny scabs of snow by the roadside. The radio spoke Monk's voice; it told us to make the right turn and go past the old Century of Progress fairgrounds. Monk said it was raining harder where he was.

Savage told me: "McGraff and McCutcheon had to be encouraged to strike out on their own."

"So they would lead you to—I may not pronounce this right—Mr. Chromospheric Eruptions?"

"That's right."

One of those involved parkway cross-overs appeared in front of us, an arrangement of overpasses and turn-offs intended to simplify things for the motorist, but looking about as uninvolved as six gray snakes in a wrestling match. We made the correct turns with no slackening of speed.

"You mean the thing had you so stumped you had to pull something like this?" I asked.

"That's about it."

"Why not just try that lie detector thing on them?"

"Oh, that? It's a lie detector, not a truth extractor. I was already fairly sure they were lying, so it wouldn't have helped us much, probably."

"I'm full of questions—do you mind telling me how you knew they were lying?"

He put the car around another motorist who was driving blissfully in the middle of the twin-lane parkway.

"Just a hunch I had," he said.

The answer was nice. He hadn't had any more to go on than I had, and I'd figured the Macs for black-faced prevaricators, too. It made me feel that I was one of the boys.

They did it to us on a road that ran through the tidal flats. The road was as lonely as a coyote on a hill. It crossed a rickety wooden bridge and S-turned its way, as slimy with rain as a fishing worm and as crooked as one, through a mud flat that was furred with brush and winter-dead grass, and the whole thing was being deluged with the rain fit to drown a duck.

Two hundred feet beyond the bridge, Monk Mayfair was suddenly beside us. The road had a starved coat of gravel and he had pulled his car, a coupe, as far off it as he dared without getting stuck.

Monk said: "They've stopped somewhere ahead. Not over a quarter of a mile. I should judge." He wore a green slicker and with his build looked like the great caricature of a frog in the rain.

Savage said: "Let's see how it sounds," and Monk handed a small case in the window. The case had about the proportions of a two-dollar novel, but there were knobs on it, a compass with a luminous dial, and it was making a high-pitched—but not loud—series of whining notes. The code letter T repeated over and over. A portable radio receiver, obviously a special job with a built-in directional loop.

Having put the thing to his ear and fiddled with the volume control a while, Savage said: "Yes, not over half a mile anyway." He rotated the thing, got a null—the signal at its least audible point—and gestured. "That way."

I was a little slow, but I got it. "The hell. You've got a radio transmitter planted on them! How did you do that?"

"There was nothing to it," Monk said. He was set, anxious and impatient. "Let's get going."

"Look, handsome, how did you plant a radio on them?" I demanded.

"We had Miss Fenisong's help," Savage said.

"Huh?"

I must have sounded like Zachariah when he saw the Angel, because Monk Mayfair felt sorry for me. "You're pretty dumb, aren't you? You didn't think Miss Fenisong had really thrown in with them, did you?"

"Of course not!" I said. And oddly enough, that was whole truth.

"Sammy, you stay here," Savage said. "Monk and I will get the lay of the ground, before we start doing whatever we can."

They went away into the darkness.

I stood there by the car. I stood in the rain, soaked to the skin, and didn't mind. Didn't mind at all. Miss Fenisong was okay. Lovely-voice was on our side—and the funny thing was that I must have known it all the time. Oh, I had been disturbed about the Macs working on her, selling her the dark stuff about Savage. But not as disturbed as I would have been without confidence. Without the kind of confidence a twenty-year-married husband must feel at a party when he notices some wolf making passes at his wife and knows the fellow will get nowhere. That's real confidence.

The pleasant thoughts were wonderful. They must have plugged my ears and blinded my eyes and put sweet mud in my head—because McCutcheon had a gun in my back before I knew he was there.

"No jump, no holler," the tall Mac said. "You'll live longer—just a little bit longer." The edge on his words could have been put there with a file.

He searched me, but found nothing he wanted.

"We'll take a walk back the way you came," he said.

"You won't get away with this," I said.

"Neither will you."

We slopped through the streaming night. The wetness softened the soles of my shoes and the gravel hurt my feet through the flaccid leather. One trouble with cheap shoes. Then the bridge was being bumped hollowly by our feet.

At the other end of the bridge, McCutcheon gave me an extra hard gouge with the gun muzzle and said: "I'm not bad on running targets, Sammy." He seemed to mean for me to stand still, and I did.

McCutcheon got down at a corner of the bridge. He floundered around in the mud and wet grass, lifted a raincoat carefully, and thrust his arm beneath it. His cigarette light flickered, the flame close to a gray cord that looked as if it had been soiled with tar. A fuse. The fuse caught fire. It spilled sparks and a little twisting smoke.

He rejoined me. "Now we move on," he said.

I asked: "How'd you know we were following you?"

"We found the little radio in Miss Fenisong's purse," he said, and there could have been acid in his mouth.

"Is she all right?" I asked around the rocks in my throat.

"What do you think?"

X

The bridge went up. It made a satisfactory—to McCutcheon—whoop of a sound in the leaking night. Judging from the jump the ground gave, and the flash, there had been enough dynamite under the bridge to ruin it. It seemed to rain harder for a moment after that.

The second explosion came quickly. Thirty seconds later, perhaps. It was at least half a mile distant.

"Another bridge?" I asked.

"The only other one," McCutcheon said. "That road runs across a stinking little swamp island. The mud is neck deep just about everywhere but on the island."

"Savage can swim, probably."

"Uh-huh. And find a house, if he knows where to look. The nearest one is about a mile. . . . But that will take time. An hour, maybe. Say it's only half an hour—that will get us where we're going."

It seemed that there was another road, better-paved than the one we were on, that cut back to this one. Presently their car came along that road, moving fast, and stopped when its headlights splashed upon us.

Short Mac looked out at me and said to tall Mac, "Why didn't you shoot him and get it over with?"

"I think he's one of Fleur's boys," McCutcheon said.

"That's what I mean."

"He might be useful."

The short one shrugged. "All right. He's your responsibility, though." He was displeased about it and, as I climbed into the car, he swung some kind of short blow to my neck that sent me headfirst into the machine, with my head full of fireworks. More of his judo. By the time things settled down, McCutcheon was in the back seat with me, had his gun in my eye and the car was moving.

There was something soft against my left side, and only one touch was needed to know what it was. "Miss Fenisong!" I yelled. "Paula! What have they—are you all right?"

She scared me stiff by not answering.

"Paula!"

She stirred a little then. There was cloth, not clean either, tied over the lower part of her face for a gag. I tried to tear it loose, but McCutcheon leaned over and struck my hand with his gun, hurting my fingers and not caring much whether he banged up Paula's face.

"You don't seem to realize," McCutcheon said, "that you're not long for this world—less if you keep it up the way you're going."

"Both of us?"

"Both of you," he said.

The car, a sedan, was traveling headlong through the night, but not so headlong that it was likely to somersault off the road. And when they came to a parkway where there was other traffic, they drove as decorously as anybody, but just a bit faster.

"Where did you get the dynamite?" I asked.

McCutcheon said, "We had been figuring on a nice bombing for a guy we know. You know him too. Anyway, it was in the car. There's even some left."

McGraff said, "What's the idea telling him that?"

"Pay attention to your driving," the tall Mac said.

"You're going to kill us?"

"Probably."

"Why? . . . Because we're friends of Savage? That will just upset him a little more."

McCutcheon shrugged. "Don't give us that. You're working for Fleur."

"Both of us? The girl, too?"

"Could be."

"Who's Fleur?" I asked.

"Hah, hah," McCutcheon said.

Apparently the doings were to be held back in town. McGraff drew the car to the curb on a side street in what was clearly the better part of town. He turned, swung his hand over the seat back to show me it contained one of the biggest guns ever to go unmounted on wheels, and made a speech cut out of raw flesh. He said: "Albert Gross was our friend in a way you will not understand unless you have risked your life for a man and had the man do the same for you—not once, but many times. Unless you have gone through hell and suffering with that man, unless you've shared troubles beyond words with him. Albert Gross is dead. Fleur killed him. You work for Fleur—"

"I don't even know Fleur!" I said.

"Working for Fleur is the only thing that would explain your involvement in the affair," he said. "The point I am making, Mr. Sammy Wales, if that is your name, is that we will go the whole way to get justice for Albert. That means Fleur will probably die, and you, and Miss Fenisong. There is just a chance, a very long chance, that we can deal with Fleur. On that chance swings your neck. Get me? In other words, act up and I'll kill you, or McCutcheon will kill you. Clear?"

"I never heard anything put clearer."

"Okay, get out and walk ahead of us into that apartment house. No, take the rag off the girl's face first. And walk with her, ahead of us."

The cloth came free of Paula's face readily enough. She didn't say anything. She rubbed, or scrubbed, at her mouth with a sleeve.

"We're supposed to lead the way, you and I," I said.

She still didn't say anything.

McGraff got the big suitcase continuing the gadget. It had been in the car trunk. Along, probably, with the dynamite left over from fixing the two little bridges. Wonder where Savage was? Wasting time out there in the rain looking for the foe? It would probably look like a trap to him.

"Paula," I said. "Did you have a radio outfit in your purse and how did they find it?"

"They just looked in the purse," she said.

"Paula—don't do anything reckless."

She nodded. "You, too."

Two words—but there was enough in them to mean a lot. Maybe fright had made my receptiveness high, but it seemed that she was a lot concerned for me. That was good. Everything else couldn't get much worse, but that was good. Why hadn't I met her at a picnic in Swope Park, and we could have looked at the animals in the zoo and watched the nuts on the playground flying their little airplanes around on the ends of wires. A good thing we hadn't, no doubt. Without seeing me frightened stiff, she wouldn't have known of my sterling qualities.

Long Mac had a key to the apartment house front door. One he'd given the janitor ten dollars for, he said.

They had been there before. They knew there would be no doorman and no telephone operator in the lobby, and they knew enough not to fool around with the boy who ran the elevator. A hungry-looking boy, this one; his uniform fitted him like something that had been blown on him by a high wind. He carried his head on a thin neck, as if it was something on a stick. He could move. Fast. But not fast enough. McGraff downed him, and took the gun the boy had half-drawn.

There was something familiar about the boy after he lay on the floor at my feet. It took a bit of recalling. But it came to me. This lad had been one of the help at the banquet the scientists held in the *Parkside-Regent*. He hadn't been out serving tables among the guests; he had kept in the rear, helping get the stuff on the trays ready to serve.

I said: "He was at the banquet!"

McGraff frowned at me. "No doubt."

"That's probably how they got a line on you fellows," I said.

"No doubt," McGraff said again.

McCutcheon said nothing; he was having his troubles making the elevator run. He'd got the doors shut, but couldn't take the cage up because he didn't know where the safety switch was.

"I used to run an elevator."

He didn't seem to hear me. He looked down at the long-necked boy. "You murderer!" he said, and kicked the boy's jaw somewhat out of shape. "Okay, run it," he said to me.

"What floor?"

He seemed to seriously consider kicking my jaw. "As far as it will go—as if you didn't know," he said.

As far as it would go was the twenty-second floor, and the Macs got progressively paler as the elevator went up. Except for the one who had the natural redness in his face, they could have passed for corpses when we reached the top. "He'll have a signal," McGraff said, staring bitterly at the boy on the floor. "We should have asked Augustino what it was." He shrugged, added, "Oh, well, if you're going to crack the egg."

He picked up Augustino and used the limp body as a shield in front of his own as he stepped out. McCutcheon used a shield also—Miss Fenisong and myself, which turned me as pale as either Mac.

I knew we were in a penthouse. They had those in Kansas City. We were in a reception room with a floor tiled in shades of browns, cinnamon walls striped in alligator green— the same cinnamon-and-green striping was carried out in such of the furniture as was not glass or plastic. A wild modernism saved the brown-and-green theme from being awful, or made it worse than awful, according to your taste. The place had enough room to swing a cat, even with the cat on the end of a long rope.

A man came through a door and spoiled our chances of enjoying the decorative motif. I'd seen this man before, too. He'd walked through the *Parkside-Regent* lobby several times while I'd been waiting there yesterday afternoon. He was a large man, hard the way a fist is hard in a glove.

"Augustino!" he exclaimed. He got that much out before he recognized the Macs. He didn't like recognizing them—he jerked to a stop, wheeled, and his feet whetted the shining shades of brown floor desperately. His feet didn't get traction. He fell down.

McCutcheon went forward, was upon the man, had kicked him in face, temple, back of neck and stomach, in very little time.

I got hold of Miss Fenisong, started her back for the elevator. She had the same idea anyway. I took, I think, two steps—and stood stony still. There had been a click of a sound like a needle breaking. I put out a hand and stopped the girl.

"Good," said McGraff. He looked at us, eyes far too

bright, over the gun I had just heard him cock. He added, "You will walk in ahead of us."

I asked, "How many more are they?"

"Two. . . . Walk!"

The next room was cream, cream walls, cream rug, and the small things—drapes, piping on the furniture—were butter yellow. There was more glass and plastic than in the hall, but no chrome. A large yellow-flamed fire burned in a fireplace that did not look like a fireplace at all, but rather like a place to store the silverware. And again there was not much time to admire the decorations.

It was the old giant this time. Spatny. He came in wearing a candy-striped dressing robe and carpet slippers lined with yellow fur. The robe was yellow and cream. He looked big, gaunt, a frame for a skyscraper before they build up the brick.

"Good evening, Fleur," McGraff said to him. "Get your hands up."

The old man smiled. It couldn't have been a smile. He stepped back the way he had come. Like a flash of lightning, he vanished. . . . He'd had hold of me the night before when we found him at the gatehouse of the place on Long Island, and I knew he was strong. But he was quick too, quicker than was possible. He was there—then wasn't. Gone.

The door he had retreated through slammed a shade before McGraff got there.

McGraff, thwarted, wanted to shoot somebody—for a couple of ice-coated seconds he had me in mind. But that passed. He bowed his head, took his upper lip between his teeth, released it to ask, "Why didn't I shoot him?"

We stood there. Spatny was alive, and Spatny was also named Fleur. Somehow it hadn't occurred to me that Spatny was alive, and for some reason or other it didn't seem at all extraordinary now that he was.

In a voice that was clear, surprised—and of all things, slightly reverent—McCutcheon said, "Countess!"

A little old lady had appeared. She was as thin as a string, not much taller than some of the furniture, and looked excessively evil. She had on a black lace gown—nightgown—sheer as imagination, and a woolly white fur wrap thrown about her shoulders. Her cheeks were painted, her fingernails and her toenails. She could have been eighty, and she wore more cosmetics than a Twelfth-Street hustler.

"So you got here," she said.

The Macs said nothing. They were afraid of her.

"Where is poppa?" she asked.

McGraff pointed at the door. He didn't speak.

"The laboratory," she said. She sounded satisfied. "That is good. I was afraid for poppa."

McGraff came to voice. He put his face close to the door, the laboratory door, and bellowed, "Fleur—you turn that machine on, and it'll be the end of you, you hear?" And then without waiting for a response, he shouted, "Savage has a thing that will make your transmitter explode. We have it here. You understand me? You turn that thing on, and we will turn this one on, and it will blow you to hell."

The old giant's voice, coming through the door, was as big as if it had been in the room with us.

"Ridiculous!" he thundered.

McGraff made frantic gestures to McCutcheon. And McCutcheon hastily put the big suitcase with Doc Savage's gadget in it on the table. He fooled with the knobs, brow wrinkled, doing it just as Savage had said it should be done.

The little old hag watched this. She made up her mind in a hurry. She went over to the door, called: "Poppa, they're not fooling."

The old giant swore a great oath. It was in German, a language I speak fluently to the extent of six words—but it had to be an oath.

"There must be peace, poppa," she said. She wheeled on the Macs. "You are fools, all of you. Greedy fools, steeped in the bloody past. Don't you realize the world has changed against you and that you are now fighting among yourselves like cur dogs?"

McGraff pulled in a deep breath. "Tell him to come out. We'll talk terms."

"Why do you say that?" she demanded suspiciously.

"I've spent the day with Savage, and I know more about him than I did," McGraff said. "That's why."

She stood close to the door and said, "Poppa, they have taken a bear by the tail and the animal will consume you all if you do not be friends with each other." Presumably she meant Doc Savage was bruin.

* * *

The old man came out. I didn't like it. Paula didn't like it either, and she fastened a set of trembling fingers on my arm.

Spatny asked: "You will furnish me money? It must be so."

McGraff looked at McCutcheon, who said, "Yes."

"Much money. I am not a cheap man."

"Yes."

The old giant snorted. "You fools would better have done that in the first place. When I first approached you for capital, it was a fair deal."

"It was a stinking deal—twenty per cent," McGraff said. "We want half."

"Preposterous!"

McGraff's voice was cold. "Albert Gross, our friend, is dead. I think you understand how close we were to Albert and he to us. A friend's life we do not sell cheaply."

McCutcheon said: "Augustino killed Albert. It was Augustino's way of killing. So we want Augustino too."

Spatny—or Fleur—grunted. "Augustino was with me in Munich, then in Griefswald and Peenemunde. He helped me get out when the Party became suspicious of me—when they discovered I was holding back the better part of my discoveries in chromospheric activities. Without Augustino, I would not be here. . . . Still, Albert was as much to you as Augustino is to me—"

"No, poppa!" the old woman said sharply. She wheeled on the Macs. "Augustino we will not sacrifice. We are too few to destroy each other."

That brought silence for a while. I was getting it straight now. The old pile of bones had been a Nazi scientist, and he had kept his discoveries for himself, fled Germany with them. He must have been a typical Nazi. He had run out of money here in America—the richness of his diggings here indicated that he could run out of money rather easily. He had approached three old friends, McGraff, McCutcheon, and Albert Gross, for financing. The result was not unexpected—they'd got to fighting over the gadget the old man had, and he'd been winning. The Macs and Gross had run Doc Savage into the picture, no doubt to frighten the old giant into coming to terms. But he'd started killing them, beginning with Gross.

McGraff broke the silence. "We will surrender the point of Augustino," he said grimly, "if he can dispose of Doc Savage."

Spatny stiffened. He called them several dark things in German. Then he said: "Why did you pick a man like Savage to frighten me with? There is no more dangerous a man."

"We underestimated him," McGraff admitted bitterly.

"Fools! It was as sensible as using a barrel of gasoline to extinguish a match."

They seemed to agree with him.

Spatny levelled an arm at me. "This fellow! You perhaps thought he was mine? He is not. He is merely an idiot with a long nose"—he glanced at Miss Fenisong—"and an eye for a pretty girl."

"Augustino can remove him," McGraff said, dismissing me more casually than I liked to be dismissed.

The old woman—she was obviously the old giant's wife, countess and all—brought Paula into it. "This girl must be disposed of also," she said.

They shrugged. Evidently it was to be Augustino again.

Spatny—or Fleur—had left the laboratory door open. I started through the door into the laboratory with the kind of fixity that a frozen man devotes to watching the snow fall. It seemed to be a laboratory that specialized on one thing, and it certainly lacked the completeness of Savage's equipment. Beyond it there was a terrace garden, with evergreen stuff growing out of tubs or boxes, and beyond that, speckled with a myriad of lighted windows, was the bulk of the *Parkside-Regent*. The hotel was not more than a block distant. It didn't take much adding of two and two to realize that here was where the moonlight must have originated the first time. It was convenient to the hotel, which explained why they had picked the banquet at the *Parkside-Regent* to introduce Doc Savage to the affair.

I looked fixedly at the terrace and my thinking began to fog. I was aware of Paula, and I knew they had decided on death for her, and knew they meant it. There was something as cold about these people as a quack surgeon's knife. They would kill us, that was sure, unless someone posed objections. . . .

There was someone on the terrace. This fact, only a little less important than the Second Coming, did not mean much. Not until I thought it out. Let's see—one of the Macs had said, as we came into the penthouse, that there would be two left. The old giant and his witch made two. That left—nobody. There wouldn't be anyone on the terrace.

He was half-way across the laboratory before I saw that it was Savage. And another one behind him was Monk Mayfair. They came quietly, but full of purpose.

I said loudly, "Well, besides Paula and myself, there's four of us in here." Then I reached for a chair, got it, and made for McGraff.

Old Spatny said, "Don't shoot him. We might have to explain a gunshot."

McGraff eyed me. He grinned. His confidence bubbled out under the lid. He tossed his gun on the table, came at me with that judo crouch that I had learned about.

I threw the chair at the short Mac. It seemed to pass through him. He just weaved, made a space for the chair to sail through, and was back in position and still coming.

This time I was going to fight him a little different. If he got his hands on me, I was sunk, probably. I threw an ashtray at him. A stool. A table lamp. He was as elusive as the fellow with his head through a canvas at a carnival pitch-joint.

This must have happened fast, because Savage wasn't in the room yet. Short Mac had me in a corner. I took a Joe Louis stance to fool him, and kicked instead. His stomach was as compact as a sack of sand, but he went down. He didn't stay down. He got my arm, did one of his tricks on it, and liquid fire went up the arm and flew out of my ears and toes. I shook him off.

Savage was in the room now. And Monk Mayfair, and the latter began yelling—there were no special words to his yelling, and he seemed to be doing it merely to show how he felt. Apparently he loved it.

There was a Scotch bottle, fifth-size, on a small table. I got the bottle by the neck, rapped it on the table, and had a scary weapon. Exactly—it suddenly developed—what I needed. McGraff's eyes got wide with horror. He backed away from me, and I chased him.

I was chasing him when I forgot not to breathe that anaesthetic gas that Savage used.

I took a swing at someone, missed him—it was Ham Brooks, and he said, "There's been a recess. Take it easy."

I sat down again. I had been unconscious. I remembered the trick gas. I was on the terrace, and they had dragged one of the yellow-piped chairs out there for me, and my face was numb with cold.

"What happened?"

Ham Brooks grinned. "The cavalry galloped. You finally got the combination on McGraff, didn't you? Too bad you had to take a deep breath of the gas when you did."

"Uh-huh. Say, how did you get here?"

"Up another elevator. Back stairs. Through a kitchen and a butler's pantry and a locker room and a service pantry—you know, this is quite a luxurious place—and on to the terrace."

"I don't mean that. How'd you find the apartment house?"

"I thought you knew about the radio transmitter we planted on them."

"In Paula's purse? But they found it."

"Oh, that one," he said. "That one was a little two-way outfit Paula was going to use in an emergency. Just insurance. The one that counted was in the suitcase."

"You mean with the neutralizer?"

He laughed. "The only thing that gadget would neutralize was McGraff and McCutcheon. It was a phony. All that show Doc put on at headquarters was phony, too. Part of the rig."

"Oh." Then I asked: "Is the fracas over?"

"Sure."

"You get all of them? The old man, his shrew, McGraff. McCutcheon, and two named Augustino and—come to think of it, I don't know the other one's name. Made of good solid stuff, though."

Ham said: "The police have them all."

"The police are here already?"

"And gone."

I didn't get that. Then I saw the old codger who had been bellwether at the scientists' banquet, old Doctor Morand Funk Hodges, who had kicked the banquet secretary's stern, in the laboratory. He was talking to Doc Savage. He would say something, take a look at a contraption they were dissecting, then say something else, and wave his arms. He seemed discouraged.

"How long was I out?"

"An hour," Ham Brooks said. "You hit your head on something when you fell."

"But my head doesn't ache!"

"Monk said it wouldn't," he said, and walked out.

* * *

Paula Fenisong was in the laboratory. She came out quickly when she saw me, and took my hands and said, "I'm so glad you weren't seriously hurt."

Her hands were warm. I nodded at the complaining in the laboratory and asked: "What's wrong in there?"

"It's technical and I don't understand it," she said. "But the elderly scientist, Doctor Hodges, claims that Spatny's device is only a slight improvement over the developments already known to have been made. Nothing particularly magical. Doctor Hodges is disgusted. He expected a great deal more. He swears terribly."

We stood there. I kept her hands. She didn't object. It was cold and clean out here, and the night air had an astringent bite that was good. There were a million lights of the city around us and cars making contented sounds in the street below.

I bent my head and thought, thought about a guy named Samuel Wales who had come from Kansas City hunting something, but not knowing what he sought. He now had a good idea of what it was. I put an arm around Paula to see how it would be, and it was even better. Then I thought about what kissing her would be like, and I tried it, and it was still better. It was better than anything could be.

Old Scientist Hodges was yelling that it was a blasted shame all that trouble had netted everyone so little.

He was wrong.

THE END

THE MONKEY SUIT

FOREWORD

Recently, after having written some one hundred and sixty-eight book-length Doc Savage novels in the conventional way, it came about that a different sort of a story saw print: A first-person piece, told by a narrator who was there. The reason: It was a manuscript told by an on-the-spot character who, while his prose might set Shakespeare spinning in his crypt like one of Mr. Mahdi's dervishes, at least owned authenticity. . . . Well, to bob the tail of what could be a long explanation and put it briefly—here is another Johnny-on-the-spot narrative.

In this case, Henry-on-the-spot would be more apt. You may not like Henry. I can well understand how you would find him personally insufferable, and yearn to lodge at least one firm kick in his slats.

Anyway, no apologies for this different sort of a Doc Savage yarn. Just a rather grim expression and—as Henry gets it in the neck from time to time—a not too repressed grin. For Henry is, frankly, best described as that unmentionable southern part of a northbound horse.

—KENNETH ROBESON

I

This one was an old-school-pal-wants-a-favor case.

"Henry, you're my godsend!" he kept howling through the telephone. "I'll be right over! You're a godsend, my reliable old pal! I'll be right there!"

Probably he was Dido Alstrong. He sounded the way Dido Alstrong would sound after these few years, if Dido was scared.

The Alstrongs had been a prosperous, grasping sort of a family, well-established for a couple of generations in the

middle-sized Missouri town of Kirksville where I grew up.
Dido was doubtless born short, chubby, eager, pushy, with
a round face and a full-lipped mouth. I'm not too positive
how he looked at birth, because he was a year older than
I—and he kept these features. By the time he attained
eighteen, Dido had indicated he was of Alstrong pattern—
he definitely preferred grabbing to earning, bluff to earnest
effort.

At eighteen, when they graduated him from high
school to get rid of him, old man Alstrong was getting
worried about the kid. I was already in my fourth year at
Missouri University, and old Alstrong told me—he didn't
ask—that he was depending on me to be Dido's shining
light. Dido took to that. He signed up for the courses I was
taking when he could, mooched off my examination papers,
cheated when he dared, and surprisingly enough, got by. I
was specializing in electronics and chemistry, so he did that
too. He got me in bad odor a few times with his grabbing at
my brains, and when I got out of M.U. and went to Cal
Tech to specialize, I was glad to be rid of him. I hadn't seen
Dido since.

But this had been Dido Alstrong on the phone. Mouthy,
with a high-pitched squeal of a voice, a way of using the
squeal as if he were having trouble with another pig.

I wondered what he thought I had that he wanted. He
must have wanted it badly, the way he had sounded.

The lab clock said ten-forty. Dido Alstrong had stated he
was calling from a drug store on Fifth Avenue. He had also
said five times, at least—that he'd be right up. New York
City transportation being good, and Dido a quick one on the
grab, he would doubtless be here soon.

I hoped so. I had a luncheon appointment with an
eminent chemist, a Mr. Andrew Blodgett Mayfair, and it was
important to me. This Mayfair had developed a solvent for
light-transmitting plastics that was out of this world. I needed
the use-rights on that formula.

The Mayfair fellow, as everyone knew, was affiliated with
Doc Savage, whom I had never met but of whom I had
certainly heard. Mayfair, an excellent chemist, preferred
adventuring with Savage to working at his profession, so he
was constantly in financial straits. Usually broke. I hoped to
lease use-rights on the solvent formula from him for the
modest sum I could afford.

The thing that bothered me about this Mayfair person was an attitude he had manifested toward me. He had inferred, if that is the word, that I was a stuffed shirt, and that I fancied myself as a boy-wonder.

Mr. Mayfair seemed rather an oaf.

But I would try being more polite to him than I intended being to Dido Alstrong.

He hadn't changed. He was an Alstrong, with that acquisitive mouth and the pushing ways.

"H'ar yuh, Henry, you mental wizard!" he came in squealing. "H'ar yuh, old school pal!"

"Good morning, Alstrong," I said stiffly.

"Henry, you haven't changed a bit!"

"Nor have you, Mr. Alstrong," I replied. He hadn't either, except to become a bit more repulsive.

"Where'ja get that Mr. Alstrong stuff?" he howled. "Henry, old pal!"

My reserved smile was intended to be a warning. I didn't intend to start calling him Dido, and the old pal stuff was quite repellant.

Dido didn't press for intimacy. He glanced about my laboratory, then burst forth in boisterous admiration.

"Some diggings, Henry!" he shouted. "By God, this is about as snitzy a layout of laboratory equipment as I've run across. Who you working for here?"

The inference was plain. He considered me to be so mouse-like that I would be forever working for the other fellow.

"I'm self-employed." My tone was stiff. "This happens to be my own establishment."

"The hell you say!" Dido roared. "Say, now, that's something! Looks as if you're doing all right for yourself, boy, old pal."

"I'm fumbling along."

He was shaking his head wonderingly. "Doing research for yourself, eh? Now that sure surprises me." His greedy little eyes appraised me thoughtfully. "Maybe you *have* changed, at that."

"In what way?"

He roared at this. "Man, I figured you would always be the unsung genius, without enough push to capitalize on your own brains. Maybe I was wrong."

He wasn't wrong, and I did a burn. I recognize my shortcomings, and they are painful to me.

"Genius," I said rigidly, "comes from the Latin *gignere*, and means a demon, a peculiar character, an elemental spirit of fire or water, a guide, a godling dwelling in a place, as well as uncommon native intellectual power."

Dido let out a whoop. "By golly! By golly, you still say things like that, don't you? You haven't changed so much!"

The fellow was upsetting me. He always did. But the irritation wasn't extensive enough to dull my wits, and I could see that he was quite frightened about something. I was remembering back to our university days—Dido always had a whooping, boisterous, overbearing manner, but it was particularly accented when he was in a scrape. I determined not to let him roil me excessively.

I consulted the clock elaborately and remarked, "It's been interesting meeting you, Mr. Alstrong. But unfortunately you have caught me at a rather busy time."

He ignored this hint for him to go. He would. "You're a sight for these sore old eyes, Henry! By God, I've often thought of you. Do you remember the time at the university that I was out with that blonde, and I told her I was you, and she was just tight enough not to know the difference, and the next day—"

"Really!" I said sharply. "I'm afraid I haven't the time to listen to you—er—reminisce. Some other occasion, perhaps."

"You mean you got an appointment?" he demanded.

"Well—yes."

"When? What time?"

"Noon," I was forced to confess. "But I must prepare my arguments thoroughly so that—"

"Hell, you got over an hour!" Dido bellowed. "This won't take that long."

"Well, I—"

"That's great!" he shouted—ignoring my reluctance, and giving the impression I had consented when nothing of the sort had happened. "I knew you would," he added.

"Would what?" I asked bitterly.

"Help me out."

"I—ah—believe you did mention a favor," I ventured. And then I added pointedly, "A trifling favor."

Dido nodded, his round little chin disappearing into his

roundish neck as he did so. "That's it, Henry," he said. "Just a trifling favor. No trouble at all. But it means a lot to me."

His tone, coupled with what I knew of his ways, warned me that it wasn't anything trivial at all.

"If it's money—" I began coldly.

He let go another whoop at that. And he yelled, "Pal you *haven't* changed. I'll bet you are as big a skinflint with a dollar as you ever were!"

"I'm no skinflint!" I snapped. "You always did confuse sensible economy with penuriousness."

"Henry," he said, "who are you kidding? Getting a nickel out of you was always just about as easy as taking the skin off a flint rock. What does skinflint mean?"

Somewhat relieved, but quite disgusted with him, I asked, "It isn't money you want?"

"Money?" He pushed out his lips like a baby spitting out its milk. "Henry, I've got a big deal on. In a few days, I'll be in a position to loan *you* money. You and J. P. Morgan. Right now, I've got all the dough I need, too."

"Well!" I said. This was the first time I'd ever heard Dido Alstrong intimate that he didn't need money. I was indeed relieved.

"Get your hat!" Dido said, suddenly taking advantage of the momentary magnanimity I felt upon discovering this was not a case of the bite. "We'll have this over with in a jiffy."

"Oh, now! I haven't time—"

"Look, Henry, all we do is walk downstairs and take a cab a couple of blocks. That's all. Your arm isn't going to drop off or anything, and it won't cost you. I'll even pay the cab fare."

"In that case," I advised him unwillingly, "I can spare not more than ten minutes."

Dido Alstrong seemed quite satisfied. It had always been his way, once he had achieved a point, to be a little nasty about what had led up to it, and he was so now. He said, "Henry, don't you ever want to have a friend?"

"I have friends," I said sharply.

He shot a glance at me. "Name one!"

He had the worst way of discomfiting a person. I had friends, several very nice ones, scientific people of high caliber. But for the life of me, at the moment I couldn't think of the name of one.

"Don't be ridiculous," I parried coolly. "What are you getting at?"

He shrugged. "Skip it." What he had been getting at, of course, was to indicate that he was aware of my dislike, and had some preposterous notion of intimating that this was my shortcoming, not his.

He clapped his hat, a garish tweed-felt affair with a yellow feather cocked in the band, on his head. I got my own dark Homburg, and advised Miss Lucy Jenkins, my lab assistant, that I was stepping out for a bit.

Dido Alstrong seemed amused by Miss Lucy Jenkins—as amused as his undercurrent of fright would permit. While Lucy may be forty-five, and not a beauty, she is certainly precise and efficient.

"That babe's as homely as a mud fence, Henry," Dido remarked when we were in the hall. "Doesn't having scenery like that around depress you?"

"Certainly not!"

He punched the elevator call-button, looked at me speculatively, and said, "I guess not. I guess you wouldn't even know when you were depressed."

"What are you doing with yourself these days, Dido?" I inquired. "You didn't follow up chemistry, of course."

"I sure did," he replied. "I'm laboratory chief for Farrar Products."

"I don't believe I have heard of the firm," I said.

"You should get around more, Henry. Farrar Products is on the way up. We're in the plastic packaging field, and doing well."

My slightly superior smile suddenly folded up—I had remembered that I *had* heard of Farrar Products and the concern was, as Dido said, an up-and-comer. Really, nothing occurred to me to say as we got into the elevator. That this bombastic goof could have achieved the post of laboratory chief for such a concern was incredible.

We were jostled out of the elevator into the lobby by the other passengers, or at least I was jostled, although Dido held his own.

It was raining outside. A slight, depressing sort of rain, it came down in soiled strings. We stood under the shelter of the awning of a shop, along with others, and Dido searched eagerly for a taxi.

Something rather odd happened.

A portly gentleman, standing a bit behind Dido and myself, and just out of line with Dido, gave out a sound. It was a sound like a boot being pulled out of mud. There was also another sound, rather as if one of the strings on a musical instrument had broken. And the stout man flung himself backward, or at least topped back, against the shop window. The window broke. There was a considerable jangling of falling glass. All of this occurred rapidly, so that it was almost one thing, without exactly being so.

The effect on Dido Alstrong was remarkable. He turned the color of a much-used dish-rag.

II

"Oh, God!" Dido Alstrong croaked. He gripped my arm. "Back inside!"

"Back—" I said uncertainly. "But we were going somewhere. You wanted a cab. Yonder seems to be an empty taxi—"

Dido seized me in the most unceremonious manner. He bustled me back into the office building. I abhor rough physical contacts, and I resisted. But there was more strength in Dido Alstrong's soft-looking porcine body than one would think. That, and also frenzy.

The other people standing there under the awning were staring in confused fashion at the portly man, who now lay on the sidewalk. The portly man was squirming about, and his mouth was making shapes, but no sounds.

"What—" I tried to assemble composure. "What happened to that chap?"

There were beads of sweat on Dido Alstrong's aggressive face. "That guy. . . ?" He hesitated. "He probably had a heart attack, or something," Dido said.

"Really? It seemed very sudden—"

"Never mind that guy," Dido said, and his voice was thickly grating with excitement. "I—I've changed my mind, Henry. I—well—I was just reminded of something."

I had a feeling of relief. "You mean you don't want me to do the favor for you?"

"Oh, no! No, Henry. What I mean—I just realized I

shouldn't take you from your work. Here's what I want you to do: I want you to get a package and keep it for me."

"Package?" I said. "What sort of a—"

"Here!" He jammed a shiny metal key into my hand. "There! That's the key to one of those package lockers in Grand Central Station. It's the locker in the men's room in the upper level. You can find them easy enough. The locker number, forty-one, is on the key. The package is there. I want you to get it for me and keep it in a safe place."

I asked blankly, "You merely want me to keep a package for you?"

"That's it. You get the packet any time you want to, as long as it's sometime today."

"But why—"

"Look, Henry, all you need to do is get it and keep it for me. It's just a little favor. You see, I may want it late at night, and I'm afraid the place where the lockers are will be closed."

Dido was a very terrified man.

I said, "I'm under the impression the gentlemen's lavatory in Grand Central Station is open for business twenty-four hours of the day."

That didn't stump him, for he said, "I—uh—may have to leave town a few days, Henry. I don't want to leave the package there that long. Ah—for all I know, they may take that stuff out and sell it for storage after a few days."

"I don't believe they do."

Dido Alstrong whipped a handkerchief from his hip pocket and blotted his face. It was not a hot day. "Hell, Henry, stop arguing with me. You've got the key. You get the package."

"What's in it?" I demanded.

He gripped my arm. "Henry, if anything should happen to me—Er, that is, if you don't hear from me in three days—you give that package to a policeman."

"Great Scott!" I blurted. "Dido, I'll have nothing to do with anything underhanded—"

"Thanks, Henry," exclaimed Dido Alstrong.

He gave me a clap on the back which he probably considered hearty, but which I found most distasteful.

"You're dependable, Henry," he said.

And he darted into one of the shops which had an

entrance into the building lobby, and also an exit into a side street.

My confusion was, to say the least, considerable, but it was exceeded by my misgivings. The temptation to follow Dido Alstrong, collar him, and demand fuller and more logical explanations, was very strong. But, as I have mentioned, I abhor harshness of the man-to-man sort, and also I didn't want to give Dido the satisfaction of seeing me confused. He had always seemed to derive pleasure from seeing me confused.

Compromising in a measure, I returned to the street, at the same time summoning my dignity, which Dido had shoved out of kilter.

Now a tightly packed cluster of pedestrians surrounded the portly man who'd, as Dido Alstrong had put it, had a heart attack. These people were like worker and drone bees around their queen bee. I was unable to obtain a glimpse of the portly man, although it was simple to gather that he lay on the sidewalk.

My curiosity, while intense, was not sufficient to give me the brashness necessary to push my way to the unfortunate fellow. It goes against my grain to elbow and shove people, although they seldom have such scruples about me. This was none of my business anyway.

I did, however, walk to the corner, and glance down the side street. Sure enough, there was Dido Alstrong. He was walking rapidly and, had he kept going out of sight, I might have dropped the matter. But he did not.

He turned into a cocktail bar.

There, I realize now, I made my second serious mistake. The first error was in ever permitting Dido Alstrong to call on me. With my hand on the key Dido had given me, which was in my coat pocket, I strode to the cocktail place and, after hesitating several times, ventured inside.

I immediately had two emotions. Delight that I had come. And disgust that Dido Alstrong should have an acquaintance with such a lovely girl.

It was a satisfaction, though, to note that this wonderful creature was giving Dido a piece of her mind.

This girl was a middling-sized butterfly girl, all liveliness and glow, with aquamarine eyes, a roguish little retroussé nose, and a skin that the sun must have loved kissing. Nature surely had turned handsprings after creating her.

She was pointing a finger at Dido Alstrong's bulbous dough-like nose and speaking sharply.

I ventured closer.

She was speaking as follows: "The only thing that got me out in this rain was your promise to buy me lunch at the Colony, and take me to that matinee. Now you say it's off. I don't like it."

"Babe," said Dido Alstrong. "I'm sorry. I'm sorry up to here. But I can't go. I tell you, my uncle in Kansas just died, and I've got to fly out there."

The way Dido called her "babe" imbued me with a wish to hit him over the head.

I didn't, naturally.

And the girl seemed mollified. "I'm sorry about your uncle in Kansas, too, of course—if you have one," she said.

"Lila, I would give anything if I could entertain you, but I can't," Dido assured her. "It's out of the question. In fact, I've got to run now. My plane leaves in an hour."

She eyed him. She has his number, I thought.

"Mind if I ride out to the airport with you, Dido?" she asked.

"Uh—no need of that," he said hurriedly. "I'll be tearing around. Not good company." He chucked her under the chin. "Remember me as I am now, toots. Fond of you as anything."

"Well. . . . You'll wire me, of course?"

"I'll sure try," he promised. "You know I'll tear my head off to do that. Well—goodbye, Lila."

"Goodbye, Dido," she said.

"A lil' kiss, huh, Lila?" he asked brazenly.

She shook her head. "After you bury your uncle, maybe," she said dryly.

With that, they parted. She remained. Dido Alstrong wheeled and strode out—I had moved a bit to one side, the interior of the cocktail place was inadequately lighted as such establishments usually are, and Dido Alstrong obviously did not notice me.

I stood there after Dido had gone, and presently something happened to me, and I made what I consider to be my third large mistake.

* * *

Verily, I do not understand my behavior. From youth I have been condemned to be an introverted sort of an individual, although I have long since ceased to consider it a matter of being condemned, but rather one of being blessed. We who are inward souls develop the greatest minds, I am convinced. But the point I am making is that I have been plagued always by thoughts, impulses, emotions, which must be repressed, and sometimes it is quite difficult to repress them, particularly when they concern women. I am, as a rule, quite successful, though. I would not permit myself to be fresh with a young one of the opposite sex, although the yen to do so might be a large one. I am uniformly polite, well-mannered, and speak along intelligent lines, when dealing with the other sex. I have never picked up a girl.

It was not like me, not at all like me, to find myself standing beside the chair at which this delightful girl, Lila, had seated herself in a piqued way.

"Oaf," I stated, "derives from the Icelandic *alfr,* meaning an elf's child, a deformed or foolish child, a simpleton, or a changeling, left by goblins on one's doorstep."

She stared up at me. Much, I suppose, as if a pink-striped toad had hopped into her lap.

"Will you," she said, "do it again?"

"I—ah—refer to Dido."

"Oh."

"I—er—am probably upset," I said lamely.

"You're acquainted with Dido Alstrong?" she inquired.

"I am his pal," I explained bitterly. "I'm afraid that I am making a spectacle of myself. I don't understand why I am. I don't, usually, so I suppose this comes under the heading of an irresistible impulse of an unorthodox nature."

She considered this, shook her head, and remarked, "I was aware that Dido had a circle of rather unusual acquaintances, so I don't suppose I should be too surprised."

"Thank you," I said.

"Me?"

"Yes, thank you," I said.

This didn't make sense to her. Nor did it to me. I was rather afloat on my emotions, but I was utterly delighted, in an ashamed sort of way, that I had dared converse with her.

"Is this," she asked thoughtfully, "one of Dido's gags?"

"No! Oh, I assure you, no!" I exclaimed. "It was utterly my own idea."

"So it's an idea," she said rather coolly.

I believe the phrase is brush-off. I was going to be brushed off. I could see it coming.

"Dido has no uncle in Kansas!" I blurted wildly. "He is from Missouri. All his uncles are there. They are all in the town of Kirksville, Missouri, and a very greedy lot they are."

This verbal imbecility intrigued her. I was most relieved and, since I had not planned to speak thus—indeed, I had no real idea of how to get and hold a beautiful girl's attention—I was rather inclined to feel that my subconscious had stood staunchly by me, and delivered in this pinch.

"This," she said, "sounds as if it might have its points. Sit down."

I sat down. I couldn't have managed much more alacrity.

"And," she added, "you can buy me a drink."

While I do not drink intoxicating beverages, I have been stuck with enough checks to know that the potions they served in places like this come very high indeed. This never entered my mind, however.

"Delighted!" I gasped.

"Who are you?" she wished to know.

"Henry," I said.

"You would be," she decided, "if you're not kidding. Is your name really Henry?"

"Yes indeed. Henry Jones."

She frowned. "Don't overdo it."

"Henry Alcibiades Ephraim Jones," I said miserably. "I can't help it."

She looked as if she wished to laugh, and presently did so, adding, "I don't get it, but if it's a rib, I'll go along for what it's worth."

The waiter came. Those hawks are always at one's elbow in the high-priced places, I have noticed. She ordered a daiquiri, and I requested buttermilk.

"Buttermilk?" she remarked.

"It's healthful," I explained lamely.

At this juncture, my memory recovered sufficiently to remind me that I had an appointment with the chemist, Mr. Andrew Blodgett Mayfair. Realizing how important a matter this was to me, it seemed best to notify Miss Lucy Jenkins where I might be found. Accordingly, excusing myself to the beautiful girl, I made a telephone call to my laboratory.

Disapproval was noticeable in Lucy Jenkins' voice when she learned I was in a rum hole. She could not, of course, know that it was a very glorified and expensive one.

"Just a moment, Henry," said Lucy Jenkins, and she spoke to someone. Then she informed me, "He says he'll join you and hoist one before lunch."

"Who?" I gasped.

"Mr. Andrew Blodgett Mayfair."

"Oh, great governor, is he there already?"

"Not now," said Lucy Jenkins. "He just went out the door. He's on his way." It was evident that she shared my misgivings about the cultural level of Mr. Mayfair.

Returning to the lovely lady, I explained sadly, "I am afraid another is going to join us. I trust you won't mind."

"Another friend of Dido's?" she inquired.

"Oh, no!"

"A friend of yours?"

"Well—slightly a business acquaintance."

"And what," she asked without embarrassment, "might your business be?"

I told her the truth. "At present, I am developing the refining properties of lithium in nonferrous alloys."

"You don't say," she said, and took a quick sip of her drink. Her lovely eyes twinkled.

Mr. Mayfair arrived with unwelcome promptness.

He did not take one look at my companion. He took several.

"Hubba, hubba," he said. "Could it be that I have underestimated you, Henry?"

Lila was inspecting Mr. Mayfair in amazement. Perhaps I should explain why: Andrew Blodgett Mayfair, while he might be a renowned chemist, gave no outward signs of brains whatever. He was short, and nearly wide enough to need to be careful to dash through doors edgewise, and there did not seem to be an ounce of anything but muscle on him. He was covered with wiry hair like shingle-nails, rusty ones. His face was something that must have terrified his mother and given his father pause.

"This gentleman," I explained to Lila, "is an eminent chemist."

"This is very interesting," Lila remarked gaily. "I'm glad I stayed."

Monk Mayfair snatched out a chair and seated himself beside her. "I'm glad you stayed too, honey," he said.

She laughed. I did not understand why.

"You I understand," she said to Mr. Mayfair.

Mr. Mayfair now turned to me, and he said, "I tell you what, Henry, let's talk about our business tomorrow. You're a busy man. Why don't you run along to your laboratory."

"Ridiculous!" I exclaimed. "I haven't even broached the subject I wished to discuss with Miss Lila—er—"

"Lila Farrar," she said.

I am not obtuse. Lila Farrar, she had said. That obnoxious Dido Alstrong had boasted of being laboratory chief for Farrar Products, and since her name was Farrar, the connection was obvious. She was the daughter of Dido's boss. Dido was just the kind of a reprobate to try to grab off the boss' daughter.

"What," asked Miss Lila Farrar, eyeing me, "was your matter, Henry?"

"A package," I said, "that Dido Alstrong wishes me to keep."

Monk Mayfair asked, "Who's Dido Alstrong, Henry?"

I tried to think of a description of Dido.

"Leech," I said, "denotes a surgeon, the edge of a sail, a cure, a veterinarian, and a carnivorous bloodsucking worm of the class Hirudinea."

"Huh?" Mayfair's mouth fell open.

Lila Farrar examined me with a degree of thoughtfulness. "Wisdom," she remarked, "can come in odd packages."

Mr. Mayfair closed his mouth, but opened it again to inquire,

"What was that you started to say about a package, Henry?"

It occurred to me that I would prefer not to discuss Dido Alstrong's package with him. It was none of Mr. Mayfair's concern. But I had started the subject, and I was at a loss how to evade.

I was spared the necessity of evasion, because just then our genteel rumhole was held up by robbers.

III

The brigands numbered two. One was slight, one less so, and shorter. They lost no time stating their purpose.

"You plutocrats!" one screamed. He was the shorter one. He used this phrase to get everyone's attention at once, it was obvious. He succeeded.

"This is a heist!" he yelled additionally. "And in case you stinking rich blank-blanks don't know what a heist is, it's a hold-up!"

The longer and slighter one calmly tossed a couple of chairs into the revolving door, effectively blocking entrance from the street.

"Get your hands up!" his companion shrieked.

The man was most frightening. Judging from his tone and manner, his state of mind was encroaching on madness, or he was in a crazed drug condition. Both of the rascals wore masks.

My heart stood in my throat. It was a kicking rabbit.

Lila Farrar sat with an arrested expression of surprise on her face.

Mr. Mayfair remarked, "Well, well, the day is filling up." He didn't seem very terrified.

The short bandit swore some more oaths, terrible ones. He had two pistols, which were not large but deadly looking, and he flourished these. His companion walked behind the bar, punched keys on the cash register, and looked inside. He seemed irritated by what he found.

"Who'n hell's got the drag-roll?" he yelled. He suddenly seized a bottle, knocked one of the bartenders unconscious with it, advanced on the other bartender, screaming, "Who's got it?" The terrified flunkey mumbled words. The bandit wheeled and advanced on a too-hard-dressed man, probably the proprietor, saying, "Cough up, you!"

It dawned on me that the drag-roll must be the larger greenbacks which the proprietor personally carried in preference to letting them remain in the cash register, in case of a holdup. Reluctantly, blue-faced with a rage, the hard-clad man surrendered a large roll of currency. He also threw

107

dreadful glances at the bartender who'd given the secret away.

The stubby thug had not cursed for a moment, but he was glaring at the customers. His eyes, small, vicious, came to rest on me. At least I presumed there must be small vicious eyes behind the mask; such people are generally supposed to be small-eyed. While I was diverted by curiosity about his eyes, the fellow emitted another of his bloodthirsty yells. He screamed, "Try to get funny, will you!"

His arm came up. His gun looked at me. It was big enough to drive a hearse through.

Mr. Mayfair said, "Yipe!" And I was suddenly flat on my back on the floor. Mr. Mayfair had done a motion with his foot, causing me to fall down.

A bullet passed. I had the distressed impression that it visited momentarily the space I had just occupied.

Mr. Mayfair proceeded to act in an amazing fashion. It seemed that a normal man would have been stiff with terror. I was. But Mr. Mayfair apparently began enjoying himself. He emitted a spine-chilling whoop, scooped up a chair, hurled it at the gun-firing brigand. He scooted down on the floor, and upset a couple of tables—this was to produce a shower of heavy ash-trays around him. He began hurling the ash-trays with astonishing accuracy. The first one he threw knocked several teeth out of the short hold-up's mouth.

The longer bandit cried out some information to his comrade.

"Say, that guy's Monk Mayfair—one of Doc Savage's pals," he said.

The two of them then fired their pistols, and beat a wild retreat.

Mr. Mayfair, in an utterly reckless manner, hurled another chair, a bottle, a small table. The bandits got the two chairs out of the revolving door, pushed their way through; one of them carried a chair, and after they were through, he dropped this in the door so it could not continue to revolve.

Thus Mr. Mayfair was blocked.

Howling, Mr. Mayfair proceeded to kick a whole panel of glass out of the door. He was assisted in this by two bullets which fortunately missed him.

Lila Farrar was staring at Mayfair.

"What a man!" she gasped.

I had, by this time, decided the area back of the bar would be a safe shelter. I grasped Lila's hand, and said, "Come!" urgently.

"Get up off the floor," she said with some contempt. "They're gone."

"They may return!" I gasped.

"If they do, they won't last long," she replied. "That Mayfair will make believers out of them."

Mr. Mayfair was creating a devil of a rumpus in the street. I did not venture outside, but Lila did. I gathered that the banditti had departed in an automobile which they'd had waiting, and Mr. Mayfair was searching for an unlocked car in which to pursue them. He was, evidently, unsuccessful, because presently he and Lila rejoined me. She was glancing at Mr. Mayfair with respect.

"Your friends," said Mr. Mayfair, "have gone. You can come out from behind the bar, Henry."

"They're no friends of mine!" I snapped.

"No?"

"No! I do not associate with such characters!"

"Well, they knew you."

Inexplicably, I'd sort of had this impression myself. But I denied it hotly. "They couldn't! I never saw them before!"

Mr. Mayfair shook his head and made a tsk-tsk sound.

"Then why did they try to knock you off, Henry?" he asked.

"Knock me off? You mean slay me?"

"Yes."

"Ridiculous!"

"I got eyes to see with," said Mr. Mayfair dryly. "If you ask me, they weren't real hold-ups, but just staged it in order to have an excuse to pot-shoot you."

I must have paled. I know that I nearly fell down. My knees became as limp as fishing-worms. A profound desire to be ill beset my stomach.

"Gracious!" I said.

"I think," remarked Mr. Mayfair, "that we should have a discussion about this, Henry."

I said that we could go to my laboratory. It was a wonder that my voice was understandable.

I got stuck with the check. It was a large one, large enough that my hair stood on end slightly and my upset stomach was not soothed. The idea of paying such a price for a few sips of an unhealthful beverage was ridiculous.

Mr. Mayfair requested my laboratory room number.

"I think," he said, "that I'll ask a couple of questions."

"Of whom?" I demanded.

"Of anybody who looks like they might know answers," he replied with asperity. So Lila and I went upstairs alone.

Miss Lila Farrar seemed impressed by my laboratory, and her attitude, which had chilled somewhat during my quite logical behavior in the course of the wild and woolly holdup, now warmed a bit.

She remarked that this was probably an efficient layout, adding, "But I wouldn't know. I've seen so much of laboratories in my time that at a very early age I got filled up, and decided to learn as little about them as possible."

This was an attitude toward serious research that I have noticed before in the human female. However, it was impossible to be critical of her. She was so utterly lovely.

I inquired, and was assured it was true, that she was the daughter of the Farrar who owned Farrar Products. This verified my deductions.

Miss Lucy Jenkins, my laboratory assistant, did not evidence much approval of Lila Farrar. This seemed mutual between them.

Mr. Mayfair returned rather sooner than I wished. Indeed, it would have been difficult to shed any tears if Mr. Mayfair had remained away permanently.

He jammed his hat on the back of his head, and twisted his homely face at me.

"You," he said, "are a lulu."

"I don't believe—"

"Why," demanded Mr. Mayfair, "didn't you mention that a fat guy got shot a while ago while standing beside you?"

This was stunning news; it was quite unbelievable. "Ridiculous," I said. "That could not be."

"Yeah? Well, this fat guy was standing under an awning in front of this building, and a bullet hit him in the chest. A bullet from a silenced rifle, or maybe a rifle fired from inside an office across the street—anyway, there wasn't much of a shot report. And there was sure a bullet in the chubby guy."

"The fellow who had a heart attack!" I cried.

"No, he didn't," Mayfair replied. "The slug missed his

heart by four or five inches. But it sure messed up his breathing apparatus.

"Oh! Oh, my!"

Mayfair examined me wonderingly. "You mean," he demanded, "to stand there with your prissy face hanging out, and tell me you didn't notice the guy was shot?"

"I—ah—" Words were burrs in my throat. There was ice-water in my veins.

"Henry," said Mr. Mayfair, "you're an oddly unobservant guy."

"Henry," said Miss Lila Farrar, "is an oddly guy. Period!"

"It must be Dido Alstrong's package!" I blurted.

IV

The gentlemen's room in Grand Central Railway Station was not doing much business.

"Put that key in your pocket, Henry," Mr. Mayfair said. There was an expression of fierce joy and extreme suspicion of everybody on his apish face. He was enjoying this, if nobody else was. "I'm gonna case the joint before we look in that locker. They might have a reception committee here for us."

"They? Who do you mean?"

"The holder-uppers and the fat-man-shooters, or their siblings," he replied ferociously. And he added, "I hope! Them guys didn't give me a good chance at 'em."

He was the most unlike a learned chemist of any I had known.

We had left Miss Farrar outside, naturally.

Enroute, they had pumped the whole story out of me, all about Dido Alstrong's unexpected entry into my life after all these years, with a demand for a favor. They had been entertained, it seemed to me, by my attitude toward Dido Alstrong, and once—much to my resentment—Mayfair had remarked, "He sounds like a guy who knows where your push-buttons are located, Henry."

Mr. Mayfair, having skulked like a panther around the place, peering into booths in a most ungentlemanly fashion, returned.

"You're exaggerating this, Mr. Mayfair," I suggested.

"Call me Monk, dammit," he replied. "And it takes a bigger liar than me to exaggerate a bullet."

"Er—I dislike nicknames. But if you insist, I will endeavor—"

"Where's the key, Henry?" he interrupted. "What's the locker number on it?"

"Forty-one," I said, producing the key Dido Alstrong had entrusted to me.

Mr. Mayfair snatched the shiny bit of metal from me, prowled down the line of grey steel lockers, found the correct one, inserted the key, and turned his head to say, "Hold your hat, Henry. Maybe there's a nice bomb fixed up in here for you."

A horrible thought. Not, in view of the other incidents, too unreasonable. "Wait!" I gasped wildly. "Wait! Let me get away—"

He did not wait. He turned the key, whipped open the locker door, and peered inside. He must have noticed my look—my heart had temporarily stopped functioning—because suddenly he banged a hand against the lockers with a great crash and yelled, "*Boom!*"

My reaction could not been been as funny as he seemed to think it was. Not possibly.

It was a box. Or presumably so, because the outlines felt like a box, cardboard, inside the heavy covering of brown wrapping paper. I have, because of my scientific work, fallen into the habit of thinking of measurements in metric terms, and this box was about five decimeters in width, one hundred and fifty centimeters in depth, and slightly less than a meter in length. It's weight, judged roughly, was about seven kilograms.

"About the size," Mr. Mayfair remarked, "of one of them boxes the store puts your suit in when you buy one."

"A bit heavier," I suggested.

"Uh-huh. . . . Okay, Henry. Let's blow. And keep your eyes peeled."

Miss Lila Farrar was waiting at a soda fountain, and a young gentleman had obviously been attempting to strike up an acquaintance with her. This fellow noticed me, and was not impressed, but then he saw Mr. Mayfair, and he literally fled.

"Wolf?" Mr. Mayfair asked suspiciously.

"Junior grade only," admitted Miss Farrar. "So that's the package?"

Mr. Mayfair handed me the package and said grimly, "You guard Henry and the package, honey. I'm going to follow junior grade wolf for a minute. I may test him for innocence."

He departed. He made, undeniably, a formidable figure of a man of the more primitive sort.

Miss Farrar stared after him.

"Quite," she announced, "some guy."

"An interesting type," I admitted reluctantly.

"I would," said Miss Farrar, "like to meet his chief. I'll bet that would be something."

"Chief?"

"Doc Savage."

"Oh."

"You knew Monk Mayfair is one of Doc Savage's associates, didn't you, Henry?" she asked.

"I—ah—believe it was mentioned."

"I'd sure like to meet Savage," she declared. "But there's a fat chance, I suppose. He's every maiden's dream, and I wouldn't have any such luck. My luck runs to characters like Dido." She glanced at me as if to add, "And you," but she didn't.

She was starry-eyed about this Savage in a way that was revolting to me.

"I imagine," I said coolly, "that he's an ordinary sort."

"What!" She stared at me. "Do you know Savage?"

"I haven't troubled," I said.

This was not strictly the truth. True, I hadn't met Doc Savage, but it was because there had been no opportunity for me to do so. I must confess that there had been a time when I had considered the man a legendary figure—his work in the fields of science was supposed to be astounding—but I had heard other tales about his possessing enormous physical strength, great energy, and being precipitated into one wild adventure after another. This ruined my illusions. Excitement repels me. I detest adventures. I had never permitted myself to have one—until today—and today's incidents were Dido Alstrong's fault, not mine. I had the impression now that Savage must be a very physical man, and I abhor physicality; I was sure the reports of his amazing scientific accomplishments must be rank exaggerations.

"Henry," said Miss Lila Farrar thoughtfully. "Are you wrong about everybody?"

"My judgment," I assured her, "is perfect."

She whistled. At least her delightful mouth made a whistling shape. And we did not exchange words for a while. I spent the interval wishing that she were more favorably impressed with me, or rather that her judgment of true worth in a man was more soundly developed.

"What?" she remarked presently, "do you suppose King Kong has made happen to him?"

"You—er—mean Mr. Mayfair?"

"Yep. He should be back."

It would be quite satisfactory with me if he did not return at all.

But the lovely girl said, "I think we'd better look into this." And I, of necessity, accompanied her. I envied other men I knew their ability to take possession of a woman's interest. I should have been delighted to do this now.

We found Mr. Mayfair on his back with water being poured on his face.

The tiled floor on which Mr. Mayfair lay was a dirty white color, and it almost exactly matched the hue of Mr. Mayfair's face. They had dragged him out of a rather dark niche in the station, and it was seltzer water they were squirting on him; a fellow from a bar was doing the squirting. Quite a crowd stood about.

Presently Mr. Mayfair regained consciousness. A quantity of seltzer water had entered his mouth and nostrils, and he erupted like a whale, spraying the bystanders. An instant later, he rolled over, doubled his fists, and mumbled, "Okay, Mabel! Okay, if you feel that way."

The man with the seltzer siphon hiccoughed. He seemed a bit intoxicated. "Hurrah for Mabel," he said.

Lila sank to her knees beside Mr. Mayfair. She inquired, "Are you all right, Monk?"

"Hell, no," he said.

"What happened?"

"I was kissed by carelessness," he replied.

"Did the junior grade—"

"Uh-huh. He did," Monk said bitterly. "With a blackjack as big as a truck tire."

Mr. Mayfair now got to his feet. In a few seconds, he was

astonishingly rejuvenated. He shook his head, gasped loudly, and clutched the head with both hands, and kept the hands in place as if feeling it necessary to carry his head that way for a time. "Whooee!" he added.

"What, may I ask, really occurred!" I inquired.

"I located the junior grade wolf, and he whopped me one," Mr. Mayfair replied.

"Was his name Mabel?"

Mr. Mayfair seemed excessively pained, but perhaps it might have been all from the knot on his head. "Mabel is a babe I know," he muttered sheepishly.

"Then," I declared in considerable alarm, "the junior grade—that chap—must have had nefarious designs on our party!"

"Put with six words where one would do—you're right," Mr. Mayfair growled.

"Incredible!"

"Just like my headache," Mr. Mayfair agreed. "Come on. Let's be on our way to further developments."

We repaired to the outdoors, but not before Mr. Mayfair told an investigating policeman the baldest kind of a lie. "I skidded and hit my head on a door," Mr. Mayfair explained, to account for his unconsciousness.

"One should never lie to a police officer," I advised Mr. Mayfair a bit later.

He scowled. "What should one do—spend one's afternoon answering questions?" he demanded. His temper was unwrapped.

The rain still fell squashily in the street. New York City was the drab thing it always is during a rain, and the people were more discourteous than usual, particularly in their willingness to seize taxicabs from under our noses. But Mr. Mayfair elbowed others out of his way and appropriated two cabs.

"We'll split our forces," he advised. "Henry, you and Lila go ahead. I'll follow in the other cab. That'll give me more room for action."

It was all right with me. I would have Lila to myself, and I intended repairing her impression of me.

The ride was an ordeal. Miss Lila Farrar insisted on talking about Doc Savage, repeating a whole string of rumors she had heard about the fellow's remarkable abilities, his generosity, his handsomeness, and his reticent ways. Much of this pap I had previously heard myself, and I utterly did not believe it. No man could be such a paragon of virtues and abilities. More likely, he was a tremendous fourflusher who had lots of people fooled. It was said that he avoided public appearances as much as possible because of modesty, but it was my secret thought that it would be a good idea for a fourflusher to keep under cover—he would be less likely to be found out.

In addition to being bored with this drooling, my mind was beset by anxiety concerning my prospects of future physical welfare. I endeavored to ascertain if we were being watched, followed, or otherwise molested. I could not tell. It was conceivable that Mr. Mayfair had said we might be in danger in order to build an unease in my mind. I didn't quite believe this, though.

Without incident, however, we arrived at the building housing my lab. Mr. Mayfair was not in sight, although his cab would probably appear soon.

"No sense standing on the street, inviting attention," Miss Farrar said.

So we went inside the building, into the lobby, and there a young man stepped alongside me, touched my arm most politely, said, "I beg pardon—aren't you Henry A. E. Jones?"

"Why, yes," I admitted, pausing.

"I'm Riley Edwards of the Calumet Research Foundation," he explained. "I'm awfully sorry to intrude, but could I have a word with you privately, Mr. Jones. Very briefly."

This young man was slender, impeccably dressed with a well-groomed if somewhat dry-skinned face. I had been exposed to so much bad manners recently that his were a relief. He was most courteous.

"Why, certainly," I said to him, and to Miss Lila Farrar, "Will you excuse me, Miss Farrar. I wish a private word with this gentleman."

"Not," she said, "too private, Henry. I'm going to keep an eye on you, bub."

The young man, Mr. Riley Edwards, was too much a gentleman to comment on her remark, which he must have thought rather odd. He manifested a very polite reserve, which I approved. We retired to a niche in the lobby adjacent to one of the shop entrances.

"Mr. Jones," he said. "I'm acquainted with Dido Alstrong."

"Oh—a friend of Dido's?" I exclaimed.

He hesitated, a mouth corner twitched wryly, and he confessed, "Well, Dido considers me so. You know how Dido is about his friends."

"Don't I!" I said violently. "The fellow is pushy no end!"

"Exactly!" Mr. Edwards seemed relieved that we held the same opinions of Dido. "I—er—consider him pushy also. And that makes it simpler to explain my mission. You see, Dido Alstrong asked me to call on you and get from you a package which he said you would be keeping for him."

"This package?" I asked, indicating the one in my hands.

"I don't know, I'm sure," said Mr. Edwards courteously. "But Dido stated, I believe, that the package was one you were to get from a locker in Grand Central Station."

"This is the one, then."

"Oh, good. Then it won't inconvenience you if I take it." Relief was a tremendous emotion within me.

"I'll be infernally glad to get rid of it!" I exclaimed, shoving the package into his hands. "There! Take it! And will you inform Dido Alstrong that I am not to be called on for any more of his favors!"

Mr. Edwards accepted the package, but seemed somewhat uncomfortable. And he said, "Well, I'll try to convey your feelings to Dido. . . . But—ah—it's rather difficult to state such a blunt thing. You know how it is."

"I know how Dido is," I said bitterly. "One doesn't find it easy to tell him anything."

"Exactly," said the polite young man. "Well, I must rush off now. I'm greatly obliged to you, Henry. I trust we may meet again soon."

"I certainly hope so!" I said heartily, because his manners were very nice, and I felt sure a further acquaintance with him would be agreeable.

He departed.

I went back to Miss Lila Farrar.

"Hey!" said she. "Where's the mystery-box?"

"Why, it's all settled," I explained happily. "That young man was Dido Alstrong's representative, he said, so I gave it to him."

"You dope!" said Miss Farrar.

Mr. Mayfair joined us at this point. "Monk," said Lila, "this witless wonder got rid of the package."

"Huh?" Mr. Mayfair's small eyes popped like those of a puppy that was being squeezed. "How?"

"A smoothie just walked up and asked for it and Henry handed it to him," said Miss Farrar bitterly.

Mr. Mayfair seized me by the front of the coat. The jerk he gave me slightly disturbed some of my teeth. "Stupid!" he said. "I don't know what I'll do to you! but I'll think of something in a minute!"

"Release me at once!" I gasped, somewhat terrified by his manner. And his face—it was something with which to crack rocks.

"Where'd the guy go?" he yelled.

"I refuse to answer—"

"Where's the guy got that package?" he bellowed.

I understood now that a loud voice and plenty of shouting was a part of his rages. This squalling meant that he was uproariously mad. And Mr. Mayfair in a rage was quite terrifying.

Before I could get my tongue unstuck from its fright, there was a commotion from inside a shop that opened off the lobby. Blows, a cry—the cry in a man's voice. It was the shop into which the polite Mr. Edwards had stepped while departing with Dido Alstrong's package.

"There!" I gasped, pointing at the shop.

"Yeah?" Monk said. "Where the noise came from, eh?" He showed great interest and dashed for the shop, retaining, however, his unpleasant grip on my clothing.

Inside the shop, two men were injured. One, the proprietor, was draped across a counter, holding his nostrils with both hands, and strings of crimson were dropping from between his fingers.

"Get a cop!" this man was yelling. "See which way that so-and-so went!"

The other victim was my courteous young friend. He lay quite still, except when he coughed, which he did infrequently and only when he could not possibly prevent himself doing so. With each cough, a spray of crimson was tossed over the surroundings. There was a dark cylindrical object protruding from his chest—a knife handle.

Monk roared at the proprietor, "There was a package! Where'd it go?"

"The one who ran away took it," the man said.

V

At midafternoon, the rain still came down in a tired way. The clouds must be very dark and thick over the city, because already at 3 p.m. there was almost a twilight, a semi-murk that pervaded like a giant's scowl. The horns of the cars in the street beeped ill-temperedly at one another, against a background of traffic sound that was a low disgruntled growling.

Miss Lucy Jenkins, my lab assistant, is a nervous soul; she had long since become so flustered that Miss Farrar suggested it would be kinder to let her go home for the day. I agreed, because I was a trifle resentful of Lucy's ill-concealed implications that I had fallen into bad company. This was probably perfectly true in the case of Mr. Mayfair, but not of Lila Farrar. Lila was having an utterly excruciating effect on me.

Mr. Mayfair banged down the telephone receiver.

"Nothing happens!" he yelled. "Polite boy is still unconscious in the hospital! The cops can't find Dido Alstrong!" He wheeled and scowled at the door, adding, "And Doc Savage isn't here yet!"

Anything smacking of peace seemed to irritate this man Mayfair, it occurred to me. This was an annoying attitude; for my part it would be suitable if nothing more happened to me in my lifetime.

"You have appealed to this Savage fellow?" I exclaimed.

"Sure."

"I don't," I informed him, "think I approve!"

Mayfair snorted. Miss Farrar had brightened in a most idiotic fashion at the mention of Doc Savage, and now asked Mayfair. "You're not kidding?"

"I called Doc," Mayfair said.

"Why, that's wonderful!" Lila declared.

Mayfair glanced at her thoughtfully, and did not look so pleased. It had obviously entered his thick head that in pressing Doc Savage into the picture, he was going to divert Miss Farrar's interest from himself.

"Hm-m-m-m," said Mayfair gloomily. And presently he added, to himself and with a hopeful note. "But maybe Doc's tied up with something else."

The hope he expressed was a vain one, for Doc Savage presently appeared.

The fellow was a spectacular sort. A giant bronze man—in fact, his stature was startlingly greater than one imagined until one stood close to him. Then he was indeed ample, in a firm-knitted muscular way. This Doc Savage, of whom I had heard such preposterous tales, was undoubtedly one of great physical powers. His muscles were mighty. But then, it occurred to me sourly, so are the muscles of a horse.

He had, I suppose, handsomeness of a sort. But my admiration does not extend to that brown, outdoorsy, knotty-wood look that so many violent fellows have, and which was a characteristic of this Savage chap. His eyes were rather freakish, being somewhat like pools of flake gold always stirred by tiny winds. They were compelling eyes, though, and about the whole man there was an air of being able to dominate if he wished to do so.

You felt, when you were close to him—or at least I felt—much the same as one does when standing beside a large, strange and powerful piece of machinery.

Miss Farrar's reactions irked me. Starry-eyed, she immediately began indulging the wiles that women use on men they admire.

I found myself wishing violently that this big man would at least turn out to be a dumbbell.

"Mr. Mayfair," I said at once, "did not have my authorization to involve you in this matter."

"Call me Monk, dammit," Monk told me. Then he informed Doc Savage: "This is Henry, an empty box as far as I'm concerned."

"I resent that!" I cried indignantly.

Savage had a quiet voice, resonant with controlled power and—this was also a disappointment to me—he put words together quite intelligently.

He asked Mr. Mayfair for the general picture.

Mayfair said: "An old schoolmate of Henry's, named Dido Alstrong, called on Henry for a favor. Dido wanted Henry to get and keep a package for him. Somebody took a shot at either Henry or Dido, and hit a fat man by mistake. Two hot-rods then used a holdup as a pretext to take another shot at Henry. We got the package, but before we could look into it, a guy crowned me. Then Henry handed the package over to a young guy who was smart enough to talk the soft words Henry likes to hear, and the young guy got knocked on the head and stabbed for his pains, and the knocker-stabber made off with the package."

Having given this brief outline, Mr. Mayfair went back and filled in the details. He appeared to have an astonishingly good memory. In spite of all that tearing around and yelling he had done, he had noticed just about everything.

"I didn't," Mayfair finished, "know what to do next. So I thought you'd be interested."

Savage turned to me. "Henry, can you clear up the mystery at all?"

"My name," I replied, "is Mr. Jones. And I am utterly at a loss."

"Henry's that way most of the time," Mayfair said. "But this is the first time he's admitted it."

He was so obnoxious that I did not deign an answer.

Savage now turned to Lila Farrar, who was waiting for his attentions as willingly as a flower waits to be kissed by the sun, and put a question. "Dido Alstrong is employed by your father?" he queried.

He spoke, I will admit, impersonally. But Lila's tone, her manner, implied that it was quite personal and just between the two of them—and she wasn't unwilling.

She said this was true.

"How long have you known Dido Alstrong?" Savage asked.

"Six months," Lila said. "He has been with father's company nearly a year, but I only met him six months ago. You see, I've really seen very little of my father during my lifetime. My mother and he were separated, but my mother died three years ago, and following that, my father insisted that I be educated in California, and I saw him only at intervals. He traveled a great deal. But don't misunderstand me—my father has always treated me kindly."

"Except," Savage suggested, "that you saw little of him."

"I hardly knew my own father," she confessed.

"But you're with him now?"

She nodded. "For the last six months, yes. He has an apartment on Park Avenue." She gave him an address in a section where it was generally known that nothing much in the way of an apartment could be had for less than ten thousand dollars a year.

"Your father's company," Savage continued, "is in the plastic packaging field? Is that right?"

"Yes. They make plastic food containers, and pliofilm covers for manufactured articles."

"And Dido Alstrong is in charge of the laboratory which does research?"

"Yes."

"Have you," Savage inquired, "much faith in Dido Alstrong's character?"

I interrupted, "I can give a picture of Dido's character!"

"Please," said Savage. "Let Miss Farrar answer."

Lila was hesitating. "I—well—I guess Dido is all right. He's amusing, aggressive, and full of ideas. A marvelous dancer. Holds his liquor well. And not tight with his money. One of those fellows who isn't overawed because he is taking out the boss' daughter."

"You like him, then?"

"We—er—I was considering becoming engaged to him," she confessed.

This sickened me. I dearly hoped, that before this was ended, Dido Alstrong would be painted before her in dark villainous colors.

"How," Savage inquired, "did your father regard Dido Alstrong?"

"Why, he made Dido head of the lab."

"I mean with reference to Dido's interest, his personal interest, in you?"

Again Lila hesitated. "That," she confessed, "was another story. He wasn't very hot about the idea."

"He objected?"

"Daddy is a pretty smooth article. He didn't object in so many words, but rather by inference."

"And he inferred?"

"Well—that Dido Alstrong was a confirmed small timer." This elated me.

"Your father," I exclaimed, "has excellent judgment!"

Things, it seemed to me, were improving. Dido Alstrong was of bad flavor with Lila's father, and I was sure she would have the excellent judgment to presently see that her father was right. And this highly touted Doc Savage, who had been flaunted to me as mental wizard, physical giant and scientific marvel, was not doing anything extraordinary. Savage was making no progress. He had lighted no skyrockets. He had not exploded like a star-shell, as the oaf Mayfair had inferred he would.

The big man jarred me a little, however, by saying, "We'll see what can be done with the fellow in the hospital."

This indicated a certain firm judgment the man might have.

But, unfortunately, it was not the sole shock. Because, when we had driven to the hospital, we did not enter. We parked nearly a block distant. And immediately we were approached by a uniformed policeman who saluted Doc Savage respectfully, then queried, "Ready for it?"

"Yes. Turn him loose," Savage replied.

Mayfair grinned like the ape he was. "So you got to work on this as soon as I phoned you, Doc," he said.

Savage nodded. He produced from a glove compartment in the car several small cases resembling hearing-aids. He handed these to Mayfair.

"Monk," he said. "There's four cabs waiting in line in front of the hospital. Go to each of them in succession, tell the drivers you're looking for an object which was lost, and open the back doors of the machines and feel over the cushions, as if searching. As you do that, plant one of these gadgets, shoving it down between the cushions of the seat and the back. Can do?"

"Duck soup," said Mayfair.

"The gadgets are numbered," Doc warned him. "Put number one in the first cab, number two in the second, and so on."

"It's done," said Mayfair optimistically.

The homely fellow departed and proceeded to do his job. For a person with no manners and such violent ways, he seemed to deceive the cab drivers smoothly.

Doc Savage himself left our car, walked to the entrance of the hospital, and loitered for a time there, but moving back and forth while he was loitering. I could not imagine what he was doing, although it did seem that he had a purpose.

When Savage returned, he at once removed a small container from his pocket and placed it in the glove compartment. The container had a perforated top, and evidently held some sort of powdered substance.

"What did you do?" I asked curiously.

"Scattered some dust on the steps," he replied. "It

might seem a bit childish. On the other hand, there's nothing like a precaution."

The man, I reflected, must be on the idiotic side.

After Mayfair returned, we moved the car to an inconspicuous spot from which the entrance of the hospital could be watched, and there we waited.

"What are we hanging around for?" I asked.

Mayfair glanced at me as if the query were extremely stupid. "For smooth-talker to come out," he said.

"What!"

"Yeah."

"You mean the chap is going to be released?"

Monk glanced at Doc Savage and said, "That's the idea, isn't it?"

"But he's wounded!" I exclaimed.

"Not very seriously," Savage replied. "The knife entered high, and did not go in deeply. He can get around all right. And as he gets around we're going to trail him and see where he leads us."

"But he was bleeding from the lungs!" I cried. "I saw him! His wound was serious."

"A bitten tongue. He was struck on the head, as well as stabbed, and he bit his tongue when struck."

"Oh!" But this still didn't make sense to me. "But surely—you say he's being turned loose! Surely the police wouldn't be such fools!"

"The police," Savage explained quietly, "are cooperating with me."

I suppose he spoke with modesty, but the implication of his words was ridiculous. The police turning this fellow loose to accommodate Savage! Preposterous!

"You mean you asked them to let him go, and they are?" I said coldly. "that is ridiculous!"

Mayfair said, "Oh, shut up, Henry. You're always zigging when you should be zagging."

I subsided. This was beyond me. I tried to think that it was a coincidence, that the young man was going to be released from the hospital at this time anyway—but the appearance of the uniformed officer a while ago rather belied this theory. It seemed that the police were cooperating with this Savage, all right. I wondered what kind of prevarications he had told them to accomplish a thing like that. Someone should warn the police about being so gullible.

Miss Farrar was gazing at the big bronze man with a fawn-eyed look. She was more beautiful to me than ever, and I felt an overwhelming wish to protect her from the influences of this big bronze bluffer.

Presently the gentlemanly-mannered young man did appear from the hospital.

He took one of the cabs in which Mayfair had planted a gadget.

"On the hook," said Mayfair dryly.

VI

The taxicab carrying our quarry moved completely out of sight. It vanished.

"You've lost him!" I said.

"Henry," Monk Mayfair said. "It's going to be a pleasure to disappoint you."

And he did disappoint me. Because they followed the polite young man with ease. They did it with a device which, because I am a scientist myself, I at once recognized. The thing they were using was absurdly simple—I understand that airplane drivers use it every day in a less complex form. It was a radio direction-finder. The objects which Mayfair had planted behind the cab cushions were obviously small continuous-signal transmitters utilizing peanut tubes and a compact battery supply that was self-contained. It was not unbelievable, because quite powerful aircraft radio transmitters are often compact enough to be held easily in the palm of the hand.

Lila thought it was wonderful.

"Why, this is amazing!" she declared. "I've heard a great deal about you, Mr. Savage—how your methods are almost magical! I'm delighted for this chance to see you at work."

He seemed to color slightly in discomfort, but it was probably another trick he had mastered.

"Isn't this a little theatrical and small-boyish?" I inquired.

Monk Mayfair thought this amusing. He said, "Henry, you're quite a guy. You're a character, you are."

Displeasure kept me in silence for a while, but presently curiosity too strong to be denied moved me to ask, "What was the powder you sprinkled on the hospital steps?"

Mayfair answered that. "Oh, it's something we use quite often, Henry."

"What is it?"

"Goofer dust."

Savage said sharply, "Stop ribbing him, Monk." Savage then turned to me, explaining, "It's simply a chemical preparation which, even in the very smallest traces, will fluoresce under ultra-violet light. You're doubtless quite well acquainted with the properties of the preparation, Mr. Jones." And he gave me the chemical symbols of the ingredients and it was as he had said. It had never occurred to me that the substance might be used in this fashion, although it was true that I had heard of sneak thieves being trapped by handling objects on which the police had placed a similar powder in microscopic quantities.

Monk Mayfair, unwelcomed by me, gave me added information. He said: "In case he didn't take a cab, and the radio gadgets would have been a flop, we had this powder to fall back on."

"The stuff is also radio-active," I remarked. "Couldn't you follow it, much as you are following now, by using an extremely sensitive Geiger counter instead of a radio receiving loop?"

"That," said Monk, "is the idea."

I was silent. I didn't wish to betray any amazement.

The apartment house stood on Park Avenue. A huge place, massive, impressive, with a genteel facade and a discreetly uniformed doorman, and another uniformed lackey, a footman, to open car doors, it bespoke the luxury of fine living and of richness within. Mr. Mayfair, who seemed to disrespect anything genteel, remarked that it reminded him of a harem queen's jewel box. "But I'll bet there's a lot of brass along with the gold in there," he added. Then, observing the address numerals on the elaborate awning from the entrance to the curb, Mr. Mayfair stiffened.

"Oh, oh!" he said. "We've brought somebody home!"

My wits seemed to be fuzzy this afternoon, because the significance escaped me.

"Yes," confessed Miss Lila Farrar grimly. "I live here."

Her voice was small, strained; she was very embarrassed and also shocked.

"You mean—this apartment—your father—this is where

you live?" I asked as coherently as my own stunned disbelief permitted.

"Yes."

"And we've followed that polite rascal here!" I blurted. Unwittingly, I'd made it sound like an accusation.

She was too upset to reply.

Mayfair then remarked comfortingly, "Just because the guy came here doesn't necessarily mean anything for you to be worried about, baby. He may live here, or he may be looking for Dido Alstrong, or he might have ten other reasons."

Miss Farrar touched the baboon's arm in a grateful fashion. I wished gloomily that I had thought of those comforting words to say.

Doc Savage parked some distance down the block, and he turned to me. "Henry," he said, "it would be a good idea if someone remained here to watch the entrance of the building—someone who knows by sight young Alstrong, the two phony hold-up men, the junior grade wolf, and the polite fellow. In other words, Henry, you could help us greatly by remaining in the car, as lookout." He indicated the others. "The rest of us will go inside with a Geiger counter, and see if we can spot our quarry."

Probably he thought he had phrased this cleverly. But the inference was clear to me. He considered me an impediment to his plans, and wished to sidetrack me.

I said nothing coolly.

Savage continued: "This car, if you haven't observed, is a special job—armor plate body and bulletproof glass. It is also gas-tight, and the doors, when this button"—he indicated a switch on the dash—"is pressed, cannot be opened until the button is depressed a second time. So you will be secure here."

The man was casting an aspersion on my courage, it seemed to me. I had not, however, noticed that the car was armor-plated, but a closer inspection confirmed this.

A grown man driving around in an armored car! It was ridiculous, as well as fantastic.

Savage spoke further. He said: "In case you see anyone who is involved—Dido Alstrong or any of the others—leaving the building, or entering, pick up the microphone here, press the button to put the carrier on the air, and state the fact. Monk and myself will have pocket receivers tuned in."

"Very well," I said bitterly.

Lila Farrar was regarding Savage with that I-think-you're-wonderful look again.

I watched the three of them enter the great apartment building, and it galled me to realize that my stature had been diminishing in the eyes of Miss Farrar. She was completely ravishing; my heart had difficulty doing its work whenever she was near me; little tingles would go up and down my spine. This was a completely new effect for a female to have upon me, and my mind logically accepted the explanation—I was madly in love with her. Nothing else would explain it. I even had—and this was quite unique for me—an absurd wish to be a hero, to accomplish a manly feat.

My mind is logical, accustomed to analysis and reason-grasping, so that it was clear to me that my growing disfavor in the lovely girl's eyes was not my fault, but due to the fantastic—and cheap, I felt—spectacularity with which this Doc Savage person and his stooge, Mayfair, were operating. They were not my type, and in comparison I suffered. In the long run, of course, Miss Farrar would certainly recognize my superior qualities. But the trouble was, I couldn't seem to compose myself for a long run. I was impatient. I wished to shine before the young lady, and shine now.

It was undeniable that, in permitting the courteous young man to take Dido Alstrong's wrapping-paper-covered box, I had acted unfortunately. The young man had met misfortune as a result. I was sorry for him. Frankly, I still believed the young man to be of good character. The suspicions of the oaf, Mayfair, and of the showy Savage, seemed to me to be very bad reasoning.

I am always sure that a courteous man is a good-hearted man.

All this was in my mind like worms. And then, as lightning flashes, an idea came:

Why not beat them to Mr. Farrar, Lila's father, and create a favorable impression? A wonderful idea! I would explain the situation, and offer my services. An important man like Mr. Farrar would be quick to recognize true worth. And I imagined the favor of a parent to be no mean asset in the suit of a lady's heart.

I left the car at once.

It troubled me not at all that this was contrary to Doc

Savage's instructions. The man had no right to give me orders anyway.

The footman and the doorman were both impressed by my gentlemanly bearing, and so was the PBX telephone operator in the lobby, because she at once rang the Farrar apartment. I had told her to announce Mr. Henry A. E. Jones, D.Sc., President, Jones Research Laboratory, on important business of a personal nature, and she did so.

"You may go up," advised the telephone operator. "Twenty-second floor. Mr. Farrar's apartment occupies the entire floor."

A man whose living establishment occupied an entire floor of a structure of this class would indeed be affluent.

Doc Savage, Mayfair and Lila Farrar were not in evidence. I visualized Savage being a man of such cunning ways that he would not think of using an open door, but would contrive around to climb in through a window—figuratively speaking. My own clear-headed methods were superior.

The elevator wafted me happily upward. Presently I stepped into a truly cathedral-like entrance hallway which, rather to my disappointment, contained no butler. It contained, in fact, no one.

Diffidently, I waited. I had no intention of jeopardizing my first good impression by being forward enough to call out, or make a racket. But, after some time dragged, I did cough discreetly.

A hard object jabbed into my back.

"Get 'em up, pie-face!" ordered a most ugly voice.

Horrified, too upset to realize the deadly danger the move posed for me. I started to turn. I didn't get clear around, but my face did revolve sufficiently that I could view my greeter.

It was the courteous young man. He was pale. He had a gun jammed in my backbone. He slapped my face. Quick, like a snake striking.

"Damn you! I said getcha hands up!" he snarled.

I complied.

"But—you seemed so courteous!" I mumbled.

He searched my clothing for weapons. His hands were as rough as a tiger's claws. Finding nothing, he stepped back. And he kicked me, kicked the part of me that polishes the chair.

The kick, a horrible thing that turned my spine to tingling stone, propelled me headlong toward a door that was closed. I tried to gasp a remonstrance at this unseemly treatment.

"Shaddup!" he said. "Open that door. And one funny move, I'll blow ya apart!"

He certainly was displaying none of the fine manners he'd shown on our previous meeting. And, as Savage had said, his wounds did not appear serious.

Impatient ferocity continued to impel the man; he kicked me again when my hand hesitated on the door. I threw the door open, and more falling than on my feet, followed it into another vast room. This one could very well have been one of those rooms in museums of arts which depict period furniture; here the period was French, one of the Louis motifs—I was too disturbed to remember which Louis, and might not have been certain on the point anyway.

There were two men in this room. I knew neither one, yet I was able to surmise their identity at once. . . . One, who lay sprawled on the floor, his hands tied behind him with a length of braided curtain pull-cord, must be the chap who had attacked the polite young man and taken the box from him.

The box lay on a delicately carved table.

The other gentleman, of course, had to be Mr. Farrar, Lila's father. The family resemblance, fine features and alert eyes, a trim moulding of the body, was quite evident. Mr. Farrar occupied a large chair. He sat very still, kept his hands in plain sight.

"Mr. Farrar?" I said.

He gave me a tense look, a slight nod.

"I'm Henry A. E. Jones, and I'm dreadfully sorry our meeting had to be under such circumstances—"

"Whassa matter with the circumstances?" demanded the polite-young-man.

"I'm afraid," I told Mr. Farrar, "that you're the victim of this chap. Am I right?"

He gazed at me stiffly and with a pale countenance. He was, one could see, the sort who under more favorable conditions would be very congenial.

"I don't know," said Mr. Farrar presently, "what is happening, exactly."

He sounded extremely confused and bitter.

"Perhaps I can explain," I began, "the situation—"

"Shaddup!" said polite-man. Incidently, he bore little resemblance to his original suave self.

I saw no reason why I shouldn't talk. "Really, I want to explain—"

Polite-man said, "How the hell'd you get here, pan-face?"

"If you mean me—" I began.

"I mean you. Answer the question."

"I'm trying to inform you that I accompanied Doc Savage here and—"

The effect of this was outstanding. The bound man on the floor gave a fish-like flop. Mr. Farrar's jaw fell, and his eyes widened—an indication that he had heard of the Savage chap, which was a little disappointing to me. But the largest response came from my bedeviler.

"What?" he screamed. "You came with Doc Savage? Is he involved in this now?"

"Yes, you see I—"

I didn't finish. One does not complete statements when one sees one is going to die. For polite-man was going to kill me. I am no great student of human nature, but I did not need to be—one could see it in his eyes, like poisonous snakes. He was going to kill me.

He said so, too. He said: "One guy we don't need is you!" He said it to me. His inference was plain.

Quite deliberately, he cocked his revolver.

Have you ever seen death? I mean, have you ever stood on legs without strength and stared into death's empty sockets? I had never. Once I had pneumonia and nearly died, but I really did not know much about it until later, when they told me; there was no consciousness of death nearness at the time. It was nothing like this. I am an abstracted soul when I walk, and I have had cars dust me off, and felt very trembly later—but even those occasions weren't like this.

For what happened next, I can only explain that I must have reverted to a primary instinct. The instinct to live, to breathe, to have consciousness, to know life—nothing else mattered. My mind must have functioned like chains of electric sparks, for it occurred to me that begging for my life would be useless. This man was going to kill.

I didn't want to die, and I whirled and hit him. I

grabbed his gun. There was no science; I have heard that soldiers and police officers have judo methods of disarming an opponent. I did not know these. All I had was madness, a desperation not to die.

The gun roared in my hands. The noise was terrible. The bullet went somewhere. I suppose it could have gone into me and I would not have known.

Strength of madness must have been in me. Because suddenly my opponent, a larger man than I, somewhat, was flying away. I followed him, screaming, spray flying from my lips. Mr. Farrar was staring at me in paralyzed wonder.

The man on the floor, the one tied with curtain cord, the one who answered the description of the fellow who had taken the package from polite-man, began floundering madly. He must have had his hands nearly free. Because he loosened them at once. He sprang to his feet.

This man ran from the room. Ran toward the exit.

Polite-man clawed at my face. I tried to knock his brains out with the gun. I had his gun now. I did not know how to shoot it; shooting it did not occur to me at all. And presently the gun was lost; it went skittering and hopping across the carpet.

We fought. Primitively. The way beasts fight. The way beasts deal death to one another. And polite-man was cursing and screaming, and not in bravery. He must have partaken of my frenzy, of my madness of effort, because suddenly he tore free from me.

Polite-man ran from the room. He, too, went toward the exit.

I ran the other way. I ran past Mr. Farrar, reached a door, tried to open it. It would not open. I was so upset that I could not even solve the simple problem of turning a door knob to get a door open. That was how nearly terror had carried me to the level of the animal.

Thwarted, unable to open the door, I turned with my back to the panel, a cornered thing. My knees gave way and I was sitting on the floor. I began to shake. Tears came.

Mr. Farrar was staring at me in wonder.

I have never been a worse mess in my life.

VII

When Doc Savage came, he was accompanied by the Mayfair fellow and by Lila Farrar. They immediately observed that something violent had happened, and Lila, with a cry of anxiety, ran to her father. He assured her that he was safe.

Mr. Farrar, after another wondering glance at me, stated, "I have just witnessed the most remarkable thing."

"Henry is that at any time," Monk Mayfair remarked, but his oafish humor fell flat.

With a concise use of words, Mr. Farrar then explained what had happened. He shook his head several times in amazement while doing so. "It was the craziest thing I ever saw, the way this fellow took that gunman."

Savage said briskly that he would see if he could find some trace of the pair. He went out.

Mayfair examined me. "I didn't think you had it in you, Henry."

It was a most difficult thing to muster my self-control, but with herculean effort, I succeeded—outwardly, at least. My wits, once assembled, enabled me to think coherently, and I saw that I needed an explanation for my behavior in trying to get out of the room after my opponent had fled. Except for that part, my actions might be construed as extreme bravery—which, the more I thought about it, they were.

"I have very little recollection of the latter part of the fight," I said untruthfully. "I was struck, I believe, on the head."

They seemed to accept this.

I continued: "I remember faintly trying to pursue the fellow through a door—but things are very vague about that."

"You mean," said Mr. Farrar wonderingly, "you weren't scared?"

It would have been very impressive to profess a total lack of fear. But it would also have been laying it on a trifle thick.

"I imagine," I said stiffly, "that I had a normal amount of apprehension. Accented, I'm afraid—or perhaps confused is the word—by the fact that the fellow had struck me over the head a couple of times before I came into this room."

This wasn't quite the fact either—it was his foot that had struck me, and not on the head.

Mr. Farrar and Lila were favorably impressed now.

But the Mayfair lout said, "Before you become too brave, Henry, you might explain how you happened not to stay in the car like you were told to do."

"I'm not," I retorted, "the sort of fellow who likes to be left in camp like the squaws and children while the braves hit the war path."

"Ho!" said Monk Mayfair.

Doc Savage entered, empty-handed from his search for polite-man and the other. He confessed his failure. But he added, "It's rather unfortunate Henry stirred up things, because Monk and myself were working out a smoother approach that would have enabled us to catch the fellow, and possibly wind the whole thing up."

"It's purely conjectural that you would have caught him—or them," I said hurriedly. "They might have escaped anyway."

He admitted this was true. He couldn't very well do otherwise.

I pointed at Dido Alstrong's package on the table.

"And I recovered the package," I added triumphantly.

Savage's expression seemed rather noncommital for a moment, then he turned to Mr. Farrar, asking, "Have you an idea what it's about?"

Mr. Farrar shook his head. "None."

"But father!" gasped his daughter. "You must have! those men were here! Didn't they say anything?"

The father stroked his daughter's hair fondly, but his facial lines were bleak.

"I didn't know either of those rascals," he said presently. "Here's what happened: the first one, the one with the package, came nearly an hour ago. He was announced by the phone operator downstairs as a Mr. Quade, on an important mission from Dido Alstrong. Naturally I admitted him—and he stuck a gun in my face."

Mr. Farrar wheeled quickly, went to a divan, reached behind it, and came up with a firearm.

"This gun," he continued. "The fellow told me to sit down, shut up, and not try anything. I did so, not being a fool and"—he glanced at me—"lacking a certain kind of courage. Well this fellow, Quade, if that was his name, which I doubt, sat down too. We waited. I tried to demand an explanation. Quade said shut up, he was expecting a visitor. And then that other rascal came."

Savage interrupted: "Was the fellow the visitor Quade was expecting?"

"Not at all." Farrar shook his head. "Quite the contrary. The second man came in unexpectedly, overpowered Quade, and tied him up."

"Oh."

"They were obviously bitter enemies."

"What makes you think so?"

"Why, he tied Quade up, didn't he? And he threatened Quade's life, and he *was* going to kill Henry, here."

Mr. Farrar had a fine, clear-minded face, and he was speaking honestly, straight-forwardly. One could heartily approve of the man.

Savage asked, "Exactly what words did they say to each other?"

"It was nearly all profanity," said Farrar. "Quade cursed the other for a meddler, a thief, and much worse. The other called Quade the same things."

"Was the package mentioned?"

"Oh, yes."

"In what way?"

"Why, I gathered the fight was about it. Both wanted it."

"Any hint as to the contents?"

"None."

"And you didn't know the men, don't know what is it all about?"

"That," said Farrar, "is correct."

It seemed to me that there was a certain wrongful attitude in the air, a suspicion directed toward Mr. Farrar, intimating he might be able to tell more. I felt this was utterly unjustifiable. He was being fine and cooperative, and handling himself well, considering how his household had been disrupted.

"It's funny," remarked Mayfair, "that them two ginzos came here."

"Dammit, that's something I can't explain!" said Mr. Farrar testily.

I saw a chance to do myself some good, and said: "Perhaps I can offer a theory. Dido Alstrong is doing something reprehensible, those two fellows are involved with him, and since Dido Alstrong works for Mr. Farrar, the men probably came here to seek news of Dido Alstrong."

"Why," said Mr. Farrar gratefully, "that's logical."

"They ask about Dido Alstrong?" Monk Mayfair demanded.

"Well—yes. Yes, I believe his name was mentioned," Farrar stated.

"You forgot to say anything about that before."

Farrar shrugged. "Dido's name was all mixed up in the cussing they gave each other. It slipped my mind." He was sharing my opinion of the Mayfair person, I noted.

"Well, we're getting nowhere fast," Mayfair said.

He strode to the table on which Dido Alstrong's packet lay.

"Let's open Santa Claus' pack and see what he brought us," he added.

Doc Savage, stepping forward hastily, said, "Henry, will you come here. Tell me, is it the same package you and Monk got from the locker in Grand Central?"

"It appears so," I replied.

"Tied with the same cord and the same knots?"

"I think so."

"What about it, Monk?" Savage asked his uncouth aide.

"Same cord. Different knots," said Monk.

"I disagree," I said.

"Miss Farrar?" Savage inquired. "What do you say?"

"I was really too excited to notice it closely," she replied sensibly.

Savage still did not open the packet, but turned to Mr. Farrar and said speculatively, "This does seem to revolve around Dido Alstrong, but so far it's just mystery, nothing tangible."

"Why don't you open that thing?" Farrar demanded. "What are you staging, a suspense show?"

Those were my opinions also.

Savage remained calm. "About Dido Alstrong—is he a creative chemist, Farrar?"

"Creative? What do you mean?"

"Is it possible that he has made some sort of valuable discovery, and the trouble is revolving around that? A fight for its possession, perhaps?"

Farrar shrugged. "Dido Alstrong is more mouth and glad-hand than ability, in my opinion. But he knows how to make other men work for him. That's why I gave him the executive job he holds."

"Then you can't answer my question?"

"I don't know that it has an answer."

Savage turned to Mayfair. "Open that thing," he said.

Since I had heard so much of this fellow Savage's profound reputation, I was naturally interested in observing his methods; my curiosity was intense to know how he had built himself up in such a degree. Now I believed I had the answer—the fellow was a showman. Take this holding back the opening of Alstrong's packet—it was senseless, but it did create an air of tension, a sort of anxious stage on which Savage stamped and pranced, showing off. This was my feeling, for I had been loath all along to believe the fellow any sort of a superman; I was glad to see my opinion corroborated.

Mayfair threw open the wrappings. He lifted the lid of a cardboard box.

"Hell!" His small eyes protruded. "What the hell!"

His sentiments were generally shared.

The box contained a monkey suit.

"The hell!" the loutish Mayfair kept repeating, as if unable to believe this.

It was a brownish sort of a monkey suit. It would fit a man of average size. It seemed, and I am not an authority on masquerade costumes, not overly expensive, previously worn, and rather faded as if it had been dry-cleaned or washed a number of times.

"A masquerade outfit!" Lila exclaimed. "But—why, this is ridiculous! All this muss over a masquerade suit!"

Savage, an inscrutability on his features—the man could certainly hide his emotions—began removing the garment from the box. He inspected it closely. He replaced it, lifted the lid of the box, and noted the name of a costume rental concern printed thereon: REX COSTUME COMPANY. He replaced the lid on the box.

"Well, what is it?" asked Farrar sharply.

"A monkey suit," Savage said dryly.

VIII

It came as somewhat of a shock to find that Savage had a plan of action. It seemed to me that the bronze man should be completely stumped, and I suspected him of fourflushing when he said, "Well, perhaps we have something to work on."

Farrar, of the same idea, pointed at the box and demanded, "You mean that makes sense to you?"

Without answering, which was rather rude, Savage advised Lila, "I think you'd better remain here. There seems to be some danger involved, as witness what almost happened to Henry, and I wouldn't want you exposed to it."

She was disgustingly put out about this. I had hoped her fascination with Savage had subsided, but obviously it hadn't.

"Won't I see you again?" she asked anxiously.

"Of course," he replied gallantly.

And the goon of a Mayfair said, "Baby, when they're as beautiful as you are, their trouble is seeing too much of us."

I was almost glad she wasn't going with us, because it would save her from being subject to such remarks from these fellows. And particularly, it would spare her Mayfair's smirking, strutting and eye-rolling.

Savage, Mayfair and myself rode down to the lobby in the elevator.

There Savage shocked me. He strode to the telephone operator, and asked, "You remember Henry calling and asking to be announced to Farrar."

She recalled.

"Who," Savage demanded, "answered Farrar's telephone?"

"Why, Mr. Farrar, of course," she replied.

"Thank you."

The meaning of this byplay was a little slow soaking into me. Then I saw it's preposterous significance—Savage was seeking to establish that Farrar hadn't been a prisoner of the fellows upstairs, because he had personally answered the phone.

"That's stupid!" I declared. "Farrar would have been forced to answer the phone by his captor."

"Naturally," Savage agreed in a rather odd fashion.

"Henry's getting to be quite a mastermind," Mayfair said.

"Phoo!" I said. "You fellows aren't accomplishing anything."

"Henry's brave as a hornet, too," Monk Mayfair added.

I wished to strike him, but he was not the sort one did that to.

On the street, Savage said, "Monk, I don't imagine Henry will feel too bereaved at not having your company. So will you do a locating job on polite-boy?"

"Sure, I'll find him," Mayfair replied. "I'll fetch him in. Take me about an hour, I guess."

The preposterous confidence of the chap!

The REX COSTUME COMPANY was on the second floor of a building just off Sixth Avenue in the part of the city that would correspond to the cuff of a bum's trousers—tired, sloppy, and not entirely honest. There was a wide stairway leading upward, but it didn't smell too well and there were bits of trash, cigarette stubs and gobs of chewing gum on the steps, if one cared to search for them.

A Mr. Ivan McGonigle introduced himself to us—or to Savage, for it was Savage who did the talking. Mr. McGonigle confessed to being the proprietor of the REX COSTUME COMPANY.

"You rent masquerade costumes?" Savage inquired.

"That's right," said McGonigle. "We supply shows, parties, and theatrical troupes."

Doc Savage placed Dido Alstrong's monkey-suit box on the counter.

"This one of your boxes?"

"That's right."

"You supply the monkey suit?"

"That's right. If there's a monkey suit in there, we—"

"Take a close look at the suit before you jump at conclusions," Savage suggested.

McGonigle did so. He was a red-faced man, brusque, with a certain shrewdness which had probably been taught to him by doing business in this district. The low-class businessman type, I should say, and quite honest, but not a sort that I particularly fancied.

Presently McGonigle was positive. He pointed out a trademark, certain repairs to the suit, and the laundry marks which compared, as he showed us, identically with laundry marks on the other costumes in his stock.

"Ours," he said. "Now what about it?"

"You mean," said Savage, "that this is just an ordinary masquerade costume out of your stock?"

"That's right. We got about a half dozen of them. Not very good renters, incidentally. Got 'em about three years ago off a show that ran a couple of weeks and closed. You see, it was a show with political significance, or so they called it, with a scene showing how this collectivism was an animal thing that was going to return us to the status of tribes of baboons—"

"Do you," Savage interposed, "recall the fellow who rented this?"

"Why, think I do, vaguely. Talkative sort, kind of high-pressure, sort of a fat face—"

"That's Dido Alstrong," I exclaimed.

"Sure. That was his name. Alstrong. You'd think a fellow like that would be more prosperous," said the man who rented costumes.

"Prosperous?" inquired Savage.

"Sure. That's how I remember the man. We do a good business here, we get so many customers, how am I gonna remember one unless for a reason? This guy, he don't have the cash to put up a deposit. We demand a deposit, you know. He ain't got the deposit, he says, so he puts up a bit of personal property."

Savage considered this. "Thank you," he said finally.

"You wanna turn that ape suit back in now?" the man demanded.

"No, not just yet."

"Hokey-dokey."

Savage turned. "Come, Henry," he said. He wore an abstracted look and I reflected, with some pleasure, that he had come a cropper. He hadn't learned anything of value. Quite probably, he didn't know what to do next.

Down in the street, Savage popped me into his car.

"Wait a minute for me, Henry," he said. "I believe I overlooked something I should have asked the costume shop proprietor."

He wheeled and re-entered the establishment. I endeavored to follow.

The presumptuous fellow had locked me in his remarkable armored car.

Savage returned in not more than five minutes. His bronze face was inscrutable. "You locked me in the car!" I said angrily. "I resent such high-handed methods."

He replied amiably, "Indeed? Did you try pressing the button which frees the locks?"

"I certainly did!"

He examined the intricate array on the dash, and said, "Why, the master-switch seems to have been open. I hope you weren't inconvenienced."

It seemed a thin explanation. I believed he had locked me in the machine merely out of a childish whim he could show me that he could make me stay put. I was also riled inwardly by his inscrutability, the lack of an emotional display on his features; I was curious to know his thoughts, and his face told me nothing.

"What did you ask the costume shop man?" I demanded sharply.

He pretended not to hear my query. He started the engine, and the car joined the traffic. He drove with the sort of carelessness which characterizes taxi drivers in New York City, the ease which some people feel comes from skill and experience in coping with traffic, but which always makes me nervous.

"What did you ask the man?" I shouted.

"Henry," he said thoughtfully. "Do you suffer from pains in the chest, headaches, nightmarish dreams, and do you occasionally awaken from sleep with violent starts?"

"Certainly!" I snapped. "I am a nervous sort."

"You should," he advised, "take things less seriously, including yourself."

"All right, don't tell me!" I yelled.

The man Savage had a fabulous laboratory. I had heard rumors of it, exaggerated, I supposed. But they weren't exaggerated. The laboratory was really superb, and particularly remarkable in that it was equipped for scientific research in many fields—it was not just a general lab; it was one in which a man could specialize in chemistry, electro-chemistry, electronics, metallurgy, surgery, and Heaven knows how many other things.

It was dumfounding. One had to be a scientist to appreciate the place. It occupied, on the eighty-sixth floor of a midtown skyscraper, the entire floor with the exception of a reception room and another room containing a scientific library that was also breath-taking.

"Goodness!" My tone was awed. "Who designed this place for you?"

"It's my own arrangement," he said, not as though he was boasting, but as if he was preoccupied with other thoughts.

I hardly believed that. It was even improbable that the mind of one man would accumulate enough variety of specialized knowledge to use all this apparatus.

Moving over to a section devoted to metallurgy, which is my field, I was amazed to note the advanced nature of the equipment, and also of the experiments that had obviously been performed there. Enough signs of the sort of work done were lying about to inform me that some of the work exceeded my own knowledge considerably. I was aware of a bitter jealousy, combined with envy.

It just wasn't possible that this man Savage had such scientific ability. There had to be another explanation.

I was speechless.

The telephone rang.

Savage was on the instrument instantly. "Yes. . . . Monk? You have? . . . That's a bad break. We'll be there in a hurry."

He hung up, turned to me, and said, "Let's go, Henry."

"Where?"

"Monk has found your friend."

"Friend?"

"The one we've been calling polite-boy."

"No!" I gasped. "Found him? But Mayfair couldn't have! He had no clue!"

Not until we were northbound in that tank-like automobile—which, incidentally didn't much resemble the rolling fortress that it was—did Savage condescend to explain.

He said: "Finding the fellow was no trick. As you know, we planted midget radio transmitters in the cabs he was likely to take, and also a radioactive powder where he was likely to get it on his shoe soles."

"The powder would have worn off his shoes by now!" I said skeptically.

"Here's what someone forgot to tell you, Henry. There was some preparation before the fellow left the hospital. One of his shoe heels was hollowed out, and an ultra-short-wave exciter placed there. In other words, another radio gadget which can be traced."

I was speechless some more. Such devices were preposterous, but I was getting to the point where almost any wild thing seemed logical.

* * *

The house was a brownstone in the upper Eighties, west of Central Park. The street was dark, fairly quiet, although a newsboy was hawking his wares at a distant corner. Savage parked and waited a while, his eyes searching different directions.

In a moment, the Mayfair fellow separated from the slightly blacker shadow of a doorway. He waddled to us, opened the door, leaned inside, said, "Ain't nothing new happened."

"Seen anyone around?"

"Nope." Mayfair jerked his cowcatcher jaw at the house. "Ground floor. Front room. Not bad diggings."

Savage said, "We'll have a look." He alighted from the car.

Mayfair gazed at me. "Henry going in with us?"

"If he wishes," Savage replied.

I had been thinking of polite-man with terror. After all, the chap had endeavored to kill me.

"Aren't you going to call the police?" I demanded uneasily.

Not answering this, Mayfair said, "Henry's liable to throw one of his whing-dings."

He was aspersing my courage, naturally. "I was struck on the head!" I snapped. "I wasn't hysterical at the Farrar apartment—it was a dazed condition."

Mayfair grinned. "Your nerve is all right, then?"

"Absolutely!"

"Okay. You can lead the way for us," Mayfair said.

Savage said impatiently, "Cut it out, Monk. Henry isn't accustomed to this sort of thing."

Not until we were in the house, and in polite-man's rooms, did I understand the grisly death's-head humor Mayfair had been indulging.

Polite-man was dead.

He lay on the floor, about ten feet inside the door of his sitting-room, lay on his side and there was an awful crimson lake that had spread from his throat, which had been incised from ear to ear.

Savage was on his knees beside the victim for a brief time.

"Couple of hours ago," he remarked. "That would mean it was done to him very shortly after he escaped from the Farrar apartment. Whoever did it might have been waiting here for him—or followed him here."

Mayfair said, "Some of his stuff is interesting."

Savage frowned. "Eh?"

"Take a look at the writing desk there, the letters and bills—" Mayfair broke off, stared at me. "The bathroom's yonder, Henry."

"I have a nervous stomach," I blurted, and made a dash for the place he was pointing.

They had their heads together when I came back, and they ended whatever they had been saying. Letters, some first-of-the-month bills, were spread out on a modest writing desk. There were many racing forms and dope sheets.

"What have you found out?"

"Polite-boy's name was Davis. Hugo Davis," Mayfair replied. "Seems to have made his living sharp-shooting. Race player." He indicated some small slips, the nature of which mystified me. "Numbers slips. The guy was a pusher for a policy racket, part of his time. Summing him up, I'd say he was a small-time plug-ugly."

"I surmised as much."

"And," added Mayfair, "Dido Alstrong paid the bills for this apartment."

"What!"

The homely chemist's enormous forefinger probed the duns. "You can see for yourself. Rent receipts made out to Dido Savage."

"But can this be Dido Alstrong's apartment?"

Mayfair shook his head. "Nope. The cops have found that. Alstrong lives in a hotel on Madison Avenue. He's not there. He hasn't been home since this morning. The cops are sitting around there with their arms open for him."

"But what crime can they charge Dido Alstrong with?"

"Search me. Maybe with having a friend who got a carving job on his throat."

"Then," I exclaimed, "this fellow must really have been Dido Alstrong's friend!"

"Could be. What's amazing about it?"

"It just occurred to me that, earlier today when he informed me he had been asked by Dido Alstrong to receive the package from me, he might have been telling the truth."

Mayfair wasn't interested in this. "Well, he's through telling the truth or anything else," he said.

Savage continued to examine the rooms. Presently he

stated, "The place has been searched. Thoroughly, too." He indicated certain letters. "And with a sort of purpose, too. These letters have no envelopes."

"I got a habit of throwing envelopes in the wastebasket, if there ain't an address on 'em I want," said Mayfair. "Maybe I ain't the only one with the habit."

"But all the New York letters have envelopes."

"Huh?"

"The letters without," said Savage, "are apparently from Hugo Davis's home town." He read some of the letters. "Two are from his mother, evidently. I gather he wasn't a very good son. The others are from a girl named Anne, whom I judge Hugo Davis had led to believe he would marry her."

"That doesn't tell much," Mayfair said.

"No, except that Anne mentions that she works in a branch of the Farrar Products Company plant in the small town where she lives. Hugo Davis got her the job through his friend Dido Alstrong—reading between the lines, I'd say he got her the job to keep her from coming to New York and bothering him."

"Hey," said Mayfair, "that should give us a line on the town."

"We'll ask Farrar about it," Savage said.

IX

Mr. Farrar received us politely. This seemed, in view of the hour, considerate of him. Also he was considerably upset, for he met us clad in a bathrobe and his hair was disheveled.

"Oh, come in," he said. "I've been trying to sleep, but with no luck. This thing has me upset."

We entered. Farrar led the way into a room which we had not seen earlier, a large library which was filled with volumes of literature and fiction—more fiction than literature, in fact, for I think of only the classics as literature. However, there was a small section devoted to the container business; mostly bound trade volumes, and a few works on the preservation of food, and the chemistry of various forms of decomposition and spoilage. It was, I was saddened to note, not a very comprehensive library. But then I imagined Mr. Farrar was primarily an executive.

Farrar was manifestly nervous. One felt sorry for the man. The way he'd explained it to us, he'd really been involved in this unwillingly, and without his knowledge.

Savage said, "We're investigating Dido Alstrong more thoroughly, Mr. Farrar. . . . I wonder if we could speak to your daughter on the matter?"

Farrar did not approve of this.

"I fail to see the point to it," he replied. "You gentlemen were with Lila a good part of the day—and I must say that the association wasn't soothing to her nerves."

"She was upset?"

"Very."

"She did not," Savage remarked, "seem so agitated when we left her here."

Farrar frowned. "It was after your telephone call that she really went to pieces."

Savage stared at the manufacturer of food-packaging containers.

"My telephone call?" he asked. "When was that?"

"Why, about five o'clock." Farrar's lean, sensitive face suddenly showed puzzlement. "You're not saying you didn't call her? You did, didn't you?"

Savage, instead of making a direct reply, turned to me and said, "Henry, you have been with me continuously. Did I make a telephone call?"

"No," I said. "You received one from Monk Mayfair. That was all."

Farrar was satisfied. His astonishment grew. "Who the hell could have phoned Lila, then?"

"Suppose we ask her about the voice," Savage suggested.

Discomfort now added itself to Mr. Farrar's astonishment, and he threw out a hand in a deprecatory gesture, enhancing it with a movement of his shoulders.

"Lila," he confessed, "isn't here."

"Isn't here!"

"Oh, there's no cause for alarm," Farrar advised. "I simply saw that she was frightened, and advised that she go to a hotel for the night. She did so. She is safe at a hotel."

"What hotel?" Savage demanded.

Farrar's chin lifted, firmed. He was the executive type, a man who would take so much, no more.

"I don't believe I shall tell you," he said grimly. "Lila needs a night's rest. I'm not going to have her further upset."

Savage clearly must not have liked this, but he did not press the matter, nor did his bronze features register much expression. Mayfair, however, scowled in the darkest and most suspicious way. Mayfair was a chap who carried his emotions in the open, as brazenly as if he was packing an uncovered barrel of nasty animals.

It occurred to me at this point, and a bit tardily, that Savage might after all have made a telephone call to Lila Farrar. There was one time when Savage had been out of my sight—when he locked me in his trick car and returned to talk to McGonigle, the proprietor of the costume rental agency. I would not put it beyond Savage to have made the phone call, then deftly trick me into testifying that he had done no such thing. I was beginning, reluctantly, to have a respect for the bronze man's mental agility.

Before I could decide whether to voice my doubts—I hesitated to do so, since to do so might wrongfully indicate that I was something of a fool—Savage got back to the bit of business which supposedly we'd come here to transact.

"Do you," he asked Farrar, "have container-manufacturing plants in small towns?"

"Three," Farrar admitted. "Besides the large one in Jersey City."

"What are their locations?"

"Is that important?"

"It might be."

"You'd better tell me why it is important," Farrar said dryly.

Instead of stating the truth to Mr. Farrar, Savage did a deft bit of walking-on-eggs. He said, "In tracing Dido Alstrong's record, we're wondering if he first worked for you in a branch plant in a small town."

Farrar considered this. "Yes, Alstrong did. I don't see how it could have any bearing on this. But he worked in the Mound City, New York, plant."

"Has he visited the other plants?"

"I imagine so."

"We'd like the times and places of his first visit."

Farrar said wearily, "He went to the Cottage Hill plant in January of this year, and the Mason City plant in March, I think. But I can't see what bearing that has."

"Maybe it has none," Savage replied.

Which was probably the truth—he had simply maneuvered until he had the location of the Farrar Products Company branch plants.

Savage continued, "Do you know a man named Hugo Davis?"

Farrar gave this serious thought. "I don't believe I do."

"You've met him."

"I think not," Farrar replied sharply.

"He was," said Savage, "the lug who tried to kill Henry. The one Henry referred to as polite-boy."

"Oh!"

"He's dead," Savage added. "Murder. Throat cut. He was, it's safe to surmise, a hireling of Dido Alstrong's. Because Alstrong had been footing his bills."

"Good God!" gasped Farrar. "Murder! This is terrible!"

Savage buttoned his coat preparatory to leaving.

"I wouldn't be surprised," he said, "if it got worse."

We went down to the street. It suddenly thundered, and there was a low bank of clouds in the west across which lightning crawled in angry crooked red rods. . . . My thoughts were too disturbed for the weather to make an impression, though. It seemed to me that odd doings were afoot, yet my mind refused to grasp their meaning; in fact I was almost sure Savage was perpetrating something, but I could not see what.

"You hardly told Mr. Farrar anything at all," I said accusingly.

"Why disturb him?" Savage replied.

"He's a fine man. He should have all the facts."

Mayfair said, "He's sure got a dilly of a daughter, anyway."

"I resent your referring to Miss Farrar as a dilly!" I snapped.

"Unbutton your collar, Henry," Mayfair replied. "Let some circulation get to your backbone."

We returned to Doc Savage's headquarters, to the place where he had his remarkable laboratory. The lab still amazed me, but there was this other thought in my mind—the feeling that something was developing, but that it eluded me.

I was irritated. I am a scientist—analysis, the selection of stray facts and the arraying of them into a meaningful whole, is my business. It was distressing not to be able to understand what was going on, when I was right there on the spot, witnessing everything.

Annoyed, I seated myself in the reception room, which had comfortable chairs, a large inlaid desk that was probably a museum piece, and an enormous old-fashioned safe that was out of keeping with the rest of the place. It was, however, comfortable. Far more comfortable than my thoughts were.

Clearly, Savage was putting something over on me. This was a galling thought. The man, whom I had considered a four-flusher, had me guessing, and the feeling of inferiority this gave me was not pleasant. It did not help to face the fact that Henry A. E. Jones had not made a too impressive showing so far. My ego writhed, and I longed to assert myself, take a prominent part, accomplish a deed.

Just then, the telephone rang and, in an assertive mood, I seized the instrument and said, "Yes?"

"Hello. Henry. Is Mr. Savage there?"

My heart turned over a couple of times. It was Lila Farrar, and she sounded distraught.

"Is there something I can do, Lila?" I asked.

"Please, Henry, is Mr. Savage there? I want to tell him something."

"I'm sorry, I'm afraid not," I said. This was at least a technical truth—Savage was not there in the room. He and Mayfair were in the lab. "But I'll gladly help you, Lila."

She hesitated over this.

Then she said desperately, "Listen, Henry, I've got something awfully important to tell."

"Go right ahead."

"No. I—I'd better say this personally."

My mind worked swiftly. "Well, Lila, suppose you come to my laboratory. You know where it is. I'll meet you there."

"But I'd rather come to Savage's place."

"That's impossible, I'm sorry. . . . My lab, Lila. I'll be there."

"Well—" Again, and reluctantly, she hesitated. "All right. Twenty minutes, or half an hour."

"Good!" I exclaimed. "I'll be there."

I had spoken in a low voice, and I replaced the phone on its cradle with care. The thing now was to get out of here. I took a moment to control my elation, then moved to the library door, then into the laboratory, and I told Savage, "I'm sleepy. Is there any reason why I can't go home?"

"Why, none at all," Savage said.

The Mayfair fellow looked at me queerly, though, and I was alarmed.

Savage added, "However—wait a moment in the reception room, will you, Henry. Just a few seconds."

I kept the worry off my face, and said, "Of course."

The wait was not long. Four or five minutes. Then Savage came in.

He had Dido Alstrong's monkey-suit in the box.

"Henry, you're the one who is supposed to have this, so you'd better take it," he said.

This didn't appeal to me much. That monkey suit had been a magnet that had attracted no little danger during the day. But I was full of a man-who-is-doing-a-deed feeling, and this overpowered what was probably my better judgment.

"Very well, I shall take it with me," I said.

"Good night," Savage said.

"Good night," I replied.

"Henry, you're a colorful character," Mayfair said.

"Well—thank you," I replied dubiously.

"Like a chameleon," he added.

X

The thunder whacked and gobbled in the west as I entered the building which contained my lab. Violent, like a noisy gathering of giants, the storm sounds none the less lacked the hot intensity they would probably attain before it began to rain. It was surely going to storm. And the cacaphony in the sky fitted my own mood and expectations. A thunderstorm is always a great show, and I too was going to make a show.

There was no trouble about entering my lab at this later hour. I do this habitually, not only because I work late, but because I live there. I had fitted up a small sleeping room and kitchenette for quarters—and not, as I had overheard someone intimate, because I am as tight with money as the skin on an apple. It was more convenient. Of course it was economical also.

Miss Farrar did not appear at once. There was time for me to ponder the Mayfair fellow's remark about chameleons. He had said I was colorful, which might be a compliment—

from anyone but Mayfair. A chameleon is a small lizard to which is attributed a facility for changing is coloration, incidentally, and thus was the nubbin at which most of my thoughts nibbled. The remark had its confusing aspects.

Fingertips, like bird-feet racing, sounded on the door. It was Lila Farrar.

"Henry!" she cried. "Oh, Henry, can't you get hold of Doc Savage somehow?"

Her obvious state of mind was both surprising and distressing. She was upset. Extremely. I longed to comfort her in a closer manner than with words, but didn't quite dare.

"What has happened?" I asked anxiously.

"Can't you get Savage?"

"I'm afraid not. What has occurred?"

She dropped in a chair. She was near tears. "Father and I had an awful row," she blurted.

"Really?" I said. "Your father—you quarreled with him? I'm—er—a little surprised at that."

Lila was opening her purse with trembling fingers. She took out a handkerchief. She looked over the handkerchief at me, and said, hesitantly, "You're—surprised?"

"Well, yes."

"Why?"

"Your father," I said, "is obviously a man of many strong points. You're very lucky to have such a fine father."

While this was my conviction, it was also said out of a desire to build myself up by speaking well of her parent. Flattery of one's family, I hold, is next to flattery of oneself.

She reacted rather oddly, though.

"Little do you know!" she said.

Taken aback, I hesitated. What could she mean? I didn't understand it at all.

She added, "Henry, you remember I said that my mother and father were estranged, and that I lived with my mother? And then, after my mother's death, my father kept me in schools in California and elsewhere—up until a few months ago?"

"Obviously he wanted you to have a fine education—"

Lila gripped her handkerchief tightly.

"I hardly knew my father!" she exclaimed wildly.

I could see that she was genuinely in need of comfort.

"My dear," I said—it took courage to say *my dear*, and it didn't come out very firmly—"your father is a fine man with your interests at heart. Mr. Savage and I went back to talk to him earlier tonight, after you had gone to a hotel, and he expressed the greatest love and concern for you."

Lila looked at me thoughtfully. "He *is* my father," she said.

"Yes indeed."

"And parental ties are very strong, I suppose."

"None are stronger," I agreed. "And rightly so, for none should be stronger. The parent fights its fiercest for its young, even in the animal kingdom."

This seemed to touch Lila deeply, for she nodded. She said thoughtfully, "It doesn't follow that the young always fight as strongly for their parents, but they should, shouldn't they?"

"Oh, indeed!"

"That's really the right way, isn't it?"

"Of course," I said. "It certainly is." I didn't know exactly—in fact I had no idea—what we were talking about. But this was sound philosophical wisdom, and one is always safe in mouthing philosophical clichés. I liked the way I sounded, too; weighty and solemn, the fatherly advisor, although my feelings about her certainly weren't fatherly.

In glancing about distractedly, Lila's eyes fell on the cardboard box containing Dido Alstrong's monkey suit. She pointed, demanded, "Is that—"

"The ape suit belonging to that rascal Dido Alstrong," I agreed.

"What is it doing here?"

"Why, I have it in my custody, naturally," I replied. "I insisted on that."

"I'm surprised Savage let you keep it," she said.

"I was quite firm," I said.

"I see," she replied, but her thoughts and manner were self-involved.

The young lady was distressed. This touched me deeply; the young lady herself touched me more deeply than anything else, though. So intensely, in fact, that I was moved to walk over to her.

"Lila," I said hoarsely. "Lila, you're worried."

She nodded bitterly. "Yes, Henry, I'm terribly worried."

"Darling," I said. "Darling, don't be."

And I put my arm around her in a manner rather more than comforting, and took hold of her chin with my other hand, and endeavored to kiss her.

She kissed me back. It was wonderful. It was skyrockets and whizz-bangs; it was fountains of honey and clouds of flying sparks. I wished I had more experience kissing, because I hadn't done very well. I decided to try again. She moved a little, squirmed.

The lights went out.

Some time later I got around to figuring out which lights had gone out. The conclusion was shocking. It was my own lights. Not those in the room.

As this dawned on me, I further realized that I was lying on the hard wooden lab floor, and my head felt awful. It felt worse when I tried to move it.

I groaned loudly. Even that hurt.

Finally, exercising some caution, I managed to get to all fours, then erect, and into the washroom where I drank some water, and examined my head. The knot on my head was not visible to the eye, but it certainly felt the size of a young mountain to my fingers.

Back at the scene of disaster, I found a large and heavy glass chemical bottle with the neck broken off, the two parts lying on the floor. This, obviously, was what had turned out my lights. And Miss Lila Farrar had wielded it, after lifting it from the table while being kissed.

Miss Farrar, naturally, was gone.

So was Dido Alstrong's monkey suit.

Both had vanished, and it was logical to suppose they had gone together. But beyond that it did not make sense. Not the slightest sense. Logic just didn't have any horse to its cart.

Naturally I began thinking of Doc Savage, and didn't feel good at all. Not that I felt well to begin the thought, but Savage's possible reactions depressed me.

I had tried to take things into my own hands with Miss Farrar. I was supposed to have custody of the baboon suit. Now I had neither, a headache, and a deflated ego.

There was a knock on the door. I wheeled, instinctively grasping my head with both hands.

"Mr. Savage?" I called.

"That's right," a voice said.

I shouldn't have opened the door. It wasn't Savage's voice at all. It was the voice of the possessor of an extremely hideous automatic pistol, and he at once inserted the worse end of the thing in my right eye.

"Now start somethin'," he said.

He had a companion. After horror stopped hitting me like lightning, recollection furnished me with their identity. The two hold-ups. The banditti who had raided the cocktail bar with the idea of eliminating me.

Short bandit swore another terrible oath. He had much the same manner he'd displayed in the genteel rum hole.

The longer one said, "Hold 'im still. I'll frisk 'im." He searched me. Meantime my eye was glued to the gun muzzle. The one doing the frisking said, "Clean. No hardware." He examined my billfold, added with considerable disgust. "And only eleven bucks!"

"Only eleven bucks!" yelled short bandit. "We oughta shoot him just for that!"

"Where's tha monkey suit?" long one demanded.

"I—uh—Miss Farrar got it!" I gasped.

"So ya know that, do ya?" he said. "Well, well, that makes you a member of the lodge. So come along, brother."

"But I—"

"Would you rather stay here?" he asked ominously.

I am not obtuse. I got his meaning.

"I guess not," I said weakly.

XI

It was past midnight when we crossed George Washington Bridge and, after rolling swiftly for a time, turned north. Eleven o'clock. The storm was on us with awful splintering streaks of lightning, and the face of the dashboard clock was visible in the convulsive blazes of red glare.

"Get a move on," the tall man said to the short one, who was driving. "Maybe we can outrun this damn storm."

"Yeah," said the other. "And have a highway cop lookin' in at Henry, here."

"Henry wouldn't tell tha cop nothin'. Wouldja, Henry?"

"The police," I said grimly, "are already looking for you gentlemen for the holdup in the cocktail establishment."

The short one sneered. "Whose afraida cops? Ask Henry if he described us to tha cops, Slim."

"Henry wouldn't do that. Would you, Henry?"

"No."

"You hear that, Pokey? Henry's our pal. Henry's our lodge brother."

"I don't belong to any lodge," I said miserably.

Tall bandit whooped. "Sure you do, Henry. You joined one tonight. When you figured that babe got the monkey suit, that's when you paid your initiation fee."

"Sure," said the other. "You're a paid-up member."

"What kind of a lodge is this?" I asked nervously.

"Biggest there is, boy."

"Sure," said Pokey. "More belong than don't. Ain't that right, Slim."

"I'm not sure I wish to belong."

"He don't wanta belong, Slim," said Pokey.

"Who does," said Slim. "But everybody joins, don't they."

"Yeah, everybody. Some sooner'n others, though." Pokey turned his head, leered. "Henry ain't got tha lodge badge yet, though. How you reckon the badge will look on him?"

"It'll look fine." Slim studied me critically. "A lily will go well with Henry's coloring."

The sky had deafening noise. The car noise was tiny, almost unnoticeable, in the storm's uproar. A bolt of lightning split a tree up ahead; there was a kind of smoke puff, whitish; it was an evergreen tree, and little flames spread all through it. Big drops of water like half-dollars began hitting the car.

"Get a move on," Slim said uneasily to his comrade. "You wanta hang around here and get lightning-struck?"

The car traveled for a long time while I waited for them to kill me.

The thunderstorm had followed us, or we had followed it, and now it should have been daylight, but it wasn't. At least all the light seemed the slashing scarlet of lightning, and the rain came down in solid wires and sheets; the wind was lions; at times it seemed the car would be swept from the highway.

Finally the car was turned on to a lane, and Pokey said, "Well, we made it." The machine crawled along the winding gravel for a time, then stopped. Pokey turned his head, demanded, "How's lodge-member?"

Slim turned a flashlight on my face. "He don't look so good. Color's kind of a mortified blue."

"Yeah," said Pokey. "That ain't a bad color. But he should be feeling better than that. He's got a lot to feel grateful over. He ain't dead."

This was true, but the future was not a thing that intrigued me.

They sat there a while. Pokey had turned off the headlights; now he blinked them twice, left them off again. And from ahead, through trees, there was a replying couple of light blinks.

"Hot dog!" said Pokey. "This is home sweet home. I was beginning to wonder if I'd took the wrong road somewhere."

Slim was surprised. "You mean you didn't know where you was going?"

"I never been here before. You know that. All I had was directions. . . . Hey, I wish we had raincoats."

"That's great, riding around all night with a guy who don't know where he's going," Slim complained. He suddenly gave me a shove. "What you sitting there for? Get out."

I alighted. My legs would hardly remain rigid enough to support my weight. We climbed a steep path. A house appeared, a rambling place, one-story, low, with wide porches and the air of being a summer home. They shoved me inside. I was in a large room where there were other people.

"Lila!" I cried.

Miss Farrar did not reply; her expression was cold, grave, and desperate. She showed, almost as much as I, the effects of a harrowing night.

A man who answered the description of the fellow who had attacked polite-man and taken the monkey suit from him stood with a gun in his hand, guarding Miss Farrar. This chap—he was certainly the one who had been a prisoner at the Farrar apartment on the occasion of my ill-omened visit there—sneered at sight of me.

He said, "You guys better not be too careless."

"With Henry?" said Slim scoffingly. "Why, Henry is the soul of gentleness with his fellow man."

"Yeah?" said the other. "Well, I seen him different." He

frowned, then added, "Maybe he'll be all right if you don't scare him."

"We wouldn't think of scaring Henry," Slim said.

Miss Farrar had said nothing. I had tried to give her a reprimanding frown, but it had no effect on her. It was difficult to be severe with her for striking me and taking the ape suit. Too many other greater fears beset me.... And clearly Lila was also a captive.

"How did you get here, Lila?" I asked.

She said nothing in a wooden speechless way.

Short-bandit, the one named Pokey, took it on himself to answer that. "Why, Henry, we were waiting outside your place when she came out with the monkey suit. We just picked her up, and sent her along here." He nodded at the one who had warned him about my reactions to fear. "Ossie brought her."

Ossie cursed him very blackly. "Whatcha usin' my name for?" Ossie demanded.

"Why," said Pokey, "Ossie ain't your name."

"Well, quit usin' any names!" Ossie snarled.

"Okay. Okay, if you feel that way about it. Okay, Nameless."

Slim grinned. He had been looking about. "We the only ones here yet?"

Ossie jerked his head at another room. "Yeah. Except in there."

Slim strolled to the door which Ossie had indicated. He peered through. "Do you wanta be Nameless, too?" he asked someone in there.

A voice called him a genial name. Not a nice one. "You two hooligans took your time gettin' here," the voice added.

"It rained. We was beset by the elements." Slim listened to the awful uproar of the storm a moment. "I hope the resta our party don't get lightning-struck."

"You get Henry?"

"We got Henry. Sure."

"Bring Henry in here," the voice said. "We might as well acquaint him with his purpose in life."

Slim came back, seized me, propelled me at the door, through it.

The voice belonged to a lean, lazy-looking man in a tweed suit, a fellow who did not look either particularly intelligent or vicious, although on the latter point his looks were obviously deceiving.

Dido Alstrong, the other man in the room, I knew, of course.

Dido Alstrong was certainly in a deplorable condition. There had always been about Dido a certain garish neatness that went with his acquisitive manners—he did not have it now. They had been beating Dido. Not with fists, either. When he looked at me, his mouth sagging open with surprise, I saw that they had knocked out, or pulled out, at least three of his lower teeth and two uppers. One of his fingernails was completely missing also, the end of the finger a bloody stump. Much as I detested Dido Alstrong, the way he looked made me a little ill.

"Henry! Good God!" said Dido Alstrong hoarsely. "Then they weren't lying!"

"Lying?" I asked unsurely.

"Oh my Lord!" cried Dido.

There had been something vaguely familiar about the lazy-looking man in tweeds, and now it dawned on me why this was. The chap had been at some of the same places where I was yesterday—standing in front of my laboratory building, and in the cocktail bar, and standing in the street in front of the Farrar apartment. The fellow had been functioning as an observer, a lookout. Now he was serving as Dido Alstrong's captor.

Suddenly, from the other room, came a bit of confusion. Feet clattered. Lila Farrar cried out, a whimpering sound.

Slim jammed his gun into my side, said, "Easy, Henry. No fits out of you, pal." And he guided me hastily back into the other room to see what had happened.

Lila Farrar had endeavored to make a break for the outer night. She had been unsuccessful. The man referred to as Ossie, or Nameless, had recaptured her.

"Hell, she worked them ropes loose," Ossie said.

"Somebody oughta work some of your hide loose, make ya a little more careful," said Slim. To Lila, Slim added, "Baby, you don't wanta do things like that. We'd sure hate to have to shoot a pretty tootsie like you."

Lila, in a voice which desperation made hardly understandable, cried, "So my own father would have me shot!"

Slim's jaw fell. "Huh?"

Ossie snorted.

Slim pulled his jaw up, asked, "What's she mean by that, Ossie?"

"She thinks her pop is stud duck," Ossie said. "Ain't that somethin'?"

"What?" yelled Slim. "She thinks old Farrar is engineering this? What makes her think that? What gave her such an idea?"

Ossie shrugged. "Damned if I know. Who can figure how a woman thinks!"

Lila stared at them bitterly. "You're not fooling me," she said.

They guided me forcibly back into the room where Dido Alstrong was seated on a chair. I noticed that his ankles were tied to the heavy chair legs.

"Henry," said the tweed-suited man. "You're a chemist, ain't you?"

"Y-yes," I confessed shakily.

"How good a chemist are you?"

"I—quite good."

"Better than Dido Alstrong?" he demanded.

"I knew more than Dido Alstrong will ever know," I said grimly, "when I was ten years old.

"Watch out, Henry!" Dido Alstrong yelled.

Slim hit Dido on the head. Dido's eyes rolled until they were all whites.

Tweed-suit looked at me thoughtfully. "You're the boy for us, Henry. You're our lad. Dido Alstrong was able to invent the thing, so you can surely figure it out. Don't you think so?"

"I—well—I don't believe I understand," I said uneasily. I had no wish to serve these people.

He crossed his tweed-clad legs casually. "Tell you what, Henry. Here's the whole story. Dido Alstrong, here, works for Farrar who has a company that makes food packaging units, and that got Dido Alstrong interested in means of preserving foods. You know about frozen foods packages, don't you?"

"Oh, yes," I said. "You see them everywhere—"

"Kinda profitable, wouldn't you say?"

"Yes, indeed. I imagine—"

"Dido Alstrong," he interrupted me, "had developed a process by which almost all perishable foods can be preserved for up to six months by subjecting them to a supersonic ultra-short sound wave gadget—I guess you'd call it that, anyway. I ain't a scientist enough to know the name of it."

I considered this. "Such a device would probably be bulky and impractical," I said. "Of course, scientists have long, understood that ultra-short sound waves have odd effects on molecular structure. But—"

"As we understand it," said tweed-suit, "the machine ain't so big nor expensive. And it preserves food just about as fast as is passes through on a conveyor belt."

I thought of this.

"Good Lord!" I gasped.

It was incredible. Such a discovery would be worth a fabulous sum. . . . Gradually, like trees falling, the significance began to grow on me. Each fresh realization was a crashing impact. Why, such a discovery would revolutionize the food packaging industry; it would have an effect on the entire way of life of men.

To say nothing, naturally, of the millions of dollars that would pour into the pockets of Dido Alstrong in the way of royalties. I thought of Dido Alstrong, the obnoxious fellow that he was, and I have never been sicker.

"That's—that's—why, Dido Alstrong isn't entitled to any such good fortune!" I croaked.

Tweed-suit laughed. "We had the same idea, sorta."

"You—"

He nodded. "We're relieving him of it. Of course, we haven't got our hands on it yet, but I think we will."

"What happened?" I blurted.

"Well, we were a little careless and Dido Alstrong found out we were after the secret, so he decided to put them where we wouldn't be able to get them."

"And where was that?"

"He gave them to you, Henry."

"Me?" I yelled. This was unbelievable. It could hardly be true either.

"The monkey suit," the man said.

"But I don't understand!"

"The monkey suit," he explained patiently, "is the key to the formula."

"I'm so confused!" I said.

"We ain't exactly in broad daylight ourselves," tweed-suit informed me. "There's one little hitch—making Dido Alstrong tell us the formula or where it is. But we'll get that done." He wheeled on Dido Alstrong. "Won't we, bub?" he demanded.

Dido Alstrong had been listening to this with all the emotions of a selfish man who was terrified about his own safety. It did not seem to me that he was at all worried about my own welfare, and I resented this, because after all he had something at stake—millions of dollars no doubt—and I had nothing. I was the bystander. I was Dido Alstrong's sucker. I wouldn't have been in this if it hadn't been for Dido.

Now Dido said, "Henry, don't believe that story."

"Isn't it true?" I asked anxiously.

"Not exactly," Dido said. "You see, Henry, there isn't any food preserving supersonic gadget. There never was. I—well—I told some people there was, and that got me into this trouble."

"Who did you tell you had such a thing?"

"I—uh—Mr. Farrar," Dido replied grimly. "And Lila, and maybe one or two others."

"You lied?"

"Yeah."

"But why?"

He said bitterly, "Old man Farrar didn't think much of me as a prospective son-in-law. I wanted to marry Lila and he was nixing it. So I told the lie about a food preserving process to fix myself up, make him think I was some guy."

"But Dido, what good would that have done you?" I demanded.

"Hah! He would have let me marry Lila."

"But he would have found out later!"

"After I was one of the family, maybe," Dido said carelessly. "What could he do then? If he got tough, I could sue him for a potful of dough for alienating my wife's affections. It wouldn't have come to that, though—I would have slid out of it by saying the process had a flaw in it that I hadn't discovered earlier."

"Then there isn't any food-preservation machine?"

"No." He eyed me anxiously. "You've got to believe me, Henry. You know I'm quite a liar."

I did know he was quite a liar, all right.

But I had no idea what to think. If there was a food-preserving machine, Dido would doubtless lie to these men, who were trying to steal the secret, and say there wasn't. On the other hand, the tissue of falsehoods and four-flushing was exactly the sort of thing Dido Alstrong would perpetrate. So I had two stories that seemed equally logical. In either case, Dido deserved the mess he was in. I wished I wasn't in it with him.

"Henry," said tweed-suit, "I'll make you a proposition. A business deal. You check this supersonic gadget for us when we get it or the plans—if there's plans, you may have to build a model—and we'll cut you in on it."

"Give me a share?" I asked.

"That's right."

It was awfully tempting. "How much?"

"Ten per cent," he said.

"Oh, I'd have to have fifty per cent, at least," I said.

Dido Alstrong laughed bitterly. "Brothers, Henry is a child where everything but a dollar is concerned. Then he's a shark. You'll find that out."

Tweed-suit was glaring at me. "We may have to do some inducting," he said.

Now came a very touching scene. It had, also, a certain hideous note.

Because another man—and this man also I had seen during the previous day at different places, not at the time recognizing him as one of the thugs—came into the place. He brought with him Mr. Farrar.

Mr. Farrar entered with his hands held on a level with his shoulders. His face was pale. When he saw Lila, his features registered the bitterest sort of stunned emotion.

"Father!" Lila cried. "They—you—"

She didn't say that she had suspected her father of masterminding the affair, but you could see that she was now convinced differently, and revolted with the very idea that she could have had such a thought.

"Lila, darling," Farrar said softly. "I—I was hoping—they told me they had you prisoner—I was hoping they lied."

Lila sobbed for a few moments. Then she turned to me. "Henry," she said. "Henry, I'm sorry I hit you and took the suit. I did it because—well—I was foolish enough to believe my father was involved."

"I understand," I said. "You wished to aid him."

Farrar did not seem astonished. He told me, "This is not news. Lila accused me of such a thing earlier last night—before you and Savage and Mayfair returned the second time.

That was why Lila was not there. She had left in a rage, revolted with me."

I stared at Lila. "That's what you wanted to tell Savage when you telephoned?"

"Yes."

"But why didn't you tell *me*, Lila, when we talked."

She said bitterly, "You just don't inspire confidence, Henry."

I was bitterly hurt. After all I had been through, I wasn't inspiring confidence. It was a nauseating development.

"I'm very distressed," I mumbled.

Tweed-suit asked dryly, "Are you distressed enough, Henry, to help us out with the gadget? You could put quite a few feathers in your nest while you're doing it."

"But what—what about Lila, Mr. Farrar and Dido Alstrong?" I asked uneasily.

"They'll be distressed, too," said tweed-suit. "And rather dead, I'm afraid."

"Oh! Oh, no—"

An utterly unexpected voice—not a stranger's voice, though—addressed us.

"Speaking of distress," it said. "I think now's as good a time as any to contribute some."

I believe I experienced an undreamed-of emotion: I believe I was glad to see the lout Monk Mayfair.

XII

Mayfair's voice was a little muffled because he stood outside a window. He remedied that. He knocked the glass out of the window. In the middle of the sound of breaking glass, his big voice—it was a normally squeaky voice, but it certainly changed when he was excited—said clearly, "The place is surrounded with cops. So act accordingly."

Maybe it was the breaking glass. Maybe they just didn't believe him. Maybe they were too desperate to care—understandable, because there had been a cold-blooded murder.

Anyway, activities commenced.

Slim began by shooting Mr. Mayfair in the chest. This discomfited Mayfair. That, I swear to you, was all it did—discomfit him. Apparently he was standing rather precariously on a barrel or something outside the window, and the bullet unbalanced him; his great arms waved like a spider's legs, and presently he fell into the room. Not away from the window. Into the room. The effect was tremendous, because he removed the remainder of the glass from the window, and his yell was like a freight-engine whistling in the room. Mayfair came erect. He came toward Slim. Slim shot him again. Mayfair still came.

Slim said, "Blanks!" He really thought his gun was loaded with blank cartridges, evidently, because he pointed it at the ceiling, which was plastered, and pulled the trigger again. A bullet from his gun ploughed a quantity of plaster loose. Quite satisfied his bullets were real, Slim prepared to fire at Mayfair again. But he had wasted too much time, and Mayfair hit him. I had not realized a mere fist could change a man's face so.

Doc Savage's voice said distinctly, "Monk, get out of there! I told you we'd use gas on them!"

"Hell, I slipped and fell in the window," Monk said.

I am afraid I have begun the description of this fight inadequately. Not that, even now, anything seems quite adequate. . . . Anyway, there had been at the beginning three victims in the room—myself, Lila, Mr. Farrar—or four counting Dido Alstrong. And the enemies were Slim, Pokey, Ossie, the tweed-suit, and the man who had brought Mr. Farrar— five. Slim was no longer interested. Four remained.

So there were now four foes, three-to-four neutrals, and bedlam. Everyone did whatever occurred to him or her at the time. I could not watch it all.

Savage came in. He had, dumfoundingly, been in the other room. The man's speed was fabulous. The tweed-suit and Ossie were levelling handguns; Savage was upon them instantly; he struck one gun away, seized the other, and got it. And then the pair were at him, and Pokey joined them.

I knew Savage could not overpower three of them. It was impossible. My only thought, the only way I could see life ahead of me, was to take flight. But I needed an excuse for it, and so I leaped to Lila, cried, "Here! I'll help you!"

She was still tied. Bound, I discovered, to the chair. Terror gave me no time to unbind her. I picked up girl and chair and made for the door. I made it, but fell down at the door; I went crashing down the steps, slammed into the ground on my face. There was mud. I was blinded.

The rain beat on me. The wind whipped my clothing. Inside the house, a gun crashed. A man screamed awfully. The mud hurt my eyes no end; I could not see a thing.

Then feet, a man's feet, hit hard beside me. I sensed—felt, heard—the force of a terrific blow that just missed my head. Someone was trying to brain me! He cursed.

Have you ever been blinded? And in a fight? It was very bad; I began to feel much as I had felt in Farrar's apartment. Not brave. Just imbued with a wish to live—to do anything, anything at all, to live.

Instinctively, my hands went up. Perhaps I was screaming in fear and rage; someone was. At any rate, and most fortunately, my hands encountered a down-slugging arm. I jerked. The other fell on me. We fought.

I hit, variously, the mud, an arm, a face, the ground again, my own leg—and I managed to bite, butt and kick almost as many objects. It was not very clear. It was too fast. It was like one fall—a great one, down a stairs, when one doesn't know what really happens.

At length the other one was still. Blinded, my eyes leaking, the mud hurting my eyeballs like acid, I lay across my victim.

A voice addressed a general statement. It was Mayfair.

He said: "What do you know! Henry wound up on the side of the white race."

Mayfair took me by the collar and dragged me into the house, on into a kitchen, and jammed my head into a bucket of water. "Wash your face, Henry," he said, and left. I cleared my eyes with all haste, then returned to the conflict scene.

The whole thing, as nearly as anyone could guess its time, had taken less than a minute. But the room was a shambles; furniture lay shattered, the air stank of gunpowder. Bodies were scattered about. Five of the latter—accounting, unbelievably, for all the opponents.

Doc Savage carried Lila Farrar inside, placed her in a chair. He asked, "You all right?"

She nodded tensely. She was very muddy.

I said, "I'm sorry, Miss Farrar, that I fell with you."

She gave me as pleasant a look as the circumstances permitted.

"I'm sorry, too, for the things I was thinking about you," she said.

This was confusing. The implication was that I had done something to redeem myself. All I had done was fight, not very gallantly either, for my life.

I wondered which of these men on the floor I had overpowered while blinded. I looked at them. None of them, strangely, were either wet nor muddy.

Dido Alstrong was still tied to the chair. Apparently he had been unable to get into the fight.

Monk Mayfair went outdoors.

Doc Savage asked me quietly, "You feel all right, Henry?"

"I—er—wouldn't call it all right," I confessed. "I'm a trifle upset."

He nodded. "Sorry about using you."

"Using me?"

He hesitated, then inquired, "Hadn't you figured that out?"

"Oh, yes," I said vaguely. This was not true.

Savage now confronted Dido Alstrong, produced a large documentary envelope, opened it, fanned the blueprints and data sheets it contained before Dido's face, and demanded, "This gadget phony?"

Dido Alstrong winced. "Yes."

"How come?"

Now Dido Alstrong repeated substantially the story he had told me earlier—he didn't have any supersonic gadget for preserving foodstuffs; he had just pretended to have one in order to impress Mr. Farrar so that he could wed Lila.

"I didn't dream," Dido finished, "that they would try to steal the thing off me, and kill me too. As soon as I was in danger, I went to that costume shop and rented the monkey suit, told the guy I didn't have enough dough for the deposit, but would leave my watch and those papers for security. . . . Hey, how'd you get that envelope?"

Savage told him how. "Henry and I visited the costume place, and the proprietor happened to mention you were short of money. That seemed queer. So I left Henry locked in the car—the more Henry knew the more trouble he seemed to be able to make—and went back and asked the proprietor what kind of a deposit had been made. He showed me the envelope. I had the police visit him and get it for me."

"Well, I guess you can see the gadget won't work," Dido mumbled.

"Yes. Obviously." Savage riffled the papers. "This one is

an interesting document. . . . Nothing to do with the phony invention."

"Uh-huh. You mean the statement of the facts," Dido said. "Yeah, I put that in because I didn't want anybody killing me and getting away with it."

"You figured," said Savage, "that in case you were killed, the police would trace the monkey suit back to the shop where you rented it, and find out about the deposit you left, thus discovering the statement?"

"That's right."

"It was a round-about way of naming your possible murderer."

"Yeah, but I didn't want no statement like that in the hands of no lawyer, who might get conscience-ridden and turn it over to the cops. I wanted it where it would be found if I got killed, and also where I could get it back if things turned out well."

"How could it have turned out well if your gadget was a fake?"

Dido Alstrong snorted. "Are you kidding? When this thing developed the way it did, I had a better hold on him than the invention, didn't I? I wanted the girl, and her dough."

Savage shook his head slowly.

"I don't think I like you, Alstrong," he said.

"That hurts me a lot," Dido Alstrong said cheerfully. "A lot. In a pig's eye."

Savage shrugged. "You got scared and fled the city. I take it. Why did you come here?"

"My pal, Hugo Davis, owns the place. I figured it a good hideout. I used to work in a Farrar plant near here, and spent time here before."

"Did you know they killed Hugo Davis?"

"Huh?" Dido paled. "They—did."

Monk Mayfair put his head in the door. "Henry's victim is waking up," he said.

"Let him wake up," Savage replied. "Then bring him inside."

I stood there with the feelings of one whose mind had separated from his body and was hanging suspended several feet distant. Because for the first time I realized who my victim must have been.

* * *

This Savage was even worse than the rumors had had him. He was the mental wizard they had said he was. He had known, it was suddenly clear to me, all the answers very early in the affair. . . .

In an utterly miserable voice, I asked, "You—you knew Miss Farrar had telephoned me at your laboratory?"

"Why not? There are extension telephones in the laboratory where Monk and I were," said Savage dryly.

"And you gave me the monkey suit, and sent me home— to serve as bait?" I blurted.

He nodded. "Monk's idea, however. . . . Yes, we surmised what Miss Farrar had on her mind—the problem of whether or not her father was a crook and what she should do."

"And you let those thugs take me, and followed us up here—"

He shook his head. "Wrong. We watched them take Miss Farrar, and followed *her* here. We were already here when you were brought."

Dido Alstrong entered the discussion.

"What I want to know," Dido complained, "is how'n hell they found *me* here! I thought this was a safe hangout. Only Henry Davis knew about it."

Doc Savage glanced at him with dislike, said, "I'm afraid I was responsible. You see, I deliberately gave Farrar the idea that Hugo Davis and where he formerly lived were important. Farrar grabbed the bait. He did some thinking, decided that since you wouldn't hide out in your own place, it was logical that you would use one Hugo Davis knew of. The first thing he did, probably, was have his men find out what property Hugo Davis owned, and they spotted this cabin immediately."

Monk Mayfair now booted Mr. Farrar into the room. Mr. Farrar showed the damage my fists and teeth had done.

Mr. Farrar did not look at me. He did not look at his daughter, either.

The police came later. Two state troopers. A detective and an assistant District Attorney from New York City. They discussed the case with Doc Savage, and it developed that tweed-suit had killed Hugo Davis. They even found Hugo Davis' wallet on tweed-suit, and presently the man offered wildly to turn state's evidence and testify against Mr. Farrar, whom, it seemed, had been a crook for a long time. He had even been operating his Farrar Products company in a dishonest fashion.

"You probably knew Farrar was a crook," I told Dido Alstrong outdoors. "You're probably as unreliable as he."

"Henry," said Dido bitterly, "the pot shouldn't call the kettle black. You stinker! I'll never forget that you were about to throw in with the gang and explain my gadget for them."

"I was just pretending," I said angrily.

"Hah!" he said.

I walked away from him. I didn't feel so tall. About tall enough to walk under a sleeping gopher.

Miss Lila Farrar was standing on a knoll. The knoll gave a view of green hills and blue distance as hazy as a blind man's eyes.

"Lila, I'm so sorry, so sorry, about your father," I said.

She had a small twig in her fingers. She turned it, looked at it, broke it. "There are many things to be sorry for," she said.

I knew she was including me.

THE END

LET'S KILL AMES

I

I'll never forget the man with the dirty face.

The least they could do, you'd think, was send a clean man. One with enough pride to wipe off his chin, anyway. It was his chin that got me. There was a piece of his breakfast on it, a bit of something that was probably oatmeal, and there is nothing quite like a two-hour-old chunk of oatmeal for chin decoration.

He wore a tan suit of which the coat was a slightly different tan than the pants, and both halves fit him about equally poorly. As if, a couple of days ago, someone had peeled a banana and hung the peel on him. He was not a big man, and he did not look as if he had been constructed for any useful purpose. The only large thing about him was his mouth, wide-spreading, round-lipped, separating his flattish head in two parts like a clamshell.

He looked as determined as he could, which still left him looking like something you'd prefer to rake away with a stick.

He said, "Miss Ames?"

"Yes."

"Miss Travice Ames?" he said.

"Yes."

He unfolded a paper that was, considering that he had been carrying it, remarkably clean. "You wanta look at this, baby?" he mumbled.

I saw what the paper was, and said, "No, thanks."

I knew who and what he was. But they still could have sent a clean man.

"You don't wanta read it, huh?" he said. "I guess you know what it is, don't you? I guess you been expecting this, haven't you?"

I moved around to the windward side of him. His breath smelled like a can of fish that had been open too long, or maybe it was just him.

"Let's skip the personal touch," I said.

"You want," he asked, "to do anything about it? In cases like this, if—"

"Never mind."

"Are you sure—"

"I'm sure," I said. "I was never surer of anything. What do they pay you for? To give me an argument?"

He nodded. "I thought probably you wouldn't," he said. "When they're as good-looking as you are, they don't usually give a damn. You take a homely one, they don't get things as easy, and they got a different attitude. They value things more."

"What is this?"

"What is what? Whatcha mean?"

I said, "Skip it," in a tired voice. And he looked at my car, at my beautiful car. It was a roadster, a convertible, one of those convertible station wagons. It was not two months old and there was not a flashier job in town, not in the whole city. Only it wasn't my car any longer. I was beginning to see that. And he said, "You got anything personal in the iron? Anything you want to get out?"

Calling a car like that an iron was a sin.

"No," I said.

So he got in my car. He drove it away. He was from the finance company. But at least it seemed they could have sent a clean man.

That was the first of two bad things that happened.

The second bad thing wasn't long following—my hotel suite door had a trick gadget in the lock. The hotel had put it there. It was one of those gimmicks they put in the lock of a guest's room when the guest hasn't paid. A French key.

I remembered that the elevator boy'd had a funny look on his face as I rode up.

And I was a little surprised at the Afton House. The hotel was, although Afton House wasn't a fancy name, one of those luxury places. I was paying—or wasn't paying—forty-six dollars a day for parlor-bedroom-bath suite. The minimum single rate was, I understood, fourteen dollars. And these had been the Afton House rates back during the depression and the pre-war days, which gives an idea. So I was surprised that they would be so *hoc genus homme* as to put a French key in a guest's lock. It was not only old-fashioned, but it was worthy of a three-fifty-a-day hotel.

So I was locked out.

The desk clerk was named Gilrox. He was a slick article, just long enough from New York that he liked to show it. His cheeks were pink, and his hair looked slick enough to have a coating of airplane dope on it. But his hands were thin and colorless, as if he washed them with Drāno.

He expected me to walk up to the desk and give him hell. He got all set for it. He gave the gardenia in his lapel a sniff. He looked as if he was going to have fun.

I fooled him and went to the main desk. There was a windowed hotel envelope. I didn't open that. There were four telephone message envelopes. I opened those, and they all said the same thing in slightly different ways. They said: Nat Pulaski had called. He had called at 2:00, at 3:10, at 3:45, and at 4:20. One said, *Planning on dinner date tonight. Love.* Another one said: *Date tonight. Urgent. Love.* And still another said: *Call at five. Important.*

None of the notes smelled of a chemical laboratory, but they should have; and my imagination easily added a faint odor of chemical reagent to them. They sounded like Pulaski. Everything was urgent with Pulaski. The sap.

The clerk, Mr. Gilrox, had stopped sniffing his gardenia. He was standing with his fingertips resting on the desk, like a student typist waiting for the speed test to begin.

"What about this?" I asked him.

"Yes, what about it?" said Mr. Gilrox. "Yes, indeed. What about four hundred and eighty-six dollars?"

"Is that what I owe?"

He nodded. "Add a matter of forty-one cents, and we have the exact total."

"And you want it?"

"We feel we would be happier with it," Mr. Gilrox said.

"I should like some of my baggage."

"No doubt."

"You mean," I asked, "that I'm being locked out with the clothes I stand in?"

"They're very lovely clothes, Miss Ames," he said. "I've frequently remarked on that to myself. What fine and expensive clothes Miss Ames has, I've said to myself. And just a while ago I said it again: Miss Ames is wonderfully dressed this evening, isn't she?" He was as polite as if he was petting a kitten, and he was enjoying himself.

"Legally," I said, "I suppose you know what you are doing?"

"Hotels usually do. You see, this isn't entirely an unusual situation." He smirked and added, "I don't imagine it's unusual with you, either, Miss Ames."

"What do you mean by that nasty crack?"

Mr. Gilrox was all ready for me. He slipped an envelope from under the desk, and he slapped it down before me as if it was a plate of caviar. He said, "Item one: The Beach Colonial hotel in Miami, Florida, a notation to the effect that you are not to be permitted to register in the future. Also a rather puzzling addition that it was necessary to replace the management of the hotel upon your departure. I take it somebody there underestimated you. . . ." There was curiosity back of his large smug eyes. He waited hopefully for an explanation.

"What a big curiosity you have, Grandma Gilrox," I said.

He scowled. "Item two: The Atlanta, Georgia, police department states you are hereafter unwelcome in Atlanta, Georgia. No details. I gather somebody there also underestimated you."

"You find this interesting?"

"That I do," he agreed. "That I do indeed. So did Mr. Coyle, the manager here."

"And you and Mr. Coyle decided?"

"That if you have four hundred eighty-six dollars and forty-one cents, you may pay it to us, and we will see that a porter delivers your bags to the street with our best service."

"I don't have four hundred and eighty-six dollars and those cents."

"How much have you?"

"Not that much."

"Have you enough to interest us in a compromise?" he inquired.

"I doubt it."

"That's very sad," he said. "I regret it greatly."

"I can see you do regret," I said. "But if I paid up, you would still throw me out. Am I right?"

"Exactly."

"Why?"

"We feel that you're a—" He let it hang. He chopped it off as if he had unexpectedly come up against it, and it had thorns on it. He stood there and remembered what he could about the slander laws. He said, "Let's put it this way: We

el that you've been underestimated in the past. We wouldn't
ke to underestimate you, Miss Ames."

"You're not calling me a tramp, by any chance?"

"Oh, no indeed," he said. He meant that.

"Or an adventuress?" I added.

With his look, he said yes, that was it exactly. With his
oice, a voice that sounded as if it wrapped things in velvet
ach time it spoke, he said, "Don't quote me on that.
didn't say it."

"Anyway," I said, "I believe we understand each other."

He said he hoped we did. And then he asked, "What are
ou going to do?"

He listened to me tell him how much of his business it
vas, but if his ears burned the glow didn't show. It might be
ossible to insult him, but a hotel guest couldn't do it. Too
nany had tried. He smiled and adjusted the flower in his
pel and probably enjoyed it.

I went over and sat in a chair in the lobby. I wanted to
nink about it. It needed thinking about, because I had in the
vhole world something like five dollars in cash.

That was how I happened to decide to let Nat Pulaski
uy me a dinner after all. Pulaski was a sucker and for two
ays I had been giving him the boot, but getting locked out
f my hotel, having my car taken back, put a different light on
. Hello, sucker.

II

Pulaski arrived with more than one thing wrong with
im. He came in acting as if there was a rattlesnake in his
lothing somewhere and he couldn't find it.

I detest short men, and Pulaski was a short one. He had
noist full lips, but otherwise his face wasn't bad, although
ow it was redder than it usually was.

He had a go-around with the revolving door when he
ame in. He was a little too slow on his feet, and the door
atted his rather ample rear, causing him to stumble, and
nen he got his topcoat caught in one of the leaves, and stood
rking foolishly at it. The coat came loose and he stumbled
ack on legs that bent at the knees at the wrong times.

Oh, fine! I thought contemptuously. Pulaski has to b
tight. Pulaski sober was no bargain.

When he spied me, his round face got the expressio
that the riders to the hounds get when they sight the fox.
thought he was going to shout, "Tally-ho!" But he just cried
"Oh, ho! Oh, ho!" And then he came over carefully enough t
be walking on golf balls, and wanted to know, "What have
done? Why do you do these things to me?"

"What things?"

"These cruelties," he cried. "These diabolical moods c
yours! These refined mistreatments you inflict on poor ol
Pulaski! A pox on you, woman!"

He was usually that way, but not always as bad. Ther
was evidently a little of thwarted ham actor in the fellow.

He rocked back on his heels, then forward again, stop
ping the tilting each time just before he upset. He continue
his complaint.

"Two days!" he shouted. "Two days, fair lady, and yo
have ignored my humble supplications. Ignored—hell! I haven
even been able to get you on the telephone." He pause
dramatically, registered what he evidently thought was strick
en grief, and then forgave me. "But your loveliness over
whelms me. Such beauty wipes all rancor from my mind.
am reduced to a carpet, a slightly rum-soaked carpet, and yo
may walk upon me if you wish." He hiccoughed. "Walk o
me if you wish," he repeated, and it appeared for a minut
that he was going to lie down so that I could.

That was Pulaski. Ham actor, amateur wolf, and—thi
evening for a change—rum pot. He did not customaril
drink, and he was showing it.

There was something on his mind that was driving hin
to drink.

I was sure of it before we were halfway through dinner.

He asked where we should dine, and I paid him off b
naming the most expensive place in town.

"Hmm!" he said. "I kiss twenty bucks goodbye."

He would be lucky to get out with a check under thirt
dollars. I ordered oysters Rockefeller, the solè *marguêry*,
green salad, planked steak, *crêpes Suzette*, and *cafe diablo*.
ordered a daiquiri first, a white wine for the fish, then
champagne. He stuck to bourbon and a steak, and did not ea
enough of his steak to give the bourbon a fight.

I saw that the waiter kept the bourbon coming. My ide

was to get Pulaski mellow, then touch him for my hotel bill. Probably he would have to be pretty mellow to stand still for a touch like that.

Pulaski was a chemist employed, he claimed, by himself. I did not know that there were self-employed chemists, and I still was not sure of it, but that is what Pulaski had said he was. He had a laboratory at 130 Washington Street—he said—and he lived at 720 Ironwood Drive, in an apartment. He said. I was pretty sure about the last, because I had telephoned him there a couple of times.

He was nothing much. A fellow I had met in Palm Beach, Florida, had been with this Pulaski in the army. The other fellow had been a sergeant and Pulaski had been a second lieutenant, and the man in Palm Beach had spent a lot of time saying what he would like to do to Pulaski, and what he would do to Pulaski if he ever got to this city and had a chance to look him up. He had several things in mind for Pulaski, including a stroll over Pulaski's face. The sort of a man who had made that kind of a second lieutenant in the army sounded like an easy mark and I had given Pulaski a ring when I got to town.

But I hadn't come to town to find Pulaski. I had come concerning a business opening with a very sharp and clever woman named Carolyn Lane, who was calling herself Lady Seabrook, and who had thought up something nice and lucrative in cosmetics. She had an angel for it, but it was supposed to be turning out so well that she was going to work the racket and not the angel. Just supposed to be. The D.A. told the Grand Jury about her the day I got there. They even put the angel in jail with her.

This town was a desert. Nothing had turned up, I was broke, and I didn't like Pulaski, but he was running after me. That was all right. Pulaski was the kind you would enjoy trimming. He wouldn't sit on your conscience.

I ordered Pulaski another bourbon.

Pulaski continued bragging to me. He liked to boast to me, I think, because I spoke his language. When he talked about fluxing and reducing reagents, saponification numbers, Elliot apparatus and molecular weights—why do the simple-minded ones always talk about their business with big words?—I could understand what he was talking about.

In college, I specialized in chemistry. Afterward, I worked at it for a couple of years. I worked for the American Union

Chemical Foundation until one of their dopey chemists perfected an improved production method for penicillin and was going to just hand it over to our employers. I had just about persuaded him to take the idea and go into business for ourselves when they fired me. They had a lawyer with bright ideas, too, but all they made stick was firing me.

Anyway, that was why Pulaski liked to brag to me. It wasn't why he liked me; it was just why he would brag to me.

But there was something eating him tonight.

I had merely thought I would stick him for an expensive dinner, and maybe for the hotel bill, although I doubted he even had that kind of money, but now I was beginning to wonder what was eating him. Whatever it was, it was taking big bites out of his courage.

Pulaski was scared. It finally dawned on me. Pulaski was so frightened of something that he couldn't keep his mouth still. He wore it like a garment. It oozed out of his pores. They say animals can smell fear in a person, and Pulaski would certainly have been a bouquet tonight.

"What," I asked him, "is bothering you?"

"Nothing," he said. "Bothering me? Nothing at all, baby. I'm just made breathless by you, is all."

Men seem to be like that. Ask them a question, and they back away, and they either want to be begged and are being coy, or they downright don't intend to tell you and will pretend that it's preposterous to think anything is nipping on them. Pulaski belonged to the latter bracket. He didn't intend to tell me anything, and was made more frightened than he had been by the fact that I had spotted something amiss.

Men are suckers. I haven't met one who isn't. They can be played like a violin if you have the right kind of a bow and know how to use it. I had discovered this several years ago, when I was about fourteen. Pulaski was an easy fiddle to play, and that was what he was, just a fiddle. The music that came out of him probably wouldn't have much quality.

An hour and fifteen minutes later. I had him giving out information. We were in a night-club now, the fanciest one the city had—there is something about extremely fleshy surroundings that makes some men want to boast. That, I had decided, was the way to get Pulaski's information out of him. Get him to take enough liquor to weaken his fences, then goad him.

I led him into making a pass or two, then gave his amour a cold reception. He complained about this.

"Listen," I said. "I'm not saying I couldn't fall for you, Pulaski. You're not bad looking. But it just happens that I have certain ideas about small-timers, and I'm not going to get all involved with some fellow who uses nickels when he should be using dollars."

He flushed. "You're mercenary."

"You think so? I call it practical."

He said angrily, "You think I'm a small-timer, huh?"

"I didn't say so."

He batted his eyes, rubbed his hand over his face as if to remove the rum film from his eyes, and complained, "You're cold-blooded."

"Pulaski," I said, "you'd be surprised. I'm not as cold as you'd think. But the kind of a man that arouses me must be a man. I don't mean he has to roll in money, but that would go with it. My kind of a man has to be one who does things—big and clever things in a big and clever way.... You're nice-looking, Pulaski. But you're not extraordinary. There's nothing exciting nor adventurous about you. If there was, well..." I let him get what he could out of some eyelash-fluttering.

This was pretty broad stuff, but the alcohol had him foggy enough that the only thing that would make an impression on him was a club. It worked, too. He got a little purple, and hit the table a lick.

He said, "Listen, baby, you're underestimating old Pulaski."

"Words," I said, "don't make it so."

"You're just a dollar-chasing wench."

I looked at him and said, "Penny-chasing."

"Huh?"

"I'm sitting here with you, aren't I?"

He blew up. "Listen, you! Don't call me cheap! I'm going to grab off twenty thousand bucks in the next two weeks. What do you think of that?"

I thought he was a liar. And pretty soon I didn't. There was the way he had said he would have twenty thousand dollars in two weeks, the way he tied the words up in fear like red ribbons, that made it convincing. And puzzling. Pulaski's type didn't get twenty-thousand-dollar fees. Not honestly. And if it was honest, if he had stumbled on some chemical formula or process, he wouldn't be this scared.

So I told him not to be ridiculous, that I was in no mood

for bragging, and to finish his drink and take me home. That made him madder, and the angrier he got, the more determined he was to prove his importance.

It took another hour to get the story out of him.

It raised my hair.

There were three men named J. X. Smith, Sonny Conover and James L. Like. There was another man—unnamed—who hated the three. This other man—if it was a man; it may not have been; Pulaski called the individual "person" throughout—had hired Pulaski to furnish an unusual poison. The poison *was* unusual. It would lay in the body tissue several months before it killed the victims. In the meantime, it could be neutralized and rendered harmless by a treatment which only Pulaski knew about. Pulaski, of course, had sold the treatment to the "person" along with the poison.

"This person I'm talking about," said Pulaski, "is going to administer the poison to the three, then demand plenty of dough for treating them. And they'll pay, too. That's the only way they can save their necks." He made a fist and added, "For furnishing the stuff, I get paid twenty grand." He hit the table again, and demanded, "Now, what do you think of that?"

"You're drunk," I said.

"Huh?"

"Or crazy as a gooney bird."

He batted his eyes at me in an owlish rage. He did that for a long time, nearly a minute, and then he said in a loose-mouthed foolish way, "Sure. . . . Sure, Ames, I was just talking."

I knew what had happened. It had finally come into his rum-sodden head that he had talked too much. He was closing his mouth, and moreover, trying to take back what he had told me.

"You're just bragging," I said.

"Yeah," he said. "Sure. . . . I just made up that stuff."

"You should fix up your stories when you're sober," I told him. "When you're tight, you think of some pretty zany ones."

"I guess you're right."

It had dawned on me by now that Pulaski's tale of three men being hated by a fourth person who was going to give them a freak poison and demand extortion money for saving them was true. If it had been a lie, Pulaski wouldn't have admitted it.

I said, "If there was such a poison, there would be no way of convincing the three they had been doped with it and would die if they weren't treated. It's ridiculous."

"The hell it is!" he said.

"Oh, don't be dumb, Pulaski. I'm getting tired of such stupidity."

The urge to brag got the best of him again, and he said boastfully, "Suppose the stuff could be detected by a Geiger counter or an electroscope?"

I think I just stared at him for a while. I was floored. He had something. It was practical—except that, as far as I knew, there was no cure for poisoning by any one of the several compounds that could be used, once they were present in the body in fatal amounts.

"There's no cure for anything of that sort," I said.

He snorted. "Oh, if it was insoluble in a salt, and there was a treatment that would cause the body to eject the salt from its tissue, it could be done."

"Ridiculous."

It wasn't, though. I was chemist enough to know that it wasn't.

He rubbed his face with his hand again, and got a fresh hold on his caution. "Sure. . . . It was just something I said to impress you."

He wouldn't drink any more. And, as he grew sober, his fear crawled on him with colder feet. He wouldn't talk about it any more, and I was careful not to pry too obviously. I pried in subtle ways, but got nothing more. I would have liked to know who was paying him twenty thousand dollars, but I didn't find out. Maybe it wasn't twenty thousand; perhaps he had lied about that. But I believed someone was paying him something, and that there really was a scheme.

Pulaski was feeling rather thwarted. He had tried to make himself out quite a big-timer, and it had flopped on him, and he was embarrassed. He still had that urge to be big in my eyes. It was, if anything, stronger. He needed to redeem himself, he felt.

I used the way he was feeling to take him for five hundred.

I said casually, "I'm in an embarrassing position. Mr. Clark, the manager of my plant in Tulsa, was supposed to wire me some money. But Mr. Clark is in Mexico, and won't be back for a week, and it's going to leave me awfully short."

I complained about that for a while, making a picture of the little girl in distress, and presently Pulaski had his hand in his pocket, and was asking, "How much do you need?"

"Oh, a measly five hundred would tide me over," I said.

The dope handed it over. He did it with a great air of what's-a-stinking-five-hundred-bucks, but his eyes stuck out a little.

Parting with the five hundred must have made him a little sick, also, because I had no trouble getting rid of him in the taxi outside my hotel. He didn't even come upstairs with me.

He just sat there and watched me walk away from the taxi with his five hundred and the story of poisoning-for-profit that he'd told me.

III

The pink-cheeked slick Mr. Gilrox was still on duty at the hotel desk. Whether he was working overtime, or hanging around to make it his business to see that I didn't get back into my suite, I didn't know. If it was the latter, the insulting I had given him earlier had had more effect than apparent at the time. At any rate, he got an I-expected-this look when he saw me.

"What, no evening dress, Miss Ames?" he inquired nastily.

"Mr. Gilrox," I said. "You can file that smirk under the heading: To be enjoyed in private. Or you can get it slapped off your silly face."

"Indeed?" he said. "I'd love to see you try that."

"You would call a cop?"

"Exactly."

"I've come for my luggage," I said. "And I can guess exactly what you will say to that."

He nodded. "You did guess it, tutz."

"Don't call me tutz."

"Very well, Miss Ames."

I got out Pulaski's five hundred, counted two hundred dollars off it and laid that on the desk under his nose.

"My, my," he said. He had watched me count it. "What do you think that will buy you?"

"My luggage."

"Oh, no. The amount you owe, Miss Ames, is not two hundred bucks. It is four hundred and eighty-six dollars."

"You refuse to give me my luggage upon my offer to pay two hundred?"

He felt pretty highly of himself. "That gentle silence you heard," he said, "was our best refusal."

I said, "Sonny, do you have a copy of the state statues handy?"

"The what?"

"The statutes. The laws of this fine state. They are printed in three volumes for the year of 1947."

"Of course not. What do you think this is, a lawyer's office?"

"Sonny, you'd better look up the law. The statutes of this state, Section thirteen thousand eighty nine, reads: 'The keeper of any inn, hotel or boarding house shall have a lien on the baggage and other property in and about such inn brought to the same by or under the control of his guests for the proper charges due him from such guests or boarders not to exceed two hundred dollars.' . . . You get that? *Not to exceed two hundred dollars*. Now, here is two hundred dollars. And you had better have my baggage down here and quick."

His face got the pulled look of a man whose collar was too tight.

"What are you trying to pull?" he blurted.

"You'd better call the hotel lawyer, Mr. Gilrox, and learn something."

"I never heard of such a thing!"

"This isn't New York, Mr. Gilrox. I imagine that's going to be quite a problem for you."

He did some cheek-blowing and some eye-narrowing while accustoming himself to the idea of consulting the hotel attorney. Then he picked up the telephone. The lawyer was named Mr. Bartlett, I noticed. He and Mr. Gilrox had an extended discussion which injected considerable color into Mr. Gilrox's face. He hung up and yelled, "Bellboy!" And then, "Bring Miss Ames' baggage at once. All of it."

I said, "Don't forget the two hundred dollars, Mr. Gilrox. And I think I'd like a receipt."

"I never heard of such a damn law!" he yelled.

"You've now heard of it."

"Yes, indeed," he said bitterly. "By God, a man never gets too old to learn. Twenty years, I've been in this racket, and for the last ten of them nobody has foxed me."

I took the receipt he filled out, indicating the hotel had received two hundred dollars on payment.

He said, "You recall that earlier I mentioned that several people in other cities had underestimated you, Miss Ames? . . . Well, just add the name of Gilrox to the list."

I told him I'd already put him on it several days ago, and the last I saw of him he was looking like a tomcat with someone standing on its tail.

IV

The Congress Hotel wasn't as luxurious as the Afton House, but it would do, and they hadn't heard of me—I was somewhat surprised that Mr. Gilrox hadn't thought of calling all the other hotels in town to warn them. He might think of that later. Or he might be the sort who would keep quiet hoping to get a perverse pleasure out of seeing someone else get trimmed. He was probably the latter kind.

I got the best suite, eighteen dollars a day, and was nasty about the green drapes—I detest green, of all colors—and they said they'd change them promptly. The first thing in the morning.

I can go to sleep instantly anywhere. Sleep is merely a matter of bringing the subconscious to the proper tranquility, and my subconscious, like my conscience, has never been stubborn.

But tonight I didn't sleep at once. I gave some consideration to Pulaski's story about three men and an enemy.

It now seemed pretty wild.

I knew, or had heard of, the three victims Pulaski had mentioned. They were local men. All were prominent financially.

J. X. Smith was an architect. He was a dark-skinned soulful-eyed man put together with lengths—long arms, long hands, long fingers, and everything else long, eyes, nose, mouth and body. These long men are usually the inward types, and he was. A thinker, a dreamer, a man who lived within himself and was perhaps a little afraid of the world and afraid of people who knew what they wanted and went after it.

Before I had been in the city long, I had learned that J. X. Smith had money, and I had given him a survey. I had gotten invited to a party where he was the guest of honor, and spent most of his time finding a corner to crawl into. The verdict: A man who frightened easily, who had to think out everything six ways from the middle before he acted. And afraid of women. He would be too much of a waste of time.

Sonny Conover, a thick-wristed, thick-necked, thick-walleted man of forty-five or so was a man I knew by sight, and I think we had been introduced once. For some reason or other men named Sonny are supposed to be scions of wealth and usually no-goods, but if Sonny Conover was a scion of anything, it was the school of hard knocks. He was clearly a self-made man, and as far as the financial part of the constructing was concerned, he had done an excellent job. Sonny Conover, was owner of the Conover Ready-Mixed Concrete Company and the Conover Lumber Company.

I had met James Like once in passing. I had bumped into him leaving the Central National Bank, which should have been named the Like National Bank. He was a perfectly prosaic-looking man of less than fifty, with, I understood, a family as conservative as he was. He was a pillar of society, the town's leading moneybags, and belonged to all the clubs which had dues of over fifty dollars a year. He had made his roll, I understood, in the construction business.

These three men, I saw, had one thing in common. They all were, or had been, connected with the building business in one way of another. Smith was an architect, Conover was a lumber and concrete man, and James Like had been a builder and financier.

These were the three Pulaski's trick poison was going to be used on.

The poison thing still seemed pretty wild after I had thought it over, and I didn't know whether there was anything to it or not.

But it gave me an idea.

I'm very allergic to being broke. And in my book, being whittled down to three hundred dollars—what I had left of sucker Pulaski's money—is the same as being strapped.

*　　*　　*

A mink coat and a confident manner were enough the next morning to get me about a hundred dollars worth of chemicals from the Cumberland Chemical Supply Company. It also got me, on rental, a gadget that the plants which manufacture certain radioactive chemical products use to check their employees regularly to make certain that they do not have a dangerous amount of undesirable radiotoxemia in their bodies. The gadget was worth over a thousand dollars. I could have paid for the chemicals and the rental out of Pulaski's loan, but there didn't seem any point in it when they were so easily impressed by a mink coat and casual manner.

I didn't know the exact poison Pulaski had been boasting about last night. That wasn't important. There are several substances which, if introduced into the body, will produce death in a period of time. These are not new.

After the first World War, there was an epidemic of delayed deaths among workers who had done nothing more exciting during the war than put the numerals on the faces of those watches which glow in the darkness. They were victims of the sort of poisoning that Pulaski had been discussing. In their case, the fatal toxic was not a part of any compound that could be eliminated from the body by treatment. So they were faced with certain lingering death.

The idea of such a death was pretty scary, and I had selected J. X. Smith for my goof. Of the three, he seemed to be the softest.

Also I had heard that J. X. Smith was engaged to be married shortly, and men in love usually think they have a lot to look forward to. Life probably meant a great deal to J. X. Smith just now.

I rigged up two phials. One contained colored water. The other contained a liquid that would operate positively on the detector gadget.

But I was sharp enough to make sure that the stuff that would give a positive wasn't a chemical that could be used to poison a man. If the thing should happen to blow up, and the police get me, I didn't want them to have anything on me that would stand up in court. It would be inconvenient to have some District Attorney trying to prove that I had intended to poison anyone.

All I intended to do was see whether there was a quick

dollar to be made. If there wasn't, I would find it out today. It seemed worth investing a day's time.

The phials were exactly alike as far as outward appearance went, and I tried them out on the detector gadget. The machine indicated positive to one phial. The headset attached to it gave off a quickened clicking sound. To the other phial there was, naturally, a negative reaction, which meant no reaction at all.

I didn't have much trouble getting an appointment to see J. X. Smith at two o'clock that afternoon. I told his secretary I was Miss Travice Ames, and that I was on the staff of a nationally known magazine. That got me the appointment. Publicity always appeals to them.

It would help if J. X. Smith was a coward. I began to examine him for courage as soon as his secretary opened the door to his office, admitted me, and closed the door. J. X. Smith looked up at me. His jaw sagged a little, and he jumped to his feet. Evidently he had expected a frumpy middle-aged woman.

"I—uh—believe I've met you somewhere before," he said.

"Oh, you probably have," I told him. "I've been in the city some time."

"Ah, then you are doing a series of articles, perhaps," he suggested.

"Not exactly," I said. "Not writing articles. . . . Let's call it preparing to save a man's life."

He was one of the those long gangling men who know only one way of handling their emotions—by hiding their feelings inside themselves. When startled, they just jerk everything inside and close a lid. He did this now, but his deadpan face didn't get me to thinking he had iron nerves. I knew that his type is more easily frightened than any other.

His office showed that he had imagination as well as money. It was a large room done in pastels and blond woods, with a minimum of chrome and quite a lot of lucite. It was the office of an egoist and a dreamer.

"I don't believe I understand," he ventured cautiously. That statement about saving a man's life had puzzled him. I handed him a shock to go with it.

"Mr. Smith," I said. "Did you know you have an enemy who is going to kill you?"

His reaction to that was normal. He probably thought I was a little crazy. He probably thought of several things to say, but what he did say was, "What is this, a joke?"

"Not at all. As a matter of fact, the enemy may be killing you now."

His mouth fell open and remained so.

"You have such an enemy, of course," I added.

He also thought of several answers to that which he didn't give. And by the time he spoke, I knew that he *did* have an enemy. Or perhaps more than one. Or he was over-imaginative enough to immediately think of many who might qualify. . . . It was all right with me; the more imaginative he was, the easier he would be to trim.

"Who," he asked, "is this enemy?"

"I'm depending on you to tell me that," I said. "I don't know myself."

He moistened his lips. "This is a bit unusual, isn't it, Miss Ames?"

"And you're tempted to add that you think I'm nuts," I told him. "I wouldn't blame you. However, you had better listen to me. This isn't something wild that I picked out of thin air. It's wild, all right, but it can happen and probably is." I had brought my apparatus and I put it on his desk. "I suggest you give me about five minutes of your time."

J. X. Smith was now a little pale. He was perfectly willing to give me five minutes. He wouldn't have grudged me a couple of days. He was going to be an easy one.

I told him I was a private investigator engaged in searching for a man named Tuggle who had embezzled some stocks from a foolish woman named Simms, and that I was hired by the Simms woman's husband, who was sorry for his foolish wife and wanted it straightened out quietly. I said that I hadn't found this Tuggle, but in the course of snooping I had overheard two men in a booth in a bar discussing the administering of poison to a Mr. J. X. Smith.

"I presumed you were the J. X. Smith concerned," I said. "So that's why I'm here."

He said that it was a remarkable story, which it was. He added, "I think we'd better call the police."

"Suit yourself," I said. "But on the other hand, it might not be desirable."

"Why not?"

I gave him part of the stuff Pulaski had mouthed. "The

poison, the way I heard it, has a treatment, but only the party who gave it to you knows the treatment. They're considering whether to make you pay plenty for the cure, or just let you die."

"This is damned ridiculous," he said.

It wasn't. I told him why it wasn't. I named examples of poisoning of a similar type, and suggested that he get on the telephone and call any X-ray or cancer specialist in the city, and ask just how practical such a method of poisoning was. An X-ray technician would probably know about it, I told him, although the poison had nothing to do with X-rays. And a cancer man would surely know, because they were familiar with the effects of activated compounds.

He listened to this, and didn't believe any of it until he used the telephone and talked to a doctor named Greenstern. Then he believed it. He had enough belief to make him a little blue around the mouth.

"I still think it's ridiculous!" he said.

"Naturally you do," I agreed. "But I came prepared to check on it and ease your mind, or at least settle the matter." I indicated the gadget I'd rented from the supply company, and told him what it was. There was no trouble convincing him, so evidently the doctor he'd just talked to had mentioned one of the contraptions. But he had plenty of suspicion and a couple of questions.

"Just where," he demanded, "do you hook into this?"

"I told you. I'm an investigator by profession. Nasty things like this are my business."

"But—"

"Oh, don't get the idea I'm a Samaritan," I told him. "It's a business proposition with me. As soon as I overheard this poison talk, I thought: I'll just make sure whether it's something real, or a piece of wild imagination. And if Mr. J. X. Smith has been poisoned, no doubt he'll engage my business services to find the antidote or cure to the stuff he has been given."

"You mean . . . ?"

"Oh, it's going to cost you—if you've been doped with the stuff already. . . . If not, it would be nice if you paid me for my trouble, but you'd really be a fool to do that because I might have just come up here with a wild story in order to hook you."

That impressed him. He had already thought of it.

He asked skeptically, "Are you qualified to test me for the presence of the stuff?"

I gave him a briefing on my experience. Some of it was genuine and some of it wasn't, but it didn't matter because he decided to let me test him.

"First," I said, "I'll demonstrate how the gadget works by giving myself a test. The result will be negative, and I'll show you exactly how and why."

He would naturally be interested in that, and it would help convince him that the thing was on the level, which it wasn't. Presumably, since he was an architect, he was a man who would be most intrigued by the mechanics of an operation.

There was not much to the demonstration. I rolled up a sleeve, explaining that concentrations of the stuff were more apt to build up in the body in the neighborhood of the major joints—ankles, knees, hips or elbows—and I was going to use my own elbow in making the test.

I explained it was first desirable to clean the skin of any possible foreign substance before applying the receptor of the gadget, and I proceeded to take one of the phials I had prepared, the one containing plain colored water, and, dabbing a bit of sterilized cotton into the liquid, mop a small area near my elbow.

This cleansing was an important part of the operation. When I sterilized his arm, I would use the liquid from the other bottle which was sufficiently activated to cause the detector device to register.

It came off perfectly. I used the tinted water on my arm. J. X. Smith asked some questions, mostly examined my legs while I was answering, and he adjusted his necktie. I gave him some large technical words and some eyelash waving of a genteel sort. He was coming along fine.

"You see," I said. "The indication is negative. The beat-note of the apparatus is unchanged, which means there is nothing of sufficient activity in my body to register."

He smirked and probably thought of some wise crack about my body, but didn't say it. He was beginning to like this. That meant he didn't think there was a chance in a million of his having been poisoned.

Okay, brother, I thought, the shock will be that much more effective.

Then calamity landed on me. I was going to switch phials now—they were exactly alike—and use the activated liquid to "sterilize" his arm. Actually this would leave a deposit that would register on the apparatus.

My fingers groped for the other phial. . . . It wasn't there. Gone. I didn't have it. . . . I knew immediately what had happened, and I wasn't proud of myself. I knew exactly where the other phial, the little bottle containing the activated solution, was—on my dressing-table back at the Congress Hotel. I had overlooked bringing it along. It was an utterly stupid oversight, and it ruined my plan.

I said, "In case this test should be negative for you, Mr. Smith, I feel it might be advisable to make succeeding ones. Perhaps daily for a time. I didn't overhear when they intended to poison you."

He grinned. "Of course. That will be fine." He was looking at my legs again.

"Why not try again tomorrow morning?" I asked. I was trying to salvage the scheme.

"Of course," he said. "But aren't you going to test me now?"

"Oh, certainly," I replied.

I applied the gadget to his arm. The measured clicking sound that came from its headset immediately speeded up and became almost a buzzing. A positive reaction.

The man had really been poisoned!

V

He came apart the way you unravel a burlap bag by first finding the end of the knitted string, plucking at it, and finally pulling the string with a great flourish, the bag coming apart simultaneously. Mr. J. X. Smith did not take to fear quickly. Not very quickly. It took about ten seconds. Then you could almost see the dry wind of terror dry up his lips.

I liked the analogy to unraveling a gunnysack. I was just a little surprised myself to find he had been poisoned—after about thirty seconds I realized the aching in my chest was because I wasn't breathing, and I would need to resume breathing. I used pains and care and did so.

He tried to take it out on me. He glared and yelled, "What is this? A damned trick?"

I couldn't actually see the pigtail of knitted string that

held him together, of course, but I took hold of it anyway, figuratively, and gave it a jerk. I said, "I resent that a great deal, Mr. Smith. . . . I think we can consider our association at an end." I made gestures of gathering my paraphernalia together in some indignation. "Brother, I came up here to do you a favor, and I don't like your attitude." I leaned forward and added violently, "But I should have expected something like this from a fellow who would have an enemy that would want to kill him that bad!"

My phony indignation probably didn't disturb him, but throwing sudden death in his face started him turning blue, and not from brimstone inside either. It was a sickly blue, paralytic, cadaverous, utterly terrified.

I demanded, "Who did it to you, Smith?"

He got as far as, "Sonny must have been right when he said—" before he swallowed it. He didn't say anything more. He fell in a chair back of his desk, and his hands began picking up ruling pens, protractors and rulers and laying them down again without the hands having told him what they were doing. His breathing was hard and audible, like someone sandpapering a bone.

He had an idea who might have done this to him, and the idea had been given him by Sonny Conover, who was also on Pulaski's list along with James Like. But Smith wasn't going to say who it was. . . . When they want to keep something like that to themselves, it's usually a sign there is something off-color involved. This last was interesting.

Smith said thickly, "What will I do?"

"Have somebody you trust run a test on you," I said. "I don't like your attitude at all, Mr. Smith. I'd prefer to wash my hands of this. As I said, I came up here to do you a favor. I thought you would appreciate it, but instead of that you're acting rather as if I was a chiseler of some sort."

He scowled sickly and said, "It *is* odd, you coming to me."

"Is it? I'm an investigator. I make my living helping other people out of trouble."

I had my equipment ready to go. A show of reluctance was, I figured, the best sort of a buildup to hand him. If the test had been a fake, as I had planned, I would have used other tactics, tried to talk him out of consulting a specialist, or, if he had insisted, I would have made sure there was enough of the phony compound rubbed on his skin to give a positive reaction on anyone's apparatus. I had planned to manage this by testing his body at several points, applying the activated liquid as I did so. The traces of the stuff would linger several days. But this wasn't necessary now.

"Wait a minute!" J. X. Smith blurted. "You think I'd better have someone else test me?"

"Since you think I'm a crook, I don't care what you do."

"Oh, now! Come, come, Miss Ames. . . . I haven't implied anything of the sort. . . . Good God! You say there's a cure for this poisoning, but only the—uh—person who poisoned me knows the remedy?"

"I don't know anything of the sort," I said. "I only know what I heard those fellows talking about."

He gave his lips a quick going over with a perfectly dry tongue and demanded. "Two men? You say there were two?"

"I saw two."

"What did they look like?"

I described an imaginary man who looked something like Pulaski, but not enough like Pulaski that J. X. Smith would recognize him—that description was an out, in case the police came into it, and I got in a spot where I had to produce a fall guy; if that happened, I would produce Pulaski, naturally—and I added, "The other fellow I didn't get too good at look at. I'd rather not pin myself down to a description of him. I think, although I'm not sure, that I might be able to recognize him. It was rather dark in this bar where I overheard the plot."

"Could you find the men?" he wailed.

"That sort of thing is my business."

"Would you—"

"Look, Mr. Smith," I said. "You'd better think this over and check to be sure you've been poisoned. . . . Then, if you want to hire me, I'm at the Congress Hotel."

Letting him stew in the juice would make him more profitable, I believed.

He mumbled, "How much would it cost . . . ?"

"Plenty," I said. "I'm not going to quote you a figure now, because it would startle you. I don't risk my life for nothing, Mr. Smith. . . . You think it over, and call me."

He grunted. He didn't get up from his desk to show me the way out, and didn't say goodbye. He was a very upset man, and that was all right with me. Let him sweat enough, and he would pay plenty.

Entering a cab, I told the driver to take me to the Congress Hotel. I wasn't afraid of the story about my being an investigator getting me in trouble. I had used that idea before, and it was so convenient that I even had a license as a Private Detective. In most states, to get an investigator's license it is necessary to prove good character, and show experience, usually four years of it, as a police officer or operative with a licensed detective agency. This was not true of the state where I had my license, but that state and this one had a reciprocative agreement which made my license in this state good. I couldn't see where I would get in trouble.

Feeling pretty good, I got out at the Congress Hotel. The doorman carried my gear inside, and I paid the cab driver and gave him a twenty-five-cent tip. The sun was shining; it was a beautiful afternoon. There was a little park across the street, with benches on which sat the seedy old men you always see in parks; and the sparrows quarreled in the tired-looking trees. There was some pedestrian traffic, most of it women who looked a little stiff in their ten-dollar girdles, their hats a little silly.

Probably I was half-way across the sidewalk when he got in my way. He was a man and there was a court-plaster on the side of his face, a court-plaster or an asterisk of soiled adhesive tape or something—I never did know exactly what he looked like. But he was a man, and he had a little paper package clutched to him, and he faced me, and squeezed the package.

He did the squeezing gently, with both hands. He must have practiced, or he was too nervous and needed both hands, or something. He just held it in the middle of his chest, two-handed, and the liquid came out in a fine stream that hit his necktie and splattered and drooled down to the sidewalk, some of it. Some of it got to me, a little on my hand, more on my frock. But not much. Not as much as he intended. He hadn't figured on his necktie. It was a brownish necktie with a yellow check, and the breeze waved it a little, but hadn't waved it enough for him to realize that it might get in front of the nozzle of that rubber syringe he had in the package.

When you are a chemist, you get to know smells that mean sudden death. This one was almonds. They call it bitter almonds, a description which probably means nothing. Except, to a chemist, sudden death.

I started walking backward. I didn't scream. I would have liked to. I tried. I don't think even any breath went out.

He saw that he had missed, and he bent his head and peered foolishly at his necktie. He didn't breathe either. He started to—but caught the air in his mouth and held it there, cheeks bloated out like the midriff of an excited blowfish. He must have been afraid to take the air from his mouth back into his lungs, because he turned with the lower part of his face still fat and round and began walking away. Walking slowly, then walking fast, and then breaking into a kind of gamboling skip-hop run.

He ran half the block and turned into a street. He disappeared into a car. I could not tell what kind of a car it was, whether it was taxi or roadster or sedan, or whether it had been standing there or moving. There were too many other cars in between.

I walked a few quick steps into the wind, head back, and got new air into my lungs. I went into the hotel lobby and into the washroom and washed my hands. I took off my dress and put it in the washbowl and let water run on it. The odor of bitter almonds was still strong, but not strong enough to kill anyone.

I gave the washroom attendant a dollar and my room key and told her what dress to fetch. She was not gone long.

She said, "Honey, I like to not of found it. Your room was sure a mess."

"Mess?"

"Things all scattered around," she said.

It had been in perfect order when I left. So somebody had gone to the trouble of searching it, I gathered.

I decided to ask Pulaski why anyone would do that.

One-thirty Washington Street turned out to be the part of town where you find all the trucks, the streets with pits in them, and the sidewalks that never get cleaned. It was in a not-so-tall building that had planks nailed over half the windows and an elevator that was more fitted for, and was being so used if the smell was any guide, a stockpen.

The elevator operator, an old character in a leather coat, said, "Pulaski? That the chemist guy? Third floor."

"Is he here?"

He blinked at me and mumbled and didn't get out any sense. The question had been too much for him.

The third floor hall lived up to advance notices and was of sparing area. One could swing a cat in it, if one used a shortened grip.

There was a door that said *Pulaski Chemical Research, Inc.* And under that it said, *Nathaniel T. Pulaski Industries.* And below that, *Nathaniel T. Pulaski, President,* and in smaller print, *Enter.* The door opened with a dry feel that was something like shaking hands with a medical school skeleton, and passed me into the sort of a room that should have a packed earthen floor, but didn't. There was one chair with a straight back, one with no back, and a desk that held together well enough to support an inkwell that contained no more ink than a blackbird, two well-chewed pencils, and Pulaski's hat.

Across the reception room was another door which stood open and showed that all the rest of the establishment was one neglect-ridden room full of the second-rate stuff that it takes to make what will pass for a chemical laboratory. The nature of the apparatus told Pulaski's story.

Pulaski had told me he was a research chemist with a considerable reputation, but I had not believed it, and I had been right not to believe it. The stuff in his laboratory said he was a hack chemist who made a living doing soil analysis and assay work and whatever routine stuff he could get to come his way.

I felt sorry for Pulaski and—thinking of poison and murder—pretty angry with him. I advanced into the laboratory. I was going to ask him who had tried to kill me, and why, and he was probably going to deny it, and I wasn't going to listen to his denials.

I didn't have to listen to him, though. He did not make any denials. He did not have a word to say. He sat in a chair and looked blankly at me and through me and beyond me. Pulaski was a short little man who had never looked comfortable when seated in an ordinary chair, but he seemed comfortable enough now. His arms and legs were relaxed and his face easy. His clothing was gathered loosely and comfortably in different places on his body as if he had done some moving about, and done it in paroxysms, shortly before he settled into that stillness. The odor of bitter almonds was barely noticeable in the air, about as obscure as a man-eating tiger sitting over his head.

I left without even trying to find out how long he had been dead.

I rode in three taxicabs, a street car and a bus, and kept looking behind me all the time. Then I found a hotel, but they wouldn't register an unescorted lady without luggage. The stores were all closed now—it was past six—but a chain drugstore sold me a fifty-six-cent suitcase for two dollars and forty-nine cents, and I bought a dollar's worth of their heaviest magazines from a newsstand to weight the suitcase impressively. The next hotel accepted me. It was called the Central Hotel. There is a Central Hotel in almost every city, but this one was a little better than the average. Almost good enough for your sister, but not quite.

Except for the hand prints on the wall around the bathroom door and a faucet that leaked as if it was dripping blood, the room was all right. I sat in it for an hour. I had not taken off my hat. I had not eaten since breakfast. I was not hungry. I had not been so scared in some time.

It's hard to say when I thought of Doc Savage. My thinking seemed to have just two speeds, a runaway, or dead stop. It was that way for two hours at least, possibly longer, and then out of nothing, Doc Savage popped into my head. Doc Savage! The answer to a maid's prayers.

After the notion of Doc Savage came to me, my thinking straightened out and made headway. It even picked up its spirits and pranced. I had never met Doc Savage, but I'd had him in mind for a long time. I'd only heard of him, but he was something you could keep in mind. He represented about the same thing that the mother lode represents to a burro-bedeviled prospector. I thought of him with the same appreciation that a safe-cracker thinks of Fort Knox.

It was, I think, in Havana that I first heard of Doc Savage, or maybe it was in New Orleans, or maybe it was anywhere, because the man was like that—you just thought, when they talked about such an individual, that it was rumor, or legend, or plain malarkey. Later I knew a confidence man named Berry in Denver, and one morning he read in the newspaper that Savage was coming to Denver to address a convention of physicians, and thirty minutes later Berry was on a departing plane. I didn't get into the convention, so I did not see Savage, but I learned more about him, and added quite a bit from time to time.

He didn't sound genuine. I think that's what first attracted me. They said he was a man whose profession was righting wrongs and punishing evildoers—which was about as trite as a statement could be. But it was true. It was true, but it was also an understatement. It was like dismissing Napoleon as a soldier, or Henry Ford as a man who had built an automobile, or Cleopatra as an Egyptian girl.

Savage really did right wrongs, and he really was a present-day Galahad. This was a little hard to believe—he probably had an angle, and the angle must be good. Of him, I had heard the following: He was a remarkable combination of physique and mental genius. He had a source of limitless wealth. He had a group of five associates, all scientists, who worked with him either singly or together. His name alone was enough to inspire terror in any crook who really knew his capabilities.

On the other hand, I had heard: He was a gnarled freak whom nobody had seen. He was really two other men. He was a front for the F.B.I., and he was really the whole F.B.I. He was financed by the U. S. Mint. He was the U. S. Marines.

Some of the last—not all of it was spoken in jest either—sounded about as sensible as the former. I was quite curious.

He sounded like a sporting proposition.

I told the telephone operator. "Doc Savage—I think his proper name is Clark Savage, Jr. His headquarters is in New York City. . . . If he isn't there, I still want to talk to him, wherever he is."

"New York is a very large city," said the operator. "Don't you have a street address, or any other information?"

"He's a very large man," I told you. "Maybe you won't need any other information."

She didn't, but I did not get through the gate right away. I found myself talking to a squeaky voice, a voice like a wet stick being rubbed on a tin car, that said it was owned by a Mr. Monk Mayfair. That was reasonable. A Monk Mayfair was one of Savage's aides, according to what I had heard.

"But I want to talk to Doc Savage!" I said.

"Sister, you have to bore a hole through me to get to him," Monk Mayfair said.

"You mean—tell you my business?"

"Uh-huh. What you want with Doc, anyway?"

I began telling him and was about two hundred words into it when he broke in.

"Hold the door," he said. "I guess this will be something that would interest Doc."

Presently I was permitted to hear the Master's dulcet tones. I was a little surprised. He really did have an extraordinary voice. It was not overdeveloped and stagy, but gave the effect of being quite controlled and capable of considerably more than it was putting out now. The voice didn't sound very interested.

"Will you repeat this tale you have been telling Mr. Mayfair," he requested.

It wasn't difficult to give him an impressive story. In view of what happened, I should be scared, and I was, and I just let the fright go in my voice. All of what had actually happened I gave him truthfully. But of myself, my motives for getting involved in the thing, and my real reasons for calling him, I told practically not a word of fact.

In accounting for myself, I gave him the same story I had given J. X. Smith—I was an investigator who had stumbled on to this thing. I gave him my license number and the state of issue. For character reference, I also gave him the name of a young policeman named Grindle, who knew the whole story of my life—not a word of it true; I had fixed Grindle up with the information for occasions such as this—and who would give a fairly rosy view of my character.

"Have you talked to the other two victims Pulaski mentions—Sonny Conover and James Like?" Doc Savage asked.

"No. . . . Frankly, I'm afraid to get out of the hotel. In case you didn't hear me or something, an attempt was made to murder me by squirting hydrocyanic acid in my face. Had the stuff struck my face as intended, inhalation of the vapor alone would probably have been enough to kill me."

"Is that why you called me?" he asked.

"What you really mean is, is that why I didn't call the police? Isn't that it?" I asked.

"The point might stand a couple of words," he said.

"I can explain that, but I don't know how nice you're going to think it is," I said. "I'm an investigator. I make my living investigating. If I had gone to the police when I should have gone—when Pulaski opened up with that wild story— the police would have done the investigating themselves. Where would I have made a profit? Frankly, I supposed

Pulaski's story fantastic. Since I found it wasn't, things have happened too fast."

"You sound," he remarked, "like a young lady who preferred the side doors."

"Look, I've had to make my own living for a long time."

"I see."

"The real reason I thought of you, Mr. Savage," I told him, "is because I've heard amazing stories about your ability, and I've also heard that you only involve yourself in cases which are quite unusual, and where the criminal or criminals seem to be too sharp for the police. Answer me this: Are those rumors correct?"

"Substantially," he admitted.

"Then what about this: Isn't this poison unusual enough to interest you? Think what a fantastic thing it is. Here's a scientific production of death that can be deflected only by a scientific treatment known, presumably, only to the person Pulaski sold it to. Do you know what is going to happen to J. X. Smith unless you interest yourself in this? He's going to die. That's what."

"Oh, you're jumping at conclusions—"

"Jumping, nothing! Name me another scientist in the country, other than yourself, who is capable of finding how to eliminate the radiant substance from the victim's body."

"Oh, there are several—"

"I doubt it. It's a job for a man who is both a nuclear scientist and a physician and surgeon. . . . You're the only combination of those that I've heard about. . . . And here's another point: Pulaski seemed perfectly confident that the victims would never find how to eliminate the stuff from their bodies. That—if you'll take my word that Pulaski wasn't entirely a fool—means at least one life, and possibly two others, depend on you."

He said, "Can you stay in your hotel room the remainder of the night—with the door locked?"

"I can't think of anything easier to do," I told him.

"Do that," he said. "You'll hear from me later."

I hung up—after he had hung up first—and tried to figure out what the conversation had accomplished. I had told him more than I had expected to tell him, and learned less than I had intended to learn. I was a little impressed, and I had not intended to be impressed, and would have sworn no one could get that done to me over a few hundred miles of telephone line.

VII

Awakening was like an icicle breaking. In nothing flat, I climbed an unseen ladder of terror a dozen feet high, and stopped at the top because there was nowhere else to go. That was the way it felt—actually, I just stood up in bed.

He had the door wide open. He stood there.

"Uh-huh. Had the door unlocked," he said. He had a soft, low voice that was a puppy sleeping.

I didn't say anything. I couldn't get my voice loose from my hair roots.

He was not tall and he had thin hips and considerable width through the shoulders. His hair was jet-black and straight, as black as a cake of anthracite on his head, and his nose was large and aquiline, his mouth also large, but mobile. He had his hat off, was holding it against his chest with both hands. The way he held the hat reminded me of the way court-plaster-face had held the syringe with the hydrocyanic in it, and I tried to float higher on that invisible spike of terror.

"I live here," he told me, "I live in the hotel, that is."

"That's fine," I managed to say. "That's just fine. You broke in to tell me that, I suppose."

He shook his head. "I didn't break in. He opened the door. He had it unlocked."

"He . . . ?" I stared at him doubtfully. "What do you mean? Are you trying to tell me someone picked the lock?"

He said, "A tall man. Very thin. Blond hair, blue eyes, in a dark suit. Do you know him?"

"Not from that description." I didn't know whether to believe him or not. "Who are you?"

"Me? . . . The bellboy," he said. "That's funny."

"Funny about being a bellhop? Why?"

"No, funny he should come to the hotel, find out what room you were in, then leave and come back later by a side door and come up here and pick your door lock."

"Oh, he did that?"

He nodded and pointed at the floor in the hall outside the door.

"He dropped something out here. Maybe you'd like to look at it," he said.

He might be fooling. He acted like a clown, but I hadn't figured him yet. While the doubts were still showing me their blank faces, he continued to stab a finger at the hall floor, and added, "I don't know what it is. Bottle of something." So I went and looked, and it was a small bottle of limpid rather colorless liquid. I picked it up and, after hesitating, gave the screw cap part of a turn then brought the bottle near enough to get that odor of oil of bitter almonds.

"What's it?" he asked. He was watching me.

"Just his medicine," I said casually, about as casually as if I was standing on my head. "He must have dropped it. . . . You say you're the bellboy? Do you have a name?"

"Futch," he said, grinning a yokel grin. "That's what they call me. Futch. Nothing before or after it."

"Well, thanks, Futch," I said. "You've given nice service, and I won't forget it. But goodbye, now."

"Wait a minute," he exclaimed. "You want me to hunt the guy?"

"Which way did he go?"

"The stairs. Down."

"You didn't chase him?"

He blushed again and confessed, "I wasn't that brave right then." He looked me over the way a two-year-old watches a Fourth-of-July sparkler. "But I might be brave enough now."

He evidently thought that was pretty gallant. He grinned as if it was.

"We won't test you out this time," I said. "But thanks again. . . . And if you see him, or see anyone else who might have an idea like he had, you could telephone me, couldn't you?"

"You bet! I'll telephone you, Miss Ames. The name is Miss Ames, isn't it?"

I said the name was Miss Ames and shut the door. I locked it again, too, but without the confident feeling I'd had when locking it last night. . . . Futch seemed to stand outside the door a long time. There was no sound of his going away. I waited for it. There never was such a sound, and when I opened the door suddenly and looked out, there was no sign of him in the hall, no sign at all.

No more than there was any trace of how the door lock had been picked.

I stacked what furniture I could move against the door after looking under the bed and in the closet and in the bathroom, then went to the window. Dawn was an angry red fever on the eastern sky, but I was more interested in the fact that the window could be aligned from a rooftop across the street. I pulled the cord that made the venetian blind slats stand on edge, and went to lie on the bed again.

Sleep was out of the question. I probably lay there half an hour, and probably not more than thirty consecutive seconds of it was in one position. They say animals can smell fear on a person. It began to seem to me that it was all around me, and I got up and took a shower bath that didn't help much, and when I shut off the water, the telephone was ringing.

"Miss Ames?... I'm downstairs—the dining-room—if you would care to come down," he said.

The long-distance telephone last night hadn't added or subtracted anything with his voice. It was still the most impressive voice I had ever heard.

"How will I know you?" I asked.

"I'll be the out-sized one."

"In three or four minutes, I'll be there." I said. "And listen—another attempt was made to kill me. Someone picked the lock of my door, and dropped a bottle of cyanic when he ran away."

"That is interesting," he said, and hung up.

There was nobody in the hall, and nobody who made me nervous in the elevator. But crossing the lobby, a shadow fell in beside me and the sleepy puppy voice said, "He's not the one who was at the door."

I frowned at Futch and asked, "Who?"

"The guy you're meeting in the dining room. He's not the one. He's bigger. He's—well, he's different the way a tiger is different from a tabby cat."

"You're keeping pretty close tab on me, aren't you, Futch?"

"I find it a pleasure," he said, and split off and went to the porter's desk.

Doc Savage was alone in the dining room. There were

thirty-odd other people eating breakfast there, but for practical purposes he was alone. He stood out like that. He wasn't twenty-feet tall and lit up with neon, but that was the general effect.

His manners were good enough. He stood up and held a chair for me, and we exchanged perfectly normal preliminary words. He was Doc Savage, and I was Miss Ames. But from there on, business picked up.

"Pulaski's body has not been found—or at least the police have not been notified," he said. "I think I'll have a look at the body. If you feel up to it, you might come along."

"I—well, I'll have to think about it.... How did you manage to get here so soon?"

"Plane," he said. "What about this second attempt on your life?"

He listened to my story. He was considerably more than six feet, but with a symmetrical build that kept him from seeming that large except when you were close to him. There were several unusual points about his appearance, two in particular—the deep bronze of his skin and an odd flake gold coloring of eyes that were striking.

Toward the end of my story about the prowler at the door, my wording became a bit disconnected. I was making an unnerving discovery about him—I couldn't read him. This was something unusual, and not expected. He had the most natural of expressions, and it changed in response to what he was hearing—his face showed logical mounts of surprise, curiosity, admiration for my nerve, all at the proper times— but I had the feeling that it meant nothing and had no bearing on what he was thinking.

"Thought of anything you forgot to tell me on the telephone last night?" he asked.

Just like that. Not a word of follow-up on the prowler. No questions about how it felt to hear a fellow had been outside your door with a bottle of hydrocyanic.

"Any thoughts," I said bitterly, "were scared out of me."

"You seem very competent," he said, and proceeded with his breakfast, letting me draw whatever conclusions came handy.

Usually my confidence isn't easily rattled. One of the best ways to pull off a failure, it was impressed on me long ago, is to let your knees get to knocking at the start of an operation. Plan carefully, don't plan too conservatively, and then get going and don't hesitate nor look back. And above all, don't get to thinking that the plan might not work.

But suddenly I was wondering if I had been so clever to draw this Doc Savage into the affair. My plan was to use him, persuade him in one way or another to do the dirty work, then capitalize on his efforts, and if it was at all convenient, give him a trimming. The dirty work would consist of protecting my neck, finding an antidote for the radio-active poison that J. X. Smith had been given, and possibly finding out who had done the poisoning and why. The latter didn't seem vital to me, but it would be interesting to know, and it might be profitable. Once Savage found the antidote, I intended to see that J. X. Smith—and Sonny Conover and James Like also, if they had to have it—paid plenty.

From my standpoint, it was going to be a business proposition. Somebody owed me for the scare I'd been handed last night.

A waiter drifted up with the coffee. A waiter, not the waitress we'd had. It was Futch. I wondered how long he'd been standing behind us, listening.

"Anything I should know about that fellow?" Savage asked casually when Futch had gone away.

"What fellow?"

"The waiter."

Evidently my face hadn't stayed as poker plain as I had thought. "That was Futch. The one who frightened the intruder away from my door. He seems to be taking an interest in me."

"If you'll pardon me a moment, I believe I'll take an interest in Futch," Doc Savage said, and arose and went into the lobby. He was not gone long. He came back and said, "Just a bellhop, apparently. A character, though."

We finished breakfast and Savage asked if I felt up to having a look at Pulaski. I said I wouldn't enjoy it, which was certainly true, but I would force myself to go along. My nerve wasn't quite that shaky, but it seemed advisable to try some clinging vine technique on Savage and see how that worked. Savage already had a car. A rented one. Futch was on the sidewalk to flag us a cab. He looked disappointed.

VIII

One-thirty Washington Street was no more appetizing at nine o'clock this morning than it had been last night. There may not have been as many trucks in the street, but they were going faster and hitting the ruts oftener and the racket was about the same. The character in the leather coat was still operating the elevator, and he said almost exactly as he had said last night, "Pulaski? The chemist guy? Third floor."

We went to the door that had Pulaski's name on it three times. It was closed, and I was trying to remember whether it had been closed when I left yesterday as Savage asked, "Anything different?"

"I don't know," I said. "The door—I can't recall closing it. . . . But maybe I did. I was in a little bit of a dither when I left here." I tried to think how my state of mind compared to words, and couldn't think of any words that shaky.

We opened the door and went in, and I knew we were not going to find any body. I knew positively that Pulaski's mortal remains were gone, that the chair where he had been sitting would be empty, that the windows would be open and there wouldn't be a trace of odor of oil of almonds. This knowledge came as a premonition. I have them sometimes. I would have bet on this one, bet my chances of coming out of this mess with a profit, even bet my percentage on taking Doc Savage for a sucker, which was the percentage any pretty girl with brains has in her favor when she starts work on a man. I would have lost, because Pulaski's body was there, looking quite a lot worse than it had last night. The almond odor was strong enough to take hold of my hair roots.

Savage began looking around. I didn't have to look—I was discovering that everything about the place, every detail had lodged in my mind last night.

"I—uh—don't think I can take this. I don't feel good," I said, not entirely faking. "Is it necessary—do I have to stay here? Why can't I go back to the hotel?"

"Aren't you afraid of another attempt on your life?" Savage asked.

"Yes," I said. "But the idea doesn't make me feel much

worse than"—I tried to gesture at what was now Mr. Pulaski—
"being around that."

"I'll call you at the hotel, then," Savage said. "The police
may want to talk to you." Then he changed it a little and said,
"Why don't you wait in the outer room a while. You might
feel better."

"I'll try that, then," I said, knowing I was not going to
feel better. There was no percentage in feeling better, because I wanted to get away from him a while.

I had thought of something.

He was examining the body closely as I went out. And
suddenly he turned away, went to a workbench and got
something and brought it back to the table where the body
was sitting. I waited long enough to see what he had gotten.
It was a microscope.

Five minutes was all I could stand in the dingy reception
room, and it wasn't entirely because, in the silence—the
clamor of trucks in the street was oddly absent here—my ears
got to ringing the way telephone wires ring on a cold day, the
way your ears can ring when you stand beside a casket.

Back at the laboratory door, I said, "I—could you tell me
something?... You see, I haven't much money, and I asked
you to take this case. And—well—I'm beginning to wonder,
will I be able to pay you?"

He was doing things with the microscope, and his fingers
had a practiced touch on the instrument. He had brought
over a fluorescent desk-light and it was turned on.

"I never work for a fee," he said, shaking his head.
"Don't worry about it.... Are you feeling better?"

That bore out what the rumors said about him. He never
took money. He labored for love. Love of what? Excitement?
He didn't look nor act that crack-brained. He must have an
angle somewhere.

"Not much better," I said. "I think I'll have to leave. I'm
not accustomed to bodies, I'm afraid."

He nodded, then said, "Before you go—how well did
you know Pulaski?"

"Not too well—a few dates." That was fairly close to the
truth.

"Know any of his friends? In this case, it might be an
acquaintance." He pondered a moment, added, "Say a man
between forty and fifty years old, with brown hair. Incidentally, the fellow would have had a haircut and shampoo yesterday."

"No, I can't think of one. . . . But that's not a very definite description."

"Not too definite," he agreed. "But I wouldn't like to be someone who answered that description too closely."

"Oh! You mean . . . ?"

Doc Savage nodded. "That prussic acid was thrown at Pulaski rather hard. It splashed quite a bit. And the killer had, I think, to hold Pulaski a few moments until the stuff began to take hold. It doesn't work instantly, you know. . . . If you'd held your victim, and perhaps had some hydrocyanic on your hands as a result, what would be the first thing you would do?"

"If you want a personal answer—pass out cold. . . . But otherwise, wash my hands."

"That's what someone did—wash his hands." Savage said. "And comb his hair. There's a comb at the washbasin with some of Pulaski's hair on it, and on top of that a couple of strands of different hair—the hair of a man between forty and fifty, who had a shampoo and a barbering yesterday. Hair can be read, you know, under the microscope. Incidentally, the man probably has a thick head of hair—brown. That's a guess, really. The cut looks as if it was done with thinning shears, the ones that have crocodile teeth."

"You've got me amazed," I said.

He glanced sharply to see if I was ribbing him. He said, "If you're really feeling bad, you might go back to the hotel and wait."

"Thanks. I think I will."

I rode down in the elevator feeling a little worried. He was sharp, all right. And what was worse, I had the feeling that he habitually didn't tell all he knew—just about one per cent of it.

Futch gave me something else to think about. He was there, leaning against the grimy lobby wall, looking too innocent.

"I have a car, Miss Ames, in case you find need for such a convenience," Futch said in that sleepy voice.

"Listen, you—you shadow! How did you get here?"

"Have I done wrong?" he asked with an injured air.

"That depends on what you've done."

He looked as embarrassed as a kid who had accidentally tripped his schoolteacher. "I'm afraid I followed you and that fellow," he confessed. "However, my intentions were good."

"Oh, they were, were they!"

"I didn't really have anything else to do, either," he added sheepishly. "I was off work. I'm—uh—a single man. I don't have much to do with my spare time. I get a little lonesome."

Somehow Futch began to seem all right to me. The more open-faced they seem and the more honest they sound, the chances are the more they need watching. Futch sounded about as honest and glib as a frog trying to swim in buttermilk.

"I don't get your point, Futch," I said.

He grinned the same kind of a grin that would come from a toe being pinched.

"I like you, Miss Ames," he said.

So that was it. It probably was, too. It was logical enough to explain everything. There seemed to be no point in being coy with him, so I laughed in his face. "You're just building up to a disappointment, Futch."

"My life has been full of disappointments," he said quietly. "You want to go anywhere? I got my car, like I said."

Why not use him, as long as he was handy? He listened intently as I gave him J. X. Smith's address, and nodded, saying, "I know about where that is, I think."

It turned out that he didn't know. He had to ask a policeman who made it even by not knowing either, until he looked in a little book. But finally we were parked in front of Smith's office building, and I said, "Thanks. You can either wait, or you can call it a day."

"I'll wait." Futch nodded at the building. "You think you'll be all right wherever you're going in there? You don't want me along?"

"Why should I want you along?"

"Search me. I never stopped to think of that," he said blankly.

The receptionist in J. X. Smith's swank office suite gave me an odd look and said, "You have an appointment? Mr. Smith isn't feeling well, and he has cancelled all appointments." I could imagine he wouldn't be feeling well this morning, and told the girl to try sending my name in anyway. I was admitted at once.

J. X. Smith gave me a look that he had been keeping on ice for the purpose and said, "I had started to wonder about you. You weren't at the hotel where you said you would be."

His barber and his valet—he probably had one—had apparently done their best with him this morning, but he still showed signs of a hard night. His eyes had the thick-lidded loose appearance of not having slept, and he had the general air of a tall mechanical toy with the spring wound far too tight.

"I changed hotels, Mr. Smith. But it didn't do too much good. Whoever tried to squirt anhydrous prussic acid in my face when I left here made a second attempt later."

"Prussic acid?" he said. Either he didn't know what it was, or his mind wasn't closely enough on my words to get what it meant.

"Oh, you've heard of it, Mr. Smith. Hydrocyanic acid. Potassium cyanide is a crystalline salt derivative. Inhalation of the vapor of anhydrous prussic will cause immediate death— so quickly, it is said, that scarcely any symptoms can be observed."

He got that all right. His jaw fell, buried itself in his expensive necktie.

"Good God."

While he was properly floored, I described the man who had stood in front of me last night and squeezed the package. The description didn't add up much—mostly it was the asterisk of adhesive tape that had been on the fellow's face. That, and the brownish necktie with the yellow check that had gotten in front of the nozzle of his gadget and probably saved my life.

"Recognize him from that description, Mr. Smith?"

"No . . . No, of course not. Great Scott! Is he the one who—who—"

"That's right. I just wondered if you knew him . . . By the way, did you go to a properly qualified doctor about that poison?"

That jolted him again—merely by throwing the discussion back to himself, which was the only thing he was interested in anyway. He shuffled over and fell in a chair, nodding his head while doing so, and still nodding it as he announced, "My whole body is saturated with a radioactive substance. Not a strong saturation, but enough to kill me slowly in the course of from four to eight months."

His doctor had probably guessed about four to eight months, because it was doubtful if there had been enough radiant poisoning cases as yet for doctors to classify the pattern of effect. That might be wrong, though. There had doubtless been considerable study of the Japanese cases and later of the animals in the Bikini tests.

He was looking at me bitterly. "I'm going to put this matter, and you, in the hands of the police, naturally."

"That's fine," I said coldly, for I was ready for this. "The police are just the boys to find an antidote for that stuff for you."

"They'll catch the party who gave it to me, and make him produce the cure," he said grimly.

He didn't stumble over referring to the poisoner as "party." Yesterday he had done some juggling with the words "person" and "uh" and something that Sonny Conover had said sometime or other. Today it was a straight, "the party who gave it to me." I rather got the idea that he had decided to keep his suspicions to himself, and I tried that out with a question.

"Decided who might have given it to you?" I asked.

"I haven't the slightest idea!" He had it all ready for me, like an urchin with a snowball behind his back.

I shrugged. "Call in the police if you want to," I told him. "But that might queer a better idea that occurred to me . . . Oh well, my idea would be expensive. Better give it to the police."

He glared at me. "Money? You think money means anything in a case like this?"

That was good to hear. It was a point. And it opened up the way for the matter that had brought me here.

"Ever hear of Doc Savage?"

He frowned—he was having a little trouble keeping his thoughts off dying—and had to rub his jaw to stir a recollection. "Savage? . . . I believe I've heard faintly—scientist, isn't he? New York. Got together some tables on alloy stresses that made quite a change in bridge construction methods and design . . ." He remembered some more, enough to make him bolt upright. "Say! That Savage is an amateur detective, or something, isn't he?"

He listened blankly to the buildup I gave Doc Savage—which I had a suspicion might be more truth than exaggeration, although it sounded as if I was describing a combination of Einstein, Tarzan of the Apes, and the F.B.I. "You can get on the telephone, Mr. Smith, and check that, possibly with the local police, or if they don't know what the score is, with the New York police."

"That won't be necessary. I'm—uh—remembering more

that I've heard of Savage... What do you have in mind, Miss Ames?"

"Hire Savage for this case."

He had heard of Doc Savage, all right. Because he said, "It's my impression that Savage isn't someone you hire."

"It could be done," I said. "I'm willing to guarantee you that it could. You see, I happen to have certain contacts with Savage."

He didn't know exactly how to take that; he grinned, or started to grin, knowingly, then wiped it off his face, and pretended to be considering something or other. The emotions he played on his face were not very effective over and above his other feelings.

He finally decided he needed a drink, and he probably did, several of them. He got out the makings—he had a trick affair on his desk: Push a button, and the whole left end of the desk suddenly became a bar with glasses, tiny cooler full of ice cubes, and almost anything you wanted in bottles. It was quite a startling effect.

He made and drank half his drink before he remembered his manners and offered me one. I told him what I wanted and he made it and I tasted it. He was not much of a bartender. With that rig, almost anyone could have done better.

J. X. Smith finished the contents of his glass. I finished mine. His manners improved and he raised both eyebrows in a gloomy question. I shook my head.

"I'm really here on business, remember?" I said.

He dropped the glasses back in the bar, pressed the button, and presto! the whole thing vanished.

"You actually think this man Doc Savage could be persuaded to interest himself?" he demanded.

"You put a thousand dollars in my hand, and an agreement to guarantee another ten thousand if Savage produces the antidote... You do that, and I'll produce Doc Savage for you."

He didn't know me well enough to pay me a thousand dollars, and said so. We argued about it. He was inclined to be as tight as the bark on a log. Finally, when he was ripe for a clincher, I told him I had consulted Doc Savage, and Savage would take the case. I didn't mention anything about Savage already being in town and on the case.

J. X. Smith began writing his personal check for one thousand dollars.

Watching him, something odd occurred to me. "You have brown hair, haven't you, Mr. Smith. And you're between forty and fifty years old."

His head jerked up. "That's obvious, isn't it?"

"And you probably had a haircut and shampoo yesterday, didn't you?"

He frowned. "Yes, as a matter of fact, I—what did you do, see me in the barber shop?"

It suddenly occurred to me that I had said too much. "As a matter of fact, I did—I was just trying to be Sherlock Holmes. Sorry."

He seemed satisfied with that, and I left waving his check to dry the ink.

Futch was waiting in the reception room. He looked sheepish, pulled at his shapeless hat, crossed and uncrossed his feet, and J. X. Smith's receptionist, a middle-aged woman with the figure of a Grable, was glaring at him.

"I thought you were going to wait downstairs, Futch."

"I got lonesome," Futch mumbled.

I let him think that would do until we got into the elevator, then demanded, "Why was the receptionist browning you off?"

He blinked a couple of times, and confessed, "Well—ah—I told her somebody wanted her in an office down the hall. I gave her the number of an office I had noticed, eleven... When she was gone I sort of cut in the intercom set. The talk-box on her desk, you know. I noticed she had the master station on her desk—you can switch in on any office and hear what's being said. She came back and I think she wondered how Smith's office got switched on."

"You eavesdropped on me!"

"I just thought I wouldn't be as lonesome if I heard your voice, Miss Ames."

"You're a liar, Futch!"

"Uh-huh," he said. "Maybe I am. A little one."

There was a bank in the building, and they gave me the cash for J. X. Smith's check. But first they telephoned Smith about it. I was afraid he had changed his mind by now, but he hadn't.

"Nice profit," Futch said casually. "But I understood this Doc Savage party didn't work for money."

"Who said he was going to get any?" I asked grimly. "And listen, you keep out of this!... On second thought, Futch, your nose seems a little long. I don't think I can stand them around when they're that long."

He looked frightened. "Gee whizz! I'm just—"

"Lonely. I know!"

I turned and walked away from him.

There was a uniformed policeman outside the bank, a policeman as big as a barn and with all his brass buttons shining, a policeman with a big melodious voice that drawled, "You're Miss Ames, aren't you? Well, we'd like to take you for a little ride."

When I got over the shock sufficiently to look around, there was no Futch. Futch had gone. He had disappeared. A magician could not have done better.

Futch, it struck me, also had brown hair. Whether he was also between forty and fifty years of age was difficult to say, but it was an item for thought.

IX

The policeman was nice. He was a wonderful policeman. How wonderful he was didn't dawn on me until we walked, after riding a while in his squad car, into the building on Washington Street where the trucks rumbled and the man with the leather coat ran the elevator. Doc Savage said, "I got worried about you, Miss Ames, when I couldn't get in touch with you at your hotel. I think, for your own safety, that you'd best stay with me." I really appreciated what a fine cop he was then.

"I was transacting some business—cashing a check, as a matter of fact," I explained.

A heavy-set, white-haired man said, "You certainly had us worried, Miss Ames. Mr. Savage told us about the attempt on your life." He turned out to be a police detective named Carnahan, in charge of the investigation of Pulaski's demise.

I expected to get a going over from the police, but what I got was a fooling. The queen of all the land wouldn't have received more deference. I tried to decide why, and got about as far as a scientist trying to figure out what is gravity, until the reason came out of Detective Carnahan's mouth by chance—they credited me with getting Doc Savage on the case. That, it seemed, made my soul pure.

It had been gradually dawning on me—not too gradually, at that—that Doc Savage was going to be one of those wonders of a lifetime, a notable who is as good as he's talked up to be. The way the police deferred to him proved it. Previously it hadn't occurred to me that the police here had more than barely heard of him.

And Savage hadn't had me brought here because he was concerned about my health, not entirely. He had a customer for me.

"Miss Ames, this is Mr. Walter P. Earman," Doc Savage said.

Earman was a man who looked long, but wasn't, and looked that way because he was of tubular construction, like sausages linked together. He was nervous. He was also full of impulses, and the one he had now was to seize my hand and give it a shaking and then hold to it. His grip was dank and moist, as if a catfish had swallowed my hand. "Terrible, terrible, terrible!" he exclaimed. "An awful thing. Poor Pulaski. The poor, poor man."

Savage said, "Mr. Earman is a former business associate of Pulaski, and just arrived in town."

"No, no, no, not an associate exactly," Earman corrected hastily. "I employed poor Pulaski at one time. That was in Cleveland, six years ago. I was a contractor—chemical plant construction work—and Pulaski was on my staff. I hadn't seen him since I dissolved my business. But I had heard from him—letters—and I thought I would look him up while I was here. I came down here looking for a location, because I'm thinking of going into business again and—"

A young policeman came hurrying past us. Only he didn't get past without an incident. He stumbled—oh so naturally—and flopped his arms, swore, fell against Mr. Earman, knocked Earman's hat off, rammed his hand through Earman's hair. It was all as naturally done as a frog jumping off a lily pad.

"You clumsy ape!" Detective Carnahan said to the young policeman. The latter said, four or five times, how sorry he was. He went into the laboratory.

Walter P. Earman, believe it or not, had not let go my hand. I got it away from him, partly by main force.

Carnahan apologized again for the humpty-dumpty clumsiness of the young policeman, then began asking Earman questions about Pulaski six years ago. I listened to that. Pulaski had been a fine boy, wonderful, wonderful, wonderful, the way Earman told it. It didn't seem reasonable that Carnahan would be satisfied with what he was getting, but he seemed to be.

Doc Savage drifted casually into the laboratory.... Presently I sauntered into the laboratory myself.

Savage was examining something under the microscope. A human hair. One of Walter P. Earman's hairs.

"Pretty slick," I said. "But shouldn't another policeman or two fall down to make it really look good?"

Savage smiled slightly. He had a nice smile. "Was it that bad?"

"Not if he's on the level. But he seems nervous.... If I was that nervous, and a cop happened to stumble just right to grab out some of my hair, I might wonder."

"That's true."

"But it was a waste of time, wasn't it? His hair is grey, not brown."

He answered that by removing the slide carefully from the microscope and handing it to the young policeman, saying, "Better have your laboratory do more than a cursory check on this. The definitely shaped pigment granules within the hair shaft show markedly darker, and there is evidence of diffuse penetration, probably by a bleaching agent or dye."

"Brown?" I gasped.

He nodded. "But farther than that, I wouldn't say."

Another officer, a fat one in plain clothes who had the air of never having pounded a beat, had been talking over a telephone in the back of the room. Now he hung up and approached.

"The F.B.I. has him under that name—Walter P. Earman," this officer said. He consulted some notes. "He operated the Four Companies Construction Company in Cleveland before the war. He was the principal stockholder and president. Two months after Pearl Harbor, his concern was awarded a contract to build an eighty-million-dollar ordnance plant in this state. A plant for manufacturing explosives. Thirty days later, his three partners approached the F.B.I. with the information that Earman was an alien, had sympathies with the enemy, and had belonged to subversive organizations. The ordnance plant contract was cancelled. The three partners, whose loyalty was unquestioned, then bid on it again and were awarded the contract. Earman was bankrupt. He was in a so-called relocation camp during the war, and since then has worked at odd jobs in Cleveland."

Doc Savage had listened to this with the proper amount of interest. He asked, "You get the names of his former partners?"

The officer said, "Well . . ." He looked at me doubtfully, and added to Savage, "There's some pretty important local names involved."

"Don't tell me," I said. "Let me guess. And let's be coy about it, too, and just say their initials are J. X. S., S. C. and J. L. Of course, if I *Smithed* my guess we can *Conover* the thing again if you'd *Like*."

The young cop thought I'd performed quite a feat, but he didn't think it was funny. He put out his jaw and said, "A lady genius. Maybe Carnahan didn't ask you enough questions."

Doc Savage asked hastily, "Was her guess correct?"

"Too correct."

"Earman's former associates were J. X. Smith. Sonny Conover and James Like?"

"That's right," said the young officer. He either didn't like me, or he did and thought I was Savage's property and was going out of his way to show disinterest.

"Those three," said Savage. "Went to the F.B.I. with the fact that Earman was an alien? . . . In effect, ruined Earman financially?"

"That's right again."

I said, "Don't look now, but isn't that a motive creeping out of the corner?"

Savage said, "It might be."

The young cop, looking at me, said, "We don't believe in lady mind-readers around here. So maybe you're something more in this than we thought."

Savage said, "Miss Ames has told me all she knows."

"I'm sorry," said the young policeman. He walked away.

"It might be a good idea," Savage told me dryly, "if you picked the right times to look beautiful and say nothing."

"I got it a little late," I said. My voice didn't shake, although it felt as if it should, along with my knees. It had just reoccurred to me that I had found Pulaski's body and hadn't said anything about it to the people that should have been told—the police—and why wasn't I in jail? "Thank heavens you seem to have quite an influence," I added.

"I'm not a genuine magician," he said. "I can't make you vanish—which may be what you'll wish to do if the police interest in you gets a bit stronger."

"I got that a little late, too," I confessed. "But I sure have it now. I'm not likely to forget it. It's tacked to my brain. And, incidentally, I'd like to tack another fact alongside it, if I could pick it up. Meaning—why are you doing me all these favors?"

"Maybe they aren't favors," Savage said.

That scared me so bad I dropped the whole thing. I didn't know why it scared me, but it did. I didn't know why he said that. But he had said it, and it was beginning to grow on me that Doc Savage was a party who used his words as carefully as the old-time buffalo hunters are said to have used their cartridges.

"That stuff with the hair sample, and the F.B.I.—you work fairly fast," I mumbled.

"Routine," he said.

And he went back into the reception room. Walter P. Earman and quite a crowd of police were still there. Savage conferred in a corner with Detective Carnahan, who gave his replies between spells of jaw-rubbing and head-scratching. Most of the policemen here now were the experts who had come to take prints, pictures, measurements and the multiplicity of other stuff the police do on a murder case—as an example, a man was taking finger-nail scrapings from the body and depositing them in a petri dish which could be covered. All the efficiency made me feel even more uneasy. Even the thousand dollars in my purse was not too much of a comfort.

Savage evidently made a deal with Carnahan to handle Walter P. Earman his way.

Rejoining me, Savage said, "We might as well leave now." Then he told Earman, "Miss Ames and I are leaving. Would you care for us to give you a lift?"

Earman accepted the way he would have taken a gold watch. Evidently he had been wondering how he was going to get out of there, and whether.

We rode down in the elevator. The man in the leather coat had a sandwich in one pocket, was eating one, and parts of a third were on the floor. He was having a big morning.

We rode north in Savage's car. He drove. Walter P. Earman was so relieved that he'd had to talk; he was so loose with relief at getting away from the police that his tongue just had to flop. But what he talked about was the city. A wonderful city, he said. Fine, fine, fine. He would like it here, and he hoped he could find some sort of suitable business, or a desirable business connection. What he said meant nothing except that he was nervous, all up in the air. He didn't even think to ask to be let out.

Savage stopped the car in front of a building that would compare favorably with anything in Kansas City or St. Louis. He said, "Mr. Earman, in view of the fact that you once knew the deceased, I wonder if you would do me a favor?"

Earman clearly didn't want to do any favors, but he said he did.

"It won't take a moment," Savage said. "I'm going in to see a party. Would you go along, just to tell me whether you recognize this party as having been an acquaintance of Pulaski when you knew him?"

"Gladly," said Earman unconvincingly. "Anything I can do that might help catch poor Pulaski's murderer, I shall be eager to do."

A second look at the building told me who we were going to see. Doc Savage was being tricky. Walter P. Earman would know the party we were going to see.

"You may come along if you wish, Miss Ames," Doc Savage informed me.

"I wouldn't miss it," I said, and his warning frown was just a thing that might have been on his bronze face.

And we went into the building, and I saw the elusive Futch. Saw him, and didn't. Because maybe Futch was there, down the sidewalk a short distance, one of the crowd; I thought I saw him, and then thought I didn't. Futch, if it was Futch, was not making himself any more prominent than a lecherous thought in a parson's mind.

Waiting for the elevator, I whispered to Savage, "I think I just saw Futch. Outside. On the sidewalk. West."

Savage didn't say anything about Futch. He did say, "I think I'll pick up a newspaper." And he went over to the lobby newsstand, and a thick-necked man who was standing there, a man who had police detective on him like white-wash, nodded imperceptibly to something Savage told him, and turned and went outside.

They certainly had their lines out.

We went upstairs and into an office without Earman realizing where he was being taken. I was sure Earman didn't know, because he did not turn any special color. The office was a little larger than necessary to store two locomotives, and was all walnuts and chocolate leathers. It was meant to impress. It did. The receptionist was blonde, had a figure that made me a little self-conscious, a high-voltage personality, and she hadn't bought a dress that achieved that stunning plainness on any forty dollars a week.

I asked Earman if he was married, and he brightened up and got busy telling me he wasn't, and didn't hear who Savage asked the receptionist could we see.

A moment later, we were shown into Sonny Conover's office.

Walter P. Earman did his color-change now. White first, then it was shaded with blue. He hadn't expected to see Conover. Meeting one of his old partners, one of the men who had tagged him as a dangerous alien and then taken his business away from him, was to Earman about the same as stepping off the edge of a tall building.

Sonny Conover was surprised too. His mouth was open when Earman's fist filled it.

This Sonny Conover had wrists and arms and a body to go with them that would have been full equipment for a village smithy. He could have taken Earman the way a swatter takes a fly. Sonny Conover was a big man. In all ways. He didn't even need his name, or his firm's name, on his office door.

But he fell flat on his back with surprise. It couldn't have been the negligible effect of Earman's fist on his teeth.

Savage went to Earman. He took hold of Earman with the casual manner of a good forward taking the basketball, and Earman seemed to try hard to do something about it and succeeded in doing absolutely nothing. Savage sat Earman down in a chair on the far side of the room. He did not appear to sit Earman down hard. The bottom split out of the chair.

"You'd better stay there," Savage said.

Earman stayed there. He watched Savage's hands with a kind of fascinated horror.

Sonny Conover turned over on the floor, sat up, dabbed at his lips with a handkerchief, and examined the red stain he got with a kind of surprised interest, as if it was lipstick. He got to his feet, snuffled around his desk and sat down. He didn't act as if being hit by Earman meant anything at all, as if it was as nothing to something else that was on his mind.

He said, "You are Doc Savage?"

Savage admitted it.

Sonny Conover said, "I've heard of you—before I talked to J. X. Smith, I mean. I talked to Smith a couple of hours ago. I went to his doctor. I've got the same thing in me that Smith has. Poison. Radioactive. I'm going to die."

He certainly believed in getting down to business quick. One speech, and he had told the whole story. Also he had explained why he wasn't thinking much about being hit by Earman. His thoughts were on dying. He hadn't had the thoughts for more than an hour, probably, and they were a fresh-born monster to him.

"Any idea who gave you the stuff?" Savage asked.

Conover's eyes drifted toward Earman, back. "Nothing I could prove," he said.

"Anything at all that would help?"

"Nothing yet. I'm trying to think of something." He wasn't fooling there. He had been grinding his brains together like rocks, and the only grist he got was whatever it meant to a man like him to die. If this office layout was a sample, it would mean leaving a lot.

Savage said, "I take it you know Mr. Earman."

"Him? Oh, sure."

"In business with him, weren't you? You, and Smith, and a party named James Like?"

Earman called Conover a dirty name. Savage glanced at me, and winced. He didn't feel right about a lady hearing a bad word. I knew worse words. Savage got up and moved toward Earman, and Earman melted back in the chair like a tallow candle being approached by a blowtorch.

"He ruined me!" Earman wailed. "The three of them did. Lied about me. Stole my business."

In the most disinterested voice, as if discussing a cravat he had worn yesterday, Sonny Conover said, "You fool, if we hadn't taken the course we did, the F.B.I. would have found out anyway that you were an enemy alien. They would have cancelled the contracts and ruined us all. But all that has been explained to you."

"You framed me!" Earman yelled.

"Oh, nuts," said Conover. "The F.B.I. found plenty on you, and nine-tenths of it we hadn't known about."

"Lies!" Earman shouted. But Savage was going to Earman again, and Earman didn't like that. He went back in the chair himself as if wanting to disappear in the upholstery. He said, "They lied," again, but it wasn't at all convincing.

"Were you an alien?" Savage asked.

"No," Earman said weakly. And then he said, "Yes. . . . Yes, but they—yes. Yes, only my sympathies were with this great, fine country. . . ." Savage stood over him now. Earman made a swipe at his lips with a tongue as dry as a sagebrush stem. "I belonged to the Bund," he confessed.

Savage said, "Then your partners were justified in turning you in?"

"Well—"

"Justified as American citizens?"

Earman bent over. He put his face in his hands. "Yes," he said. In a moment, a puppy-like sound escaped between his fingers. "I'm afraid," he whimpered. "I don't know what is happening, and I'm afraid."

Sonny Conover didn't seem at all interested in this. He pretended to be interested in the top of his desk, but nothing was there. And then he looked at me. He wasn't interested in me, either, but he seemed called on to be something, and he asked, "May I inquire who you are?"

"Miss Ames," I said.

"But what part . . . ?"

"I've been sort of Doc Savage's advance agent in this thing," I said. And then, because I didn't want Savage to notice particularly the statement I'd just made, and give out the correct idea of my status, I added hurriedly. "There's another man who may possibly be involved in this. Mr. Conover. James Like. He, too, was a partner of Earman's six years ago. Is that right?"

"Jimmy was one of us, yes."

"Have you discussed this with him?"

For answer, Sonny Conover—the name Sonny certainly didn't fit him—snapped down the lever of an interoffice communicator, similar to the one which Futch had done his eavesdropping at J. X. Smith's office, and addressed his secretary. "Miss Spellman, have you gotten hold of Mr. Like yet?"

The young woman said she hadn't.

"Where have you tried?" Conover demanded.

The girl had a list of places and friends, most of the places being bars, and most of the friends women. "No one seems to have seen Mr. Like for a couple of days, Mr. Conover," the secretary reported.

Conover said, "Thank you, Miss Spellman," snapped up the lever—he wasn't fool enough to have the intercom master set on his secretary's desk, as Smith had been—and asked us, "That answer your question?"

"You are trying to get hold of James Like and can't locate him?" Savage asked.

"That's the general idea."

Earman made no more puppy sounds, but he still held his face in his hands as if it was made of thin glass.

Savage studied Conover thoughtfully. "Figured out any measures, or had any advice, on treating that poison in your body?" he asked.

Conover's control split a little. He had been doing well, but now there was a crack. Not much escaped. Just a shudder. One that would have waved a malted milk.

"Good God!" he croaked. "Figure out something! You're crazy, man! The doctor tells me there's no known treatment for radiant poisoning. That it's a tissue destruction effect that doesn't show up until later. Months later."

"Perhaps in this case—"

Conover had another of the shudders, then told us the reason for it. But first, before he told us, he cursed his doctor, or J. X. Smith's doctor. He called the doctor much worse than he had been called by Earman a few minutes ago, but Savage let it pass. Then Conover said, "That damned doctor. The blankety-blank morbid so-and-so showed me some pictures of the Hiroshima victims. Why in the hell he did that, I don't know. I was scared bad enough without that."

Savage said patiently, "It's possible there may be a ready available cure in your particular case." He turned to me and said, "You might repeat what Pulaski told you."

I had forgotten Pulaski's exact words. But I gave Conover the gist of it—that the radio-activated substance was carried in an insoluble salt, and that the salt itself could be eliminated from the body by the proper treatment. "If that's true," I said, "these cases aren't the same as ordinary radiant poisoning due to exposure—for instance, the sort of exposure they fear in working around an atomic pile—nor quite like the thing that happened to the victims in the pictures the doctor showed you. . . . That was the basis for the whole extortion scheme."

"I'll pay plenty to get out of this, if that will do it," Conover said bitterly. "I suppose the smart thing is to say I won't pay a damn cent, but what's the use of kidding."

He looked at Earman when he said that. Earman didn't take his face out of his hands.

Savage now stood. He said, "In case you think of anything that might help catch whoever gave you that stuff—and if you are contacted, and a payment demanded—get in touch with me."

Conover nodded. "It may take some nerve to do that—if I'm told not to do it by whoever contacts me."

Savage didn't argue with him about it. "That will be up to you," he said.

Apparently the interview with Sonny Conover was over. We had learned quite a lot, accomplished nothing. Savage went over and took Earman's shoulder and raised Earman out of the chair. It looked as if he had picked up a coat. "We'll be going now, Mr. Earman," he said.

We left Sonny Conover braced back in his chair, staring fixedly at the ceiling and the end of life, and crossed the reception room that would hold two locomotives and some to spare, went along the hall again, rode down in an elevator that I now noticed would itself hold a small truck.

Futch wasn't around on the street, not noticeably. The solid-looking police detective who had left the cigar stand to look for Futch was standing at the curb trying to disguise himself by reading a newspaper. He didn't particularly look at us, but shook his head, whatever that meant. We got in Savage's car.

Earman got in beside Doc Savage and sat there a minute. Then Earman's breath went out in a long shrilly audible rush, as if an alligator had hissed.

"I'm afraid I've lied to you somewhat, Mr. Savage," Earman said.

That will probably be the understatement for today, I reflected.

X

Doc Savage drove the car three blocks—no doubt to get way from the police detective's large ear—and slanted the machine into a clear space at the curb, stopped it, shut off the ngine, and told Earman, "I was wondering when you would egin to see some advantage in the truth."

Earman didn't get it out at once. He wanted to, but he ad been holding back his fears as if they were handfuls of ats, and they began getting loose. Most of them got as far as is throat and filled it.

"I didn't exactly lie," Earman gasped, after two or three ninutes of tough going. "I—uh—said I came here from Cleveland to investigate a business proposition. That was ight—substantially. But I was paid to come here. A man amed Rilling—Theodore Rilling—the letter said he was a nan—there were two letters in all—the first one was three veeks ago, but I told Mr. Lilsey that—"

Savage interposed, "You're getting a couple of carts efore the horse. Suppose you take a deep breath and tell it he way it happened."

Earman gripped his knees with both hands and tried gain. He said, "God, I'm afraid! I think I've been framed."

And for another three minutes, he found ways of saying e was afraid and had been jobbed. Savage waited patiently, vatching Earman with a rather clinical calculation, as if he hought Earman if left alone would get himself back on the rack. This was right.

Earman had been working for a Mr. Lilsey who owned a adio shop in Cleveland. Earman sold radios for Mr. Lilsey. A etter came for Earman from a Mr. Theodore Rilling. The etter said he, Mr. Rilling, had once been employed by Carman and still remembered the fine treatment Earman had given him and all his other employees. Mr. Rilling was grateful, the letter said. Gratitude, said the letter, had moved Mr. Rilling to offer Earman an executive job beginning at two undred dollars a week in Mr. Rilling's organization, a firm vhich was expanding in the prefabricated housing field. That vas the first letter. Earman accepted by mail. Why not? For

selling radios, he was averaging about thirty-five a week. Th
second letter from Rilling had contained eight hundre
dollars—a month's advance—and instructions to come to th
city and register at the Segrew Hotel, and take things ea
until Mr. Rilling showed up. To be in no hurry. It might be
week. Two. But don't worry if Mr. Rilling didn't appear
once, because Rilling was a busy man and might be delaye
making the territory.

By this time, Earman sounded like a barrel that had lo
some of its staves.

"I've been here three days," he said. "Rilling hasr
shown up."

"Who is this Rilling and what does he look like?" Savag
asked.

"God, that's what terrifies me," Earman cried. "I neve
remembered such a man. I don't know whether I even had
Rilling working for me. I can't recall the name."

"Then why did you come?"

"Eight hundred dollars," said Earman miserably.

"Have you these letters you mentioned from Rilling?"

"Oh, yes! Yes! Damn, I'm glad I have, too," Earma
blurted.

He handed Doc Savage the letters, one at a time, ar
Savage read them, then passed them back to me. They wer
what Earman had said they were.

Earman was shaking now.

"Do you think I was decoyed here to serve as goat?" I
cried. "Do you? God, I think I was! What am I going to do?

If Savage had an answer to that, he kept it to himself. H
started the engine again, twisted the car away from the curl
and drove north. Then he asked, "Miss Ames, do you kno
James Like's home address?"

"Why would I know that?"

He said pleasantly, "I merely thought you might hav
looked it up."

He was right. I had looked it up, last night. But the fa
that he had decided I had was disturbing—while it was
small thing, nothing in itself, it did indicate that Savage wa
deep water and seeped into unexpected places. I was feelir
pretty good up to then—our interview with Sonny Conov
had gone just about the way I wanted it to go. But now I ha
the impression of being undermined, surrounded, and th
Savage was doing it, or had already done it.

"It's on Kay Street, 116," I said quite thoughtfully. "That's an apartment district. The best one."

"We'll try there," Savage said.

There were lots of flashy roadsters on Kay Street. The baby carriages were all pushed by nurses who wore nice uniforms. One-sixteen was twelve stories of dignified dark brick and the entrance was Colonial white and the brass didn't have a spot on it. There was a doorman and a PBX operator and three uniformed elevator operators. There was an argument with the PBX operator, then with the manager, and it wasn't settled until the manager telephoned the police. That settled it quick.

We went up to the seventh floor, and the manager unlocked a door with a master key, and we went in to see if James Like was at home. He was at home.

James Like was another man between forty and fifty with brown hair. He had a sun-tanned look and wore sporty tweeds and a checked wool shirt. There was a cloth sport hat on the stand table beside him, and leaning against the stand table was one of those canes that men take out to the race track with them, the kind that can be made into a seat-rest. James Like looked like a sporting man, and the apartment was a sporting man's apartment.

The ceiling had great stained beams and the plaster was finished rough, like waves on a small lake. On the walls were stuffed animal heads, a giraffe and an elephant and some others with big mule ears and long horns like toothpicks the names of which I didn't remember. There was a Kodiak bear from Alaska, stuffed whole. The bear was only a little bigger than a horse. The apartment was full of stuff like that, the apartment of a big man who had liked to do big primitive things in a hard direct way, the sort of a man who had plenty of courage and would be a great help to everybody in a case as grim as this one was.

The only trouble was, he was dead. His hands were on the armrests of the chair, and he had died peacefully. If there is such a thing as dying peacefully.

"Heart," Savage said. "Probably he just thought he was feeling sleepy, and so he took a nap.

"But isn't a heart attack sort of a coincidence?" I asked.

"Rather," Savage said, and looked at me. There was speculation in his eyes, and a deep-seated curiosity, and perhaps other thoughts that I couldn't fathom, and wouldn't have liked if I could have. He said, "You're a very stabl person, aren't you, Miss Ames? Death and terror and me lying themselves blue in the face all around you, and you'r not too much affected."

"I'm affected, all right," I said. "With a little more of thi encouragement, I think I can shake up a first-rate set hysterics."

"Don't," he said. "It might not look well on you."

I had heard somewhere that he was afraid of women that he didn't understand them; that, as a matter of fact, h had a phobia about the point, and never allowed himself t form any kind of attachments of that sort. Just because h couldn't figure a woman out. It would be nice if that wasn' the hooey I was beginning to think it was.

He didn't go farther into my psychology. Instead, he go a small case out of his pocket, and I knew what it was at once and wasn't too surprised that he should be carrying aroun something of the sort. It didn't have one twentieth of the bul of the radioactivity detector I'd rented and used on J. X Smith, but it was probably as efficient.

He adjusted the gadget and it began clicking. It wa quite audible. He stood on the far side of the room and w could hear it going in measured time, a little like a clock. H came toward the body of James Like. The clicking quickene and became a clatter, a buzz, a whine, a wail like the chil ghost of all the banshees trying to get back into purgatory.

There was evidently enough radiant material in Jame Like's body to set up in the atom bomb business in a modes way.

"But I didn't know that stuff would stop a heart!" I said.

Savage shrugged. "None of us know too much abou radiants. We haven't been around them long enough. . . . Or i may have been the carrying medium for the radiant, th metallic salt or whatever it is."

Walter P. Earman now set up a diversion. He didn't his this time, didn't make a puppy sound; what he did make wa a wail like a cat on a high pole, after about the third day. Tha was all he did, make the sound.

"What is the matter with you now?" Doc Savage asked him.

Earman moaned noisily. "He's the one who reported me to the F.B.I."

"But I thought all three of your ex-partners—"

"Yes, yes," Earman said. "Like was the one who did it.

mean—he's the one who knew I was an alien. He found it out first, and sold the idea to the others."

"In other words," said Savage, "James Like is the one you hate the most?"

"Yes," Earman said. Then he changed his mind fast and said, "But you see, I don't hate any of them. That's all out of my heart."

"Then you have nothing against J. X. Smith, Sonny Conover and James Like?"

"Nothing. Nothing in my heart," Earman insisted.

Anyone could see how much he loved his three—now two—ex-partners. About as much as an elephant defies the law of gravity.

Savage said, "It's good to be pure of heart."

He had been accusing me of being too calm, but I had never seen a set of self-controls kept on ice better than he was keeping his. If that pure of heart wasn't sarcasm, it would do until there was better.

I gathered that Savage wasn't completely satisfied with progress. Which, all in all, was understandable.

I said, "About now would be a good time for you to pull a great feat, wouldn't it?"

"What do you mean?" He didn't change expression much, but he was annoyed.

"Why, Mr. Savage, I understood that you made quick packages out of things like this. Here you've been with us—how long is it—several hours? And all we've done is find bodies and men who have an excellent prospect of becoming bodies."

He didn't say anything. He went to the apartment door and gestured, meaning we—Earman, myself and the apartment house manager who was with us and as weak as last year's campaign promises—were to leave. He said, "We'll telephone the police from downstairs."

Riding down in the elevator, I said, "He got a much heavier dose than the other two, didn't he?"

Savage didn't say nothing.

I said, "That might make it easier to find out how it was given to him, and if we knew how, we might learn when and who."

He still didn't say anything.

So I said, "It looks like I've hurt someone's feelings."

"Not seriously," he said.

The elevator, all gold and mirrors, arrived at the ground

floor with a halt no more violent than a golden wedding kiss, and the doors slid apart. Savage stepped out, a little sidewise— by now I had noticed that he had taken to watching everything around him—and there was an old woman in a long coat waiting, and she crowded in, crowded past him without waiting for us to get out. The operator started to say, "Please let them off—" and got part of it out when there was about the same sound that a rug-beater makes on a rug. The elevator operator didn't fall down for a while; he only leaned foolishly into the corner, propped up by his stool and the fact that his coat front was hooked over the control lever.

The old woman was closing the elevator doors now. Working fast. But Savage was fast, too, and got a foot in the doors and kept them from sliding entirely shut. The old woman labored against the lever which threw the doors shut, and at the same time began shooting—using the gun that had slugged the operator—indiscriminately at the door, at Doc Savage's foot. It didn't take Savage long to get away from the door. I didn't think he was hit.

The gunshots in the elevator were louder than you would think any sound could be.

The old woman was a he, naturally. But I wasn't impressed by that so much—not that I wasn't impressed, however—as by the fact that, having closed the doors, he turned and showed me the face that had the asterisk of adhesive tape on it last night. Here was the party who had tried to spray me with lethal hydrocyanic.

"Hello, Walter," he said to Earman.

The man—there was no tape on his face now—jerked at the elevator operator, who fell away from the controls. The man threw the lever over, and the cage got going upward suddenly enough that my knees bent a little.

"Walter, you're looking fine," the man said dryly and bitterly to Earman. The latter's eyes, mouth and nostrils, and probably his pores, were as widely open as they could get and staying that way. He didn't reply.

The man—I hadn't the slightest doubt now that I was going to die presently, and he would be the cause of it—had time to give me a vague look. He probably made it vague deliberately, and it was supposed to mean something, perhaps to scare me. Nothing could have scared me any further. Anyway, he had only time to give me the studied look—and the elevator stopped. There was no foolishness about its halting—*chuck!* I was a few inches off the floor, and settled back.

I knew what had happened. Savage down on the lobby level had shut off the current somehow and done it fast.

The man, ex-tape-face, knew what had occurred also.

"Walter," he said. "Walter, your big friend is trying to make us trouble."

Earman, who was flattened against the wall now, had no words. The other didn't seem to expect any. He didn't waste time jiggling the useless control. Instead, he came down hard against the door lever and broke the doors open, looked out.

"We get a break," he said, pleased with what he saw. "Fifth floor. That'll get us out on a roof next door."

The cage wasn't quite at the fifth floor, but it was near enough that, jumping up, clinging to the shaft-door, the man was able to reach the device that opened the floor-level doors with his fingertips. He did some fumbling and yanking, and presently had a way out.

"Get going, Walter," he said.

Earman looked at him in a pop-eyed way that might mean anything, and began, "But should I—"

"I would, Walter. Indeed I would, if I didn't want to be guest of honor at an electrocution."

So Earman climbed out. He made a hard grunting job of it, was helped by the other, who then followed him up and out, then turned and looked down at me. He was on hands and knees. "Miss Ames," he said. "You did manage to make a lovely mess of this after all, didn't you?" He had a gun in his hand now. No more foolishness with prussic acid.

No more foolishness at all. He was going to be practical and shoot me. He had concluded he would get out of the elevator before he did it, probably not wanting to get himself spattered. Still, he didn't look like somebody who cared too much about being neat. But he did look practical. He should have done it this way last night, probably.

About that time, I got against the lever that closed the doors, the lever that was shaped like an elbow. I came up hard against it, and I was strong, stronger probably than any woman in the world ever was. I could have bent a horseshoe barehanded. The door began closing. He said something nasty. His gun spoke a loud noise and a yard of flame.

But the door was closing. He grabbed at it with his hand that wasn't holding the gun. All that got him was his fingers pinched. The doors slid together and got his fingers and his gun barrel. Out of the gun barrel, more fire and sound. Then he took the gun barrel from the crack. But he had more trouble with his fingers. We fought over the fingers, me trying to pinch them off with the door, he saying things and trying to keep his fingers. He got them.

I didn't hear him go away. I didn't hear Walter P. Earman go away. I stood braced there, pulling at the handle, forcing the door to stay shut with all my strength, working at it until I ached all over. It probably wasn't necessary, but I didn't want that door ever to open.

It wasn't so good. My knees began to go first; I was pushing up against the handle so hard that they wouldn't take it. The sensible thing to do was quit pushing, but I couldn't do that; it would have been easier to stop breathing permanently. It was the first time I knew my knees would fold both ways, but that was what they seemed to be doing. My legs are long and nice, and pretty soon they weren't good for anything; they didn't even have any feeling in them. I began to feel as if I had been swallowed by a tiger that was dead.

And just then Doc Savage's voice called, "Miss Ames! Ames!" He was outside the door. "Ames! Are you all right?"

I said something. "Go away," I think it was. "I've had enough." The words were clearer than they should have been.

"Are they in there?" he asked.

"I don't think so," I said.

"Where did they go?"

"Out. One said something about a roof."

"That shooting—"

"Just go away," I said. "Just go away. And never come back."

Savage said, "You stay in there." And then he went away, but not because I had told him to.

I didn't stay there. I opened the door, crawled out, made my way down the hall by using the walls for supports, and found the inside fire escape stairs. I started up—intending all the time to go down—and had climbed half a flight before I got that straightened out. Then I went down. Five and a half flights, five and a half miles. Nobody was in the lobby but the P.B.X. operator and she didn't say a word, just stared with big glassy eyes. The air in the street tasted sweet, like wine. But I didn't stay around to sample it.

XI

Sonny Conover's secretary gave me a bit of special treatment—she went into Conover's office herself to tell him I was there. It didn't take her more than five seconds to come out again.

Conover was right behind her, crying, "You have news for me? You've found some way of helping me?"

He had aged noticeably since I had last seen him. That had been about an hour ago. But he had aged—five years, just about—and it led me to wonder how old he had been that morning, before he had a conversation with J. X. Smith on the telephone and learned that there was a new kind of poison around that killed slowly, taking several months to kill, and which just possibly might—and might not—be curable. If curable is the word for poison.

I strolled past him into his office, saying, "I don't have what you want to hear, probably, Mr. Conover. But I do have some news for you."

Confidence had better be my keynote now. Because I was going to take two thousand dollars out of him, put it with J. X. Smith's thousand, and be on the next airliner that left the city. He was in a mental state where he might be easy for more than two thousand, but I wasn't sure and didn't want to take a chance. I hoped their would be an airliner ready to leave just as I got to the airport.

"Mr. Savage overlooked a detail when we were here a short time ago," I said. "Possibly he overlooked it on purpose. He does, sometimes. And I have to go back and explain that it was overlooked, and it's rather embarrassing for me." My diffident smile was intended to be embarrassed, "I'm sure you'll understand."

He didn't understand, but he jerked his head up and down anyway, and went around the fell in the chair back of his desk.

"It's a matter of fee," I said.

"Fee!" he echoed foolishly.

"Two thousand retainer," I said. "And an agreement that you will pay an additional eight, making ten altogether, when and if Savage produces an antidote for the poison and you are pronounced fully recovered." It wouldn't hurt to put in some more, and I did so, saying, "The matter of your recovery, in case of dispute, shall be settled by a board of arbitrating physicians, you to pick one, Mr. Savage another, and they to agree on the third. However, I'm sure there'll never be any question."

"Ten thousand," he muttered. He had something to think about now. He was evidently a man who put a high value on ten thousand dollars.

The secretary was still standing in the room. He looked at her; there was nothing particular in the look, but she left hastily. Something mechanical began whirring and ticking near me, and scared me more than a little, until it proved to be nothing more deadly than a stock ticker spitting out the latest quotations on a tape.

"Two thousand only, just now," I said. "It isn't much."

"Isn't much!" he said bitterly. "The hell it isn't."

This might be only instinct talking. He was a man who had made a great deal of money, and he probably had the habit of striking a bargain. I hoped so, and waited. The waiting got tiresome, and so I said, "It's hard to put a price on life. James Like, for instance, would probably consider it pretty cheap right now. Or maybe not."

"Jimmy?" He snorted. "Listen, that guy never spent more than fifty dollars on anything but a rifle or a shotgun. Not on anything. Even his women were cheap."

"I doubt if it worries him now, though," I said.

Conover scowled. "Now—why are you using that word. Now! Why now! He wouldn't change in a day. Not Jimmy."

"It may have been yesterday, then."

"Huh?"

"He's dead. He was given a heavier dose than either you or Smith. I gather it would have finished him in a couple of weeks anyway, but his heart jumped the gun. We don't know too much about radiants—maybe they do have a direct effect on the heart. Anyway, he's dead."

That made it a sale. He sat there a while, not long, then he reached over, leaning down, and turned back the corner of the office rug. There was a little safe embedded in the floor under the rug—a wall safe, only it was flush-faced and in the floor instead of the wall. He gave the dials a few turns and opened it, and the office door opened again about the same time. It was his secretary.

"Doctor is here," the secretary said, and my face started getting red, for I thought she meant Doc Savage.

But this doctor was a crisp young man in his early thirties, who came in briskly with a satchel and raised his eyebrows at me rather pleasantly, noted my legs, and otherwise showed few signs of the old-fashioned practitioner. Conover knew him, they exchanged hand waves, and Conover forgot to introduce me, and the young physician took care of that formality himself. He was Doctor Cavanaugh, he said, radiologist.

Answering the questioning look thrown at him, Conover said, "Miss Ames is familiar with the situation."

"Oh, yes! Yes indeed," said Doctor Cavanaugh. "I realize who Miss Ames is now. She's the private investigator who unearthed all this affair." He gave me a big grin and said, "You must be a remarkable person. Mr. J. X. Smith told me of you—I made the examination on him which corroborated your earlier findings, Miss Ames." He made his grin larger and added, "Mr. Smith gave me quite a different picture of you from reality."

"Not favorable, eh?" I said.

"Well, I find it enchanting now that I've met you," the doctor said. "Mr. Smith seems convinced you're an unshakeable sort—as a matter of fact, I supposed from his description that you would have few feminine traits. I can see he was wrong."

Sonny Conover, who clearly didn't think I had any femininity either, muttered that they'd better get on with it. He had called Doctor Cavanaugh up to re-check the presence of the radiant in his body. Unconvinced, probably, that such a thing could really happen to him. When they had the habit of success the way Conover had it, sometimes they get to feeling ugly things just don't come their way.

The doctor opened his case and brought out his gadget. It was similar to the one I had rented earlier, but a later model and more efficient. Curious as to how much he knew about what he was doing, I stood close and watched.

He fiddled with the controls, frowned, pulled the headset away from his ear and let it snap back, and made more adjustments. He stepped back from the contraption, then approached it again; he made some more tests for body capacity by moving his hand to and from the thing.

The young doctor finally looked at me, said, "Would you—uh—mind stepping back, Miss Ames?"

I stepped back. I wasn't concerned. . . . Then there was an expression on the young doctor's face. Just a loosening of his lips, a rounding of his eyes—but it took hold of every separate hair on my head and stood it on end.

"Good God!" he said.

"You—I'm not—"

He nodded. "Yes. You—unless you are carrying a radiant on your person? Are you?"

I wasn't. I stood there and looked at nothing and died twice. There was nothing radioactive that I was carrying that would work his machine, nothing at all. But to be sure, I tossed my purse away and came close again, and the infernal machine squealed. I was poisoned, all right.

The young doctor said sympathetic things, nice things; I think he was genuinely shocked and sorry. Doctors can't afford to be too concerned about their patients, but he was concerned. It was nice of him, probably. But I have no idea what he said, the tone he used, the words, or how he felt. My ears didn't ring, but my cheeks got that foolish dull burning and the rest of my body was just something made of nothing and attached to my head.

Finally the young doctor, having said all he could say, put on his hat and took his little case and left. He probably said he would see me again.

Sonny Conover pocketed his hands and scowled at me.

"Ten thousand dollars to find the treatment, and two thousand in advance!" He emphasized what he thought of it with a vulgar gesture; he spit on the floor. "I guess not. I guess you'll find it for nothing, won't you?"

My voice was gone, along with everything.

"I guess I'll just wait until I see whether you *do* find a treatment, before I put out any two thousands," he said.

I picked up my purse and left. I must have, because presently I was in the hall.

Conover laughed somewhere behind me. The sound was not real humor, just a yok-yok of a thing. Maybe a little mad.

Then later I was sitting in a car parked at the curb in the street in front of the building. It was Futch's car, and Futch was in it. Why Futch should be there didn't give me any pause for thought at all, and I didn't wonder why I was sitting there. Perhaps I had just crossed the sidewalk and gotten in, or Futch might have waved, or called, or even gotten out and taken my arm.

Futch said, "So you found it out? How? By accident?"

Suddenly there was a coat of ice all about me. "You said that more than once, didn't you?"

"You don't seem to be hearing too well," he said, nodding. "You found out you had a radiant in your system, didn't you? Nothing else would put quite that look on your face. Am I right?"

"But you already knew it?"

He nodded. He took a small case out of his coat pocket. It was one of the detectors, about like the one which Doc Savage had used, which was more compact than either mine or the one the young doctor had used.

"That's right," he said. "You had time to figure out who gave it to you?"

"Pulaski," I said. "Last night. He talked too much, and when he knew he had, he gave—"

"Oh, no," Futch said. "Pulaski was dead before this morning. And this morning you didn't have it. Not early this morning."

I looked at him. *"Who are you?"* I think I probably half screamed it.

"Just a guy who gets lonesome," he explained. "But I don't get lonesome because I'm entirely without brains. You and me, baby, have got this thing by the chin-whiskers. We got two facts in one hand and two facts in the other hand, and we add them together and what do we get? Four. Two and two make four. So we know who Pulaski sold his poison to, and the cure—if there is one. I think there is. I'm just guessing, but it's a pretty good guess, because there wouldn't be any profit to it if there wasn't a cure. And profit would be the only motive for—"

He didn't finish it. He had been too interested in saying it, so interested he had neglected something he needed to do to guarantee continued good health—keep his eyes open. Suddenly, but without any commotion to speak of, there was a thick tube of steel, the speaking end of a gun, resting on the edge of the window. A man leaned down behind it—ex-tape-face. He said, "You won't mind riding three in the front seat, I hope."

He didn't mean himself. The man he put in with us was

a very sick-looking Sonny Conover, and then he got in the back seat.

"I'll tell you where to drive," he said. "And, oh yes, there's one other piece of information—you may all live through this. You could, you know. But getting reckless and shouting at policemen isn't the best way to do it."

XII

It was a long drive out into the country that we took. No policeman stopped us. They must not have been watching the roads, or didn't know about the ones we took. Our guide, who spoke nothing but directions, and those very sparingly, certainly knew some backwoods lanes. He didn't object to our talking, until ten or so words had been said.

Sonny Conover said them. He said, "Just after you left, Miss Ames, he came in with a gun—"

"No, no," the man said. "No words."

So after a great deal of silence except for the grumbling and knocking the engine did, we were on a road that climbed over a series of ugly red clay hills made more ugly by starved trees, weeds and leprous-looking abandoned fields that were no more than two or three acres in area. Even these signs of a vanished decadent civilization were no more and we rooted along a still narrower trail, brush whacking the side of the car, and came to a cabin which seemed to be our destination. It dawned on me that we probably hadn't driven nearly as far as it had seemed.

"Hey, you," said Futch, who had driven. "This where we stop?"

Hey-you said it was. He also advised conservatism for our conduct. "You'd enjoy the drive back much more. Better stick around for it," he said.

The cabin was impractical. The location was impractical. Both had one thing that highly recommended them—the view. The cabin was situated on the crest of a great roundish hill, standing about where the cowlick would be if the eminence was a man's head, and overlooked a semi-mountainous valley and a lake of surprising size that was probably one of the government-built reservoirs for hydroelectric purposes which spotted this part of the state. Without referring to the scenery, Hey-you herded us into the cabin.

The matter of a name for Hey-you seemed to disturb Futch, who asked, "What do we call you? You got a handle?"

"Shaddup," the man said.

The cabin hadn't been lived in for several months, then had been opened up an hour or two ago, perhaps as long ago as last night, but not long enough back that it had lost the old-trunk smell that long-closed places, even cabins get. The odor of mice, spider webs, dust, stillness and faded memories.

The man stood three kitchen chairs in a row near a wall. Then he upset the chairs.

This was, really, the first time I had had a look at him under any but firecracker conditions. Not that the situation was so placid right now. But at least it was a chance to examine him without an aura of devil horns and spike tail. He wasn't big, he wasn't small. Not thin, not fat. He was just nothing that was out of the ordinary, not handsome and not ugly enough to remember. He was somebody you would pass and not remember, a man with average features and average black hair and an average voice. Black hair. Black hair—that was something to think about. The killer of Pulaski had had brown hair—or maybe whoever had combed and washed in Pulaski's poor down-at-the-heels laboratory hadn't been the killer at all. It might have been anyone, come to think of it. Anyone who had brown hair and who'd gotten a haircut and shampoo yesterday. But looking average and not having brown hair didn't make this man seem a bit less like a skull-face with death a shadow in the eye sockets. A dramatic way to put it. But I felt dramatic that way, and apparently so did Futch and Sonny Conover. Sonny Conover particularly. He would pay almost anybody two thousand dollars cheerfully right now.

"Step in those chairs, one of you in each chair," said average-man. "Put your feet down between the rungs, and out through the bottom, and then stand there."

I wondered where Doc Savage was? Still chasing average-man and Walter P. Earman? I hoped so. Not that it seemed likely to do much good. And where, come to think of it, was Walter P. Earman?

We learned something about kitchen chairs. When you stand in them with both feet through the spaces in the rungs, any quick moving around is apt to be awkward.

Our host searched Futch. He seemed surprised with a

gun he found—the gun seemed to be a trick automatic or machine-gun pistol of some sort; I had never seen one like it, and it was amazing that so much gun could have been so inconspicuous on Futch. The man was pleased with money he found on Futch, and his feelings about Futch's radioactive-substance-detector were less definite. I doubted if he knew what it was. Which seemed odd, if he was perpetrating this ultra-scientific poisoning.

Where was Walter P. Earman? We didn't find out just then. But J. X. Smith was in the next room. Average-man stepped through the door, and came back in no time at all dragging Smith.

Smith gaped at us. "How did you—"

"Shut-up!" said average-man.

"Listen here, Stone—"

"Shut up, I tell you!"

So average-man's name was Stone. It probably wasn't, but it would do, although it didn't fit him. He should have been named Smith, and Smith should have had another name, one that meant a man with lots of money who was very scared and perspiring like a glass of beer in August.

Smith was given a chair to stand in.

Futch asked, "How did he get you here?"

But Futch didn't mean anything to J. X. Smith and he didn't answer. So I asked it, too: "How did—did he kidnap you the way he did us?"

"He brought me here at the point of a gun," Smith said.

"When?" Futch asked.

Smith just looked at Futch.

"When?" I asked.

"Not long ago. I've been tied up in there," Smith said.

Stone—to call him that; it was as good as anything—said, "Now you're all here, and you know how you got here. When I tell you why, you'll know everything. And the why is this: We want our dough and we want it damn quick."

"Who's *we*?" Futch asked.

Ignoring him, Stone continued: "You all know the deal by now, or should. . . . You've been poisoned. There's a cure. You can buy the cure off us, or die. Take your choice. That's putting it quick and fast, but that's the way it has turned out."

He looked us over unpleasantly before he continued.

"I don't mind telling you that this started out to be a leisurely thing, with you being given the poison and having plenty of time to think it over," Stone went on. "But it doesn't seem to have turned out that way. The young lady" —he gave me an un-nice look—"got too much information out of Pulaski last night, and Pulaski got to thinking about it, and thought he'd been quite a fool and had better tell us. He did tell us. We saw that indeed he had been a fool, and there was not much to do about it except knock him off. We did. . . . Now wait. Let's see. I'm not making a confession. I didn't kill him myself. I haven't killed anybody." He glanced at me again. "Although I tried a couple of times, on the young lady here. But I didn't kill anybody."

Futch said, "But you're saying Walter P. Earman did?"

"What?"

"Did Earman—"

"I should be so foolish," said Stone, "as to name any names. Here's what I say: I never heard of Walter P. Earman."

"Never saw him, either, I suppose," Futch said.

"That's right."

"It's clear now," Futch said.

Stone seemed pleased with the exchange, which didn't make any sense to speak of except that he had implied that Walter P. Earman was his boss without saying so.

"Let's wind it up," Stone said abruptly. "Doc Savage got mixed up in it, and we don't like him much. We want our dough. We want to go away. The leisure and the time-for-thinking-of-death is out. You pay. You get the cure. We leave. See how simple it is?"

J. X. Smith, his voice up with the birds, asked, "How much money do you want?"

"We want a half million," Stone said.

Nobody spoke.

"But we'll be reasonable and take a half million," Stone continued. "Does that sound funny? Then have a good laugh, because we—my boss, anyway—doesn't think so damn much of you, Smith, or you, Conover. . . . I'll tell you something I've noticed by observation—I don't think it would hurt my boss a bit to go off and let you two die. And the hell with your money."

Smith wailed, "How do we know the treatment will cure?"

Stone grinned sourly.

"You think you got us there? You haven't. We can give you some of the stuff, and you can take it, and by tomorrow

morning you can see that the radiant has been partly eliminated from your bodies. But not entirely. There'll still be
enough in you to kill you. And you'll need more medicine to
get well."

Smith, the fool, said, "We could have the antidote
analyzed—"

"Not," said Stone, "if I dose you with it here. Which is
what I was going to do—providing you pay off."

Nobody spoke. Stone waited. The silence, without starting
off that way, gradually became a matter of finality. The cards
were on the table. The trigger had been pulled. Now it
would be one way or it would be the other.

Smith, bubbling a little, finally said, "If—if we don't—
what would—"

"Why," said Stone, "I'll give you a sample of what will
happen if you don't."

Futch moved then. Futch must have been a mind-
reader, or possessed extrasensory perception—he had something, anyway, that let him know Stone was going to shoot
him, and know it ahead of everyone but Stone. Futch jumped.
Not up, to get free of the entangling chair rungs; that would
have been a waste of effort, and probably an impossibility.

What Futch did was spring upward and forward, take a
kind of arching dive, hit the floor with his hands, go on over.
It was a marvelous flip-flop; it was stupendous under the
circumstances. Futch's feet, and the chair, crashed into Stone.

Stone, driven backward, had the worst sort of tragedy
befall him. He lost his gun. He had been too confident with
it, anyway. The weapon jumped out of his fingers, hit the
floor, did some crow-hopping, and Stone pursued it.

I tried to go into action, and fell down. Ignominiously,
awkwardly, when my life was utterly in danger, I sprawled
over on the floor. For some unknown reason, I had forgotten
all about standing in the chair.

But mine wasn't the only odd behavior. Futch was
yelling something that didn't fit the occasion.

Futch was shouting: "Doc! Watch it, Doc! The fool was
going to shoot me! We'll have to end it now!"

Futch's voice had changed a bit. It was quite educated,
for one thing.

Stone had almost reached the gun he had dropped. All of
this was happening in nothing flat. Futch nearly had his
hands on the gun, and the hands had their fingers splayed

until they were like eagle-claws. But Futch did more gymnastics with the chair, struck the gun and knocked it across the floor, twirling as it went, to a point near J. X. Smith.

J. X. Smith now fell forward, picked up the gun, aimed with the deliberation of a man examining the back of his own throat in a mirror, and shot Stone in the brain.

Sonny Conover solved his status in the proceedings neatly. He fainted.

Doc Savage came in through the door. He looked twice as big as he had before, and somehow discouraged with the way things had gone.

Stone finished his dying. He had not made much of a fuss about it.

This, I thought, ended the present phase.

XIII

I ended it like the French getting licked ended the Second World War. Futch twisted the chair off his feet, swung the chair around his head once and let it fly at J. X. Smith. This thwarted temporarily, but not permanently, J. X. Smith's intention of shooting Doc Savage. Then, quite probably, he would have shot Futch, Conover and myself.

Smith ducked, and this caused him to stumble forward on all fours. I now noticed that he had one foot out of his own chair. He freed the other foot with alacrity, fired the gun, did not hit anyone, gained his feet, and headed for another door, the one through which he had been escorted by Stone a while back.

Savage was going for Smith. They had a two man race for the door with Smith leading, losing ground, but going to make the door.

J. X. Smith probably made his last serious mistake then. He paused to shoot Savage. The bullet—it was pretty apparent that Savage wore a bullet-proof vest—only turned the big bronze man somewhat sidewise and made him a target half as wide. Smith went on into the other room. He tried to get the door closed, and didn't succeed, and Savage was in the room with him.

The sounds that came out of the room didn't last long,

and seemed to please Futch, who lost no time going into the room himself.

"He's alive. . . . Why, thank heavens, he's perfectly all right," I heard Futch say.

He didn't mean Smith, but Walter P. Earman. Because he came out of the room in a few seconds, leading Earman and helping Earman get ropes off his hands. There was a gag, a huge one made of adhesive tape and rags, that covered the lower part of Earman's face, and Futch let Earman remove that himself.

"Will you find some water," Futch told me, "and pour it on Mr. Conover? If you will do so, Miss Ames, I imagine Conover can clear up a point."

He didn't sound like Futch. He sounded Harvard.

After I had found the water and was pouring it on Sonny Conover as directed, Savage came back into the room dragging J. X. Smith by the shoulders. Smith didn't look at all the same, wasn't worrying about it at the moment, but would later.

When Conover stopped sputtering, blowing water, and yelling questions, they had one question for him:

Did you and James Like have any idea recently that J. X. Smith might be short of money?

Conover said, "Yes, and Jimmy had some notion that Smith might have lifted some securities belonging to him and worked a forgery and sold them. He talked to me about it, but we didn't quite think Smith would do a thing like that."

Conover filled a minute or two with words telling how the three of them had enjoyed a prosperous wartime period when anybody who had a cost-plus contract with the government could make money, and how after the war J. X. Smith had not been as successful, although he hadn't retrenched nor cut down his expenses, and had seemed to think he could keep on as if the government hadn't shut off the spigot.

"You mean," Conover broke in on himself suddenly, "that J. X. and not Walter P. Earman was doing this thing to us?"

"That's right," Doc Savage said.

"But how did you—"

"Know it? We didn't, for sure—or we wouldn't have let it get this far along," Savage explained. "But Smith had brown hair, and the police dug up for me the fact that he'd had a haircut and shampoo this morning. And when Miss Ames showed up with the poison in her system, we were fairly certain. . . . You see, my associate, Mr. Ham Brooks, had been keeping very close tab on Miss Ames, and the only time she could have been given the poison, we thought, was when she had a drink with J. X. Smith at his office earlier in the day."

Conover nodded. "I guess he would, at that. He was the one who dug up that alien case against Earman in the beginning. We sometimes thought he dressed up the evidence against Earman somewhat."

Earman had seemed dazed by the whole thing, but now he came out of his trance sufficiently to yell, "I was framed! Smith framed me! I'm going to sue—"

"Oh nuts!" Conover told him bitterly. "You were an alien, all right. And belonged to the Bund to boot. So don't get funny."

If all this seemed to mean that everyone had forgotten the really important matter—was there a cure for the radiant poisoning we had in us—it was wrong. Because Conover suddenly began shouting about it, and wouldn't shut up when Savage told him to do so.

Futch finally went over and bellowed in Conover's face: "Of course there's a cure! A sure-fire one, too."

"How in the hell do you know—"

Futch levelled an arm at Smith. "He took some of the stuff himself so absolutely nobody would suspect him. . . . Do you think he would have done that if he didn't have a cure?"

That was the kind of logic that leads you to know an apple will fall if you let go of it in the air. It was absolutely irrefutable. There was a treatment for the radiant. Smith wouldn't have taken a chance of there not being.

The stuff, it developed, was on hand. In the next room we presently found a small canvas bag, one of the fifty-nine-cent ones with a zipper that now sells for two dollars eighty-nine, and in it was some stuff in a bottle, and some other substance in powder form in pill boxes, that seemed to have possibilities.

Doc Savage asked J. X. Smith, who was now conscious, if this was the antidote. Smith said sneeringly it wasn't.

"Then," Savage said calmly, "We'd better destroy it. It's probably some of the radiant poison material, and we don't want any of that around for someone else to be tempted."

Smith waited until he was convinced that Savage meant to destroy the stuff—Savage was actually dumping boxes of the powder into the stove—before he began screaming not to do away with the chemicals. They were the antidote. All there was in existence, too.

Savage eyed the hot stove regretfully. "Too bad you didn't say so earlier," he remarked. "You let me burn so much of it that there may not be enough left to treat you, after we get Miss Ames and Conover out of danger."

That, presumably, was to soften up Smith for a confession. Because I had come across Savage a bit earlier outdoors. He was putting ordinary road dust in the boxes he'd chucked into the stove later.

"Futch," I asked thoughtfully, "what did he call you?"

"Who?"

"Doc Savage."

"Oh, you mean called me for being sucker enough to let Stone get a gun on me and bring me out here?" said Futch. "Well now, he hasn't gotten around to calling it yet. I imagine it'll be plenty."

"A while ago," I said, "he called you Ham Brooks. . . . Who is Ham Brooks?"

"That would be the name of a lawyer, one of Doc Savage's associates."

"You're Ham Brooks?"

"Yes."

"I see. He put you to watching me last night."

He grinned. "I didn't mind the work, after I got a look at you."

So I had been pretty smart. I was the one who was going to use Doc Savage to rake the chestnuts out of the fire, then I was going to grab the chestnuts and leave him with a foolish expression. Sure, I had been smart, the way a cat is when it sticks its head inside the milk bottle then discovers that the head that went in easy won't come out.

I remembered that I had left my purse in the car. I went and got it and took a look inside. The two thousand wasn't there, and it wasn't too much of a surprise. I had a pretty good idea that I wouldn't say anything about my vanished profit.

And I didn't, and a couple of weeks later I got an awfully nice letter from a cancer research fund, thanking me for the fine donation of two thousand dollars. So I didn't feel too foolish.

THE END

ONCE OVER LIGHTLY

I

Out of a clear sky came this telegram. It read, MISS MARY OLGA TRUNNELS: IF YOU ARE MAKING LESS THAN HUNDRED A WEEK QUIT YOUR JOB. I HAVE BETTER ONE FOR YOU. FINE SALARY, LOVELY SURROUNDINGS, WONDERFUL PEOPLE.

It was signed, GLACIA.

That didn't sound like Glacia should sound somehow, so I wired back. HAVE YOU TAKEN TO DRINK?

This should have drawn a sassy answer, but it didn't. It got this:

WIRING YOU TRANSPORTATION. JOB IS SUPERB. HONEY YOU MUST COME.—GLACIA.

The telegrams were coming from a place named Sammy's Springs, California, and it did not seem to be on the map. A place called Sammy's Springs sounded as if it belonged in California, but it still wasn't on the map. I looked.

Being a conservative girl sometimes, and also still feeling that all this didn't sound quite like Glacia, I tried the telephone. The operators seemed to have no trouble finding Sammy's Springs.

"Glacia," I said. "What has gotten at you? Have you married a monster, or something?"

Glacia had a voice that went well with champagne and little silver bells, and she used it to tinkle pooh-poohings at me. Then, speaking rapidly, she told me in five different ways that it was a wonderful job out there, and asked me four different times to come out in a hurry.

"I'll rush down and wire you a plane ticket this instant," Glacia said.

"Why should *you* wire the ticket? Why not let the purveyor of this wonderful job do that. And by the way, who is my future employer?"

"Oh! You're coming! Fine! Wonderful! Oh, I'm so delighted!"

She kept saying this in various ways for a while, then said well this was costing me money, long-distance calls didn't come for nothing, and goodbye and she would meet the plane with bells on, then she hung up. She hadn't told me who the job was with, nor what it was.

I decided that it had been Glacia I was talking to, because it was Glacia's voice, but that was about all. Glacia hadn't demanded a cent of grease for getting me the job. Not like Glacia, that wasn't. She wasn't one to do a favor without getting her bite, and she was brazen and hard-headed enough to have it understood ahead of time that she would want a cut.

I lay awake for a while trying to figure it out, and about midnight, just before going to sleep, I began to wonder if Glacia hadn't sounded scared, really. Still, it would take quite a fright to jolt a dollar out of Glacia's mind.

The next morning, I went to work at the office, and waited for Mr. Tuffle to make a mistake. Mr. Tuffle was my department boss, and could be depended on for a mistake every day. He was the vice-president's son-in-law, which put him in a position where he could blame his subordinates for his stupidity. I began to think he was going to miss today just to spite me, but about two o'clock he came over to my desk roaring to know where the Glidden Account papers were and why in hell I hadn't turned them in on time. I had turned them in on schedule, and further than that, I knew just where he had misplaced them the afternoon he rushed off early for a game of golf. I went to his desk, dumped the drawer contents on the floor, grabbed out the Glidden Account papers, and raised hell myself. I carried the stuff into Mr. Roberts' office, raised more hell, and got fired.

That took care of the embarrassing matter of having to quit the job without the usual two-week notice. Incidentally, it did the office morale some good. They gave me a party that night.

Glacia had wired the airline reservation herself. I inquired about that, and she was the one who had sent the ticket.

The plane was one of those super-duper four-motored stratosphere jobs. It got me to Los Angeles in less than ten hours, and they were paging me over the public address system there. I was wanted at the reservations counter, the loudspeaker was saying.

"Oh, yes," said the reservation clerk. "This gentleman is waiting for you."

The gentleman was a very tall Indian, with two feathers in his hair. He was having trouble with one of his feathers, which was cocked forward over his left eye. He straightened it, and looked at me.

"Ugh!" he said presently. "You the one, all right. You answer description." And then he asked, "You got heap strong stomach?"

"I don't know about that, Hiawatha. Why?"

He put a large copper thumb against his own chest. "Name is Coming Going," he said.

"Glad to meet you, Mr. Going." I said. "Now why this interest in my stomach?"

"Got lightplane," said Mr. Coming Going. "Supposed to fly you like a bird to place named Sammy's Springs."

"Oh," I said. "You mean that you are a pilot who has been employed to furnish me transportation the rest of the way to my destination?"

He nodded. "That would be long-winded way of saying so," he admitted.

"Who hired you? Glacia?"

Coming Going lifted his eyes as if he were looking at an eagle, and whistled the wolf-call.

"That would be Glacia," I said. "All right, lets get my suitcases and be on our way."

"Ugh," he said, and we got my suitcase. He must have expected more in the way of baggage, because he seemed favorably impressed.

"Squaw with one suitcase!" he remarked wonderingly. "Wonders haven't ceased." Then he examined me again, with more interest than before, and said another, "Ugh!"

That "Ugh!" was the end of his conversation for the trip. I found out why he was interested in whether or not I had a strong stomach. The plane he had was a little two-place grasshopper affair, sixty-five horsepower, the pilot seated ahead of the passenger. A kite with an engine. We flew for three hours over desert and mountains and the thermals and downdrafts tossed us around like a leaf. My stomach stood it, although there were times when I wondered.

The only comment Mr. Going had on the durability of my midriff was another, "Ugh!" after we landed. It was slightly approving, however.

Glacia came running and screaming, "Mote! Darling! You did get there! How divine!"

Glacia was blonde, small, lively, and wonderful for gentlemen to look upon, with hair falling to her shoulder, widely innocent blue eyes, a tricky nose, and other features to nice specifications. She did not look as if she had a penny's worth of brains, although she actually had some—in an acquiring fashion.

I told her she was looking wonderful—she was—and then asked what about this job, and didn't get an answer. I got a lot of conversation, the gushing sort, but no specific data on the job.

Glacia had a car waiting. A roadster. Seen after dark, the color of the car wouldn't put your eyes out, but now the desert sun was shining on it, and it nearly blinded me.

"You must have taken some fellow for plenty, honey," I said.

Glacia had no answer to that, but plenty of other words, and we got in the roadster and drove through mesquite, cholla cactus, yucca cactus, barrel cactus—I didn't know one cactus from another, but Glacia gave a running comment on cacti as we drove—and after a few miles it became evident that we were approaching a rather odd sort of civilization.

"You'll love this place, dear," said Glacia.

We got closer.

"For God's sake!" I said.

"There!" said Glacia. "I told you. Quaint, isn't it?"

"You mean this is a hotel?"

"Yes."

"But what—"

"Oh, it isn't a bit like the ordinary hotel," Glacia explained. "That's probably what makes it *the* place to be seen. Lots of Hollywood people come here. Nothing around here is supposed to be quite commonplace."

I could see that it wasn't commonplace. The buildings were made of native stone and enormous logs in an utterly bizarre architectural plan, like one of those hairbrained plans that artists think up for the magazines when they are handed a story of a visit to Mars or some other planet to illustrate. The structures hadn't been skimped on size, either, I discovered, when we drove into a tunnel-like portico that would have accommodated a locomotive.

There was a whispering sound, a big door closed quietly behind us, and we were greeted by a rush of cold conditioned air that seemed approximately zero. Outside the temperature must be past a hundred.

"You'll love it," Glacia said.

"You're not," I said, "implying that this is going to be my place of residence?"

"Certainly. Why not?"

"There's a slight matter of dollars involved. Or don't they use them for legal tender around here?"

"Oh, that's taken care of," said Glacia.

"Is it? You don't say. I'd like to know—"

What I wanted to know about was this job, which was rather elusive it seemed to me, but three more Indians stalked out of the place and without a word captured my bag and disappeared inside with it. Two Indians carried the bag. The other walked behind them. They hadn't made a sound.

"Do they scalp anybody?" I asked.

"They're bellhops. Don't be silly," Glacia said.

"What do they charge you for a room around here?"

"They don't call it a room. You're a tribe member. That includes your lodging, food, recreation, everything."

"Don't beat around the bush, dear. I asked you the charge—"

"Nothing—for you. It's taken care of."

"Just the same, I'm not going to sign the register."

Glacia laughed, and I found out why. There wasn't any register, or if there was one, I never saw nor heard about it. This hotel, or resort, or whatever you would call it, was the screwiest spot imaginable.

My room was swell. Glacia managed to deposit me in it without telling me what the job was, and then skipped, saying, "You'll want to scrub up, honey. You look like you'd been pumped here through a pipe." Which was more like Glacia. She normally wasn't a very civil person, to people she could bulldoze well enough to call them her friends. I'm afraid I belonged to that category.

The room had a stuffed buffalo in it, but otherwise it was normal. The walls were pastels, blues mostly, and the furniture was what one would probably find in the forty-dollar-a-day suite in the Waldorf. But the buffalo rather dominated the place.

I went to the window to see whether the scenery was in keeping. It wasn't. The scenery was all right, a swatch of authentic desert equipped with the varieties of cactus Glacia had named, sand dunes, mesquite, probably sidewinders and scorpions too. The mountains were not far away; they were remarkably dark mountains that tumbled and heaved up to a startlingly cyanite blue sky, and if there was a shred of vegetation, I failed to see it. The scenery was unique in a bleak, tooth-edging way. It didn't look at all genuine, but then that wasn't unusual in Southern California.

The scenery seemed to have an effect on me, though, or perhaps it was the hotel. Or wondering about this job. I showered and changed, and didn't feel any more confident, and tried to find a telephone to get in touch with Glacia. There didn't seem to be any room telephones. I went into the hall, and an Indian, presumably another bellhop, was passing, and I asked him. "What about room phones? Don't they have any here?"

"Ugh," he said. "Takeum buffalo by horn and talk to him." He walked off.

I yelled, "Listen, Pocahontas, what room is Miss Glacia Loring in?"

"Mink," he said, not looking back and his feathered headdress not missing a bob.

So I went looking for mink. The suites weren't numbered either, it seemed, but were designated drawings of different animals and birds on the door panels. The place was screwy enough that this touch seemed quite sane and practical.

Glacia had changed to a bathing suit. It was small, a dab here and there. Not enough to do her figure any harm.

"Angel," she cried at me. "I want you to meet Uncle Waldo?"

"Whose Uncle Waldo?"

"Mine."

"I didn't know you had one," I said. "Listen, you beautiful wench, if you're trying to pass some antiquated boy-friend off as—"

"Oh, don't be so stinking moral," she said.

"He's really your Uncle?"

"My mother's brother. God help her," Glacia said.

That should sort of prepare me for anything, I thought. I hadn't known Glacia's family too well when I was a kid growing up in Kansas City, because we lived in the part of town where we had backyards and washings were hung there. The Lorings had lived four blocks over, not a great distance, but quite a long way measured in the snobbery scale. Glacia Loring and I ended up attending the same high school, and we must have found something in common—as I recall, we were both going to become actresses at the time, and got together in school theatricals—and we saw quite a lot of each other.

Were we friends as kids? I don't know. I doubt it, but it would depend on what the definition for friendship was. We were together a lot. We fought over the same boys, and got stuffed at the same soda fountains. I suppose we sort of rubbed off on each other. I toning Glacia down a little, and she giving me more glisten. But I don't know about that either. I do know my mother didn't approve of Glacia's folks, and Glacia evidently had similar trouble at home, because she never took me there.

Not that Glacia's folks were snobs. They were screwballs. They just plain resented common sense, and they maintained that the conventional and the ordinary was slops for pigs. I think Glacia's mother and father were married in an airplane circling over Kansas City as a publicity stunt, and I knew that her grandfather on the maternal side had maintained that he, not Peary nor Cook, had been first to discover the North Pole, and that he had sued, or threatened to sue, both Admiral Peary and Cook for daring to lay claim to the Pole. This old fellow would be the sire of Glacia's Uncle Waldo, if there was really such an individual. And since Uncle Waldo was a sprig on such a goofer-tree, anything might be expected of him.

It might have been the cockeyed hotel, but I expected to find Uncle Waldo covered with monkeys. I wouldn't have been surprised, anyway.

What I met was a nice-looking old gentleman, not much taller than I am, an old gaffer made of oak and weather-cured hide. He wore tan flannel trousers with sandals, and a terrific checkered shirt. He was sitting in the bar which overlooked a swimming pool, and he was the only person in the place with a glass of milk in front of him. He looked me over.

"A seaworthy seeming craft," he remarked.

That didn't sound too much like a compliment, but I gathered it was. He had no more to say until he had given Glacia's scanty bathing costume a disapproving nose-wrinkling, and watched me order a drink. I ordered ginger ale with nothing in it, because my stomach was still in some doubts about what to do over the lightplane ride. Apparently, what I ordered met with approval, because Uncle Waldo got around to dropping an oracular opinion.

"She'll do," he said.

Glacia blew out her breath.

"Darling," she told me. "Now I can tell you about the job. It's working for me."

"For you!"

"Oh, don't look so shocked. What's so bad about that?"

"I don't know what's tough about it," I said. "But I'm sure something will develop."

Uncle Waldo chuckled. This sounded like a steam engine snorting once.

"The pay is good," Glacia said hastily. "You'll get fif—" She paused and examined my expression. "Eighty a week," she corrected.

"That's too much," I said. "Or is it?"

"Don't be so damned suspicious," Glacia said.

"So there's something I should be suspicious of?"

"Of course not!" She didn't sound convincing, although she tried hard enough.

"What is this job, baby?"

Glacia evidently had an answer all ready, but suddenly decided I wouldn't believe it, and got busy trying to think of another. While she was doing that, Uncle Waldo summarized the job.

"You hold niece's hand," Uncle Waldo said.

He meant Glacia, of course. By holding Glacia's hand, I hoped he didn't mean what I thought he meant. Anything that would make Glacia want her hand held probably wouldn't be easy on the nerves.

II

The job had a snake in it somewhere. But two days passed and nothing happened and I was lulled into a condition that might be called somewhat puzzled peace of mind— the kind of an attitude where you don't think you'll have to swim, but you take your bathing suit along just in case.

The two days had incidents enough in them, but they weren't significant incidents. Except, it later developed, one incident was going to lead to something. For I saw Doc Savage.

Glacia was with me at the time. We came into the lobby and there was an air of hush and bated breaths like the Second Coming.

"The redskins must have arisen," I said.

"It's always like this when he's passing through," said Glacia.

"What do you mean?"

"You'd think," said Glacia, "that if he wanted a vacation, he would go where no one knew him . . . Still, that place would be hard to find, I guess."

At this point the magnet for all the gaping interest appeared. He was a bronze man with flake gold eyes—that description sounds a good deal more casual than it should sound, probably. But that was all he meant to me at the time. A bronze man with flake gold eyes. I did not notice that when he passed near another person or a piece of furniture to which his proportions could be compared, there was the rather odd illusion that he became a giant. Not quite seven feet tall, but almost. Otherwise he was just an athletic-looking bronze man with gold eyes. Striking. But nothing to fall over on your face about.

Not until he had passed through the lobby and was gone did it seem permissible to resume breathing.

"Well, well, quite an effect," I told Glacia. "Who might he be?"

"Don't you know?"

"Should I?"

Glacia looked at me as if she considered me thoroughly stupid. "You mean to tell me . . . ?" She shook her head wonderingly.

"Has my education been neglected?"

"You evidently forgot to put on your brains this morning," Glacia said. She seemed genuinely disgusted. "That was Doc Savage."

"So?"

Glacia's eyes popped a trifle. "I honest-to-God believe you've never heard of him."

"Am I supposed to have?"

Glacia said she could cry out loud, said a couple of other things not complimentary, and added, "You must be ribbing me, dear."

"Just be nice for a change and tell me who he is?"

"Doc Savage, the Man of Bronze, the righter of wrong and the nemesis of evildoers."

The way Glacia said it was odd, and I looked at her. She had put considerable feeling into it, not as if she was irked at my not knowing who this fellow was, but as if it was a personal matter with her—as if Savage himself was a personal matter.

"Oh, a detective," I said.

Glacia said, "Not so you would notice," without bothering to shake her head.

"G-man, then?"

But Glacia shook her head and said, "Skip it, baby." And the rest of the afternoon she was rather sober.

Later that evening, I found my redskin pilot, Mr. Coming Going, near the swimming pool. He wore a swim suit and two feathers, was having trouble with one of the feathers drooping over an eye, and was sitting with his legs cocked up on a table, watching female guests disporting in the pool.

"Ugh!" he said to me.

From that beginning, I worked the conversation around to Doc Savage, and asked for information about the star guest. I had touched a sympathetic chord, because Mr. Going's eye brightened. He said "Ugh!" a couple of times enthusiastically, changed to perfectly good Kansan City English, and told me that Doc Savage was a noted celebrity, a righter of wrongs and punisher of evildoers.

"I got that same line from my girl-friend-employer," I said. "But it sounds a little screwball."

"That Savage fellow is no screwball," said Coming Going. The glint in his eye was probably admiration—not for me, but for Savage. "What gave you such an idea?"

"That evildoer nemesis and wrong-righter stuff," I said. "It's straight."

"Gadzooks. It sounds like strictly from the place where the bells hang."

"Well, that's what he does."

"You mean that's his profession?"

"Yep."

"How does he make it pay off?"

Coming Going shrugged. "I'm not his historian. Strikes me you should have heard of Savage. How did you miss it?" He gazed at me with more approval than he had evidenced hitherto. "You seem to be a pleasantly ignorant wench. The type I admire, incidentally."

I noticed that Mr. Coming Going had blue eyes. "Just how much Indian are you?" I asked.

He pretended to be alarmed lest we be overheard. "My pop once bummed a cigarette off Chief Rose Garden, but don't tell anybody on me."

"What tribe did Chief Rose Garden belong to?"

"Kickapoo, I guess. He was selling bottled Kickapoo Snake Oil off the tailgate of a wagon that stopped in our village for a while."

I left Mr. Coming Going without being certain whether I was being kidded.

That night, Glacia asked me to share her room. Somehow I did not seem at all surprised when she did so, which must mean that I had sensed something of the sort coming. Glacia was off-handedly high and mighty about it. "You'd better move in with me, and cut expenses," she said. And added, "I've already had your things brought to my suite."

It was all right. After all, she was paying me—she really was; I'd collected the first week's pay in advance—and she was entitled to give the orders.

About ten o'clock, Glacia said something else that seemed a bit odd. "I'm going to say good night to Uncle Waldo," she told me.

"If I'm not back in half an hour, will you check up?"

"What do you mean, check up?" I asked.

She said angrily, "Just see why I haven't returned! You ask too many questions!" She flounced out, slamming the door.

I went over to a chair and dropped into it, waiting for the clock minute-hand to move half an hour. And presently I noticed that I had instinctively or for some other occult reason selected a chair facing the door. My hands seemed to have a peculiar unrest of their own—they wanted to hold something, and the fingers were inclined to bite at whatever they gripped, the latter objects alternating between the chair armrests, my knees, a handkerchief and an Indian warclub that I chanced to pick off the table.

The warclub, it presently occurred to me, was out of place. It didn't belong in the room, which was otherwise a fine modern hotel room. The screwball atmosphere of the hotel didn't extend to any of their suites—except for one little touch like a stuffed buffalo or something of that sort. And that reminded me—I looked around for the screwball item in Glacia's suite. But there didn't seem to be anything, because the warclub wasn't enough of a zany touch to qualify.

Presently I was worrying because there wasn't a stuffed buffalo or the equivalent in the place. The logical conclusion to be drawn from that was I must be getting a loose shingle. The nutty desert resort, and the intangibility of my job, might be getting me.

Twenty minutes later, I decided I was scared. There was no other emotion that would quite account for my goose bumps. Frightened. Why? Well, Glacia wasn't back yet. But that didn't quite account for it. Something was giving me the feeling—Feeling indeed! It was more than an impression. It was utterly conviction—that there was considerable danger afoot. Where the notion came from, I hadn't the slightest idea.

In the next five minutes—Glacia had been gone twenty-five now—I formed a sound notion of what was making the roots of my hair feel funny. It was this: It didn't make sense, but it was this: Something was waiting around to happen, and it was something violent. I had arrived at the desert resort and found an air of suspense, of expectancy, concealed waiting, tension, fear, danger and God knows what more. How did I know I had found these things? Somebody would have to tell me.

I was in the right mood to jump seven feet straight up when the door began to open with sinister slowness. It had been twenty-nine minutes since Glacia left. The door to the hall opened a fractional inch at a time. I didn't jump straight up or straight down. I just turned to stone.

Nobody more dangerous than Glacia came in. She gave me a rather odd smile.

"It's late. Why don't you go to bed?" she said.

"What for?" I asked. "I won't sleep."

But evidently I did sleep. I think I did, anyway, because there was a period when nightmares and nighthorses galloped through a zone of muted terror. And once I possibly sat up in bed and looked for Glacia and she was gone. I say possibly, because I'm not sure; I only know that I lay back—granting that I ever sat up in the first place—and worried for a long time through a ghastly series of dreams about what I should do about Glacia being gone. Then finally I got the answer—I should get up and find her. Whereupon I awakened, unquestionably this time, and looked, and there was Glacia asleep where she should be on the other bed. I didn't go to sleep again that night. It wasn't worth the effort. I was scared of the dreams, too.

The sunlight was splattering in through the windows when Glacia arose, showered, wrapped a housecoat about herself and said, "I'll see how Uncle Waldo is feeling."

"Is he ill?"

"He wasn't quite himself last night," Glacia said vaguely, and left.

She came back with her face the color of bread dough that had been mixed two or three days ago.

She said, "Uncle Waldo is—is—" She gagged on whatever the rest was and arched her neck, all of her body rigid. She held that for a moment. Then she said, "His face—his brains are all over his face."

Then she went down silently on the floor. Fainted.

III

He was a short, wide, furry man with one of the homeliest faces ever assembled, and he wouldn't have to be encountered in a very dark place to be mistaken for an ape.

"Oh, Yes," he said. "Another female admirer. We comb them out of the woodwork every morning. . . . Well, what do *you* want?"

"I wish to see Doc Savage," I said.

"That's not hard to arrange. Doc will be passing through the lobby at nine-fifteen. Just be on hand. I understand they're thinking of putting up grandstand seats."

"Aren't you funny?"

"Not very," he said. "Just sarcastic. Look, baby, do you think it's very lady-like to pursue—"

"I want to talk to Doc Savage."

"I know. But it will be harder to arrange. Still, some do. It happens. One did in his car yesterday, and assaulted him with a pair of scissors. It scared the hell out of me, but she only wanted to cut off the end of his necktie, which she did."

"Stop being a stuffy fool!" I said.

He grinned faintly, examined me with more interest, and

whistled his approval brazenly. "If I thought being sensible would get me anywhere with you—"

"There's a man dead," I said.

"Uh-huh. It happens every—" He paused, his head jutted forward and down and turned sidewise. "You levelling?"

"He's dead."

"Natural death?"

"I wouldn't say so."

"Where?"

"Here in the—I can't get used to calling this silly ranch a hotel," I said. "His name was Loring. Waldo Loring."

He nodded and said, "Oh, that. Yes, I heard one of the guests had been killed in an accident."

Accident. That was right. That was what the hotel had said it was, which was about the only normal thing I had seen about the hostelry so far—hoping to make their guests think a murder hadn't been committed. So they had said it had been an accident.

"The accident," I said, "was an Indian warclub. It happened several times to his head. There was quite a change made."

He considered this, and there were some subtle changes in his manner, somewhat as if a racehorse had heard the rattle of fast hoofbeats.

"Now I want to talk to Doc Savage," I said.

"I'm Monk Mayfair. I'm Doc's right hand and catch-all. Won't I do?"

"Listen I've told you—"

"Oh, all right, but you'll just get tossed into the waste-basket, and I'm the latter. Doc is on a vacation out here." He paused and looked at me thoughtfully. "I guess you won't be satisfied until he tells you that himself, though."

He went away, leaving me in the living room of a suite which was clearly one of the larger ones. I looked around for a stuffed buffalo or the equivalent, and was peering behind things when Monk Mayfair reappeared and asked dryly. "You hunting something?"

"Stuffed bison," I said. "But I suppose you'll do for a substitute."

After he scratched his head without thinking of a reply, he escorted me into another room where Doc Savage was making a coffee table and room-service breakfast look small by sitting before them.

Monk said, "Doc, this is Miss—"

"Mote," I supplied. "Mary Olga Trunnels, formally."

"She hunts buffalo, but thinks I would do as a substitute," Monk added. "Mote, this is Doc Savage,"

Doc Savage arose, gave me a surprisingly pleasant smile, and indicated a chair. But, probably lest I get any idea the visit was to be on a social plane, he said, "Monk tells me you have a matter of a dead man and a warclub."

"That sounds a little like hello and goodbye," I said. "Am I dismissed already?"

"Not at all. What gave you that idea?"

"I just got a long lecture on lady necktie snippers and wastebaskets from Mr. Mayfair. I gathered I was only to be permitted a bow, and that just to humor me."

Perhaps he thought that was entertaining. I couldn't tell. His bronze face was handsome, but already I could see that it only showed the emotions he wanted it to show. So the fact that his smile flashed again might mean nothing.

He said, "Mr. Mayfair is watchdog today. He prefers to watch pretty girls. I presume that was the gist of his lecture."

"That wasn't its gist," I said. "But it might have been the hidden meaning."

Monk Mayfair took a chair. He didn't seem disturbed.

Doc Savage said, "If you have the idea I don't care to listen to your troubles, perish the thought." He picked up the coffee percolator, asked me if I could use some, and I said I could.

"I'm Mary Olga Trunnels, and up until a few days ago I was employed by the Metro Detective Agency in New York City. It's a private investigations firm, doing all sorts of jobs that detective agencies do, but mostly insurance company work," I said. "Have you got time to listen to me begin the story that far back?"

"Start as far back as you wish," he said.

So I began still earlier, in Kansas City when Glacia Loring and I were brats together, and gave him a picture of the nonconforming background Glacia had. I carried the briefing down to a couple of years ago, when I had last seen Glacia—she had quit a modeling job in New York to come to Hollywood and be a movie star, without having achieved the latter, however—and skipped the intervening time. Then I told him the events of the past few days, and they seemed rather flat, somehow, except for the death of Waldo Loring.

"I think Glacia really hired me as a protector," I said,

"because I happened to be working for a detective agency, and she felt that sort of job qualified me."

"I gather Miss Loring hasn't flatly told you that?"

"No. Intuition and guesswork told me that. But I know a scared girl when I see one, and Glacia is scared."

"Of whom?"

"I don't know."

"Then I presume you don't know what is behind it?"

"Look. I haven't been Girl Friday around a private detective agency for better than three years without learning a little about human nature. Glacia is terrified. I'll stick by that. She is doubly scared now, but she had it before her Uncle Waldo was killed. I can't cite you case and example for proof, but I do know how it feels to sit on a volcano when it's getting ready to erupt, which is the way it has been the last couple of days."

"What about the deceased man, Waldo Loring?"

"Waiting. Secretive and waiting. I had the feeling he was a hunter in a jungle full of wild and dangerous game, a hunter standing behind a tree with his rifle cocked. Waiting to shoot, but at the same time not knowing what instant one of the wild animals might pounce on him. Last night one of them pounced."

Doc Savage tasted his coffee. "Let's leave your intuition a little more out of it," he suggested.

"No. Because I wouldn't have much left," I said. "And I know my intuition. I'll bank on it."

"Did Glacia discuss her Uncle Waldo with you?"

"Never... Of lately, nor before. I didn't know she had him."

"He wasn't around previously, then?"

"No. I got the idea they'd only met recently—that is, Glacia hadn't seen him for a number of years, and he had looked her up a few days ago at the most. Uncle Waldo had been a seafaring man, I think. He talked like a sailor. A real one, not a phony. I would guess him as not a navy man, but a commercial sailor, and an officer, perhaps the captain of a freighter."

"Is that entirely guesswork?"

"Deduction, my dear Watson. I know the difference between navy and commercial jargon. Uncle Waldo was commercial. You can spot a man used to commanding by his manner—at least I can. That meant Uncle Waldo was an officer on a ship. And officers on passenger liners develop polite manners. Ergo, he was a freighter captain."

"A freighter captain waiting for something to happen to him," Savage said dryly.

"Or waiting to make it happen to someone else, if he could get in first lick."

"You mentioned an Indian warclub in the room occupied by yourself and Miss Glacia Loring. Was that the instrument used on Uncle Waldo?"

"I don't know. But the warclub is gone."

"You also mentioned a nightmare last night during which you thought Glacia had left the bedroom."

"I'm not sure about that."

"I would mention it to the police anyway," Doc Savage said. "The warclub. The nightmare. Both items."

"I'm mentioning them to you," I said uneasily. "Isn't that enough?"

"I hardly think so."

I slapped the coffee cup down on the table. Some of the coffee sloshed out. I jumped up. "You mean you're not going to help me?"

"Help you?" His bronze face registered a great deal of astonishment, all for me. "Good Lord! This is a matter for the local sheriff. A murder. Why should I be involved? Particularly when I'm on vacation."

Why should I involve him? A question of great logic. I could look a long way and not find an answer. But he had sat there for fifteen minutes and let me recite my troubles, and so I told him just what I thought about it. My thoughts of the moment, worded just the way they came to me.

"My, my," said Monk Mayfair. "Language."

"So you two let me in here and big-shot me!" I said. "I don't know why I didn't expect that, but I didn't. All right— I've entertained you for a quarter-hour. Now you can go ahead and enjoy your day without further help from me."

Doc Savage did not say anything. He was examining the inside of this coffee cup, and his neck seemed a little deeper bronze.

Monk Mayfair got up hastily, said, "Mote, you seem to be a capable article, and I wouldn't want you to—"

"With that funny face," I yelled at him, "You don't really need all those wisecracks. You're hilarious enough without them!"

I left them. There was a chair in my way, and I kicked that. The door was too heavy to slam well, but I gave it a good try.

IV

There was a tall sunburned man wearing dungarees and a checkered shirt in front of the door of the suite in which Glacia's Uncle Waldo Loring had died.

"What body?" he said. He listened to me explain that I knew about the body because I was an employee of the dead man's niece. Then he said, "Oh. I see. Well, what do you want to know?"

He had a deputy sheriff's badge pinned to the pocket of his shirt. From the same pocket dangled the paper tab on the end of the string that was attached to his tobacco sack. He had been holding a stick of sealing wax over a blazing match. Now the wax got soft, he jammed it against a strip of paper he was sealing across the keyhole, and implanted the impression of a coin, which he took from his pocket, on the soft wax.

He added, "The deceased is still in there. The Sheriff called in a crime laboratory guy from Los Angeles. The expert can't get here until this afternoon. I'm sealing the suite meantime. What did you want? Anything out of the room? If so, you can't have it."

"I just wanted to know what arrangements had been made about the body," I said.

"No arrangements. The arrangements we hope to make is to put the pinch on somebody for murder. The Sheriff said that. The arranging is his job, and I'm glad it is. Me, I would be baffled."

He didn't sound much like a native of the desert, so he probably was. He said his name was Gilbert. He showed me the coin he was using to seal-mark the wax. It was an early California gold piece, worth about ten times face value as a collector's item, he said. It was his pocket piece. Then he said he would finish waxing the lock in a minute, then why shouldn't we have a drink?

I said no, thanks, and left.

Now I wasn't angry. I was getting a little scared. I had been put out with Doc Savage because he hadn't jumped to our aid, but that had evaporated. The anger had drained out of me, and the hole had filled up with something that could get a little worse and be terror.

I went to our room. Glacia was sitting in a chair, her purse open on her lap and both her hands in the purse.

"You feeling better, honey?" I asked.

She took her hands out of the purse. She was a trifle clumsy doing so, and a small blue .25-caliber automatic pistol slid out on her lap. She had been sitting there holding it. Gripping the gun and watching the door.

"I feel all right," she said.

She didn't look it—her gay, crisp, alert, predatory blondness was awry. She was like a china doll that someone had been carrying in his pocket.

"Who were you going to shoot?" I asked.

She jerked visibly. "Nobody. Don't be ridiculous." She jabbed the gun back into the purse, and threw words out. "Where have you been? Why did you run off and leave me?"

"Baby," I said, "you'd better not hold out on me any longer."

Her head came up, and her eyes tried to meet mine, but couldn't. "Don't be such a fool," she mumbled.

It was obvious that she wasn't going to open up. I didn't pick at her, because it would have done no good. I dropped in a chair and waited. Glacia got hold of herself with an effort—you could see her doing it, like a sparrow drinking water. She would look at me, take an intangible drink of what she probably supposed was my calmness, and her throat would tremble. But it trembled a little less after each look.

When she had herself nailed down again—proving she wasn't scared enough to lose her head, at least—she conducted mining operations in the purse. It wasn't a little blue lady-gun this time. It was an envelope. In the envelope was a key.

"Uncle Waldo gave me this to keep for him," she said, displaying the key. "It's the key to the hotel safe deposit box downstairs."

I didn't know that the zany hostelry supplied their guests with private boxes, but it did not seem a bad idea, and some hotels did it. After hesitating, Glacia got around to explaining why she was showing me the key. "Will you go downstairs with me and we'll look in the box," she asked.

"Glacia," I said. "Why did you hire me in the first place?"

She looked hurt, and sounded a little like a kitten mewing for its milk as she said, "You're such a competent person. Mote. You—you're the kind of advisor I need. Stable. And not afraid."

"You want advice?"

"Yes."

"Then take the local law along when you go down to investigate Uncle Waldo's box."

Still like a kitten—with its tail stepped on—she yowled. "That's ridiculous! I'll do nothing of the sort! Why should I?"

"Murder is a tiger that doesn't care who it scratches," I said, probably stupidly. "You start searching a murdered man's safe-deposit box, and you're likely to get scratched plenty."

"It's mine, too. Some of my jewelry is in the box," Glacia said.

She didn't say it cunningly, so I supposed it was true. Anyway, she wasn't going to take a policeman along, and if I didn't go, she would eventually work up the courage to go by herself. So we went downstairs, me wondering if she really had any jewelry in the box, and how she would lie out of it if there wasn't.

They let her have the box without an argument, but she did have to sign a slip. I got a look at the slip—the box was in her name as well as Uncle Waldo's. That made it partly all right, or enough all right that they wouldn't jail us immediately. Let's hope.

Sure enough, Glacia dug out a piece of jewelry. An amulet studded with rhinestones and worth all of thirty cents, probably, on the Woolworth market. But I knew it was hers, because she had worn it as a high school kid.

Glacia became sentimental over the gaudy. "Uncle Waldo gave this to my mother," she said in a small voice. "He was very touched when he learned I had it."

Suddenly I decided that Waldo Loring *had* been her uncle. This decision came as a surprise to me. I'd been under the impression that I had given in to the notion that he was her uncle, but evidently I hadn't until now.

The other object in the metal box was an envelope, and I put a hand in the way of Glacia's hand when she reached for it. "It's still not too late to start using your head." I said.

"Damn you, Mote," she said. And then she asked bitterly, "What would you suggest?" I thought she was going to take a swing at me, and I know she was considering it. "If it's another lecture about going to the police, you can just chew it up and swallow it again. I haven't done anything the police can arrest me for."

The police were out, I could see that. Glacia didn't want any part of them.

"The alternative," I said, "might be to break loose and tell old Mote all. I can't say I'm anxious to be the collection-plate for you troubles. But it might help."

"Help what? Your curiosity?"

She had something there. "Help me decide whether I'm heading for jail by associating with you." I said.

Glacia got angry again. She called me an impossible wench, and a damned fine travesty of a friend. It didn't mean too much the way she said it, I decided. She was putting on and taking off her emotions—rage, sentiment, fear, hesitation, decision—the nervous way a man about to be married probably tries different neckties.

"What went wrong with you?" she demanded. "Where did you go right after the body was found? You went somewhere, and something happened to jolt you. What was it?"

All right, you asked for it. I thought.

"I went to ask Doc Savage to investigate the mysterious murder of your Uncle Waldo," I said, and waited for that to sink in and take effect.

She fooled me. She didn't show surprise, or not much of it. She even seemed interested. And she was alert enough to guess what had happened.

"He turned you down," she said.

"That's right, and with trimmings, I agreed. "It wasn't just that I got turned down, either. It was being exposed to their curiosity and then tossed aside that burns me. They opened me like a box, looked in, didn't care for any, and pushed me out."

Glacia's lips were parted a little, as if she was all set to blow out a candle. Her way of showing breathless wonder. "What was he like?" she gasped.

"Eh?"

"Doc Savage... what was he like? Did you really get to talk with him, Mote? He must be a wonderful person."

"That big bronze chew!" I said. "I didn't see anything so wonderful about him."

Glacia began to look as if I was putting verbal toads in

the conversation. "Your trouble is, you're not impressed by anything!" she snapped. "Doc Savage has a reputation. Some people are scared stiff when they as much as hear of him. Why by just appearing here, he—"

She bit it off.

She had almost said something, then hadn't. She had nearly said that Doc Savage, by appearing here at the odd hotel, had caused something. Then she had caught herself, and hadn't said what. That was what she'd done. It was as clear as the nose on an anteater. But I did a delayed take on it—delayed about half an hour. At the moment, I didn't even notice that she'd almost said something. All my wheels weren't turning.

I said, "The great Doc Savage is a thin trickle as far as I'm concerned." We were still standing over the safe deposit box and I pointed at it. "That letter is addressed to you. Are you going to open it?"

Glacia opened the envelope that had been in Uncle Waldo's box, and writing on the one sheet of paper that was in it said:

My dear niece:

Feeling that death by violence may possibly come my way, I am penning these few words with the intention that they constitute my last will and testament.

I bequeath to you, Glacia Mae Loring, all my worldly property including Keeper. I ask you to take good care of Keeper. In case Keeper is not in your hands by the time you read this, I direct you to contact my attorney, C. V. McBride, Lathrop Bldg., Phone Cay 3-3101, Los Angeles, California, and have Keeper delivered to you.

(Signed) Waldo D. Loring.
(Witnessed) E. P. Cook.
(Witnessed) Royalton Dvorak.

This was dated two days previously.

"Is that a will?" Glacia asked blankly.

"It says so, and probably is," I told her. "What is this inheritance of yours?"

"Keeper?" Glacia stared at me foolishly. "I don't know what Keeper is. I haven't any idea."

"Oh, all right," I said wearily.

She seemed to think she had been called a liar, and said

sharply, "I really don't! It might be—oh, I don't know what. I haven't any idea."

"A profound mystery, eh?"

"Oh, stop acting as if I was pulling the legs off flies! What's got into you, anyway?"

I told her what was wrong. "I'm just getting a little tired of going in here and coming out there. With the same dumb look on my face."

She said that didn't make sense, and she didn't want to hear any more about it. She handed the strongbox—she kept the piece of jewelry and Waldo's letter—back to the hotel employee.

She was really angry with me. She didn't say where she was going. She just marched off, jamming the document in her purse, then carrying the purse clamped with both hands. I followed. Glacia was going back to our room, apparently, but she passed up the elevator and took the stairs. She did that to torment me, I imagined—I do not like stairsteps, because I go up and down them awkwardly and with a certain fear, having fallen twice and been injured while on a stairway. It isn't a phobia. I just avoid stairs whenever possible, and have done so since childhood. Following Glacia up them now, I wondered if she had chosen the steps deliberately to provoke me. It was not above her to do so.

On the other hand, Glacia, who was wiry and alert and objective, expressed her emotion with action. She was the kind of a person who walked off her troubles. Her answer, when someone else was feeling under the weather, was: "What you need is some exercise!" One of those people. She might be merely climbing the stairs because she was upset.

Possibly it wasn't important. Certainly there were bigger things to do my thinking about. There was murder, my boss hiding things from me, and there was Keeper.

"Race horse," I said.

"What?" Glacia asked.

"Keeper. Maybe Keeper is a race horse. We could get one of those turf annuals or magazines and look in it for a horse with that name."

Glacia didn't say anything.

It seemed to me there was quite a time when she didn't say anything. A long time. I got the idea it might be fifteen minutes or so.

"Well?" I said.

Glacia still didn't say anything.

"Well, could Keeper be a race horse?" I asked.

I didn't see Glacia, and she didn't answer. I looked around for her. I looked hard. All I could see was the ceiling.

"Well, could it?" I said. Then I said, "Well?" a couple more times. After that, I gave the word-making a rest.

Things were very odd. All that was up there was the ceiling. I seemed to be lying on my back on something, evidently a floor.

V

It took some time to accept the fact that I was on the stair landing exactly where I had been when I was asking Glacia whether Keeper could be a race horse, maybe. One square look showed that it was the stair landing, but accepting the fact took somewhat longer. But that's where I was. Now, why was I lying down?

I worried about having laid down for a while, then got to my feet. Apparently I was as good as new.

"What did you say?" Glacia's voice asked.

I turned around. She was sitting on the steps where they continued on upward from the landing.

She said, "A race horse? I don't know. Could be." She also got to her feet. She touched her blonde hair absently with a hand. "What happened? Did you fall down?"

"I don't know," I said truthfully.

"I didn't hear you fall," she said. "But you were on the floor."

"Why didn't you pick me up?" I asked.

"But I had barely turned—I didn't even hear you. You were getting up when I saw you."

"Look, honey, I'm getting damned tired of your denials!" I said sharply.

"What denials?"

"You were sitting down when I woke up. What were you doing, sitting there waiting for me to pick myself up?"

She opened her mouth. Denial was there. Then—her lips remained parted—she looked stunned. Shocked.

"I was—sitting down, wasn't I?" She mumbled.

"Glacia!"

She shook her head vacantly. She had trouble with her words, taking them out one at a time as if they were frightened little animals.

"What did—I don't understand—Oh, God, what happened to us, Mote?"

Her frightened small words dived into the silence and were gone.

Jumping forward, I seized her purse and opened it and found the envelope from the strongbox was still there. Uncle Waldo's last will and testament was intact in the envelope. I slid it back into the envelope, dropped that into the purse, and snapped the thing shut.

"Why did you do that?" Glacia asked wildly.

"Because I think we were unconscious. But don't ask me how long or from what cause."

She didn't ask me. I don't think she believed me—for a while. But then she did, and she said again, "I was sitting down, wasn't I?"

We went to our suite, and I told her, "Take a drink. You'll feel better." But she just sat on the edge of a chair, her fingers biting at things, breathing inward and outward deeply.

Later she took up the telephone and put in a call for Los Angeles, for the attorney mentioned in Uncle Waldo's testament, an attorney named C. V. McBride. The call went through, and she told McBride who she was, and that Waldo Loring was dead.

Attorney McBride's voice was deep, but staccato. I couldn't understand his words, but I could hear what his voice sounded like. Like a large drum being thumped.

The lawyer's deep voice began pumping and Glacia only managed to insert words, fragments of sentences. Things like: "Yes, Mr. McBride, I'm staying . . . But Mr. McBride . . . What is . . . This morning . . . But . . . What is Keeper . . . Yes." A "No," and three more "Yesses" finished up the conversation, and Glacia moved the telephone around in the air vaguely until it found the cradle.

There was confusion in her eyes as she told me, "He's coming at once. He's bringing Keeper."

"He had quite a few words, didn't he?"

Glacia folded her hands and said, "Damn him! He out-talked me!" This seemed to be a belated conclusion that she had just reached, and was angry about.

"I take it he didn't tell you what Keeper is."

"That's right. He didn't."

"And you didn't tell him much either," I reminded her dryly. "You left out several things, murder being one of them."

Glacia didn't say anything.

I asked, "Are you going to keep secrets from everybody?"

"You're fired!" Glacia snapped.

I got up and left the room, and as I was closing the door, she called "Mote!" sharply. I didn't look back nor go back. I closed the door behind me, hurried down the hall, took the stairs, and stopped in front of Doc Savage's suite.

The furry and amiable Monk Mayfair opened the door at my knock.

"Ah, the beautiful buffalo hunter," he said.

I pushed past him saying, "You've already demonstrated how funny you can be, so could we skip further proof?"

"Hey, now! There's no call to be—"

"Tell the Great Man I'm here for a re-take," I said. "Or do I just walk in?"

"You sound determined," Monk Mayfair scratched his neck with a fingernail. "I guess you *are* determined. Okay. But let me announce you. I was supposed to keep you out of here."

He crossed to a door and opened it, hung his head through and said, "She got in anyway, Doc. She has a look in her eye." He kept his head in the door for a while, then sighed. He told me, "I guess I'm in the doghouse," and held the door wider open.

Doc Savage was wiping his fingers on a towel. He stood beside what could have been a portable chemical laboratory— the table was covered with the odd-shaped glass gadgets that chemists use—and there was an odor of acid fumes in the air.

"Good morning," Doc Savage said.

He was big. I suddenly got all involved with trying to accept just how big he was. It wasn't just his physical size that I was feeling now, although there was plenty of that, without it being out of proportion, and without his being in any sense a physical freak—except that he could probably tie knots in horseshoes.

It was the intangible size of him that was flooring me. Because he was all that they said he was, and more. The way they had looked at him in the lobby yesterday, the awed way the phony Indian named Coming Going had spoken of him. Glacia's idea that I was a dope for not having heard of him—those were the things that had told me what he was. He was all they indicated. he was probably more.

I said, "You're Clark Savage Jr."

He seemed surprised. "Yes."

"I was pretty slow getting it," I told him. "For some reason or other, the name Doc Savage didn't mean what it should have. I guess I don't know how to meet a legend. Or don't know one when I meet it."

"I don't believe I understand—"

"I have heard of you the way little boys hear there's a pot of gold at the foot of rainbows," I explained. "But I'm not a little boy, nor even a little girl—I'm twenty-four years old. That's too old to believe in anything at the end of rainbows, except maybe rain. But a while ago, Glacia Loring and I went to sleep on a stairway. And then I knew."

He said, "Really?" The word meant two things—that he was suggesting I didn't know what I was talking about, and that he knew I wouldn't believe his suggesting.

"I've heard of that gas."

"Oh."

"I even remember where I heard about it," I said. "It was at one of those lectures the F.B.I. give law enforcement officials. The F.B.I. agent who lectured was named Grillquist, and he said that your anaesthetic gas had been considered for general police use, but that it wouldn't be used. It was too good. Crooks might get it, and use it on people, and the folks they used it on wouldn't know, because most of the time they wouldn't even know they had been gassed."

He didn't say anything. "This is quite interesting. It sounds fantastic."

"Not to me, now that I know you're a fantastic person . . . You did it to have a look at what Glacia had taken out of the strongbox downstairs, I suppose?"

"You take some mighty long jumps at conclusions."

"Just a hop, that time."

"Does your—ah—employer share your rather unusual hallucination?"

"Glacia? She hasn't said so. She hasn't said anything much, really. But I doubt it."

"I see."

"Glacia," I said, "is in the middle of some kind of a plot, and knows it."

"Indeed."

"She's scared stiff. But she's not giving up. She's going it alone, if necessary. She just fired me."

"You're probably fortunate."

"Lucky that she fired me, you mean?... No. No, because I think the silly little blonde is going to need help, and I'm going to stick by her."

He thought deeply. The thing he was thinking about was whether or not he should shake his head negatively. He shook it.

He said, "If I were you, I'd catch the one o'clock bus for Los Angeles."

"No, if you were me you wouldn't do anything of the sort. I've heard about you, remember. If you had a friend who was foolish enough to let greed get her into trouble, you'd stick."

He said nothing to that.

"She telephoned the attorney and he's bringing the inheritance," I said.

It was hard to tell whether he reacted to that. His flake gold eyes weren't composed. But they were not composed at any time—the gold in them seemed always in motion, alert, wary. Presently I found I was staring at his eyes and they were getting some sort of hypnotic spell on me, or I thought they were. I stopped staring.

"You're in this yourself," I said. "I think you were in it before I was."

"Indeed?"

"That's just an idea that came to me. Would you mind verifying it?"

"You should catch that bus," he said.

I stood up. "All right. Not all right about the bus—just all right, I see I'm not getting anywhere with you. I just thought I'd drop in and let you know I'd figured out that fainting stuff.... And to get another look at the great Doc Savage. The first look didn't count. You have to know what you're looking at, to appreciate scenery."

If he thought I meant that as flattery—and I didn't—he did not rise to it. "You've made the morning interesting," he said.

Maybe he was just being cagey. But on the chance that he was being smug, I pointed at the chemistry stuff on the table. "Notice you were doing an iodine vapor check for latent fingerprints. How's it turning out? Find out who killed Waldo Loring?"

For the first time he showed a little emotion. He looked slightly pained. He crossed to the door, opened it, followed me through. Monk Mayfair was in the other room, and Savage told him, "Our visitor has an active imagination."

Monk Mayfair was looking at my legs. His lips phrased but he did not say aloud, that was not all I had. He got to his feet, assisted Doc Savage with the goodbyes—and I got a pretty good idea of what he would presently do, and was not surprised when he did it. He opened the door after I had left and was walking down the hall, and said, "Oh, by the way, Miss Mote."

I stopped. Monk came up. "I said, "It's either Mote, or Miss Trunnels, but not Miss Mote, please. Don't tell me I forgot my handkerchief."

"You were probably very careful not to do that," he said amiably. "Look, I didn't follow you just to shine my eyes at you, although that would be interesting too. I've got a question. . . . Are you going to stick with this thing?"

"If you mean stick with my friend Glacia, that's what I plan."

"Okay. Then I got a wee bit of advice. Be careful of new friendships."

"Eh?"

"In new acquaintances can lie danger, whereas old friends are to be trusted, or at least you know which one of them is a stinker."

I looked at him for a moment. "How do you want that interpreted. You sound like a thirty-cent fortune teller."

He grinned. He was so utterly homely that there was something pleasant about his grinning. "It's just a dab of wisdom. Tee it up and take a mental swing at it if you have spare time."

"You mean there's going to be a tall dark man in my life?"

"Search me. The tall and dark ones I wouldn't worry so much about, though."

"How about short ones?"

"If they're short and wide, and run quite a lot to jaw, I'd walk as if I was on eggs."

"Would those that look like that have names?" I asked him.

"Names can be changed. Jaws can't."

"Thanks, pal," I said.

Glacia had a reception ready for me when I got back to our suite. She had the door locked, but the purple carpet of welcome was spread out inside. The door was merely locked because Glacia was scared stiff—she was so frightened that she didn't trust herself to recognize my voice, but made me repeat the name of the kid who had put the civet cat in the teacher's desk when we were going to school in Kansas City. The kid's name was Dan Burton, and I came near not being able to remember it. Then Glacia unlocked the door and threw her arms around me. She made my shoulder wet with tears, told me several different ways that she was glad to see me and then swore at me. "Damn you, Mote, why did you walk out like that? I thought you had deserted me."

"The way I heard it, I was fired."

"Don't be silly," Glacia said. "You just had me upset, is all."

"Upset? Honey, your nerves are vibrating like harp strings."

"Pshaw! I'm all right."

"Uh-huh. Do you know a short, fat man with a jaw?"

She gave me a thoroughly blank look. "What are you talking about?"

"I had another round with Doc Savage," I said. "This time I was properly respectful—or anyway I knew I was before the master. He didn't admit a thing, but he did put out a piece of advice—leave the lodge. But his court jester, that Monk Mayfair, followed me out in the hall and was a little more explicit. He said to beware of a short fat man with a jaw, who would be a new acquaintance."

"All men have jaws," Glacia said woodenly.

"I gather this one is special.... Glacia, why are you looking like that?"

The way she was looking was somewhat the same as when she had walked into our room that morning and told me how Waldo Loring was wearing his brains on his face. But she didn't faint this time. Instead, she dived for the telephone. She put in a call for the lawyer in Los Angeles.

Waiting for the phone call to go through, Glacia looked at the floor, the walls, at nothing, and used a voice that was two tones higher to ask me, "Is Doc Savage—did he come here to the lodge because of—of Uncle Waldo?"

"You do the guessing," I said.

When the Los Angeles connection was made, her voice went up another tone, and she demanded to speak to Lawyer McBride. The reply she got was a quick piece of news. She hung up.

"He's left. He's already on his way here."

"With Keeper?"

"I—suppose so."

"Why didn't you ask whoever you talked to what Keeper is?"

"I—" Her eyes went different places, helping her mind hunt for words. "I never thought of it," she said.

"Or you already know what Keeper is."

Glacia shook her head dumbly. "Mote, I really don't know."

She didn't get mad, so probably she didn't know. And after that she wouldn't get ten feet from me. But she wouldn't tell me of what she was afraid, or what she thought might happen. I felt sorry for her. I seemed to be the only person she trusted, and she was too frightened to trust me much.

I spent about an hour with my imagination, picturing different things that could happen when the lawyer got here, different things Keeper could be, and various ways of being a murder victim. By that time, I had scared myself into needing sunlight and fresh air badly, so I suggested a walk, and Glacia agreed. Rather, I said I was going for a walk and Glacia, following her new policy of staying within two jumps of me, reached for her own hat.

It didn't occur to me that things might not wait to happen until the lawyer got here.

VI

The portly gentleman was about fifty, gray-haired, with a distinguished face that ran extraordinarily to jaw, and he managed to carry more air of dignity than one would have thought could be gotten away with by a ponderous old boy in a bathing suit.

The dubious redskin, Coming Going, brought him up and introduced him.

"Mr. Montgomery, ladies," said Coming Going. "Heap anxious meet you. Okay?"

We were sitting near the pool trying to look as if we were enjoying a couple of cold drinks, and as far as I was concerned, it wasn't okay. Mr. Montgomery had too much jaw for me to want any part of him.

"Goodbye," Coming Going said suddenly. He must have been watching my face.

"Mr. Going," I said, standing quickly. "Will you show me your tribal totem pole. The one you were talking about." I took his arm and hurried him into the thicket of different kinds of cactus, mostly as large as trees, which bordered the pool and made the lodge grounds a thorny jungle. When we were out of sight on the path, I stopped the puzzled redskin.

"Now," I asked, "where did you get him?"

"Ugh. What tribal totem pole?" he asked.

"Never mind that, Hiawatha. The fat man with the jaw—where did you get him?"

"Didn't. He got me."

"He asked you to introduce him to us? How come?"

"Service to guests." He was uncomfortable, and took off his heap-big-Indian manner and explained, "He asked me did I know you two girls, and I said yes before I thought, and he asked would I introduce him, and I thought of how hard good soft jobs are hard to find these days, and so I did: Did I do wrong?"

"Is fat jaw—Mr. Montgomery—a guest here at this dopey hotel?"

"Sure."

"How long has he been here?"

"Couple of weeks."

"By any chance did he arrive about the same time as my girl friend?"

Coming Going shook his head and the feather that was always getting out of order dropped over one eye. "Before her. He got here about two days after her uncle arrived, the way I recall it."

"What else do you know about Mr. Montgomery?"

"He's a mining man—he says. His daughter and a gentleman secretary are with him. Daughter's name is Colleen. Gentleman secretary's name is Roy."

"How come I haven't noticed them, or at least Mr. Montgomery—around?"

He was fiddling with the feather. "They have been staying pretty close to their rooms."

"Do you know anything else I should know, Tecumseh?"

He grinned and shook his head. "It's my turn to ask a question. I hear your friend's uncle met with an accident. This odd curiosity of yours got anything to do with that?"

"Accident—is that what they call it around here when a guest gets his brains bashed in?"

That shocked him. The feather fell over his eye. His jaw sagged. Everything else had gone out of him to make room for the surprise, and genuine surprise it was.

I walked off and left him. I thought I had him measured now. A nice young boy, no more an Indian than I was, who liked the play-acting that went with his job. Probably he was a thwarted actor from Hollywood. Murder had floored him, and he was no doubt thinking that I was a hard case. He wasn't fooling with his feather, the last I saw of him.

I went back to the table near the swimming pool. Glacia was worried about me. She jumped to her feet when she saw me, and then sat down again, rather weakly with relief.

"You shouldn't run off like that, Mote," she wailed.

"Relax," I said. "The redmen aren't taking scalps today."

Mr. Montgomery sat at the table. He leaned down, brought Glacia's purse into view, and placed it on the table—conveying the idea, he no doubt hoped, that she had dropped the purse and he had picked it up.

"I don't believe the boy is an Indian at all," he said cheerfully. "Most of them around here aren't. Or am I disillusioning you two young ladies? I'm very sorry."

"Sorry enough to let us stick you for a drink?" I asked, pulling out my chair.

He said he was that sorry, and began waving at a waiter.

He was a well-cared-for old man, all right. He might not be as old as the white hair and the dignity made him seem. He might even be as young as fifty. He was certainly browned by the sun; it had taken a lot of sun to brown him that much; he must have spent years sitting around beaches and swimming pools in a bathing suit with a good drink in his hand. The fingers of his right hand were permanently curled from holding good drinks.

Finally my wondering settled down on one point. What had he taken from Glacia's purse, and where had he hidden it? His tight bathing trunks didn't offer much space for hiding things.

Mr. Montgomery got the attention of a waiter, and began ordering for us. He didn't ask what we wanted. He just said he had something special, and told the waiter what it was, and how the bartender should make it. That took some time.

A young man came around the corner of the hotel. He stood looking at us. He was a rather slender young man with a round baby-like face and soft brown eyes. He was wearing a white linen suit, white shoes, white shirt and a startlingly yellow necktie.

The newcomer did not approach, but gazed at us with puppy-like friendliness. He wanted to approach.

Mr. Montgomery stopped in the middle of telling the waiter how the bartender should pour the creme de menthe over a spoon just so. Presently he smiled rather strangely. He smiled at the young man. The smile would have frozen grain alcohol.

"Yes, sir?" said the waiter hopefully.

Mr. Montgomery gave him the rest of the recipe. He probably slighted the rest of it. Then he arose and went to another table and picked up a chased silver cigar case, a lighter and a heavy knobbed walking stick. He came back with these.

The young man raised his eyebrows. There was a question, and a prayer, in the gesture.

"You'll love the drink I have ordered," said Mr. Montgomery to us. He spoke vaguely. "It's a specialty I picked up—ah—in Cairo."

"Cairo, Illinois?" I asked.

"Eh?"

The young man had taken a tentative step forward. Mr. Montgomery renewed the ice in his smile. He lifted the walking stick and stroked it with his hand.

The young man in white stopped. There was a butterfly almost as yellow as his necktie fooling around a cactus that grew out of an urn nearby.

"Cairo, Egypt, then," I said.

The young man raised and lowered his eyebrows. He turned and went away. Just before he disappeared, he held both hands out at his sides, the palms up, in a gesture of resignation.

"Was it Cairo, Egypt?" I asked.

Mr. Montgomery closed his eyes tightly, and they remained shut for a moment. Then he picked up his cigar case and looked in it and it was empty.

"Will you excuse me a moment, girls," Mr. Montgomery said. "I must get some cigars. My special brand. Will you forgive my absence briefly."

He tucked the walking stick under his arm and went away. His jaw did not seem so prominent, oddly enough.

"Glacia," I said. "Let's see what he got out of your purse."

She looked at me, eyes and mouth three round circles in a round face. "What?" she gasped. Then she snatched at her purse, wrenched it open, and dug into the contents. "Oh my God! It's gone!"

"What is gone?"

"The envelope—Uncle Waldo's will." Her face flamed with rage. "That old man—why, damn him! He won't get away with something like that!"

Glacia sprang up and raced off in the direction Mr. Montgomery had taken. She was angry enough to have forgotten that she considered me a bodyguard.

I didn't follow her. I sat there and chewed over a theory I had. Mr. Montgomery's jaw had seemed prominent as anything when he first arrived at the table, and hadn't later on. There was a reason for that. The jaw, when he first came, had been in motion. Mr. Montgomery had been chewing gum then.

It was a good process of reasoning. Sherlock Holmes and J. Edgar Hoover never had a better basis for deduction. I was proud of it.

I moved to the chair Mr. Montgomery had occupied, put my hands under the table—and didn't feel so puffed up. But I wasn't going to let any fat man with a jaw make a fool out of me. I shed dignity, got down on hands and knees, and looked at the underside of the table as if I was reading hieroglyphics.

It was all right. He had just been cunning, and used his chewing gum to stick the envelope to the bottom of the table in front of my chair. He was cute, all right.

A cute fat man. I looked at the outside of the envelope to make sure it was Uncle Waldo's testament and at the inside to see whether the works were still there. They were. I scraped off Mr. Montgomery's chicle and tucked the thing inside my frock where no one with good manners would find it.

I was getting to my feet, and hurried it up considerably when Glacia began screaming. She was doing her yelling off to the left somewhere in the jungle of cactus and desert plants. I and at least twenty other people ran in the direction of Glacia's shrieking, but a dozen others had arrived ahead of us.

Glacia, suddenly without noise, was pointing at the base of a cactus thicket. Her whole arm shook somewhat.

It was the young man in white. He lay on both shoulders and one hip and one leg was extended, the other leg drawn up and bent at the knee in the position for riding a bicycle. His white suit contrasted, alabaster to absinthe, with the palmetto dagger-like leaves.

His tanned face now had a mongrel coloring; it was marble that had received one coat of inadequate walnut stain. The blood that had left his nostrils was not much, but it had run down—his head was cocked up by the rocks on which it rested—and made a startling woodpecker's head blotch on the gay yellow of his necktie.

I looked hard for death in his face. I couldn't tell. His facial muscles were loose, but there was still some of the puppy-dog friendliness with which he had gazed at Glacia, myself and Mr. Montgomery a bit earlier.

Somebody got down on their knees beside him and began saying, "Hello, there!" in a shrilly voice, as if they were talking to a baby.

If he doesn't answer, I thought, I'm going to exercise feminine rights and scream like hell.

Just in case he didn't answer, I got away from there. It wasn't easy. I didn't know who he was, who had bopped him, why, how. . . . My bump of curiosity about him had grown into moose antlers. But I got away from there. I was worried about Glacia.

A quick pass through the cactus jungle in the vicinity got me nothing but lack of breath. Glacia was not around. Ice began to collect around the roots of my hair.

I went into the hotel, found the fellow who had given Glacia the strong-box to open, and handed him the envelope that Mr. Montgomery had temporarily lifted. "Can you put this back in Miss Loring's box?" I asked.

He shook his head and said, "Not without her key, or a

meeting of the board of directors, practically. You see, there are only two keys to each box. The guest gets one, and the other is in escrow as it were—you have to convince about six people you're entitled to use it."

"But I want you to keep this envelope—"

"Why not a box for yourself. It's included in the service. No charge."

The simple solution left me speechless. I watched him arrange the lock box, signed something, put the key in my purse and said, "Will you have Miss Loring paged?"

"Certainly."

In the course of the next five minutes, I wore the upholstery off a lobby chair with my squirming. Glacia wasn't answering to the paging.

I tried the clerk again. "Can you give me Mr. Montgomery's suite number?"

We were old friends now. He gave me the information without an argument. Mr. Montgomery was in the second floor corner suite, northeast exposure.

The second floor hall was cool, almost cold after the desert heat of noontime beside the pool. The air was redolent of sage. They probably had a machine that manufactured the odor and squirted it into the conditioning system.

I listened at what I had been told was Mr. Montgomery's door for a long time, for such a long time that I grew weak as from starvation. Nothing in the rooms on the other side of the door made any more noise than a fly scrubbing his eyes, so I tried the knob. It turned. I pushed on the door. It opened. I gave it a little shove, and it swung wide and hit the wall with a little bump. Later I went in.

It was a wonderful room. Plenty of room for a couple of Russian ambassadors, with huge solid plate glass windows that picture-framed the mountains, and doors to the right and doors to the left. The plurality of doors was bothersome—my mind by now wasn't in a state where it could make a choice readily, even a choice between two doors. Right or left, which should it be? Finally I just started walking. Left, it happened.

That door also opened readily—into a bathroom. The color motif here was pastel blue and green against ivory, and the place was neatly departmentalized. Each department was enclosed in a little glass booth of its own, booths of etched glass and chrome. I tried to imagine how a stuffed buffalo would look in here.

"Good intentions are sometimes like curiosity," said a voice. "Except that I don't know that good intentions kill cats." It was Mr. Montgomery's voice.

I turned around. Mr. Montgomery was backing out of a door across the large room, and he had spoken to someone in the bedroom beyond the door.

He took his time turning to face me, and by then I wasn't there. I was in the shower stall, with the etched glass door closed.

VII

Mr. Montgomery moved over to the table, picked up his walking stick and examined it; with a slight grimace, he picked a brownish hair, complete with root, from the heavy head of the cane, carried it into the bathroom and washed it down the drain. Then he applied soap to the cane, scrubbed it, towelled it dry, and placed it by the window in the sunlight where it would dry.

He did none of this with much urgency, nor was his manner anything but placidly brisk, the air of an elderly gentleman who was self-satisfied.

I saw part of what he was doing—the shower booth door was sprung and wouldn't quite close, leaving enough crack for observation, and to scare me stiff—and there were enough assorted sounds to keep me posted about the rest of his activity.

Meantime, the sound of a typewriter, in the sporadic rushes of creative composition, had started coming from the adjoining room.

Mr. Montgomery tipped a finger of Scotch into a glass, added ice and a jump of soda, then a second hiss of soda after he had tasted the drink. He carried the glass along and went to investigate the typing.

By moving my head half an inch, I could see from the bathroom across the living-room into the other room where the typist sat.

She was a smooth, polished svelte number of about twenty-five with dark hair and rather small features. Strictly a custom job. Her slight excess of lipstick was used well, although her large harlequin glasses needed a more exotic face.

Mr. Montgomery was gazing over her shoulder at what she had been typing.

Presently he chuckled. "Very effective, Colleen. I imagine, if I were the young man, I should palpitate. Passionate sentiments, very." He rocked gently on his heels. His smile was contemplative. He added, "Dryden, I think it was, who said: 'Pains of love be sweeter far, than all other pleasures are.'"

His Colleen took two puffs off a cigarette. "If you think I'm in love with the guy, you're nuts."

Her father—he was her father; you could see signs of family resemblance—seemed pleased with that. "That pleases me, my dear. Young Swanberg was an impressionable, callow, easily deluded jackass. His one asset, an overabundance of wealth, hardly entitled him to a passing grade in this life."

The daughter laughed. "Scram, Monty, will you. I can't compose this stuff with you grinning over my shoulder."

"Why compose it at all, my dear? Why bother?"

"Any old port in a storm," she said, shrugging. "If there should be a storm."

Mr. Montgomery's eyes glittered like knife steel. "There won't be."

She swung around slightly to face him. "There could be. After all, you could have hit Roy—"

"The fool! The disobedient oaf!" said Mr. Montgomery bitterly.

"Are you sure you didn't hit him hard enough to crack his head?"

"Bosh! You underestimate both the thickness of Roy's cranium and my experience. As a matter of fact, I also tapped him on the parietal, well back of the coronal suture, which is a substantial area of the skull. When you have occasion to hit a man with a cane, my dear, pick that spot." The old gentleman sipped his drink. "Roy will carry a substantial headache as a reminder. That is all."

"Roy," said his daughter, "didn't mean anything."

"Well, I certainly did when I hit him!" said her father.

"Roy was lonesome. I hadn't been entertaining him according to his ideas of entertainment. His taste runs to blondes, and pretty cheap ones."

"Lonesome, eh? Not as lonesome as he could become in Alcatraz. Even though, as is well within the bounds of reason, he might have us along for company."

Colleen shuddered. "Do you have to put such damned ugly ideas in well-rounded words, pop? Why not just say Roy might get us all in the pokey by showing himself where Doc Savage could see him?"

Mr. Montgomery waved his drink distastefully. "Let's omit Savage from the conversation. I'm allergic to the man's name. It makes me nervous."

The hall door opened. I couldn't see who had come in, but the way the Montgomery family jumped to see the arrival was impressive.

"Ah!" said Mr. Montgomery. He sounded relieved, as if he had nearly fallen into a tank of ice water.

Roy stumbled into view—the boy in white with the yellow necktie. To a nervous man in a business suit who was with him, he expostulated. "I'm all right. I fell, is all. How many times do I have to tell you that?" The man, evidently an assistant hotel manager, said the expected things about the hotel regretting any accidents and then left.

Sheepishly, Roy glanced at Mr. Montgomery. He did not say anything. He went over and lowered himself in a chair and laid his head back gingerly against the chair. His eyebrows went up, down, painfully.

"Colleen," said Mr. Montgomery with bitter sweetness. "Will you be so kind as to place a cold ice compress on Roy's head."

Colleen came into the bathroom for a towel. I could name her perfume. Forty dollars an ounce. I tried to remember whether I had used any perfume myself that morning, and couldn't remember even a little thing like that.

Roy sat in gray-faced shame while Colleen dumped ice in the towel and handed it to him. The glances that came from his brown eyes were injured ones

Mr. Montgomery kicked the dog while he was down.

"Well, Roy, how did you like your brief look about the hotel?" he asked blandly.

Roy winced. "It was all right."

"Up to a point, you mean?"

"Yes. Up to a point."

"The point should have happened earlier. Prior to the

ecution of your foolish deed—in other words, before you
epped out of this suite."

"Okay," Roy mumbled.

"Common sense, if not respect for my commands, should
ve induced you to stay bottled up here."

"Don't rub it in," Roy muttered.

The old man's jaw was quite prominent now. "I shall rub
I I damned please, and you shall like it," he said.

"Yes, sir."

"I am—I really am, Roy—irritated with you. Of our
oup, the only one Doc Savage might recognize is yourself.
ould he get one glimpse of you, imagine what might
ppen."

"But Savage only saw me once, years ago," Roy complained.

"Yes, Roy, but the man's mind is a photographic record.
et us not, at this late stage, start underestimating Savage."

"Yes, sir," said Roy. "Who were the babes I saw you
lking with? The pocket-sized blonde . . . she's old Waldo's
ece. Right?"

"Correct."

"Then the other one would be the lady sleuth she
ought on from New York as a friend in need."

"Correct again."

"The lady shamus wasn't a bad looker. But should we
orry about her the way you've been worrying?"

Mr. Montgomery scowled at Roy for long enough for me
 feel surprised that I had given anybody cause for worry.
hey were afraid of Doc Savage. They were afraid of me, too.
hat put me in the big league. I felt rather puffed up.

Making a little speech, Mr. Montgomery said, "Roy, you
ve been using your brain. That is a poisonous thing. We
se only one brain around here—mine. I did hope you
nderstood that."

"I understand it," Roy said uneasily.

"You are a stupid incompetent, Roy," said Mr. Montgomery
ith the heedlessly playful air of a farmer discussing a coming
utchering with the hog he is going to butcher. "There is too
uch involved in this affair—in case you feel I am being
verly severe—to take any chances."

"Oh, I know—"

"You know from nothing, Roy! Let me point out the
ndamentals to you."

The fat man stuck three fingers of his right hand under

Roy's nose and began bending the fingers one at a time as he enumerated points.

"One," he said. "Old Waldo Loring had a secret fabulous value to sell."

He bent down that finger.

"Two," he continued. "Waldo Loring approached me serve as broker. He knew I had contacts with people wh would pay handsomely for what he possessed. But we cou not come to terms—the old sea dog didn't want to pay me proper commission."

Down went another finger.

"Three. I thereupon began bending my efforts towa acquiring the fabulous item by whatever means feasible."

He had run out of fingers. That bothered him, and l frowned at his hand. He solved the problem by starting ov again with three more fingers.

"Four," he said. "Waldo Loring was brained by a prowl he caught searching his room. This was unfortunate, becau a dead Waldo could not be induced to tell where he sa that—ahem—where is hidden the item he had for sale."

He paused to shake his head and cluck sadly over th development.

"Five. Waldo Loring was throughout a man frightene by the incredible magnitude and deviltry of the deed he w trying to perpetrate, and in his fear he sought comfort fro the presence of his niece, Miss Glacia Loring. He invited he to join him here. I do not know how much of the truth h told her—but he told her some, because she in turn wa terrified and had recourse to the only friend she probab has, this lady sleuth from New York."

He was down to the last finger again, and he knocke that one off quickly.

"Six," he said. "Miss Loring has inherited an unknow quantity called Keeper. She apparently doesn't know wh Keeper is. But we know—and she must suspect—that Keep er is the answer to where old Waldo Loring's secret now lies

Through with the fingers, he rubbed his hands togethe briskly, then picked up his drink again.

Roy grunted. "You left out plenty. How did Doc Savag happen to get wind of it and show up here? That's what I like to know."

"That's not a fundamental. I just gave you the fundamen

:als. And the conclusion you should draw is this: We must lie
.ow and grab Keeper when the latter appears."

"Huh? And not bother about Savage, I suppose?" said
Roy skeptically.

"Bother? How do you mean? Concern ourselves over
how he got a smell of the affair? That would be pointless. It's
easily explained, anyway, if you use a little imagination.... Waldo
Loring's secret was of such magnitude that its existence has
no doubt traveled the grapevines, and it wouldn't surprise me
:o find that Doc Savage is here representing the interests of
:he nation. Does that sound too startling, Roy? It shouldn't.
The destiny of humanity might well be at stake here, Roy.
Savage is a humanitarian, in his rather unorthodox way."

Roy closed his eyes and didn't say anything. He apparently thought the portly old gentleman was using too many
words. So did I.

"You mustn't disobey orders, Roy," said Mr. Montgomery.
He was a man who liked the sound of his own voice,
apparently. He continued, "Actually, Roy, we should both be
able to retire after this job. Retirement, you being a young
man, may lack appeal. But if you wish, and we are successful,
I imagine you could, young as you are, put yourself out to
pasture the rest of your days. Now you understand why my
feelings were a bit urgent when I tapped you with the cane."

Roy grimaced. "I don't see why you had to knock me
cold. It made a rumpus."

"My temper got the best of me," said the fat man
blandly. "I'll tell you why. I haven't mentioned it.... While I
was sitting at the table near the pool with the two young
ladies, I filched from Glacia's purse an envelope containing
Waldo Loring's testament."

Roy brightened and sat up straight. "You think it'll tell
where—"

"We shall never know, I'm afraid," said Mr. Montgomery
bitterly.

"Huh?"

"Listen carefully, Roy. I stuck that envelope to the
underside of the table with a bit of chicle. Then you appeared
and upset me so that I went to hunt you and urge you to
return to our rooms. I did not find you at first, and then I
chanced to observe Glacia's friend in the act of recovering the
envelope from beneath the table. She had found it. I was

naturally enraged with you, and when soon afterward I foun
you, I expressed my feelings."

"Good God!" Roy blurted. "They're wise to you?"

"Thanks to you, I'm sorry to say," agreed Mr. Montgomery

Whereupon Mr. Montgomery slapped Roy. The fat han
was a broad poisonous serpent's head; it darted out and ther
was a pop of flesh on flesh. It must have been a harder sla
than seemed logical, because Roy fell back in the chair agair
and his eyes turned in their sockets like white mice investi
gating their own tails.

"My dear boy," said the fat man. "I'm very irritated,
assure you."

I wasn't exactly irritated, but neither was my mind goin
tra-la. I hadn't dreamed that Mr. Montgomery had observe
me finding the envelope—and it followed naturally that h
knew what I had done with it after finding it. If he sti
wanted it, I might be in for some trouble. Because M
Montgomery was a lot worse article than I had anticipated.

Where was Glacia? I still didn't know that, and the fac
that the fat man hadn't mentioned doing Glacia any harn
within the last half hour didn't mean a thing. There wer
probably many things in Mr. Montgomery's life that he wasn
mentioning. The things he didn't mention were the ones t
worry about.

I began to have a vague idea that I'd underestimate
almost everyone and everything. I'd underrated the fat man
I'd missed the boat on Doc Savage—because I hadn't reall
believed he was involved. Oh, I'd told him he was. I'd tol
Glacia he was. But I'd been telling something I didn't quit
believe. As for mysteries and fabulous secrets—well, I hadn
even been playing in that league.

I'd supposed the thing, even if it was pretty complicated
would be a matter of Uncle Waldo having done someone
dark deed, and the donee getting even with the donor for it
It seemed there was slightly more to it than that.

Apparently I now knew everything but a couple o
salient facts. Uncle Waldo'd gotten hold of something terrific
and he'd tried to sell it, and the selling had gotten a trifl
complex and now Uncle Waldo was dead and nobody knev
the whereabouts of the merchandise Waldo'd had on th
market. That was what the scuffling was about. Where wa
the button?

Mr. Montgomery had just gone over all this with Roy

but I went over it again just to be sure. It sounded far-fetched, even though I had stood in a shower bath booth and heard it. But I was sure it was true. Mr. Montgomery had left out just enough to make it sound like truth—he had left out what Uncle Waldo's secret was, and he'd omitted the matter of who murdered Waldo. He knew the details. Or he'd guessed at them. It followed that he might know who killed Waldo, or might be the one who had done it.

Probably I wasn't gaining a thing by standing here re-stating facts to myself. But it made me feel better, so I did it. Far better, it was not long developing, that I should have looked to business closer at hand—was there, for instance, a bathroom window through which I could make a flying exit?"

There was no window, but maybe it would have done no good anyway. Because Mr. Montgomery's voice, not quite calmly, said, "I don't know what bard said familiarity placed a blindness on one. Maybe one didn't say it. He should have."

He had the shower booth door open by then. He was fast for a fat man, which was no surprise. Not nearly as much a surprise as seeing such a large gun in his hand. Somehow I'd imagined him as a deft old gentleman who disdained firearms.

"It was a long time dawning on me that a shower curtain doesn't have quite your silhouette, young lady," he said.

He must not have liked the way my head went back.

"Don't!" he said. "Don't scream. I shouldn't like it."

It was a good thing he said that. I didn't want to do anything he shouldn't like. Not when he had that look on his chubby face, lips loose like a kid's collapsed toy balloon, eyes big and all whites like boiled eggs.

"Colleen," he called over his shoulder. "Colleen, will you step in here and bolster me in misfortune."

Colleen came forward walking with lithe strides. She looked about as scared as a cat at its cream saucer. "It's Nell-the-girl-detective," she said. "Well, snatch my girdle and call me unrestrained!"

"Search her," said Mr. Montgomery.

Colleen did an experienced job with her hands, and I was invited into the living room. Roy still sat in the chair and did not look any different, except that he had probably forgotten his headache.

"What I want somebody to tell me is how the hell she got in here?" remarked Colleen.

"That really should concern you, since she entered while you were here alone, obviously." Mr. Montgomery didn't sound too kindly toward his daughter. "Your search was also inadequate. Take her into the bedroom. Find that envelope containing Waldo Loring's final testament."

"I'm afraid of her," Colleen said with disapproval. "Me alone in there with her? She'll probably wring my neck."

Mr. Montgomery said coldly, "I am in a frame of mind to enjoy the act by proxy if she does. Get going. Find that will."

Colleen got me into the bedroom. There were two of the latter connecting with the suite, I noticed. "Pops is in a bad mood, honey," Colleen told me. "I'd be very meek, if I were you."

I didn't argue the point about her father's mood. If she said it was bad, I would take her word for it. I was convinced he had brained Waldo Loring while feeling a bit irritated, the way he was now.

One search didn't satisfy Colleen. She did it over, then inventoried my purse, sneering at the brand of my lipstick, and counting my few dollars before she folded them neatly and tucked them in her stocking. She wasn't happy about settling for the receipt for the lockbox they'd given me downstairs, but she settled for it. She carried it in and tossed it down before fat papa.

"She probably locked it up," she said. Then, not liking the boiled egg look her father's eyes got again, she added hastily. "That's right. They stamp the time on those receipts. That one is stamped not more than forty minutes ago."

Mr. Montgomery scooped up the receipt, eyed it, threw it on the floor.

He swept up the gun. "Step over here, dear," he said.

I stood exactly where he wanted me to stand. The look in his eye told me where. I stopped there, and registered as much cooperation as I could.

I wasn't scared. I was paralyzed.

He asked, "You have a good memory? You will recite the exact contents of that document. Beginning in five seconds."

"I don't remember," I said.

That was the wrong thing. I should have waggled my mouth around and let nothing but squeaks of terror come out. I should have been too scared to speak. That wouldn't have been hard to do, if I had thought of it.

Mr. Montgomery drew in a deep breath, a deep one. And he smiled. A little smile.

Roy came up out of the chair. He didn't stand up. He just seemed to rise somewhat on the cushions, as if he were being, hauled up by the hair. His face looked that way too.

"Father!" Colleen screamed.

They knew him, so they must know what his expressions meant. I didn't know him, but I thought I understood his grimace too. Because it wasn't really a smile.

He was going to kill me. Shoot me. He was a suave, egotistical, show-offish old gentleman with too much soft flesh and too many words. But he was blowing his cork.

The only reason he didn't shoot me—quite a good reason it was, too—was the loud noise knuckles made on the door.

Someone at the door didn't change Mr. Montgomery's glazed madness. But it electrified his daughter and Roy.

Roy pushed Mr. Montgomery down into an overstuffed chair. He tried to take the gun away from the old man, but Mr. Montgomery wouldn't give it up, so Roy compromised by shoving the old fellow's hand down beside him, between the cushion and the side of the chair—the hand and the gun.

Colleen grabbed me and hustled me into the bedroom. The last I saw of Roy for the nonce, he was walking toward the door with his eyes wide and tragic. The fist was banging the door again.

I heard who the visitor was. I was in the bedroom, but I recognized the voice.

"Heap sorry," it said. "Got short-circuit in wiring."

Coming Going. My redskin pal.

"There's no trouble with the wiring in here," Roy told him. Roy sounded all right. A little shaky with the last couple of words.

"In switchbox," Coming Going argued. "Got to take a look. Electricity in other rooms won't work. Fuse box in here. Take a minute. Okay."

"There's no switchbox in here, you crazy Indian."

"Look anyway. Okay?"

At this point, I woke up to the fact that there was a man outside the bedroom window. He was standing there, apparently on thin air, but probably on a ladder. I knew him. another pal. Monk Mayfair.

Now that I had finally discovered him, Monk Mayfair shrugged—the shrug meant I'd certainly taken my time about noticing him—and then he made little circles in the air with a finger. Indicating I should persuade Colleen to turn around. He illustrated my next move for me—he popped himself on the jaw with a fist.

"Colleen," I said. "There's a man behind you."

She had a little gun. Where she'd gotten it from I didn't know. She sneered over the gun and said, "Nuts, darling."

"There really is."

"Keep your voice down," she breathed viciously.

"Oh, but there really—"

Monk Mayfair helped out by tapping on the window. Whereupon Colleen went off as if she had exploded. Her arms flew out from her sides much as if she was spreading them preparatory to flying. Her mouth opened, but whether she would have screamed I never knew, because I closed the mouth again, hard. It wasn't a very orthodox punch. I think I used both hands. Both at once, the way you lift a heavy weight.

VIII

Colleen took plenty of time deciding to drop. The small gun fell. She showed lots of eye whites, let her arms down to her sides, managed two steps backward and one to the right, before deciding on the floor.

I was already passing her. The window was locked. I unfastened it. Monk Mayfair started to climb inside, which complicated matters. because I was endeavoring to climb out.

"Take it easy," he said.

"Get out of my way," I said.

A gun went off in the living-room. If there had been any preliminaries in the way of words, they had been softly spoken. But the gun was definitely loud, almost as noisy as the second one that answered it.

I passed Monk Mayfair. Probably I crawled over him. I went down the ladder, and halfway I passed Doc Savage. I had never imagined two people could pass on a ladder with so few formalities.

"Is it safe to go into the hotel room?" he asked.

"Certainly not," I said.

He looked up and shouted, "Monk! Stay out of there!"

Monk Mayfair was already through the window. He didn't answer.

The shooting continued inside the hotel for a few moments, then came to a spotty end. I was trying to reach the bottom of the ladder as if it was everything on earth that I wanted, and it was. Then I got down there on solid earth— and didn't know what to do.

It hadn't occurred to me that there would be any question about what to do next once I reached terrafirma and liberty. There were many courses open. Run was the first one. Then there were the assorted organizations I could hurriedly notify that a fat man had been about to kill me, these including the police, the sheriff, the F.B.I., the hotel house sleuth if it had one, and the U. S. Marines. Now, though, that I was on the ground and comparatively safe, unless hit by a ricochetting bullet, or someone leaned out of the hotel window and took a shot at me, I somehow did none of the obvious things. I waited to see what Doc Savage would do about all this. I tried to tell myself that I was curious about how the great man worked. Actually I probably thought his neighborhood was about the safest available spot.

Whatever went on in Mr. Montgomery's suite happened in comparative peace. There were no more shots. Doc Savage, having demonstrated that he had no control over Monk Mayfair when the latter was excited, went the rest of the way up the ladder himself and disappeared in the window. That was my cue to start re-climbing the ladder. Whether Savage wanted to be a protector or not, I was going to elect him.

Not too happily, I crawled back into a hotel suite I had quitted not so long ago. Mr. Montgomery, Colleen, Roy, were gone, as was Monk Mayfair, while Coming Going was walking around yelling and ruining an expensive rug with the blood that was coming from at least two holes in him. The theme of his yelling was that he was calling on hell to open wide and receive the United States State Department.

"Where did they go?" I asked.

Coming Going looked at me and yelled, "Out! Where did you suppose they went?" And he had been so cute and kindly with his heap-big-Injun ways.

Doc Savage was hauling a chair across the room. I watched him. He got on the chair, and unscrewed a light bulb from the ceiling chandelier, selecting one particular bulb.

"The fat man's party left hurriedly, as Mr. Going intimates," Savage told me. "Monk presumably followed them. They were all gone when I got into the suite."

"Aren't you going to—won't Monk need help . . . ?"

"He won't get it, if he does. But he won't need it. Monk never does."

I thought that was a pretty dirty trick. The notion must have shown on my face, something like the look the baby rabbit gives the alligator that is going to swallow him. Because Savage looked patiently pained himself.

"We've been watching Mr. Montgomery's party for days," Savage told me. "We didn't want him alarmed. Monk will alarm him—which, incidentally, is my understatement for today."

I admitted that being alarmed by Monk Mayfair would probably be rather special. "But suppose he needs help. That Montgomery isn't exactly a lamb."

"If Monk needs help, he'll call for it." Savage said briefly.

He wrapped the light bulb he had removed in a handkerchief and pocketed it carefully.

Pointing at the pocket, I said, "Don't tell me that's a microphone?"

He nodded. "Yes. Only one we have in the fifty-watt size, too. It's a special job—practically indetectible even on inspection. It lights like an ordinary bulb, as well."

Coming Going asked hell to also keep its gates open for all meddling human females. He was looking at me.

"Oh!" I said. "Oh, I see now. You were eavesdropping on what went on in here, and you had to change your plans and save my life."

"Something like that," Savage admitted.

"I don't see why it should gripe your redskin friend so," I said.

"He happens to understand how disastrous this setback may be."

"I see. Pardon me for having a neck that needed saving."

Nobody had any more to say until we had carried our bad tempers out of there—curious guests were just beginning to collect and ask what had happened—and adjourned to Doc Savage's suite. Savage began dressing Coming Going's injuries—bullet paths in, respectively, an arm and a neck muscle. Savage was deft, knew his business. Coming Going had stopped importuning hell to take care of me and the United

States State Department, and sat on a straightbacked chair. The back of his neck, the backs of his hands, became wet with perspiration that pain made.

"Mr. Going," Doc Savage told me, "is with the organization he has just been condemning with such sincerity—the State Department. He was the man first assigned to investigate this matter. It was at his suggestion that I was involved."

"Oh," I said, in a small way.

I dragged out and inspected my previous idea that Coming Going was a dopey ham actor from Hollywood whose speed was playing phony Indians. Just a nice, harmless boy, I'd thought him, who had been floored by the news that Waldo Loring had been murdered. The idea was like some others I'd had in my time. Rather sour.

"Then you're all secret agents," I said.

Savage snorted slightly. Quite a display of emotion for him. "Mr. Going might be remotely so classified. But I haven't been able to do anything secretly for years."

He might be right. Come to think of it, his presence here at the lodge had been as unobtrusive as the arrival of a circus in town.

"I don't get it," I said.

Coming Going looked up at me. "Neither have we. And now we may never get it." His feather was over his eye again.

"It's partly your own fault," I snapped. "God knows, I came running to you both for information. And what did I get? Big-eyed innocence." I was pretty upset about it. "What was I to do? My friend, Glacia, was in trouble, and it was up to me to help her."

"Some girl-friends you pick," said Coming Going.

"There's nothing wrong with Glacia except that she's money-hungry!" I yelled. "She wouldn't harm anyone intentionally."

Doc Savage patted the air vaguely with his hand that was holding a bottle of antiseptic and told me, "We know more about Glacia Loring than you do, and probably know things about you that you've forgotten. We should—there have been nearly a hundred agents sifting you both the past few days."

I asked a question that I had been afraid to ask.

"Where is Glacia?"

Savage caught Going's eye, hesitated, finally said, "We don't know."

Both of them watched me for a time. Going finally

muttered, "For God's sake, either faint or stop looking as if you're going to."

"You mean—she's not at the lodge?" It was my voice, coming from a spot several feet distant, the voice of someone who had been swallowed.

"We don't know," Savage said again.

"But surely—Glacia left me at the pool, ran off in a rage to hunt Mr. Montgomery because he'd rifled her purse. . . . Oh my God! She didn't find him and he—"

Savage's hand was up, his voice sharply urgent. "No, no, she didn't find Montgomery. We kept track of her for a while—or Coming Going did, but—"

"I wish you'd stop calling me Coming Going, or Mr. Going," the phony Indian snapped peevishly. "My name is Lybeck. Joseph Lybeck. . . . No, Mote, I lost track of your friend. She didn't lose me consciously. I just zigged when I should have zagged, and lost her."

"There is no reason to think she isn't perfectly safe," Doc Savage told me.

"No reason! When there's been one murder! And that fat Montgomery was going to kill me in cold blood if you hadn't—" I took hold of myself with both hands, my knees anyway. I could feel them shaking. "I'm sorry," I said. "Glacia may seem a little screwy to you fellows. But she has done a few things for me, enough nice things to outweigh the other kind."

"You think a lot of her," Savage said. It was more statement than question.

"Yes. A lot is right. Call it the attraction of opposites or whatever you want to. But the fact is that I swing my last punch for her if necessary."

Savage nodded. "She knows that. It's why she sent for you."

"Probably."

Savage's expression and manner now showed that he had a problem to solve. The result of what I'd said, evidently. I didn't know what it was.

I didn't know, either, why we were staying in the room making small talk. Action seemed called for. Glacia was missing. Monk Mayfair was missing. Mr. Montgomery and party had flown. Yet we were here, doing what never solves problems—talking.

When he had finished patching Coming Going—I couldn't

think of him as anyone named Joseph Lybeck, although I had no trouble accepting him as a federal agent—Doc Savage stepped back. He told Coming Going. "I think she should know the whole story."

Coming Going said, "Ugh!" He added, "Oh, all right. Everybody else seems to know everything anyway."

Savage went into another room to fetch a small radio that was not a conventional table model, but more resembled the communication apparatus that amateurs use. He switched it on. After it warmed up, the speaker did not emit the usual static cracklings, but a slight high-pitched hissing. I knew what it was. A V.H.F. outfit. Very High Frequency radio.

Without explaining why he had turned on the radio, Savage told me, "Your guess about Waldo Loring's previous profession was accurate. Exact. He was a ship captain. Master of freight steamers."

My nod was probably just a gesture I should have made. I was thinking of Glacia.

"I won't bore you with a lengthy summary of Waldo Loring's life," Doc Savage continued. "It was a rough life, and there was some sharpshooting in it, but probably no more than the average tough sailor does. . . . We'll skip down to the year before the war ended, the month of September. That was when—"

He jumped, bit off his words, eyed the radio. It had emitted a deep sound like a long steady breath. Savage watched the radio. Coming Going watched it. The radio stopped making the breathing sound without making any other.

"September. A freighter. The Victory Tumble. Captain Waldo Loring commanding." Savage still had his eye on the radio. "The Victory Tumble loaded a cargo at a Canadian port. Destination of the cargo, England. There was the greatest secrecy—even Captain Loring didn't know the destination. Only a Lieutenant Commander Roger Peelman knew that. Peelman was U. S. Navy. He went aboard with orders that made him Captain Waldo Loring's senior in command."

The radio for a moment proved more of a magnet for his interest than the story he was telling. After about a minute, he pulled away from it enough to continue:

"Perhaps if the Navy man had been more diplomatic, none of this would have happened. Waldo Loring was an egotistical, hardheaded old sea dog, and his opinion of the

Navy was considerably lower than the Navy's opinion of him. Captain Loring and Lieutenant Commander Peelman did not get along well. Peelman complained to Washington about it before sailing, but nothing was done about it—a bad bit of neglect, probably."

"Something happened to the ship?" I asked, jumping at a conclusion.

"It sank. . . . Some three weeks later, a destroyer picked up a lifeboat containing the survivors. They consisted of Captain Loring and some of his crew. Peelman had drowned. The story they told—the ship damaged by an enemy torpedo, then a storm, and the ship going down—was corroborated by all survivors. The logs checked. Apparently the ship had sunk in deep water, three hundred miles at sea." He hesitated, then added, "Apparently."

"Apparently?" I said.

"Well, yes. You see, after the war, the Navy took pains to check enemy submarine reports and they found that the *Victory Tumble* had been torpedoed, all right—but a couple of hundred miles from the spot Captain Waldo Loring named."

"What about the log-books, aren't they reliable records?"

Savage shrugged. "Easily altered. Captain Loring kept the master's log, which was a digest of the day-log. He could have made false entries and no one else would have known."

"What about the crew members who were picked up with him?"

"Seamen, No officers. They wouldn't have known. Every pain was taken to keep the *Victory Tumble*'s cargo, course and destination secret.

"Oh."

"Because of the nature of the cargo," Savage continued, "the Navy kept Captain Loring under surveilance. They checked enemy sub reports after the war, as I told you. And then they really watched Captain Loring. They watched him and they watched people he contacted—and they found out, a few weeks ago, that Captain Loring was trying to sell the cargo of the ship that had sunk."

"You mean his vessel didn't sink?" I gasped.

"Oh, it went down all right. But not where Loring claimed—the Navy had sounded the whole area, and made Geiger counter tests—"

"Wait a minute!" I yelled. "Geiger counter? I've heard such a gadget mentioned, or read of—"

"Naturally. A device for indicting the presence of radio-activity."

I thought I had it now. "This cargo wouldn't have been atom bombs?" I demanded.

"No. . . . On an unguarded ship? Certainly not."

"Then what—"

Savage glanced questionably at Coming Going, who shrugged, said, "Might as well tell her. The State Department has the delusion that only three people in the world know what that cargo was. They won't mind this lady being a fourth. Much."

"Want to bet I can't name at least two nations with aggressive notions who don't know by now?" Savage demanded. "Particularly since Waldo Loring has been trying to sell the stuff to them?"

"I was just being funny in my odd way," Coming Going said bitterly.

"Uranium," Savage told me. "Not freshly mined ore. Processed. That is, it had gone through the two preliminary processing stages. Intended for atom bombs, of course."

"But why on a steamer going to—"

"Let's not go any deeper into top secret stuff," Savage said. "You know that England and Canada were working with us on the bomb."

"But why is it so valuable? The war is over—"

"Over? There is some doubt about that in a few quarters. Let's just say that all uranium sources are closely guarded and every speck of ore accounted for since the war ended. There's enough ore on that ship to furnish the makings of quite a few bombs. Enough to be worth—well, the destiny of a few nations, perhaps."

Coming Going, with grating vehemence, said, "Don't underestimate the value of that cargo, honey."

I decided that I wouldn't. I had read those conjectures about what a dozen or so bombs planted in American cities, perhaps months ahead of zero hour, and timed to let loose all together, would do to our defense plant. Pearl Harbor would be nothing.

Glacia. . . . Glacia was involved in something like that. My silly, self-centered, dollar-hungry little friend. . . .

Doc Savage came over and placed a hand on my arm. "Don't get the wrong idea, Mote. Glacia doesn't know it's uranium. Waldo Loring told her it was gold, and I think she believed him."

My face felt dry and like bone and it must have looked like bone because Savage looked concerned and went to a writing desk, hauled open the drawer, and took out the Indian warclub that had been in Glacia's room.

He said. "You were worried about this club, I believe. You needn't be. Monk got it from your room—to run a few tests to see if it could be the murder instrument. It wasn't."

"I knew Glacia didn't kill him," I said tightly. "I never let that quite get into my mind."

He tossed the club on a chair. "Well, it's not comfortable having such things around trying to get into one's mind. You can forget it."

The radio did what they had been waiting for it to do. It made the husky breathing sound again, added words, remarkably clear words—Monk Mayfair's voice—and said, "Doc, I ran into something too rough—"

There was urgency in Mayfair's voice. Not fear, but sick urgency. A quality that made my hair feel as if it was being combed the wrong way.

"—no out for me," Monk was saying. "Get this quick, Doc! It's not Montgomery! It's another one who knows where the ship lies. It's nobody we suspected. Watch out for her—"

That was all. I don't know what a radio transmitter sounds like over the air when it is being smashed. Probably like the sound that came from our receiver.

IX

It was quiet in the lodge bar now, and cool and semi-dark, rather like a sepulchre, for the day was done and a couple of hours of the night had gone, and they were having a party in another part of the lodge, which accounted for the bar being empty. A party. On the house. Everyone was there. The dead are dead, and the living must live. The bar was dank and still, a repository for me and my fears.

I moved my glass back and forth and it made wet smears on the table and they were symbolic of something or other, the mess things were in, probably. The waiter went past silently, like a ghost walking on eggs. There was only one waiter, and he would look at me each time he passed. He didn't seem to see me.

I knew what was wrong with the waiter. He didn't like what we were doing. We were even. Neither did I.

The waiter didn't have a friend who had vanished into thin air, and I didn't imagine anyone had tried to kill him today. He hadn't spent an afternoon locked in his room with little cold-footed fear-things stampeding over his skin every time someone walked down the hall. He'd probably spent the afternoon shooting pool. And he was getting twenty dollars for what he was doing. Twenty, and the privilege of assisting the great Doc Savage.

Not that I'd decided Doc Savage was less than the reports said. He was good. He was marvelous. He had functioned all day with the acumen and skill of the F.B.I., Sherlock Holmes and all the fictional sleuths ever created with words. The trouble was, he hadn't been good enough to find Monk Mayfair. Nor Glacia.

My sitting here was Doc Savage's idea. I didn't necessarily need to be in the bar, but my room had gotten too much for me. I had stayed in that room until I began seeing things walking on the walls. I felt as if I could walk on them myself. So I was in the bar. Being at the party wouldn't do—I was supposed to be in mourning. I had lost an uncle. My uncle Waldo Loring. I was Glacia Loring.

The waiter would say I was Glacia Loring. Or he would if he earned his twenty dollars. The desk clerk would say so too. That had been arranged.

"Miss Loring?"

It was the waiter. He had walked straight to me and I had watched him and hadn't quite seen him. I jumped. "Yes, waiter," I said.

"A gentleman inquiring for you. A gentleman named McBride."

"Show the gentleman where I am."

"Very well, Miss."

"Wait—what does the gentleman look like?"

"He's about forty-five, Miss."

"Show him me."

Attorney McBride didn't look forty-five, or wouldn't with the worried look scrubbed off his face. He was about thirty, but he did appear very tired. He was a large bushy young man in slacks, Hollywood shirt, sunburn and a deposit of desert dust.

"Miss Loring?" he asked. "Miss Glacia Loring?"

"Yes," I said, and wondered how well he remembered Glacia's voice from having heard it over the telephone.

"This is certainly a relief." Apparently he didn't remember it so well. "I'm Attorney McBride."

"Oh, yes indeed. I spoke to you on the telephone."

"That's right." He dropped on the seat opposite. "Oh, man! Whoeee!" He looked at the waiter. "Can a man get coffee laced with whiskey in here?"

"Certainly, sir."

"Then produce it," said Attorney McBride. He turned to me and said, "If I seem dithered, you can rest assured that I am."

"Has something happened?"

He nodded. "Your uncle was the damndest client."

"How do you mean?"

He blew out his breath. "How? Whoosh! I never heard of a client, much less had one, who left the sort of a legacy he left you, Miss Loring."

"Keeper, you mean?"

"Oh my Lord, yes," he said.

The McBride voice was not as yapping as it had sounded over the telephone—from what I had managed to overhear of Glacia's conversation with him—but it was not exactly dull.

"Did you bring my inheritance?" I asked.

"My Lord, yes," he said.

"Could I see it?"

"It? . . . Oh, I see. Uh—you apply a very good word to the inheritance. Calling it it, I mean. Very appropriate. I had thought of some words for it myself, but they wouldn't bear repeating in polite company."

"Mr. McBride. I have no idea what Keeper is," I said.

He sat back. His jaw dropped. His eyes were as round as shotgun barrels.

After wincing and hesitating, he asked, "Have you had dinner, Glacia? I may call you, Glacia, mayn't I? If you haven't had dinner, you'd better. You'll need your strength."

"Look here," I said sharply. "I don't know why you are so excited, but I'm beginning to wonder. What are you trying to do, upset me?"

"Upset? Oh, no. Forbid and preserve," cried Mr. McBride.

"I only want your courage at full tide, bright and sparkling, so you'll have the nerve to take it off my hands."

"It?"

"Whew! I mustn't frighten you. Oh, no! I mustn't!" gasped the attorney.

I tried to pin him down with a frown. "Just what is wrong with this inheritance?"

"I don't believe I'd better start answering that, because I want to start back to Los Angeles tonight. . . . But if you want a fault, here is one of the milder ones: It eats a hell of a lot."

That settles it, I thought. A race horse. "How many races has it won?"

"Races? Eh? Can it run?" He couldn't have been more confused if I had stood him on his head and put a carrot in his mouth.

"Isn't it a race horse?"

"Oh, no. Well—no!" said McBride. "Race horse? Good Lord, what a description for—well, never mind." He mopped his forehead, although the desert nights weren't hot and the hotel air conditioner was still going. "What a characterization—race horse. Whoee! whoee! What ever gave you such a wrong idea? Oh, I see. . . . Uh, what *did* give you the idea anyway?"

"You," I said, "seem to be twittery. Keep it up, and we'll both be that way."

"McBride is twittering, all right," the attorney-at-law said. "Oh, thank God!" The last because the waiter had finally come with his coffee and a side of bourbon.

I decided to wait him out. This might be an act. I didn't know what it was.

Doc Savage might be able to make a head or a tail of it. . . . I took a chance and moved my purse a little on the table, edging it to a spot where it would better pick up our conversation. I supposed that moving it would make a terrific rumpus in the little microphone. Because there was a microwave transmitter—that was what Doc Savage had called it, whatever that was—in the purse. The theory was that I was a traveling broadcast station, and I was supposed to pretend to be Glacia, and that was supposed to lead to something. We hoped.

Lawyer McBride finished his laced coffee. He looked at me as if he was very sorry for me. He blew out a considerable breath. "Miss Loring," he said, "you might as well see the bad news."

Whereupon he led the way outdoors and toward the parking lot. The desert night was clear. They were probably always clear, the sky cloudless, because the adjacent country didn't look as if a drop of moisture had ever fallen on it.

Attorney McBride approached a trailer. With misgivings. "I usually announce myself by throwing a rock," he told me nervously. "But this time, we'll take a chance."

The trailer was an unlighted, beat-up affair, and he knocked timidly on the door. No response. Without more preliminaries, McBride snarled, "Why the hell should I worry? I'm getting shut of him!" and he hauled off and kicked the trailer door. That got action.

"Oaf," stated a deep-throated male voice inside the trailer, "derives from the Iceland *alfr*, meaning originally an elf's child, a changeling left by goblins, therefore a foolish or deformed child, an idiot, a simpleton. Hence it may refer to one person who disturbs another. Will you go away."

"Harold!" said McBride. "Harold, your new owner is here."

There was a prolonged silence from inside.

"Harold!" said Mr. McBride.

"Yes, sir."

"Come out. Miss Loring is here, who inherited you, is here."

"I don't want to come out," the voice said. It sounded as if it was being manufactured in a barrel.

"Harold," said Mr. McBride patiently. "You wish to be fed, don't you? And guided, and managed, and cared for?"

"Yes, sir."

The lawyer yelled, "then get the hell out here and meet the nice lady who has inherited you."

Oh, Lord, I thought—I was beginning to react like Attorney McBride. I had, or Glacia had, inherited something that talked with a man's voice.

Presently it opened the trailer door. . . . Older than I had thought. Too old to be very interesting; at least more than forty. And fat. Not short, but tremendously fat, egg-shaped.

"This is Harold," said Attorney McBride.

Harold's head was quite large, like a melon placed crosswise, and his mouth was large out of proportion, as were his eyes. In front of the latter, he wore shell-rimmed glasses that, regardless of what they did for his vision, certainly made his eyes startling. None of his clothing fit well, all either too large or too small.

"Harold, this is Miss Loring," added McBride.

"Girl!" exploded Harold. "Girl was originally the name of the Goddess Vesta, or the human young of either sex, but the term is now applied to the female child, a maiden, a mare or filly, a maid-servant, a sweetheart, or a roebuck in its second year."

He slammed the trailer door in our faces.

There was a silence.

"The last one fits me," I said.

"Eh?" said McBride.

"The roebuck in its second year."

"Oh." McBride cleared his throat. "You—ah—I have a paper for you to sign. A receipt for your inheritance. If you will sign same, I will be going."

"Wait a minute, brother," I said. I gripped his arm. I led him a few yards from the trailer, and he held my purse so the gadget in it would be sure to pick up and relay what we had to say. "What's the matter with Harold? Is he nuts?"

"Nuttier than a fruitcake," said McBride.

"Who is he?"

"Harold Keeper. You've inherited him. Now, if you will sign this paper—"

"How come, inherited?" I said, gripping the attorney's arm. "Give. What is this, anyway? Waldo Loring never told me what Keeper was. Who is he?"

McBride sighed elaborately. "Harold was the old man's—your deceased uncle's friend. Sort of a flunky, I surmise. A sailor. Harold was a sailor on your uncle's ships."

"Oh, Harold is some crazy sailor whom Uncle Waldo was taking care of?"

"Well—yes. Only your uncle did say that Harold had not always been—shall we say cracked. It seems that during the war uncle's ship was torpedoed, and your uncle and Harold were in the boatload of survivors. They suffered great hardships in the open sea in the small boat. The experience affected Harold's mind. Your uncle feels, or felt, duty bound to care for Harold."

"I don't think I like this," I said.

"I was afraid you wouldn't," McBride said wearily. "Are you going to sign—"

"Not," I said, "until I think it over."

"You can't do that to me!" yelled McBride. "My God, unless you accept Harold, I'm stuck with him!"

I walked back to the lodge. McBride hopped along beside me, complaining that I was cold-blooded and arguing that Harold had good points. He tried to enumerate Harold's points, and couldn't think of any.

"Listen, I'll talk this over with you in the morning," I said.

"But—"

"You've done enough to me for one evening. Good-night. Mr. McBride. In the morning. Say about eight."

He stamped into the lodge. I could hear him screaming at the registrations clerk about the price they were going to charge him for a room. A very excitable nature, Mr. McBride.

I moved a few paces and stepped into the shadow of the lodge, waited. Presently, without noticeable sound, there was a large form beside me. Doc Savage.

"Did the gadget work? Did you pick all that up?" I asked.

Doc Savage said he had.

"Were you surprised?" I inquired. "I was. Keeper a man, a screwball. That's the last thing—"

But Doc Savage had something more urgent on his mind than a discussion. His hand touched my arm. Not a hard grip. But as solid as a stone building.

"Let's watch the trailer," he said. And that was all he said until we had reached another wedge of darkness beside a parked car thirty yards or so from the trailer, which was still dark.

"Why doesn't Harold turn on the lights?" I said uneasily. "He—he gives me cold chills. I never did like psychos, and—"

All of a sudden, I wondered if I was going to lose my balance wheel. This whole thing of Harold Keeper, the way it seemed to bear no relation to Waldo Loring's murder, or Glacia's disappearance, or a shipload of uranium ore, was unnerving. It was like starting to a funeral, and finding you were in a circus instead.

"I'm coming loose," I mumbled. "I didn't expect anything like this. My stomach feels unfunny."

He tried the door of the parked car. It was unlocked, and he opened it. "Sit down here," he said. "Not in the seat, where you will be seen. In the door.... Now, just what is upsetting you?"

"It's Glacia!" I blurted. "No word from her. And I thought this Keeper would be a document or a map or something that would solve everything. It hasn't. I feel so damn thwarted."

Savage said, "You've made a lot of progress."

His voice was wonderful. It built confidence underfoot as solid as a concrete sidewalk.

"Waldo Loring never had a friend named Harold Keeper," he said.

"How do you—"

"Waldo Loring's past has been investigated every way possible. We can almost tell you what he ate every meal for the past five years. We would know if Waldo Loring had Harold Keeper. Rest assured, we would know that."

"He was supposed to be in the lifeboatful of survivors—"

"No. He was not. I know where every man in that lifeboat can be found. And not one of them will be found in that trailer."

I felt better. Chilly, Nerve chills, but they were better than the awful feeling that I wasn't helping Glacia. I just sat there. The big bronze man had seated himself on the ground beside me, between this car and another. He was silent. Somewhere far off there was a giggling and yapping, and it sounded like several girls noisy from too much to drink. But it was coyotes. We were in the desert. Close to wild nature. But nature wasn't as wild as some of the humans around here.

"What is the rig?" I asked. "What are they trying to pull?"

"No rig any more, lady," said a voice.

It wasn't Doc Savage's voice. But it was close enough to have been. I looked up. I didn't make it out at first, except that it was big and hung with gross flesh. Why I didn't seem to understand that it was Harold was a mystery.

"Not any more," Harold said. "The rig is off. We have left just what is in my hand. So don't move."

We didn't move. Harold's gun was a big thing. Anybody but Harold would have needed a wheelbarrow to cart it around.

The night was still around us for a moment. Except for the coyotes far away, about as far away as my mind seemed from my body. I think my mind had fled that far because it couldn't stand staying in a place as scared as my body was.

"Lady, if you faint, do so quietly," Harold said.

X

One of those impatient men, Harold. He waited for me to swoon, and I didn't, but I probably tried. Savage had not moved, which showed good judgment.

"Lie down on the ground. Spreadeagle," Harold told Savage.

"Face up or face down?" Doc Savage asked.

"Down, of course."

"Whatever you say. But a man can get going from a face down position a lot quicker."

"You can give a demonstration of it if you want to," Harold said grimly. "It's about as wide as long with me."

There was a little silence, then Savage lay down on his face. Even lying on his face, obeying the order of a grossly fat devil with a gun, he did not surrender any of the competence that was always with him. Even in the darkness, where there was barely enough light to distinguish more than the presence of a hand on the end of an arm, he kept that feeling of ability. Harold got the same idea, evidently. Because he made a hissing sound through his teeth, ugly and serpentine.

"Mr. McBride!" Harold called softly.

The darkness stirred nearby, then the figure of Attorney McBride shaped up in it. He lingered a few yards distant. He seemed to be wishing he was a dried leaf and could blow away.

"Come here, Mr. McBride," said Harold.

The lawyer ventured closer. As if he was pushing his way through steel.

"This is Doc Savage, Mr. McBride," said Harold.

If Mr. McBride was breathing, he didn't show it.

Harold said, "You have heard of the sun that makes the tides, the U. S. Marines that make whatever marines make. Well, Mr. McBride, that gives you some idea. Because this is no less than Doc Savage."

McBride had no words.

"We didn't fool the great one, it seems," Harold said.

McBride replied with a deep breath. It shook coming in, and shook going out.

"We wasted our time," Harold said. "We went to a lot of trouble fixing a deal. And did we fix us a deal. Brother!"

Harold grew tired of McBride's answers.

He asked me, "Mote, isn't that what they call you? Mote. Well, Mote, didn't you think it was a nice deal?"

"It took me in," I said.

"That didn't make it good enough." Harold sighed, and in that pile of body, it was like steam going through a heating system. "You know what the deal was, don't you?"

"No," I said.

"Baby, you should see it by now. I was going to be your puppydog, see."

"Why?"

"Just to be around. Eyes open, you know. There were some flies in my ointment, and I was going to do a little fly-catching. Specifically was Doc Savage on this case? How much did he know—enough that we would have to knock him off? . . . The answer to the last is yes. Yup. Maybe we didn't waste all that finagling."

He seemed to have plenty of words. I didn't know what he was doing, trying to button up his own courage perhaps. And I didn't know how much of what he had said was lying, beyond the part of wanting to know where Doc Savage was involved in the case. He had known that all right, if he knew anything at all about what was going on, and he did.

Pretend to be Keeper so that he could find out just who was suspected of doing what and how much? That was more logical. It must be quite a mental strain to have someone like Doc Savage on your trail, and have him pretending that he wasn't. The temptation to do something about finding out just where the firm of Savage was going to do business—the temptation would be great. It would, when it ate on you long enough, be irresistible.

Yes, I could see where Harold would want to learn what Doc Savage was doing. It was even logical that Harold would go to the length of doing something slightly foolish in order to learn where the ax was going to fall.

And now I knew what was eating Harold. He was thinking along the same lines—he was reflecting what a damned fool he had been to pull Harold Keeper on us. The ruminations weren't doing his temper any good.

Evidence of how accurate my notion was, Harold now kicked Doc Savage in the side. He did it twice, grunting both times with the effort.

If this did Harold's ego good, it wasn't noticeable in the deep-in-a-barrel voice when he spoke. The barrel was pretty tinny. "Search him, Mr. McBride," Harold said.

McBride didn't move, didn't speak, probably didn't breathe.

"McBride," Harold said. "Do you wish him to pull some gadget on us? The man isn't lying there letting me kick him in the ribs because he is afraid of me."

"Shoot him!" McBride blurted, finding his voice.

"I wish to God that I dared," Harold said. "On proper provocation, I probably would. But my brother wishes to consult him. . . . Damn you, McBride, search him! You're as useful as lipstick on an old maid."

McBride, operating as if he was driven by gears, got along with searching Doc Savage. While the hunt was in progress, Harold said, "I know about that anaesthetic gas you use, Savage. I'm holding my breath." I thought he was, too, part of the time.

"Feels like he's got a bulletproof vest on," McBride gasped.

Harold wasn't impressed. "I've been aiming at the back of his neck, anyway. . . . We will retire to the trailer and do this more thoroughly." He cocked his gun impressively, and the sound was like a well-thrown horseshoe ringing the stake. "Let the retiring be of good judgment."

We entered the trailer, and I could see why Harold would feel disgusted. He had gone to a bit of trouble to decorate the trailer interior with the personality of Harold Keeper. He had filled it with dictionaries, nearly a hundred of them, all shapes, sizes and colors. I remembered how he had started off impressing his character on me by orating cockeyed definitions. Girl, the roebuck in its second year. He had evidently intended that to be his theme.

McBride began searching Savage again.

"Strip him," Harold said.

They did that, let me turn my back, and supplied Savage with what Harold said was his bathing trunks, and they gave Savage the appearance of a bronze statue standing in a sack.

"Throw his stuff in the back of your car," Harold told McBride. "We'll dump it somewhere. I imagine it's full of bombs, or something. . . . Oh yes, then hook your car to the trailer."

McBride went out, and Harold took my purse and spent five minutes stealing glances into it and cracking open the little portable U.H.F. radio transmitter. He seemed to know what the latter was. "Ingenious," he said. "But no more than I expected."

I had been watching Doc Savage. I couldn't help it. The man's physical development was astounding, so much so that it was a little unnatural. Harold was impressed, too. He said, "You bat an eye at me, Savage, and I'm going to shoot you. Because looking at you scares the hell out of me. I don't know how I had the nerve to bring you this far. I must be crazy."

There was the sound of an automobile engine, followed by a slight jolt from the trailer, and metallic clanking. McBride showed us a face the color of an unbaked biscuit and said, "I'm hooked on."

"You know where to go," Harold told him. "Go there."

"But . . ." McBride swallowed quite audibly. He was having trouble with the simplest sentences.

"But what?"

"The trailer—the people at the hotel know it was here—won't they—it being gone—"

"I don't know what you're talking about," Harold told him. "But if you're saying we should be cunning some more, it's ridiculous. I'm winding this up with a bang."

"But we'll be suspected!" McBride wailed.

"Suspecting and catching are two different birds," Harold suggested. "We'll solve that problem in a broadminded way. We just won't be there."

McBride didn't think much of that. "You mean flee? Leave my law business?"

Harold sneered at him with his melon face. "Leave what law business? I thought you did a deal with us because you didn't have any law business."

"Oh, my God!" McBride wailed. "Where will we go?"

"I know a little place in Patagonia, right next to where Adolph Hitler lives," Harold told him bitterly. "You can go along with me if you wish."

"I'm not joking," gasped the lawyer.

"Neither am I, brother. What about getting this caravan in motion? Are you giving that some thought?"

McBride ducked out of sight and Harold told us, "We

had all better sit down. I have a hunch he is going to tow this trailer like a nervous bull dragging the chain in his nose."

He was right.

Later, when we seemed to be on a highway. I asked Harold a question. He appeared to like conversation anyway, because he had been doing plenty of it.

"McBride had the location of the *Victory Tumble*, the ship loaded with the processed uranium?" I asked.

"So you know about that, too." Harold said. "I guess it was a good thing I didn't leave you behind."

"I'm surprised Waldo Loring would give a lawyer information like that," I said.

Harold commented on this. "He didn't. Not exactly. He left an envelope with Attorney McBride. You should have seen the envelope—more wax seals on it than a high-school diploma. We were even scared to open it. Thought it might be booby-trapped."

"Oh, you've opened it?"

"Uh-huh. You want to know how that came about, honey? We were very clever—yeah, very. Just like sticks of stovewood are clever. But we finally ferreted out that Waldo Loring had a lawyer, and the lawyer was just about as shady as he was unprosperous, and so we presented the lawyer with a business deal. Sure we got a look at the envelope."

"Was the location of the *Victory Tumble* given?"

"Sure."

"Then you feel pretty good about everything, don't you?" I said.

"Shouldn't we?"

"I suppose so. You managed to kill Waldo Loring without anybody suspecting you."

"Thanks," Harold said. "I'm glad to hear it. I was having some doubts."

I had caught Doc Savage's eye. He had given me the slightest nod of approval. Not that he probably hadn't guessed all this far ahead of me, but he liked the way I was checking it.

"Was the envelope named Keeper?" I asked Harold.

"That's right, dear."

I thought Doc Savage had shaken his head slightly.

"So you killed Waldo Loring, Harold?" I asked.

The melon face looked at me. It became different.

"Baby, if I said yes to that, what would then have to happen to you?" Harold asked.

I knew why Savage had been shaking his head. He had known that I would talk myself into something. I had. Harold was still watching me and the melon face was now something that even the devil wouldn't like.

XI

It was a ranch. It had to be a ranch, because they couldn't just camp out on the desert, for that would be a little conspicuous. But what surprised me was that Mr. Montgomery had owned the ranch for quite a while. Long enough for his name to be painted on the mailbox and for the weather to peel away most of some of the letters. The mailbox was one of those capacious ones, big as an elephant's stomach, which you see along the roads out in the open spaces where the mail-order houses do most of the business.

There was also a LAZY-M RANCH printed on the mailbox, and from that there was two miles of dusty road, then a squat adobe ranch house and bunkhouse and corrals made in the Mexican fashion, of living devil's-walking-stick cactus.

A reception committee of three rifles and Mr. Montgomery, his daughter Colleen, and his flunky, Roy, was on hand.

Harold peered out of a window. He could read Mr. Montgomery's moods readily, it seemed.

"My brother is angry," Harold said.

I really believed then that Harold and Mr. Montgomery were brothers. And I was sure of it when I saw them together, for there was a sameness to their fatness, and they had identical ways of over-using words.

Mr. Montgomery used plenty of words when he saw Harold. All profane words—they came from the gutters of many parts of the world and some of them from the best dictionaries, and the last ones were even worse. The total of it was that Mr. Montgomery felt Harold had wrecked everything. Not in those words. Not in words that anybody would want to say the way they were being said by one brother to another.

"All done?" Harold asked.

"No."

"Okay—this is just to fill in while you get your breath, brother. . . . You make me laugh. Me ruin the pitch by grabbing Savage and the lady sleuth? Why, you fat jackass, you shot that phony Indian twice. Shot a federal gent—that's who that Coming Going was. You're wanted for that. You're hiding out here. How could you be in any worse fix?"

"But you—you weren't suspected." Mr. Montgomery yelled at him. "Savage didn't even know you existed. You could have played Harold Keeper, the half-wit the girl had inherited, and strung along and kept tab on Savage for us."

Harold went yok-yok bitterly. "That was your stinking idea, brother, and I'll tell you what I think of it sometime when I have half a day," he said. "It didn't work. Savage caught on before I even got the chair warm."

He went on to tell Mr. Montgomery exactly what had happened. Half the words he used were brotherly opinions that came to him as he went along.

"We've got old Waldo Loring's chart of where the ship lies on a bank in water shallow enough for any fourteen-year-old kid in a bathing suit to reach," Harold finished. "Waldo is dead. Nobody knows for sure what was what—even if Waldo had the ship spotted and for sale. Savage, the lady sleuth, Savage's big monkey, are all here. We can dead them, too. Then we can take a nice trip until the skies clear. Now tell me more that's wrong?"

The recital had sobered Mr. Montgomery.

"Why didn't you shoot Savage on the spot?" he yelled.

"And make the world a present of his body?" Harold yelled back at him. "That would make some stink, that would."

Mr. Montgomery said, "Oh!"

Harold continued bellowing. "But if you want the plain truth, I was afraid to kill him. I'd rather assassinate a president."

Mr. Montgomery started to sneer. Harold stopped that.

Harold said, "Now you tell me why you didn't knock off Monk Mayfair? Or even the Loring girl. I want to hear it."

Mr. Montgomery was slow with his answer. "Come in the house," he said.

"You were afraid yourself, that's why?" bellowed Harold.

"Come in the house."

I said, "Glacia is here!" I think I said it, because nobody else looked as if they had made the funny little wailing.

Glacia was dead. That was what I thought. Mr.

Montgomery had killed her, and killed Monk Mayfair, and that was why he wanted his brother to come into the house. He wanted to display the handiwork.

We all went into the ranch house. It was still night, and the lights were on. Kerosene lanterns, two of them smoking from poorly trimmed wicks. The stuff in the house had been used hard a long time ago, and then not used for a few years. Nobody had taken the trouble to brush away dust, and Glacia's face and clothing had collected quite a bit of it.

Glacia was a mess. A thoroughly scared mess, but she looked wonderful because she was alive. She had only to be breathing to be gorgeous. She looked at me, and she bleated, "Oh, Mote, they've got you, too!" And she turned—or turned as much as she could, tied to a table—and called Mr. Montgomery words I didn't know she knew. She didn't equal Mr. Montgomery's recent performance on his brother, but she did make herself clear.

It wasn't about herself that Glacia was angry. It was for me, because they were bothering me. I wanted to fold my knees, just fold everything, and sob. Because Glacia, although half of the time she might be mean and self-centered, would come through when someone else was in real trouble. Not that I'd been afraid she wouldn't pay off in blue chips. Or had I? Maybe that was why I wanted to cry.

Monk Mayfair was tied to a table. Under a table, really. So was Glacia. There were two heavy tables, evidently from the days when the place had a heavy complement of hungry cowhands, and the prisoners had been placed under these, roped to the four legs. The whole effect was ridiculous, but I could see that it was efficient. Mr. Montgomery's imagination had been at play, probably.

Monk Mayfair had first word. "How's Joe Lybeck?"

"As fine as anyone can be in the hospital," Doc Savage said.

Who was Joe Lybeck? for a minute I didn't get that one. . . . Coming Going. Joe Lybeck was Coming Going.

Monk pointed at Harold with chin and glare. "That one was my downfall," he said. "I hadn't placed him as in this. Him and the lawyer. I tried to tell you to watch out for her inheritance—meaning Glacia's inheritance, which would be so-fat here—just as they got to me."

"How did they trap you?" Doc asked.

Monk said, "I'm ashamed to say it, but they didn't. They

just walked up and pointed a gun at me. I tried to talk to you and he smashed the radio, and brought me here."

That seemed to settle that, so I asked Glacia, "How are you, dear?"

"I'm great," she wailed.

"They scare you much?"

They had scared her enough that she didn't want to try to tell me how much. Instead, she howled, "There's something so damned undignified about being tied under a table, you feel like a dog." And she burst into tears.

Mr. Montgomery liked to make little speeches so well that he made us one now. He said, "Yes, indeed, there are few less dignified places than under a table. If you want to undermine an individual's morale, just tie him under a table—"

"Oh, shut up," Harold told his brother.

"All right, brother," said Mr. Montgomery.

"Words all over you all the time like fleas," Harold complained.

They looked at each other. They weren't angry. They just looked at one another, and the question being argued visually didn't have a thing to do with words. It was: Who is going to do murder wholesale. Kill the prisoners. You? Me? Roy? Lawyer McBride?

They both looked at Roy.

Roy said, "Huh-uh. Not Roy." He got it out in little gulps, as if someone was trying to give him poison.

They looked at Attorney McBride. But not for long. He was more than pale; he was beginning to turn a cyanosed blue. He wouldn't be slaying anyone. He might even die himself, unaided.

Finally they glanced at Colleen, and she didn't say or do anything, did not even smile.

Doc Savage spoke. His voice doubtless wasn't as quiet, even, unfrightened as it seemed. It couldn't have been. But compared to the other voices that had been making words, it was deep peace. It made me realize how terrified everyone else was—the brothers of the job of killing us, and us of being killed.

Savage said, "This is a logical time for our side to be grasping at straws. Will you take that into account, listen to me a moment, and accept the fact that what I say isn't straw-snatching?"

"Shut up!" Harold said.

"It won't take long. Two sentences," Savage said.

"Let him say two sentences," Mr. Montgomery growled. There were beads of perspiration on his forehead, neck, the rim of his jaw, the places where nerves were close to the surface.

Savage said: "You carry a cane habitually, Mr. Montgomery. Don't you know that portable radio gadgets can be made small enough to fit in a hollowed-out cane of the size of yours?"

Nobody said anything for longer than I was able to hold my breath. Then Harold asked, "You got that stick here, brother?"

Mr. Montgomery said something that had no sound. It did not seem to be the word yes, but it was assent anyway.

"The girl sleuth had one in her purse." Harold advised. "It was smaller than a hearing-aid."

His brother wheeled and went into another room and came back carrying the large walking stick. He brought it close to one of the kerosene lamps. The sweat on his palms had made shiny spots on the nodular surface of the wood. He put his eyes much closer to the stick than the stick was close to the lamp, and for something like two minutes the loudest noise in the room was made by a fly walking across a window pane.

When Mr. Montgomery lifted his face, it had come apart. His jaw had sagged far down in his chins and only the rubbery lips were visible.

"It may be just a scratch," he whimpered.

Harold screamed, "Has that stick been tampered with?"

"A scratch," Mr. Montgomery said, using stark horror instead of breath to make the speech.

"Break it!" Harold yelled. "Goddam it, break the thing open. Let's see what they've done to us. How the hell could they have gotten that stick?"

Savage said, "We've been watching you for days. Mr. Montgomery was very careful with that walking stick. He stood it in the left rear corner of the clothes closet each night."

Mr. Montgomery bought that.

"The left rear corner—oh my God" he wailed. "They did! They—"

"Break it open!" screamed Harold.

Savage said, "The purpose of a tiny radio transmitter, of course, would be to keep accurate tab on your whereabouts. The other agents working with me will naturally have located you here and—"

Somewhere somehow I had gotten the idea that Doc Savage never told a lie. Where the notion came from, I don't know. But it was a lie. There was no radio in the walking stick. Or maybe, the way he had told it, he had merely stated a hypothetical possibility so convincingly that it seemed untruth.

Because, when Mr. Montgomery brought the cane up— high over his head—to slam it down on the table and smash it into bits, every eye was on it. Every eye, all of everybody's attention.

It was buildup. That was all. Done wonderfully. Everyone thought there was a gadget in the cane, and nobody was thinking about anything else.

Savage stepped to Harold and sank hand, wrist and some forearm into Harold's midsection. The effect was somewhat as if a partly inflated inner tube had been squeezed, causing the rest of the inner tube to suddenly fill out. Both Harold's arms flew out from his sides, stiffly; he looked like something in a Macy parade.

A bright object flashed past me. Harold's gun.

Going about his business, Savage brushed against Colleen, knocking her into my arms. I went to work on her. Her hair first, with both hands.

Roy tried to run backward and use his gun at the same time, but it wasn't a success. His feet merely beat up and down on the floor, and his hand raked the rifle hammer twice, trying to cock it, but couldn't get the hammer far enough back to stay on cock. He was trying vainly to fire the uncocked gun when Savage hit him.

Mr. Montgomery appeared to be frozen in an attitude of high sacrifice, holding the walking stick aloft. Probably that was an illusion, the result of things happening rather rapidly.

Monk Mayfair was having convulsions under the table. Trying to take the legs off the table. He seemed quite disappointed with the results—as if he'd never entertained a doubt but that he could jerk all four legs from the table with ease. But he wasn't doing it. He began to yell.

Most of this impressed itself on me in a detached fashion, because Colleen was doing enough to me that I could hardly be classed as a spectator. Colleen knew some sort of judo. Anyway, I was very busy trying to keep her from taking off one of my arms.

The lawyer, McBride got a running start and left his feet head-first for a window. His window-diving technique was correct. He hauled his coat up over his arms and head to protect his face as he hit. But there was a detail he hadn't noticed. The window was covered on the outside with heavy planks spiked in place. He knocked himself out neatly.

The ranch house shook a little, possibly from Mr. Montgomery falling, and I think I yelled for fifteen minutes for someone to detach Colleen from me. Somebody finally did.

XII

It was exactly 8:10 a.m. and the sun had finally managed to climb over the tops of the mountains in the west. It was throwing a great deal of angry light, and already some heat, over two blanketed and feathered phony Indians who were stuffing the luggage of a departing guest in the back seat of a sedan. The automobile departed, and the redskins began an argument concerning the tip they had received. It was a dime, and the argument was about exactly what word they should use to describe the guest if they wished to refer to him during the day, which they probably would.

Coming Going said, "Let me look at that map again." Later he said, "Now this is what I like. A regular honest-to-God treasure map."

Monk Mayfair suggested, "The old guy didn't show much imagination."

"Who wants imagination? If old Waldo Loring had any imagination, he'd have known anybody who would buy a shipload of uranium these days would knock his brains out.... You say Mr. Montgomery had this on him?"

"Right in his hip pocket."

"Tell me more," Coming Going urged. "What was really in the walking stick?"

"Nothing." Monk said. "We hadn't touched it. Doc just remembered that you had searched the room, and said the cane was standing in the closet while they were asleep."

Coming Going grinned happily. "I wish I had been there."

"I would have sold you my part of it cheap," I said.

"Mote, you were wonderful!" Glacia said delightedly.

I nodded. "That's right. I gave the star performance. I was the only one on our side who got licked."

They had converted a second-floor room with an eastern exposure into a hospital room for Coming Going, alias federal agent Joe Lybeck. . . . Presently Doc Savage came in with the news that the fat brothers and Colleen and Roy were locked up, and that attorney McBride had nothing more serious than a fractured skull.

Then Savage asked Glacia and me if we would care to have breakfast with him. He got an acceptance halfway through the invitation.

"We certainly played hard to get that time," I told Glacia when we were in our room trying to make ourselves look as if we hadn't been up all night letting people frighten us.

"He's a gorgeous hunk of man," Glacia said. She hung stars on the statement.

I was starting to put on a shoe, and I just sat there with it in both hands. It was all right, probably. Glacia was Glacia, and a little thing like last night wasn't likely to change her. But she was so damned objective. She knew what she wanted, and went after it. It was pretty obvious that right now she had Doc Savage in mind. And was I upset about that? I'll tell the world I was.

I put the shoe on carefully. I straightened the seam of a nylon. I hoped I looked cool and collected, because I wasn't. It had just dawned on me how interesting life could be. It probably wouldn't be. But possible? Who knows?

They don't shoot you for hoping.

THE END

I DIED YESTERDAY

The new client was a long-faced, sack-suited young man who came in wearing his lips drawn flat against his teeth. I remember having a first thought about him.... He needed the sun.

Miss Colfax came forward and bent her shining head at him, and he asked, "What is this place? A beauty shoppe?... Okay. I'll take the works."

I walked on. I was just passing anyway. Miss Colfax was an iceberg, and she was hired to preside at the door and throw out fat women who thought they could just walk in and become customers. It was part of the system. To become one of our customers was a shade more difficult than being presented to the court of St. James. That was part of the service they got for the prices we charged.

Miss Colfax could handle him. Miss Colfax could freeze a battleship, Admiral included, and send it rocking away with no steam left and full of respect. Miss Colfax was master of the most queenly snub yet invented. She was well-paid for it.

But she came into my office a few minutes later. "Miss Savage, I'm awfully sorry to trouble you," she said.

"Yes?"

"I've got one I can't handle," Miss Colfax said.

"The young man who came in a while ago?"

"Yes."

I thought about the young man for a moment. There had been something that was odd about his way. But then, what would you expect of a man who walked into an exclusively female establishment the way he had? Or even walked in.

"Intoxicated?"

"I think not," Miss Colfax said. She didn't look upset, but then she never had, and probably never would.

"Exactly what seems to be the difficulty?"

"He just walked in and asked for the works. I gave him my best *no*. He walked past me. He walked until he came to an analysis room, and went in and sat down. He won't budge."

"Is that all?"

Miss Colfax nodded. "Shall I call a cop?"

I left off frowning at the ceiling, and frowned at Miss Colfax. She wouldn't normally refer to a policeman as a cop. Not Miss Colfax; she would have more regal terminology for a cop. So she was flustered after all.

"What is he doing, Colfax? Chasing our girls around and around the furniture?"

Miss Colfax did not smile, and said, "Quite the contrary. I imagine some of them wouldn't be adverse. He's not bad-looking." Then she lowered her eyes to her hands and examined one of our best ten-dollar manicures. "I think they're looking forward to watching you throw him out," she added.

"Who is?"

"The hired help."

"Oh, they are, are they? And what is behind that kind of anticipation?"

Colfax lifted her head at my tone and said, "You've got me wrong. . . . It's just that they've heard about you."

"What," I asked, "have they heard about me?"

"Things. About excitement."

"I see."

"I'm afraid you haven't been living up to your reputation," said Colfax quietly.

I told her that some others hadn't been living up to their reputation around here, one of them being Miss Colfax, who was supposed to brush off pests. I said I would brush off this pest personally, then we would go into the other matter, the one about maintaining reputations.

"Yes, Miss Savage," Colfax said.

She wasn't very impressed, and I thought about that for a minute. Colfax was supposed to be awed by me, even if she wasn't spellbound by anyone else. Hitherto she had been. She wasn't now. She was even giving me, her employer, a little of the sass that our prestige-minded customers paid money for. There was just one answer—Colfax was right, and I hadn't been keeping up my reputation as a hair-raising adventuress, and I was losing standing. That sort of thing was bad. It could trickle down to the customers, and business would get bad.

"Throwing one obnoxious young man out won't prove anything, Miss Colfax," I said. "But I'll throw him out anyway. Where did you say he is?"

"In Analysis Room Three."

Our analysis rooms were like the settings they made for ten-carat diamonds; they were intended to emphasize the richness of the merchandise. Number Three was done in blonde mahogany and pastels of azure and dove, and it was calculated to make a frustrated customer feel that she had stepped upon the threshhold of symphonic harmony with nectarian living; it was a room ambrosial with the muscadine vibrations of the psyche aesthetic and the body sublime—that was the way the decorator had put it, or words almost like those, and he had achieved something that would be about like that if put into words. There was a more earthy way of putting it: the room was guaranteed to impress over-moneyed, overjaded rich-witches who were accustomed to being impressed. It did the job, too. We charged them fifty dollars for just being in the room.

The young man I was going to throw out had certainly made himself at home. He was stretched out on the astral blue couch, the one that was like a psychoanalyst's consulting couch. His fingers were laced together, his eyes were closed.

He was, as Colfax had said, not bad-looking. His gaunt good looks were of the Lincoln and Eamon de Valera sort, and his sacky tweed suit indicated he wasn't unaware of his typing and not above enhancing it a little with an outdoorsy motif. But his paleness detracted from the effect considerably.

Opening his eyes wearily before I could speak, he said, "Where am I? Would you mind telling me that?"

"Why bother? You won't be here long enough to make it important," I said.

"It's quite a fancy trap, whatever it is." He closed his eyes then, and I noticed that his face looked weary, infinitely tired and spent. The weariness was almost an ugliness. "You're not such bad bait, either."

"I'm glad we're not going to have any polite preliminaries. I was afraid we'd be delayed by them." I told him.

"You're beautiful," he said. "You're as lovely as the golden morning sun on a spring raincloud. I didn't see you very well. But I'm sure you are."

"You think so? Wait until—"

"There's more shines from you than just startling loveliness," he continued tiredly, his eyes still closed. "There's more, an electrical quality, a vibrating force. I think it's like a chemical reaction in a test-tube, like the mingling of strong acid with helpless fluid. You have a strong effect on everyone around you, don't you? Going out with you would be about as placid as carrying a lighted candle through a gasoline refinery, wouldn't it? Where did you get that combination of bronze hair and flake gold eyes?"

"Listen, I've had that kind of ammunition shot at me by experts," I said. "You might as well save your breath."

He turned his head away a little, with his eyes still shut. He wasn't concentrating on me, or on anything.

"It don't amount to one little thing how lovely you are." His voice was low now, thin and far, a weak thing that didn't reach the walls of the room. "I wish it did. I sure wish it did."

I began to think seriously of throwing him out the hard way. I'm supposed to be pretty good at judo.

"Would you like to go out head-first or feet-first?" I asked coldly. "We don't usually extend a choice, but you're beginning to seem like a special case."

"You effervesce," he said. His voice crawled further back into him. "That's it. You effervesce. You sizz. You're a Fourth-of-July sparkler. You're self-igniting, and you must be lovely to watch. . . . I can't see you. I wish I could."

"You might try opening your eyes."

"Why trouble? It wouldn't do any good. . . . No, I prefer to keep them closed, and that way I can compare you to Lucia. Lucia makes quite a contrast. Lucia isn't like you. Her misfortune. . . . And mine."

"So you've got woman-trouble?"

"Maybe I have. . . . I haven't thought it all the way out yet—but maybe I have. Could be."

"Name of Lucia?"

"Lucia. Yes."

"Doesn't Lucia appreciate a great big lanky hunk of man like you?"

A smile that was nothing but the spirit of a smile haunted his lips.

"Lucia is married to a helluva nice guy named Rich Thomas," he said.

"Oh, you've been jilted?"

"Lucia married Rich ten years ago," he said. I went a few steps closer, because his voice was now dying before it reached me. I listened to him add, "Lucia carries the world on her shoulders. That's her trouble."

"It looks to me," I told him, "as if Lucia isn't carrying you, but let you drop with a thud."

"Lucia should have been born God."

"Lucia sounds stuffy."

He didn't seem to be hearing me. "But it is the other way around," he continued. "Rich *was* born God. Rich is going to remake the world, and it won't take him any seven days, either."

"This seems to be rather divine company you've been keeping," I told him coolly. "Now let's get back to fundamentals. We can't use you around here. Even if you're an assistant Angel, which could be the impression you're trying to give, we still couldn't use you. How about taking a walk?"

He loosened a little more on the couch. There wasn't any animation in him anywhere. He might have been more pale, or it might only have seemed so. I had to lean forward to get the sound of his voice where it stopped, which was no more than six inches from his lips.

He said, "Would you run an errand for me?"

"Errand?"

"As far as the door," he said. "Go see if they've come in yet to finish killing me."

I went to work on him then. I could see that there wasn't any more time to lose, and that it was quite possible that too much had been lost already. What was wrong with him wasn't easy to find. He helped me a little; he had barely enough left in him to do that. He managed to get a hand around to his back and lay a finger on the spot.

I couldn't tell exactly what they had put into him, but it had a thin blade, and they had broken it off, snapped off the handle or whatever had been attached to the blade. There was just a small bead of bluish blood, and when I pressed on it with a finger, I could feel the sharp edge of steel underneath.

II

I walked to the door, threw it open, and told Colfax, "Get Farrar in here fast."

Colfax stared with pale, detached wonder. She wasn't alone. All the other employees who could decently loiter there were present, waiting to see me in action. But they hadn't expected to see a young man possibly in the act of dying, and on their faces was the thin shrill silence of horror.

"Pat, is he—" Colfax made a wooden movement with her hands. "I'll get Farrar!" she cried, and whirled and ran.

Farrar was my plastic surgeon, and he was also, with the exception of one man, probably the best in the business. The exception, the one man better than Farrar, and better than any specialist was likely to be for a number of generations, was my cousin, Doc Savage. But Doc Savage didn't demean his skill by sculpturing the faces of vain women, and Doc didn't work for money anyway, and also he wasn't too long on approval about my beauty salon business; and so Farrar was the best available.

Farrar came in a hurry. He began doing what he could.

"Colfax," I said. "You were at the door when he came in."

"Yes."

"You see anyone following him?"

"Who would—"

"Someone thrust a thin blade, ice-pick, or something of the sort, in his back, trying to kill him. He came in here to escape them."

Colfax's head came back stiffly and fear stirred in her eyes, like pale smoke.

"I saw no one." She said this with her lips only.

I said, "I'm going out and look around. Help Farrar. If he needs an ambulance, call one. Get him anything he needs."

"You're going out and—No! No—they may still be there!"

I went into my office, opened a cabinet, and took out a family heirloom, a little more than four pounds of old-fashioned single-action six-shooter. Hoglegs, those implements of mayhem were called in their day. I had inherited it from my father, who hadn't exactly used it as a paperweight in his time. I could stick five matches in a crack in a fence post at thirty yards and light at least four of them with it, and that was my father's doing too. He had shown me how.

Stowing the family treasure in a handbag a little smaller than a valise, I went out to look for murderers.

The hired help, who were never called by anything as vulgar as hired help, watched me depart with a collective expression of hair-on-end. My reputation was on the up-swing, I gathered.

It wasn't quite as devil-may-care as they seemed to think it was. I gave some thought to that, to the effect that excitement seems to have on me, while I was sauntering along the hallway looking for anything suspicious, and the result of my thought was a thankfulness that Doc Savage was not there watching. Excitement in any of the three forms it usually takes—danger, suspense or anticipation of violence—undeniably has a stimulating effect on me, and this trait, if it should be called a trait, must be a family inheritance just as much as the six-shooter in my handbag. Doc Savage once told me that it was a blemish that passed along in the Savage blood. He said this unhappily. He also said that he was going to cure me of it, and he said the same thing on other occasions, but never very confidently. Firmly, yes. Angrily, also. But never with much certainty.

My cousin Doc Savage has the same blemish himself, although he just looked erudite and poker-faced when I pointed this out. He was a victim of the same intoxication about excitement that I was, because nothing else would very well explain the odd profession he followed, a profession which was—and nobody should be fooled by the Galahadish sound of his work—righting wrongs and punishing evildoers who were out of reach of the usual law enforcement agencies.

Doc Savage, who had been literally lifted from the cradle by a rather odd-minded father and put in the hands of scientists and specialists for years of training, was a remarkable combination of scientific genius, muscular marvel and mental wizard. To say that about Doc sounds melodramatic and a little ridiculous, but the fact remains that he was a startling individual. He was primarily trained as a surgeon, and could easily have led that profession in practice. He was also an electrical engineer, chemist, and several other things, of startling ability.

But Doc followed none of these professions. He did research in them, sporadically, and contributed his discoveries, which were outstanding, to the general welfare. The rest of the time, he followed adventure, in the company of five specialists—Monk Mayfair, the chemist; Ham Brooks, the lawyer; Johnny Littlejohn, the archaeologist and geologist; Renny Renwick, the engineer, and Long Tom Roberts, the electrical wizard—men who had the same liking for adventure that Doc Savage had.

Doc Savage led a wonderful life. His name could make

men shudder in the far corners of the earth—the sort of men who should shudder, that is. Someone tried to kill him at least once a month. It was always the very best talent that tried, because the idea of going up against Doc Savage would scare a second-rater green. Doc was appreciated, too. He could, by making the mildest sort of a request, get unbelievable cooperation from any governments of the right sort. He did things daily, as a matter of course, greater and more exciting than most people achieve in their lifetime. He really did. He was my cousin, and members of a family usually underrate the accomplishments of the rest of the kinfolks. He was probably even better than I thought he was.

Doc Savage and I had our differences. Personally, I could use money, and I didn't mind chipping it off those who were heavily plated with it. Doc was independent of money. He had—and this was true, far-fetched or not—a lost tribe of Mayans in Central America who supplied him with fabulous quantities of gold, out of gratitude for a service he'd done them. That was the way Doc Savage was. A little unbelievable.

But the main difference, and point of dissension, between Doc Savage and myself was this first matter of liking excitement. Danger affected me in a way that was—well—a little abnormal, as I am sure it did Doc also. To me, excitement was a heady thing, irresistible, fascinating, drawing wildly at me. Not that I didn't have fear at the prescribed times. Whether it was a normal amount of fear, I don't know, because who can measure a thing like that in himself or herself? What do you use for a yardstick?

Oh, to sum it up, Doc Savage and I were bitterly at odds on one point—he wouldn't let me take part in the wonderfully exciting adventures he was always having. He called it keeping me out of trouble, because I was a girl. He was stubborn as a mule about this. He didn't even let me know when he was in New York part of the time, for fear I'd horn in on something.

Naturally, I jumped in whenever I could. Who was I to defy a family trait? It was too interesting not to defy it.

I nearly didn't find the killer, due to the fact that I almost overlooked a kindergarten item that every policeman knows: Murderers don't necessarily look like murderers.

He was a bobbing little fuss-duddy of a man. He should have chirped as he hopped along. He looked like a bird, a drab one, a sparrow.

He came out of an office and went into another one. He came out of that one, and entered still another, and I followed him into that one, not really suspecting him yet, but interested in him because I couldn't figure what business would take him into the office of an oil-well tool supply concern, a fashion magazine, an insurance agency.

He took off his hat, and his hair was the same coal smoke grey as his suit. He said to the receptionist in that office, "I was to meet Doctor Cleagle here."

"I'm afraid I don't know Doctor Cleagle," he was told.

"But I don't understand. . . . I was told the Doctor came— there had been an accident—a young man, something had happened to him."

"Sorry."

"Perhaps, if I described the young man who was— ah—injured . . ."

And so help me if the little sparrow didn't describe young Abraham Lincoln-De Valera who was lying in my establishment with the sliver of steel in him.

"No, sorry," said the receptionist, who then turned to me and asked, "What can I do for you, Miss?"

I leaned over the desk and told her that I would like to see Mr. Illminer—one of the names on the door—about some insurance. Not a bad idea to have insurance, either, I thought. I could see the little man from the corner of an eye. He was looking absently at me, not at my legs but at a spot on my back that corresponded to the resting-place of the thin steel in the lanky young man, or so it seemed to me. It was quite a creepy sensation. Then he took out a handkerchief, a neat white one which he unfolded, and he blotted at his face. He turned and left while the receptionist was telling me that I would have a short wait to see Mr. Illminer, and I said sorry, I'd have to run along.

The business end of my big gun had a satisfyingly firm feeling when it came against his back. We were alone in the office-building hall. Just to make it better, I put the gun nose to the spot where the steel reposed in the other man.

"This is a gun," I told him. "And if you have any preconceived notions about women, don't be misled by them."

He twisted his head around sufficiently on a thin neck to see that it was a gun, and his eyes, brightly round and bird-like, came out a little.

"I understand," he said.

"Remember, don't be misled."

"I won't."

I pushed on the gun so that it gouged into the significant spot on his back, and asked, "Remind you of anything?"

He said, and it sounded surprisingly mild, "I'm afraid visions of my long and misspent life aren't going to flash before my eyes, as they are supposed to do. Really, young lady—"

"It was in him right at that spot."

"I don't believe I—"

"It was a small blade. It didn't make the commotion that this thing will if I let it go."

He stood as still then as the statue of General Grant on Riverside Drive, and he began to get a little of the General's marble coloring. His shoulders became concave, a trifle saucer-shaped, trying to get away from the hard iron touch of the gun. And he was thinking. His mind was chasing ideas like a fox after rabbits.

"You heard me asking about young Thayer," he said finally. "Yes, you followed me into that office and heard my inquiry. Well, I can explain that. You see—"

I said, "You've had time to think up a nice lie. I'll bet it's interesting, but let's save it a minute. . . . Do you think you could perform a simple act like raising your hands without provoking me into shooting you?"

"You wouldn't shoot me."

"You think so? Try me and see."

His shoulders squirmed a trifle more, and dropped a bit in discouragment, or I hoped it was discouragement, and he said, "I wish I had taken a closer look at you. You seemed to be a very lovely girl, the sort who would howl like anything at a mouse. Yet now you sound—there's something about you— I can't be sure—"

"And you're not a mouse. The hands up, do you mind?"

He lifted his hands then, and I noticed that they didn't tremble, which was a bad sign, a warning to be careful with him. There are ways—they teach them to policemen and soldiers—of taking a gun from another person, and they work astonishingly well. I watched those. He had a billfold. And a camera. Nothing else. Absolutely nothing else.

The billfold contained a hundred-dollar banknote, two tens, three ones. No cards. No identification. But it was an old billfold and its shape showed that he customarily carried cards in it.

The camera was a tiny, expensive job. A 35-millimeter, with an F2 lens and shutter speed up to a thousandth of a second. It evidently contained film, and fourteen exposures had been taken.

"Mind giving me the camera back?" He was looking over his shoulder at me now, like an owl twisting its neck.

"It'll be safe. I'll turn it over to a policeman, if you like. He'll take care of it for you."

"Very funny." His voice was a little guttural. "That camera cost me plenty. I don't want it stolen from me."

"It won't be."

"I'm going to argue with you about the camera," he said sharply.

"All right. But let's have a referee. Let's go into my place, and perhaps call an attentive policeman—"

He was beginning to turn slowly, swinging his head around first, then his shoulders and the rest of his body following in a slow wheeling that was almost imperceptible, and his eyes were fixed on mine. That was the gimmick—he was holding my gaze, and gripping by intention by that slow wheeling, not turning fast enough to start anything, but still turning so that I noticed it and would give it attention. That was the whole purpose. To hold my attention. But he slipped a little, and his eyes left mine for an instant, crossed my shoulder, and there was a kind of wild appeal in them. It's probably an old trick to tell someone with a gun there's another person behind him; anyway it has been worked to death in books. But he wasn't doing that. He was too subtle about it. *He had a friend behind me.*

It was a bad moment then. This fellow was no amateur; the moment he knew that I knew there was someone back of me, the instant that fact had all my interest, he'd take my gun. He probably knew how to do it. That pelted through my mind, and a lot of other things. . . . To move slow? Or move fast? Or stand there? Or was I wrong? . . . I decided to move in a hurry, but he understood that I knew them, and he did that whirling striking motion that the judo instructors teach the rookie policemen. He went for my gun He didn't get it. But then I didn't have it either, for it was knocked from my hand and sailed through the air.

I was after the gun fast. I was after it while it was still in the air, before it hit the shiny parquet hallway floor—after it and praying it wouldn't bang off a bullet in my direction when it hit the floor. It was an old gun built for simple business, and it had no foolishness like safeties.

The sparrow had a friend in the hall, a very young-looking boy with skim-milk skin and eyes that were large, calf-like, benign, and the color of ripe dewberries. He was a big boy, too, with football shoulders. But he had a single-track mind, and he was still looking foolishly at the spot where I had stood.

"Get her!" the sparrow gasped.

The broad-shouldered young one took this and thought about it. His jaw lowered, his brow furrowed. He had to take it, arrange it, understand it.

The old six-gun didn't discharge when it struck the floor. But it did skid, and I kept after it.

The small man was completely unlike the other in his thinking. He must have been chain-lightning. He evidently weighed everything, his chances of getting to the gun ahead of me, the likelihood of his being able to do himself good if we reached it simultaneously, and the unfortunate things that might happen to him if he over-guessed himself. He debated all this. For time, he used nothing flat. And he reached a sensible conclusion, and turned and ran.

"Get the camera!" he yelled at his slow-witted young giant. "Take the camera. Quick! Get the camera, Abraham!"

He strung this out behind him as he left, mixed it with the frantic whetting of his feet on the floor, and by the time the last word fell, the large young man—Abraham, if that was his name, and there was no one else around to answer to it, so evidently it was—had stopped. Abraham halted ponderously, the way a truck halts at a puzzling crossroads. He didn't look after his fleeing companion; he didn't gaze at me particularly. Abraham had stopped to take a new idea.

The old gun was hard and heavy and good in my fingers now, and I turned, still crouching, ready to shoot the sparrow in a leg. But I didn't, and for a good reason—his angel of evil was riding with him, and an elevator door had opened. It was chance. The pure ugly luck that the devil hands out. The elevator doors had eased back with no more sound than flame on a match. The sparrow flicked inside, his coattails out straight as a board from speed.

That left Abraham, and I pointed the gun at him, let him

look into the large round cavity where the noise could come out. I didn't tell him to stand still, nor raise his hands; it didn't seem necessary. He could see the bullets in the cylinder, and they should be looking as large as skulls to him.

Abraham was to be an odd one. How odd, I now got an inkling.

He asked blankly, "What do I do now?"

I didn't know he meant the question seriously, because I didn't know Abraham yet. He really wished to know what he should do.

"You can run," I said sarcastically, "if you think you can dodge some lead."

He accepted the first part, took it literally. Because that was the way Abraham was; he could accomodate one idea at a time, if it was a small idea in two or three words, and not handed to him crosswise. I had told him to run, and so he ran.

I was so astonished I didn't shoot him anywhere.

The elevator was waiting, and his friend heard him laying his large heavy feet on the corridor floor. It must have been a disturbing sound, and the view-mirror beside the elevator door must have given a picture of what was happening. Because the small drab man screamed. "Get the camera, Abraham!"

But Abraham steamed ahead for the elevator. Perhaps he hadn't noticed any camera.

The sparrow shrieked imprecations. Mostly what he screeched was incoherent. He tried to hurl the sliding doors closed. But Abraham was there now. He gripped the door, wrenched it open, his great shoulders bunching, with no more effort than opening an envelope. Abraham went into the elevator.

I was there by now, in front of the elevator doors, and I had pushed astonishment aside, and was ready to let the six-shooter take up the argument. But there were half a dozen innocent passengers crowded in the rear of the elevator, and nowhere to shoot without hitting one of them if the bullet went through its target, which it would.

"What do I do now?" Abraham asked the sparrow.

The little man was fit to be strait-jacketed. He emitted one more screech, while he was falling against the doors, and he got the doors sliding shut.

My right foot in the crack of the closing door was the

best I could do. He kicked it out. The door shut. The elevator left with a thick whispering that backgrounded, but did not cancel out, the things he had to say about Abraham and Abraham's ancestors.

III

Within five minutes I knew they had taken an express elevator—it would have made no difference; they wouldn't have let it stop enroute down anyway—and at least ten people had as many different descriptions of the sparrow and his single-witted companion. The ten were trying to tell it to anyone who would listen in the lobby. There were four different opinions of which way and by what method the pair had departed, but three of the opinions were by taxicab, so that was probably right.

Miss Colfax had a high shrill look in her eyes when I came back.

"I—I hear you tried to shoot a couple of men," she said.

"News travels fast, and ties itself into knots getting there," I told her. "What does Farrar say about young Thayer?"

"Thayer . . . ?" Colfax looked at me blankly.

"The young fellow who dropped in here to do his dying, and I'll bet you that turns out to be his name," I said.

"Doctor Farrar had him removed to his office," Colfax explained.

I found Farrar dabbling his fingers in a large tray of fixing bath in which an X-ray negative reposed. The red darkroom light gave his face an unreal, satanic cast that enhanced the worry he was wearing, and presently he switched on the white light behind the viewing box, lifted the wet negative from the bath, washed it briefly, and slapped it against the illuminated glass.

"So you X-rayed Thayer already," I said. "That's quick work."

"Thayer?" Farrar was puzzled.

"I met a small drab man in the hall, and the resulting conversation led me to believe that might be your patient's name."

Farrar nodded vaguely, not understanding but not partic-ularly upset about his lack of comprehension, and used the tip of a pencil to indicate certain parts of the negative. He said, "A vertebraic perforation, and an incipient myelin rupture. I was afraid of something of the sort." He did some more poking and peering. "That isn't good." He straightened, and his face was sober. "It isn't good at all."

I knew, of course, that the vertebrae are the backbone, but the word myelin was only doctor's abracadabra as far as I was concerned. I asked him to explain that, and anything else he could get across in plain English.

Farrar said, "The blade, which seems to be an ice-pick, actually passed through the backbone, breaking off a small spear-shaped fragment of bone which, due to the position in which it is lodged is almost certain to be forced into the spinal cord when the blade is withdrawn. You can see how pressure of the blade in the position it occupies is holding the bone dagger forced away from the spinal cord."

"Won't an operation do any good?"

He got out a handkerchief and wiped his face. "Not one chance in a thousand, unless we had a man capable of doing it."

"Do you know a surgeon good at that sort of thing?"

Farrar shrugged. "The woods are full of specialists. . . . But this isn't an ordinary job. I'd say that—well—you can guess who comes to my mind. Doc Savage."

"Could Doc do it?"

"If anyone can," Farrar said, nodding.

"All right, if Doc is in the city, he's our man," I said.

Farrar rubbed his jaw, and began dubiously, "Well, if you think he'll touch—" He stopped, looked uncomfortable, and finished. "Of course, Savage would be excellent."

"What did you start to say?"

He glanced at me, looked away, pocketed his hands and complained. "Something I shouldn't have started to say. I've—uh—heard rumors that you and Doc Savage are not on—uh—shall we say, the best of terms."

"You heard wrong. We're on the best terms. The very best. We have some of the most dignified fights you ever listened to."

"Very well. If you think Savage will do this job."

"He will when I get through outfoxing him."

Reaching the door, another thought came to me, and I turned back to indicate the X-ray darkroom and ask, "Can you develop a camera film in there?"

"What kind?"

"A 35-millimeter film, one from a small candid camera."

Farrar shook his head. "Not with X-ray developer. Too hot. Give you a grainy negative. . . . Better take it to a place where they do line grain work."

It was not difficult to get Doc Savage's headquarters on the telephone, but getting through to him was a different matter. The first hurdle, a private detective agency which was hired to monitor and screen all calls on his listed phone, was easily circumvented—I knew Doc's unlisted number, which got me as far as Monk Mayfair.

Monk's small, squeaky, child-like voice had the same sort of distinction that a cricket has in a barrel. It didn't sound like Monk looked, nor did Monk act in keeping with Monk's reputation. Monk was an eminent chemist; it could be said without much exaggeration that he was world-renowned, but he had the manners and dignity of a fourteen-year-old hooligan from the wrong side of the tracks.

"I'm supposed to say no," he said to my inquiry as to whether Doc Savage was in town.

"You mean no just to me?"

"That's what I mean," said Monk cheerfully. "You're the kitten who drags the big, terrible rats into our parlor."

"I'd like to talk to Doc."

"No can do. We're in the process of unofficially disowning you. . . . What have you got on your mind?"

The thing that would interest Doc Savage, and the only possible thing that would persuade him to let me come within a mile of him when I was even faintly tainted with excitement, would be an appeal to his Galahadish side. Doc would function as an angel of mercy, but he wouldn't even listen to me if I came with a ready-made package of trouble. He would welcome the trouble separately, if it was interesting trouble, but he wouldn't tolerate a package deal with me included.

So I told Monk that a young man had walked into my beauty shoppe with an ice-pick blade in his back, and was going to die if Doc didn't do surgery and save him. I made it dramatic, coating the story with terror and tears—you could lay it on as heavy as you wished with Monk, because he was a sucker for any female. He would accept the most preposterous lie for gospel, if a woman told it to him.

"Holy smoke, I'll get Doc on the wire for you," Monk gasped before I had nearly all the stops out.

Then Doc Savage's marvelously capable voice was addressing me with all the enthusiasm of a banker interviewing a client trying to float a loan on an honest face.

"It has been some time since you came skipping in on us with a little case of trouble that would scare a normal person green," he said. "I knew it was too good to last."

I gave him the same story I'd put to Monk, minus the trembling and tears. And minus some other points. I didn't tell him I'd gone hunting the stabbers, had found them, had come out unfavorably in the encounter, and had a camera and some weakness in the knees to show for my efforts. He wasn't fooled.

"That tale sounds three-legged to me," he said.

"You're unfair."

"No, I've just had some experience with you," Doc said. "You say Farrar examined the fellow? Put Farrar on."

Doc Savage spoke to Doc Savage for a while, breathlessly as if he was being received by the Master. Mostly they talked big-worded medical nomenclature, things like anterior poliomyelitis and spastic paraplegia due to bilateral cerebral lesion. Farrar was earnest, apologetic, and in the end gasped with relief, "I'd like to observe you do the surgery!" Then he handed the phone to me, explaining, "The Doctor would like to speak to you again."

"Pat," Doc Savage asked, "did you invite the victim into your place of business?"

"Good Lord, no!"

"Why did he pick on you?"

"I don't know. Accident, I suppose."

"I think somebody took a round-about way of laying something in my lap," Doc Savage said dryly. "What do you think?"

"But this fellow Thayer didn't even seem to know where he was—"

"That, toward the last, could have been the result of the injury to his spine. I imagine he knew very well where he was going when he walked in there."

"That was a sad error he made, wasn't it? I mean—he mustn't have known I never participate in your adventures, mustn't he?"

"That's not very subtle sarcasm, Pat. And if he knew you never get me in trouble, he knew something that I don't."

"Oh, then you're going to let me go along with you on this one—"

"Now you know better than that."

"But what do I do now?"

"You may return to the practice of that refined piracy you call a beauty salon, young lady. . . . And just let me make one flat statement—you stay out of this, you understand?"

"Yes, I understand you clearly," I said—a statement that was for the benefit of Farrar, who was standing there listening to my end of the conversation. I hung up then, and raked back over what Farrar had heard me say, concluding it might, with a little deft addition, be enough to fool him.

"Farrar, I'm going to work with Doc Savage on this mystery. We're going to find out why young Thayer was stabbed, and also what Thayer meant by saying that a woman named Lucia *should* have been born God, but that her husband Rich Thomas had been, because husband Rich was going to re-make the world, and not in any seven days either. I think Thayer was saying something important when he said that. It should be investigated."

Farrar looked at me oddly. "You're going to work with Doc Savage?"

"Of course."

He pocketed his hands, shifted his gaze uncomfortably to the floor, and advised, "It so happens that Doc instructed me specifically that you were not to be involved. . . . More exactly, you were not to know as much as what hospital Thayer was taken to for the operation."

I tried something that I knew was not going to do any good. Tried to stare him down. "Farrar, you're not going to go along with such nonsense?"

"I'm afraid so, Miss Savage."

There was some temptation to ask him if he recalled who was paying his salary, but fortunately I got that one stopped in time. Farrar would have replied, politely and stiffly, that beginning now, nobody was paying him a salary. That was exactly what he would do. And I'd have lost the best plastic surgeon who was available.

"Farrar, you seem to place Doc Savage very highly."

"Very highly," he agreed.

"You're a good man, Farrar."

There seemed to be no point in carrying it farther, but if they thought they had me boxed in, they were mistaken. I went into my office, called Colfax in and told her, "I want you to get me Thayer's hat and coat. Bring them here."

"How will I—"

"Just walk in and remark to Farrar that you'll take care of Thayer's coat and hat, then bring them here. And step on it, will you. Time is important here."

She was back in hardly more than a minute with the tweedy coat and the hat. Both were distinctive garments. "Thanks, Colfax. Now, I want the mannequin—the male one—we used a few weeks ago in the lobby display. It's in the storeroom. I want it—a wheeled stretcher—the rubber-tired one that is in the storeroom—and two blankets, a pillow, everything in the storeroom. Take the coat and hat in there too. I'll be with you in a minute."

Colfax nodded and went out, looking excited in her glassy way, and I took the big old six-shooter out of my purse and laid it on the desk. I frowned at the elderly cannon—knowing now, when it was a little too late, that I shouldn't have depended on it. . . . I should have used some of Doc Savage's gadgets.

Doc Savage, earlier in his career, had shown a flair for creating gadgets which he employed in his adventures. He no longer used them as much; I sometimes suspected that was a phase of his life that he was trying to live down. Doc had explained it a little differently: "A man who has a good tool is inclined to come to depend too much on that tool, and if it's taken away from him, he's helpless," he told me once. "I used to think that applied particularly to a man with a gun, which is why I've never carried one. Now I've concluded it applies to any mechanical aid, and so I'm not depending as much on tricky gadgets. A quick wit and a sharp mind are better. You can't be disarmed of those so readily."

That was fine, if you could devote a lifetime to developing a quick wit and sharp mind, as he had. For the rest of us, who didn't have a tribe of grateful Mayans to keep us in spending money, gadgets were not to be sneezed at.

Personally, I had been grieved that Doc no longer made as much use of gadgets. His astonishing scientific devices, which he pulled out of his hat at the most unexpected times, had given him a great deal of color and a weird touch that I liked. His contraptions, and some of them were stunning in their ingenuity, were symbolic of Doc's wizardy. Yet he seemed determined to drop away from using them, and that spoiled a lot of Doc's special flavor for me.

The fact was, I'd made a collection of his past gadgets. Sort of a museum of them. I had enlisted his aides—principally Monk Mayfair, but the others had helped too—to assist in assembling them. I had a couple of hundred of them—and I didn't have near all of them, which gives an idea of Doc's prolific ingenuity—and I knew how to use them. I'd rigged a special room, adjacent to my office, for their storage. Someday, when I'm a doddering old lady, the Smithsonian will probably be very grateful for them. In the meantime, I had them, had learned to use them—and I intended to make use of them now.

It required only a couple of minutes to collect the gadgets I would probably need. It was that simple because I had copied Doc's system of carrying them. I changed shoes, put on a trim grey suit, a snappy dark hat, re-did my hair slightly, and carried a different handbag. I was wearing them now. Maybe it took more than a couple of minutes, but not much more.

Colfax was waiting in the storeroom. She had read my mind, and she had the male dummy wearing Thayer's noticeable tweed coat and hat, and lying on the litter under a blanket.

"This what you wanted?" Colfax asked with a perfectly expressionless face.

"Fine. Colfax, you're a wonder. Phone the garage to have my station-wagon waiting out front—"

"I did that."

"You *are* wonderful!... All right, we'll get this into the hall through a side door, and into an elevator. I don't want Farrar seeing me. He's fallen in with Doc's starry-eyed notions about woman's place being in the home."

It went smoothly for us, with the station-wagon there and waiting, and the elevator starter and an operator helping us load the dummy as carefully as if they were handling a wounded man. Five dollars and a brief explanation accomplished the latter.

Colfax, a little pale now, asked, "Do you wish me to go along?"

"Want to?"

Colfax shook her head. "No, thank you—I'm already scared stiff. . . . Isn't this likely to be dangerous?"

"What possibly could be dangerous about hauling a dummy around the streets?"

"If they tried to kill him once, they'll want to finish the job," Colfax said dryly.

"Could be."

"Bait," said Colfax, shaking her head again, "is something I don't crave to be. Not bait for murder."

"Everyone to their taste, Colfax. That's what makes it such a diversified world," I mixed a smile with that, so Colfax wouldn't get the notion her courage was in doubt. It wasn't, either, because Colfax had all anyone needs.

"How long," asked Colfax, "before I send out a posse?"

"Oh, give me an hour. And after that, if I haven't turned up wearing the smile of the cat beside the empty canary cage, you'd better make it the cavalry, the U. S. Marines, the whole works."

"Doc Savage?" she asked pointedly.

"That's what I meant."

"I'm glad," said Colfax, shuddering, "that I don't have the sort of malady that makes one crave danger."

"Without the disease, you'll never have the wonderful fever that goes with it, Colfax," I said, and slid behind the wheel and drove the station-wagon away.

I felt, then, a little foolish. Because this was a very long shot I was taking, no more than an arrow loosed generally into the darkness where there were wild animals. It might hit nothing. Nobody might try to finish off my supposed passenger. If that didn't happen, the arrow would be for nothing and I would feel very silly indeed.

And before long I understood why I had done a thing like this. It was because Doc Savage might have done something of the sort—but when Doc did them, they always seemed to pay off, and now I wasn't so sure I would have that luck. Doc had a way, a kind of magical perception. Sometimes I thought I had it too, but often I wasn't so sure.

The excitement began to wear off. Bank-fishing with a cane pole and getting no bites isn't my style. I stewed.

Impatience, presumably, is a sour taste that everyone has in varying degrees. Some bear it better than others. We Savages, I think, carry it poorly. I know my father was that way, and his father before him; our grandfather had been little inclined to sit in his log cabin waiting for the Indians to attack, but had gone out looking for them instead. A grand old guy. There were villages named for him all over the northwest.

It was a long drink of sour-silly tasting impatience that I had, but there was a tart olive at the bottom of it, and a violent one. It took the form of a truck. An enormous truck, full-bodied as a house, but drab-looking and not conspicuous as trucks go.

A fantastic thing, but I didn't have time to think of that. Not until it was gone. The truck had angled in front of me with that loutish air that trucks and many large things seem to have. A traffic light showed a green eye, and everything stopped, the truck ahead of me, and then the truck inched forward a little, a few feet. The whole back end of the truck fell down, flopped down like a hinge, making a sort of ramp. And then, with a stunning power—not a crash, just a shove, gentle and then hard and powerful—a car behind me gave the station-wagon a shove. My vehicle jumped forward. The car behind followed, pushed—my station wagon was boosted up the ramp and into the van body.

I turned the wheel hard now, but it was too late; the swerve of the station-wagon only jammed a fender against the inside of the van. The car behind, backing away, raced its motor noisily, and then there was a grinding of machinery followed by darkness.

There was a feeling of motion then. The truck was carrying me away.

IV

The station-wagon engine idled gently with the rather startled sound of a big cat, and I thought of how swiftly the exhaust would pour poisonous carbon monoxide into the tight small room that was the inside of the truck. So I switched off the engine.

We were not moving fast enough to interest a traffic cop, and the street sounds, while audible, were surprisingly faint. The inside of the van was thoroughly sound-proofed with heavy quilted material. I waited until there was no motion— probably we had stopped for a traffic light—and put back my head and screamed for help. It seemed like a deafening effort, but possibly it wasn't much outside. And all it got me was radio music. I could hear in a moment, a car radio playing loudly in the cab. That took care of the screaming; it wasn't much use.

There wasn't a lot of appeal to the idea of crashing the station-wagon out through the back of the truck, but being hauled off somewhere helplessly was less appealing, so I started the engine again, meshed the gears in reverse, and stamped the throttle down hard. The station-wagon jumped back all of two feet, stopped with a jolt that snapped my head back. It hadn't even hit the rear of the van. I got out and looked, and found there was a steel bar contraption, or rather a series of steel bars, which had been released and dropped down to pen in the station-wagon.

"Tried everything, baby?" The voice—hoarse, guttural— had the obvious unnaturalness of being disguised.

"Can you hear me?" I asked.

"Like you had that pretty head on my shoulder, baby."

Now the voice could be located—it came from an ordinary public-address loudspeaker mounted overhead.

"This trap is something," I said.

"Impress you, does it, tutz?"

"Fixing a truck up like this took a couple of weeks work, didn't it?"

"Think so?"

"That much at least. It has been less than an hour since I got involved in whatever I'm involved in, so it follows that the truck wasn't prepared just to catch me."

"That's sure logical, ain't it, tutz," the voice said cheerfully.

"Just how did you happen to be all set for me?"

"Honeychild, we always go loaded for bear."

"I'm going to set this thing on fire."

"It's fireproofed, baby."

"There's plenty of gasoline in my station-wagon. I'll bet I make some smoke that attracts attention."

"I'll bet you're hotter than a firecracker before any smoke shows."

He had a point there. It would be foolish to start a gasoline fire in the van body, which I recalled as being made of sheet steel.

There was one more thing to try. "Mr. Thayer is very seriously wounded and needs an immediate operation," I said earnestly. "He's going to die if you don't let me take him to a hospital. If that happens, I'm sure you will be charged with murder."

"Yak, yak, yak," the voice said. "I'm shaking in my boots, if I had boots."

I climbed back into the station-wagon, and sat loosely there, deciding I was completely shaken by surprise. Actually, I was probably scared until all the threads were loose. But it was no time for a case of terror, and so I told myself it was just surprise—that it was incredible they could have been so well-prepared against the rare chance that I would move Thayer from my place in a car, and be all set to trap me in this bizarre fashion... Still, it wasn't too illogical, because they must have known how seriously Thayer was wounded, and surmise that he would be moved in an ambulance. With this truck contraption they could have caught an ambulance as easily as they had taken my station-wagon.

There was another chance, to which I tried to pin hopes—someone must have seen the station-wagon being bumped headlong into the truck. Anyone seeing it *should* give an alarm. But had they? Thinking it over, I decided they probably wouldn't, because the incident was fantastic, and New Yorkers have a way of regarding anything too unusual as being a publicity stunt or a zany gag. New Yorkers are afraid of making fools of themselves; they're exposed to the unusual so much that they become immune to it. Oh, the story of a big truck swallowing a station-wagon might seep out eventually, and the newspapers might even publish a squib about it—too late to do me any good.

The rest of the ride could be summed up as about an hour of acute dissatisfaction during which I lost at least two pounds. Came a jolting, a heaving around of the great truck as if it were crossing the disgruntled body of a huge animal, really only a rough lane, no doubt, and stillness came. No motion. No sound at all.

"Hello?" My voice was thinner and higher than I liked. "Are we there? Have we arrived?"

"Baby," said disguised-loudspeaker-voice. "Baby, do you like it in there?"

I hesitated, then suggested, "There might be worse places—and I'm not fooling."

"There could be. There very well could be. . . . But it's

nice you like it in there. I'm glad to hear that. Because you're going to stay there for a while."

"Stay in this truck? For how long?"

"Oh, a week or two."

"But Mr. Thayer—"

"He can keep you company, tutz. The lucky stiff—and I'm not just kidding. He wouldn't be a stiff by now, by any chance?"

I didn't say anything. I didn't want too much interest aroused in Thayer, lest they—or one of them, if there was only one, and I had heard only a single voice so far—discover that Thayer was a beauty-shop show window mannequin.

Presently, in a disgruntled way, the voice said, "Oh well, if you're off speaking terms, it's okay by me, baby. . . . But now you listen to me: I'm going to open the side door—there is one, in case you hadn't noticed it—and slip you some canned tomatoes. You probably won't like canned tomatoes afterward but they'll do you for a diet."

I got ready for him then. I hadn't been entirely doping off during the ride, and I had the collection of Doc Savage gadgets I'd brought. The trinket I selected was one Doc Savage had used as much as any other, a little glass globule that contained a liquefied anaesthetic gas that would vaporize instantly, and nothing perceptible in the way of color or odor, and would knock a person senseless in what practically amounted to nothing flat. It was wonderful stuff, that gas; its potent agency was oxidized and nullified by the oxygen in normal air in approximately forty seconds. You could hold your breath—almost anyone can hold their breath fifty seconds or a minute in a pinch—while the stuff knocked out the other fellow, then be on with your business. The victims were usually out for about fifteen minutes, with not much more than a foolish feeling for after-effects.

A latch clucked on the side of the truck—or what sounded like a latch—and I watched the spot expectantly, the globule of anaesthetic gas poised. The minute my friend looked in, he was going to get it in the face.

The silence was like time stopped. Not another sound for twenty seconds, forty. . . . The door didn't open in the side of the van; as a matter of fact. I couldn't distinguish any sign of a door by the reflected light from the station wagon headlamps, which was the only illumination I had.

There was a sudden pell-mell of sound behind me—a

door whiffed open, a heavy object thumped inside, the door whacked shut. I'd been foxed. The door was on the other side of the van!

"Yak, yak," said my tormentor from the loudspeaker presently, "Fooled you, didn't I? Sissy, if you'll look at the box I dumped inside, you'll find it's a case of canned tomatoes, and—"

I went around to the other side, found the spot that was cut out in the padding for the door, and pried it loose near the bottom. Into this spot I inserted another Doc gadget, this one a grenade, too. But not gas. This one, not as large as a grape, was concentrated violence. I got into the station-wagon, rolled the windows down so there wouldn't be as much flying glass, got the blankets off the dummy and wrapped them around my head and hands.

The explosion was better than a bargain. It changed the shape of the side of the station-wagon, and changed my ideas about ever using one of them in such close confines again.

Dizzy, deafened, I found the hole in the side of the truck and tossed out one of the gas pellets. That came near being too hasty a move; holding my breath for the needed minute was enormously difficult.

The breath-holding, the latter part of it, was made pleasant by having heard a man, evidently of some bulk, falling to the floor.

I crawled out into what proved to be a large and unused barn to learn what my gadgeteering had bagged. He was a squarish bulk in a careless suit and he occupied an attitude of restful sleep on the floor. He had bumped his nose in falling, and it was leaking crimson very slightly. It wasn't a large nose, and it was no asset to a wide and remarkably homely face—I was tempted to kick it further out of shape.

I sat down and waited the fifteen minutes that it took him to get over his whiff of anaesthetic. By that time, I was full of words.

He sat up, felt of his nose, and said, "That was a dirty trick, Pat."

"You should know," I advised him. "Since you're an authority on dirty tricks."

He was Monk Mayfair. He ran to breadth and pleasantly homely baboon looks, and, as I mentioned, he was a great chemist when he took time out from chasing excitement to practice his profession, which was rarely. Since he was one of

Doc Savage's five assistants. I had a fair idea of what had happened to me.

"You look kinda irritated," Monk ventured.

"You think so?" I asked.

"Now wait a minute! I don't like that expression in your eye! Just because I outfoxed you—"

"Outfoxed—me? Take a look at your ankles. Notice the nice rope tied around them? I could have tied your wrists too, but I believe in giving even a dog half a chance. Now, I've got a nice hypodermic needle here, filled with stuff that will make you sleep about a week. I'm going to use it for a little game of pin-the-tail-on-the-donkey, with guess who for donkey."

"Pat!" he yelled in alarm. "My God, it was only a joke—"

"Oh sure, Monk, all a joke—"

"Wait! Be reasonable! It was Doc's idea—"

"I knew whose idea it was as soon as I saw your silly face," I told him. "All right, I'll listen. What is the story?"

"Why, Doc thought he would teach you to stop horning in on our little shindigs." Monk looked at me uneasily. "After you telephoned him, he hung up and looked at me and said, 'Monk, Pat sounded innocent, and that's a bad sign. I'm sure she's going to jump headlong into this mess, if she hasn't already. So we're going to stop that right now.' And then he told me what to do with the truck."

"Who was driving the car that rammed me from behind?" I asked.

"Oh, him. The private detective who screens Doc's calls. You talked to him earlier in the evening before you got hold of me."

"That's fine—run in strangers. What were the plans for me?"

He grinned uneasily, knowing he wasn't going to like the way I would react to what he had to say, and explained, "Well, Doc thought if we left you locked up in the truck a day or two, while we got to the bottom of the trouble you stirred up, it would give you a chance to meditate. Maybe mend your ways."

"A fine cadaverous idea. . . . And I didn't stir it up. Thayer just walked in on me."

"That's not too logical, Doc feels."

"Logical or not, that's the way it was. . . . How did you know I didn't have Thayer in the station-wagon?"

"I phoned up to Farrar to make sure."

I admitted grudgingly, "The whole thing was a nice piece of crystal-gazing on Doc's part—guessing I'd try to use a phony Thayer for bait. Or did Farrar get wise and tip Doc off?"

Monk snorted and said, "You must have forgotten there's a fellow named Doc Savage. You're underrating him."

"I'll underrate him, all right. I'll make him into catmeat, if he doesn't watch out. What's the idea, pulling a thing like that on me?"

"This I'd like to see," Monk said doubtfully. "Listen, you're not going to stick that needle in me, are you?"

"That's certainly my plan."

"A fine way to treat a pal," he complained, completely overlooking the part he'd had in Doc's shenanigan upon me. "A fine thing, is what I say. Don't you know who your friend in court is? Why, I even said to Doc: 'Why not let Pat jump into the thick of it for a change? Maybe she'd get her fill of excitement.'"

"And Doc said?"

"He wasn't impressed. He said who ever heard of a kitten getting too much cream?"

"Monk—I'll make you a deal."

"Oh, oh!" he said suspiciously. "Here goes my shirt. I don't think I'm going to be interested—"

"All right, if you'd rather have this stuff shot into you and sleep for a week—"

"I'm listening," he said hastily.

"You're going to be the little pal you say you are, Monk. You're going to cut me in on this case. You're going to do it by tipping me off to where the explosions are going to be, so I can be there. Either that, or so help me, I'll empty this hypo needle into you, and add another for good measure."

Monk argued, cajoled, threatened, for about five minutes before he came around. "All right," he grumbled. "But nobody is going to like this, including you."

"No doublecrossing me!" I warned.

His homely face could show more injured dignity than a frog that had accidentally hopped into a cream pitcher. "My word is as good as gold."

"That," I said, "is one we could argue about, but won't."

I untied his ankles and tossed the rope in the barn, to one side. "You don't tell Doc about our little side arrangement. You understand?"

He rubbed his ankles to restore the circulation. "How much inside dope have you got, Pat? Do you know who stabbed this Thayer?"

I described sparrow and his thick-witted young friend, and gave Monk a rough idea of how I had met them, leaving out the parts that might lead him to think they'd made a fool of me, a construction that wouldn't be too hard to attach to the episode.

"Of course, I didn't actually see either one put the ice-pick into Thayer," I finished. "But they knew about it, were hunting Thayer, and were rough boys."

Monk nodded. "That almost votes them into office, don't it. . . . Now, why are people sticking ice-picks into other people? Tell me that."

"I don't know."

"Huh?" His jaw fell.

"Lucia, who carries the world on her shoulders, and should have been God," I said. "And Rich Thomas, Lucia's husband, who's going to re-do the world."

Monk said, *"Huh?"* more loudly, with his jaw farther down.

"Oh yes, and in less than seven days," I added.

Monk scratched around in the reddish pig-bristles that he used for hair, and finally asked, "Is that supposed to mean something?"

"My guess would be yes," I told him. "But don't ask me to draw any pictures. Here, I'll tell you how I picked up that little charade." He listened intently to my explanation that Thayer had said these enigmatic facts, and said them seriously, and was already shaking his head when I ended on, "Now, what do you think?"

"We'll have to shake more out of the bushes than that," said Monk.

Inasmuch as the barn was on an isolated and uninhabited farm—I stepped outside and looked, and it certainly seemed isolated enough, the nearest house almost a mile distant—we concluded to drive the trick truck back to the city. The little grenade had blown the truck side-door open and it was jammed against the wall of the barn, we discovered. We looked about for something to pry it free, Monk suggesting a fence post. There were no loose fence posts, so we compromised on a rail that formed part of one of the stalls in the barn, and were yanking at that when our visitor arrived.

She came in with no more commotion than a fly walking in a sugar bowl, and said, "I hate terribly—believe me, I do hate terribly—doing this."

Monk and I turned. We probably did it while we were two inches off the packed earth barn floor.

"Please!" she told us earnestly. "Please don't provoke a disaster."

She didn't explain what she meant by disaster, but the object she was holding in her hand described it fully. It was one of Mr. Colt's latest models.

V

This was Lucia. Somehow I knew this, although she wasn't bearing the world on her shoulders, which were a little too pointed for the job. Not that she was an ugly woman. She wasn't. She had a remarkably pure pale beauty, done in marble, that was striking in a sepulchral way. Ash-blonde was her type, and she wore it clean-scrubbed and without cosmetics.

"Lady—lady—" Monk was paler than she was, had raised his hands, and was trying to point at her gun with one finger of one of his lifted hands. "Lady—that thing is cocked."

She was younger than went with that ash-blondness. She should have been a stone angel standing in front of a tomb in some cemetery where no birds sang and the passers-by stepped silently.

She said, "I followed you here. We—we did, that is. You will—and please understand I won't be circumvented—raise your arms while I search you."

We followed instructions, and she did an amateurish but earnest job of frisking us. Amateurish, because she didn't find a thing on me, and I was loaded with trinkets designed for coping with just such situations as this.

"Now, you will walk with me, but ahead of me," she said.

I tried out my guess about her identity with, "What are you going to do with us, Lucia."

A kind of angelic composure touched her face and scared

me badly because it was the kind of a look that didn't exactly go with sanity. It didn't quite pass away, and kept Monk and myself meek and actively complying with her wishes. She herded us outside, and onward.

The afternoon sun was cresting western clouds with hot silver and putting brassy shadows among the trees and in the underbrush that edged a crooked, rutted heat-cracked lane which we followed for a while, for about a hundred yards. No one said anything. I turned my head. She was floating along behind us, a pure-faced wraith attached to the big blue gun.

Her car—I knew it was her car because of its hearse-like character—stood silently in the lane, gleaming black among the green trees which almost buried it. And the squarish shape of a man stirred inside, then a very red, excited face looked out at us.

Her companion, whoever he was, was driving her car. But he wasn't a chauffeur, unless chauffeurs have taken up two-hundred-dollar tailoring and three-carat diamond rings. His name was Burroughs, she let us know.

"They know my name, Mr. Burroughs," she said. "At least *she* knew it."

He hadn't liked waiting there in the car, or anyway it showed clearly on his face that there was *something* he hadn't liked, and he wasn't much more pleased now. His hands lifted, the fingertips making little clutching movements—but whether seeking peace of mind or knowledge, it was hard to say.

"I've been very worried, Lucia," he said. And then added, more wryly, "I'm quite distressed by it all."

She said calmly, "We've discussed that, Mr. Burroughs. Please let's not again."

Burroughs looked at her, and then away from her; he set his attention on infinity with extreme concentration. He was fifteen years older than she was, I guessed, which would make him past forty-five. Probably fifty. There might be a five-year swing in his age either way, because he was a man who kept himself groomed, manicured, and sun-lamped. His skin was good velvet and the tan it carried was reddish copper like an Indian's.

With gun, eyes and chin, Lucia told us to get into the back of the shining limousine.

"I must ask you to journey with us. It is not a far distance," she said.

I glanced at Monk, wondering what he thought about our Lucia, and he made question marks by waving his eyebrows. I nodded. That was the way Lucia affected me, too.

When we were settled—Lucia in front, half turned on the front seat like a little girl, but not looking like a little girl—and before he started the engine, Mr. Burroughs felt it necessary to introduce himself.

"My name is Preston Burroughs," he said.

Introductions didn't seem to fit the situation, but he had started it, and so I went along, pointing at Monk and saying, "Mr. Mayfair—Monk Mayfair—a Doc Savage associate," and at myself to add, "Patricia Savage, distantly related to Doc Savage and, I'm beginning to think, species of jackasses."

Lucia looked at me with the angelic firmness of a saint turning a sinner around and giving him a gentle push toward tophet.

"Lies have no place in this. Please don't," she said.

"You don't think we're connected with Doc Savage?" I asked.

"Please don't," Lucia said.

Monk nudged me, and his ugly face was waving a look of alarm from side to side when I glanced at it. Monk didn't understand Lucia, and he thought she might be something worth being afraid of. It could be.

Preston Burroughs drove, and he was a little too heavy and often with brake and accelerator, but otherwise did well. The sunlight broke lances of gold on the long black hood, and the big engine made no more noise than a good electric fan. No one spoke. No one seemed particularly happy.

We came to one of those crossroads places, two service stations, general store, antique shop, and Lucia told Burroughs to stop. He did.

"Telephone my husband," Lucia told him. "Instruct him to meet us at—well—a half mile down that road yonder." She pointed.

Burroughs squirmed. "Lucia, I don't approve—"

"Please!" Lucia's voice was clear and hurt, as if she'd been soiled by his beginning to object.

Burroughs went into the general store, came out and went into the antique place, and five minutes later he was back with, "Rich is coming. He seemed stunned. I don't blame him."

By now my fingers were itching to try another of Doc's gadgets, and I asked Monk, "You want to go through with this?"

"We haven't much choice," he said, heartily enough to show that he did want to go along. He added, "maybe a little drop of information will leak out of this somewhere eventually."

We drove half a mile down the road Lucia had indicated and parked in the cool green-tinted shadows of a great sprawling tree. Lucia turned then, and gave us a lecture, one that sounded as if she had been rehearsing it.

"Do you understand predestination?" she opened.

Big words always flabbergasted Monk, and she had addressed both of us, so I let Monk take that one and fumble with it. He saw what I was doing, scowled, and told Lucia, "If you mean have I gotta follow a plan that was laid out for me before I was born, I think it's bunk."

Lucia was shocked. She was as startled as an old-fashioned roll-on-the-floor evangelist who'd heard a sinner say there wasn't any hell. She didn't even try to convince Monk that people are born for the Purpose; she believed it herself so strongly that it didn't permit argument; this Belief shown in her calm deep eyes.

Lucia said, "All who achieved greatness in history were equipped for it. Whether their greatness was for evil, or benevolent, they came into life bearing their tools ready-made. They were prepared. Their way was ready for them. Take any of them—Alexander, Genghis Khan, Edison, Napoleon, Hitler. . . . Choose any of them at random, and you will find you have a man with a god-given quality or more than one quality that fitted him for his ordained place in the human race."

She stopped for breath, and I said, "Let's take one fresh in mind, that late—we hope—Adolf Hitler. What would you say his pre-equipment was?"

She looked at me from a cool distance and said, "He was a man ordained for evil, and he had the tools he needed, intensity and a hypnotic sway over men. That's a good example for you to choose. You see what I mean? Greatness is pre-arranged, ordained—the plan is all made and the individual tailored to fit it."

"Oh, what pap!" I said.

Lucia stiffened, lifted her chin two degrees, and addressed me as a misguided child. "No doubt you haven't investigated the subject, and there is no time to enlighten you now, even if there was any reason to do so."

"For my money, it's piffle."

She ignored a skeptic pointedly, continued with, "Accidents can happen in all things. It happens in plant life, I understand, when a new plant of entirely different type, called a sport, appears. . . . Still, that hardly makes my point. What I'm trying to say is those shining knights who enter this world destined for greatness carry their armor and weapons with unmistakable splendor, for everyone to see."

If this was leading up to a point, or had a point, she was keeping it a mystery, and I was getting mighty curious. I watched her lifted face, intent eyes, aesthetic expression. She had the air of someone who wished to see a vision, and perhaps thought she might.

"Rich can't be," she blurted suddenly. "If he was destined, I should certainly know. . . . After all, I'm his wife."

I got it now. She didn't think her husband was cut out to shake the world. She couldn't see that he was carrying the ordainment, whatever that would be. . . . This tied in with what Thayer had mumbled about Lucia should have been born God, but Rich Thomas, her husband, had been instead. It hooked together, but it didn't make sense.

"Monk," I said, "what do you think?"

He had a thought that was as good as any of mine. He said, "Maybe the boys with the butterfly nets missed her."

Lucia stiffened at that. And Preston Burroughs reached over, patted Lucia's hand comfortingly, and murmured, "Never mind, Lucia. They don't understand."

But her feelings were hurt, and we had silence in large chunks until her husband Rich Thomas arrived at sixty miles an hour in a palomino-colored roadster that was new and expensive.

"Lucia!" he yelled while his tires were still shrieking to a halt. "What in hell's going on here?" He vaulted out of the car and strode toward us.

Rich Thomas appeared to me to be a perfectly nice uninhibited guy who wouldn't know a pre-destination if he saw one. He was not too handsome, not too athletic, not too sober-looking, but neither was he particularly deficient in any of these things. About thirty-five, with no hat and a cropped bullet head of tan hair. The kind of haircut the young scientists have gone in for.

"Who are you people?" he shouted at us. He looked at Preston Burroughs—without marked liking—and roared, "Press, what is my wife into?" He saw the gun Lucia was holding. "My God! She's got my new revolver!" he said.

Preston Burroughs opened his mouth to answer, but Lucia made the words.

"Rich, listen to me," she said, "Leo Thayer was stabbed this afternoon. About noon. These two people did it and—"

"Hold it, Lucia," I said. "You've got the wrong stabbers."

She threw me a coldly aloof look and brushed my statement away with, "You arranged it, I'm quite sure. Poor Thayer was headed straight for your place. Two men actually did the stabbing. They were trying to keep Thayer from reaching you, weren't they?"

"I wouldn't know," I said.

"Lucia!" yelled her uninhibited husband. "Start with something that makes sense? Thayer stabbed! I don't believe it! Why?"

"Listen to me, Rich," Lucia said with saintly calm. "Leo Thayer thought someone was trying to steal It. He was investigating his suspicions. Thayer told me he felt someone was after the Discovery. But he wouldn't tell me who he thought was after the Secret."

She said it like that, her tone capitalizing the words It, Discovery and Secret.

But I was staring at her husband now. I think we were all staring at him. A drawn grey look had whipped across his face, and his lips were stiff and drawing as if being pulled invisibly at the corners.

"Shut up, Lucia!" he gasped.

"Rich, I'm telling you why young Thayer was—"

"No, Lucia," he said in a thin high voice of anxiety. "Don't say more."

"But Thayer was still stabbed," said Lucia calmly.

"How do you know? Did you see it?"

"I saw it. I was following Thayer. Do you want to know why I was following him, Rich? . . . It was because I wished to know whom he suspected. He wouldn't tell me. I thought I might learn whom he visited, and draw some conclusions."

Rich Thomas moved a hand vaguely across his face. He was sick. His wife, by saying It, Discovery and Secret—the way she had said them—had made him ill.

Thickly, from a dull throat, he took: "What happened then, Lucia?"

"Why, I was disturbed," his wife explained. "And I felt the need of advice. So I telephoned Mr. Burroughs."

Rich Thomas looked at Burroughs, and some of his former bounce flickered back, and he asked unpleasantly. "And what help did you think he would be?"

"Mr. Burroughs and I see human values similarly," she told him.

"The hell you do!" he said thoughtfully.

His wife ignored his tone with the tranquillity her pure feelings gave her, and told him the rest of it. "This young woman left the building where Thayer had gone. She had Thayer on a stretcher. Mr. Burroughs and I followed in my car. We saw a rather unbelievable incident—this young lady's station-wagon was forced inside a large truck, which then hurried her away, a prisoner, to the country near here. Mr. Burroughs followed, and I took her and this man, the driver of the truck, prisoner. Then we called you."

"Great God, did you go off and leave Thayer wounded—"

"It wasn't Thayer. It was a papier-mâché dummy."

I liked the way Rich Thomas said, "Whoosh!" Now he dug out a large white handkerchief and blotted his face, which still wore the still paleness. "Throw some more fire-crackers," he invited.

"There are no more."

"You mean," he demanded. "That you don't know who stabbed Thayer?"

Patiently, showing faint surprise at his density, speaking elaboratedly as she would to a child, Lucia described the sparrow and his dull-witted giant. "They did the act." She inclined her head at me. "Hired by these people."

Rich Thomas examined me, and decided, "Lucia, you picked a nifty-looking number for the mastermind, anyway." Then he frowned, stroked his jaw again, rubbing the jaw hard with the heel of his right palm. He was thinking. His eyes brought Burroughs, then his wife, into whatever he was debating about. And abruptly he asked, "Lucia, why did you do that?"

"Do what?"

"Well—follow Thayer, for the first thing."

"I wished to know who—"

"Baby, I told you, when this thing first came out of a test

tube, that you were to forget about it. Frankly, I didn't like the look that came into your eye. I told you to forget all about it, remember?"

"But Rich—"

"This isn't like you, Lucia. This concealment—you didn't tell me that young Thayer had suspicions. I can understand Thayer not telling me—he didn't want to worry me because it might interfere with the experiments. Thayer is excitable and imaginative, and I'd warned him before about grabbing at the tail of every wild idea that came along. Yes, I see why Thayer didn't tell me. . . . But you, Lucia, you've pulled a new one on me. What got into you?"

"I wished to learn—"

"All right, baby, you wanted to know who had designs on my brain-child. . . . But why? What were you going to do when you knew—I take it you weren't going to tell me, from the way you acted."

She gave him a look of high glory. She was Madonna. She was the essence of all purity. She was garbed in the shining light of righteousness, and she was destiny's little helper.

Lucia said: "I was not going to interfere with destiny. If the one in quest of It seemed to wear the robes of ordination, I was going to see that he got It."

Her husband thought about that for a minute.

"Baby, do I get this right? . . . You were going to help some stinker rob me of something I've worked all my life on?"

She was sweet and sad now, and inward and knowing, righteous and certain. "Rich, my dear—my dear, dear Rich, you have not the qualifications of destiny. You were an accident, Rich darling. You're a fine husband, but it was never intended that you should hold such greatness in your hands—the power to change mankind, the shape of history, the way of the world. You have it now, Rich, but it was given to you by accident—it had to be. Rich, don't you understand that?"

He showed how well he understood it by saying, "Well, I'll be a flop-eared duck!" And showed what he thought of it with: "A lot of fine wifely ideas you've picked up!"

She was ice on an altar. She said, "You're a fine earthly and lovable man, Rich. Great destiny does not fit you. It was an accident."

Her husband had other notions about it, and he looked darkly at Burroughs, demanded, "Look, Burroughs, did you put these butterflies in her head?"

Burroughs stiffened, passed a dry pink tongue over his lips, and shook his head. "Old boy, I assure you I had nothing to do with it. I don't even understand what the scuffling is all about."

Rich Thomas made his hands into fists and put the fists on his hips. "Let me give you some advice, Burroughs. Chop us off your acquaintance list. Do you think you could do that?"

"Really, old fellow, I shouldn't like—"

"Either that," Rich Thomas said, "or I'm going to smear your nose all over your face. . . . I don't like you, Burroughs. I shouldn't have neglected telling you."

Burroughs, embarrassed, face a fire-engine red now, was unhappily, and perhaps prudently, silent.

Rich Thomas then swung on Monk and myself, saying, "Lucia seems to be wrong about nearly everything. Is she wrong about you people?"

"She," Monk said, "hasn't hit a right note."

"Who the hell are you?"

Monk, who didn't include modesty in his vices, gave himself a buildup as world-renowned chemist and Doc Savage aide, and did almost as well by me as Doc's cousin and beauty salon operator. But he didn't quite sell Rich Thomas.

"I've heard of Doc Savage, of course," Thomas said suspiciously. "I admire the man enormously, as who doesn't. I'd know him by sight." He scowled at Monk, and said, "I've heard of you, too—if you're Mayfair. But I don't know you by sight."

"That makes it tough," Monk admitted. "But if you'll look in my pocket, you'll find a billfold with cards, a driver's license—"

"I wouldn't believe anything I found in your pockets," said Rich Thomas calmly. "But in your head—that might be a different matter."

"Huh?"

"$HC_2H_2O_2$," said Thomas. "That mean anything to you?"

Monk said, "That's the formula for acetic acid. What's it supposed to mean to me?"

"I guess you're a chemist anyway." Thomas shook his head, scowling, and added, "But it doesn't prove much—

there are chemists back of every bush. . . . And what if it did?
I don't want any part of you." He drew in a heavy breath,
pocketed his hands, darkened his scowl, and said, "Yeah, I
don't want any part of outsiders."

Now he swung on his wife again, demanding, "Is the
tow-rope still in the car?. . . Oh, never mind—if it's destined
to be there, it will be." And he went around and jerked open
the sedan baggage trunk, to return presently carrying a
Manila tow-rope. "Stand still," he told Monk and me.

Monk, his patience worn thin, said, "Wait a minute,
brother! What's the go?"

"I'm going to tie you up, telephone the police, and let
them pick you up here," Rich Thomas advised him.

"The heck you are!"

"You think not, eh?" Rich Thomas went over and took
the big revolver from his wife's fingers, turned with it, and
added, "We can argue about it all you want to." He waved
the gun. "This is my argument."

I tried out another Doc Savage gadget. It seemed about
time for one. And since I had started out with grenades, I
stuck with them. It was simple stuff, perhaps a little childish,
and I could have been a bit more complicated, ingenious, and
spectacular, because I was equipped for it. But nothing
outstanding seemed called for.

This one was a button. A row of buttons ran down the
front of my suit coat, and were rather thick and elaborate—
but not obvious because since when is a flossy button on a
woman's suit anything unusual. It was the third button. I
pulled it off, let it go quick.

The button didn't make a great deal of noise opening,
but then it wasn't designed for noise. It was as quiet as night
coming, and blacker than the darkest midnight. It made, in
the first twentieth of a second, a black object—smoke—about
the size of a bear. This didn't change for about another
four-fifths of a second, then it really spread. Suddenly I
couldn't see a thing, and that was frightening; it was like
being in the abysmal blackness that eternity may be.

I said wildly, "Monk—" But Monk had already moved.
He was familiar with Doc Savage's trinkets, and he had gone
in on Rich Thomas. I could hear his feet, hurried, frenzied
sounds; I could hear his hands on Rich Thomas, Thomas'
gasp of pain. And Thomas' gun gave a great blatt that spiked terror
into the darkness.

Then a clash, steel into steel, and a whine that was the limousine starter urging the big engine. I had expected that, and I went forward, not for the limousine door because I thought more of my looks than to have a scratching match in that smoke with Lucia. I headed for the front of the limousine, the engine hood, and got to it; the slick black metal was under my hands. The engine had caught and was throbbing, and the big car began to move.

I had another button now. I ground it against the ventilating louvers at the side of the engine hood; I could feel the wetness of the stuff from the button, feel the biting cold as it evaporated. The car lunged, was gone past me, and I fell back, wondering wildly if the chemical was something that would disfigure my hand. I didn't know about that. I had never asked—I'd just turned the original material into an expert chemist, and engaged him to make up the stuff enclosed in a button that could be crushed if one really wanted to crush it.

The late afternoon breeze moved the smoke away—not smoke, really, but a chemical nigricant. And Monk was sitting there, sitting on Rich Thomas' chest.

"You all right, Pat?" Monk asked.

"I'm fine."

Monk pointed down the road. "There she goes, riding on destiny," he said.

"Destiny will soon get out of breath," I said, and had barely said it when the limousine engine died and the car—it was going uphill—made no more than fifty feet farther, and stopped.

Monk told Rich Thomas, "Don't let this worry you—I've rapped many a skull in my time, and killed nobody yet," and he whacked Thomas alongside the head with the revolver. Then Monk loped toward the stalled limousine, waving the gun, bellowing. He was a figure that would have frightened a tribe of Indians. He howled, "Don't start anything!" And Lucia and Burroughs didn't.

When we had assembled them, Monk looked at me thoughtfully.

"What stopped their car?"

It was a little trouble telling him, because I didn't know the exact chemical composition of the stuff, only that it was a vapor that would be sucked into the limousine engine through the air intake and, mixing with the gasoline vapor, form a mixture that was absolutely useless for locomotion purposes.

"Uh-huh, I know that stuff," he said. "I helped Doc develop it."

"Did you?"

He looked at me again, intently and speculatively. "You're loaded down with little things like that, aren't you? . . . Pretty good job of it, too. I hadn't noticed."

"I'll bet you," I said, "that you can't name half of them that I have left."

He grinned faintly. "I thought, when you asked me a few months ago to collect some of those gadgets for you, that you wanted to start a private museum."

"I did. I'm wearing part of it."

He indicated our prisoners. "You going to proceed along your own lines? Or take them to Doc?"

"Why, I wouldn't think of denying Doc a little excitement," I said.

He was clearly relieved.

VI

They stood, a group of fifteen or so nurses and internes, in the little anteroom that was the professional entrance to the hospital. They were wide-eyed, subdued, expectant; there was not much conversation, and one interne was doing most of that—he'd seen the operation, and he was telling two other internes about it, his voice a song of breathless wonder. . . .

I thought: *I wish they'd wait with bated breath this way to see me pass by. I wish that I'd done one thing in my life, just one, to make me worthy of that.* And I turned and went back to the limousine which we'd parked in the sweeping driveway, and Monk asked, "Is Doc coming?"

"In a few minutes, they said."

The amount of prestige that Doc Savage had—where it counted, with people with enough specialized skill themselves to understand Doc's skills—always awed me profoundly. It wasn't just a thing like being hero-worshiped; that sort of idolatry means little and tomorrow is gone. This was fundamental, sincere, and I don't think any of the hospital people loitering there envied him as much as they sincerely admired his ability. I know that people have worked a lifetime for just a little of what he was receiving here.

Monk was watching me speculatively, and he asked, "What's eating on you, Pat?"

"Something that always sort of gets me. They're waiting in there, to see Doc walk past."

Lucia and husband Rich and Burroughs stirred a little in the rear seat. Monk looked around, and they were quiet again. Rich Thomas was resting his fingertips gently against the bruise Monk had put on the side of his head, but he wasn't injured much.

Presently Doc Savage came from the building and moved toward us, swinging out with a kind of power in his stride that was smooth and natural. Doc Savage was a big man—not fat, just big—but I don't think anyone quite realized it until they stood close to him. Not what a giant he was, really.

Doc was, unlike many unusual men, distinctive in almost all ways. He did not cultivate it—quite the contrary; he practiced a considerable effort to appear inconspicuous. It was about as effective as trying to make the Empire State Building look like one of the buildings in St. Louis. Doc's size, his metallic bronze from tropical suns, his flake gold eyes, the remarkable regularity his features achieved without being pretty, were a combination he couldn't bury.

He grinned slightly at me and said, "What, you're not spending the day in a truck?"

"Hello, Doc. That idea was a little pixyish for you, wasn't it?"

"I'm slightly ashamed of it." He glanced into the rear seat. "These your collection?"

I introduced Lucia, her husband and Burroughs to him. Lucia had a look on her face that said you-see-what-I-mean; men-of-destiny-wear-it-on-them. She was as impressed as if a house had fallen on her. Burroughs was pale-faced, wet-lipped, and looked a trifle ill. Rich Thomas grunted agreeably. He said, "My signing name is Richard Welfred Thomas. I'd be rather flattered if you'd heard of me."

"Thomas on Lecoplasts and Chloroplasts in the Sexual Cells of plants," Doc said.

Rich Thomas leaned back. He was as pleased as a school kid who had found his name on the passing-grade list.

I asked, "Doc, how did the operation go?"

"Fair enough."

"Has Thayer talked yet?"

He pretended not to hear this—indicating I shouldn't have asked the question—and said instead, "We'll drop in at your place of business, Pat. Okay?"

I was rather pleased, which shows my head wasn't cut in, and said it would be fine. Doc flicked down the jump-seat and rode in the back with our three guests. He exchanged no word with them; instead, he said nothing at all, except to answer a question of mine.

I asked him, "What are Lecoplasts and Chloroplasts, Doc?"

"Portions of the protoplasm in plants." he replied. "Chloroplasts carry green color. They're quite a mystery to science."

I was satisfied. But I noticed that Rich Thomas wasn't— he had become rather pale, his lips were flat against his teeth, and his eyes looked worried. . . . Had what I said upset him? I didn't see why.

"Are you allergic to chloroplasts, Mr. Thomas?" I asked.

He said nothing. He looked a bit more ill.

My place of business was functioning as if nothing had happened. Miss Colfax bent her shining head at us, and her voice was only two points cooler as she asked, "The young man, Leo Thayer, is his condition satisfactory?" I said it was, and Doc told her that Farrar was still at the hospital. We went into my private office.

"I'll make a cool drink," I said.

"You needn't bother. We'll hardly be here long enough for that," Doc Savage said quietly.

"I'll make it anyway." I went into the room where I kept my collection of Doc Savage gadgets. I had Lucia's purse with me—naturally I wasn't letting her carry it, while she was a prisoner.

I put a trinket in the handbag. It was about two inches long, the size of a cigarette. I slit the lining in an inconspicuous place, and inserted it.

I carried another gadget, a little continuously-operating micro-wave radio transmitter—a wonderful thing for spotting with a direction-finder—with me through a side door. I found Colfax.

"Put this in the shining black limousine downstairs," I told Colfax. I described the machine, and gave her the license number, which she wrote down. "Get it out of sight.

Under a seat cushion might do. Be sure they won't spot it readily if they jerk up the cushion and look."

Colfax went away with the radio. It was about two-by-four-by-one inch in size.

Returning to the office, I looked Doc in the eye. "What did you mean—you wouldn't he here long enough for a drink? I got to thinking about that."

"We're not staying," he said calmly.

"No? Where are *we* going?"

"You're not."

I nodded. "I think I get it. You're tossing me back into the dull, drab, work-a-day world where there's no nice excitement. That it?"

He nodded also. "Where you're not likely to get killed," he added.

"We've been over this trail before," I said.

Doc shrugged, turned to the three prisoners, and apologized, "Pat shouldn't have been involved in the beginning, of course. I hope you'll overlook the harsh words she will probably have to say now. . . . You'll go somewhere else with me to give your stories."

Rich Thomas was pale. "Stories?" He put out a jaw that was now made of colorless stone. "There'll be none."

Doc Savage's bronze face was normally expressionless, but not from any innate woodenness. He had an excellent actor's ability to register emotion when he wished, and now he showed a profusion of injured surprise.

Doc said: "But your friend, Leo Thayer, has been the victim of an attempted murder. Surely you wish to help find and punish the—"

"That's your idea," Rich Thomas said. "Do it without us."

"Rich, dear," his wife said sharply. "Rich dear, I think—"

He swung on her like a frightened cat. "Think—if you want to. But keep your mouth shut!" he snapped.

Lucia drew herself up. She shone her soul out at him. She wrapped herself in shining white righteousness, and she said, "Rich, how can you fly in the face of things so clearly pre-ordained and arranged? How can you?"

"That, again!" said her husband.

She was unaffected, and she said, "Destiny has taken you by the hand, Rich, and you're trying to jerk away. You mustn't!"

Rich Thomas looked tired, frightened, and everything but uncertain. "Shut up, Lucia," he said.

She said: "Mr. Savage may be the man destined to wear the cloak of greatness that dropped by mistake on your shoulders. Rich, it could be. Oh, it could be. I think he is!"

He said, "Nuts!" wearily. And then, scowling, "Honey, you're hell-bent on giving my little discovery away, aren't you?"

"I'm afraid for you, Rich," she wailed.

"I'm afraid, too," he growled. "But not that afraid."

I was looking at Lucia, and I saw that she *was* afraid. That cool shining stuff she had been wrapping around herself—it wasn't goofy psychic stuff, but plain unadulterated frost-edged fear. Our Lucia was scared just a bit beyond being a normal woman.

"It's too great for you, Rich," Lucia whimpered. "Oh my dear, I so wish you would put it in other hands."

Her husband was unimpressed, or too frightened himself to be impressed. He jutted his jaw toward the door, said, "Get going, Lucia. We're leaving."

Lucia was a pillar of ice. "Rich, I'm going to tell Mr. Savage—"

Now her husband went toward her, having a little trouble with his long legs because he didn't seem aware what he was doing. And that was the way he slapped her, as if it wasn't quite of his own volition. He slapped her, and then pushed her toward the door, turning his head as they went, saying to Doc Savage, "You might keep us here. You might manage it. But damned if it will get a word out of us—"

"Stop them, Doc!" I gasped. "They know why Thayer was stabbed! We can get it out of them, I'm sure."

Doc swung on Monk, said, "Monk, stay here and keep Pat. Don't let her follow me." And then he was out of the door after Rich Thomas and his paper-faced wife.

Monk suddenly stood between me and the door. "Huh-uh," he said. "We stay here."

"You big clunk!" I told him. "Let's not miss this!"

"Ixnay."

"There's going to be more excitement that a Yaqui war-party. Doc is going to try to get the wife loose and pump her, and the husband is going to raise cain. . . . And what the woman says to Doc is going to be interesting. This world-shaking destiny stuff has me intrigued."

But Monk was adamant. He explained sheepishly, "I loused up the job Doc gave me of keeping you out of this. I don't think it would look good if I flopped again."

"You're no pal of mine!"

"That," he said, "should save me some bruises."

It dawned on me that Burroughs had followed the Thomas pair and Doc, that he had actually preceded them through the door. I said, "At least go out and collar that Burroughs, Monk. We can work on him. Doc won't mind, and it'll pass the time."

Monk was tempted, but shook his head. "Nope. Doc wants you out of the whole thing, and he wouldn't like you questioning Burroughs."

"I was a sucker to bring the three of them to Doc. I knew better."

"I thought it was pretty wise."

"The man has no gratitude. . . . And don't you start preaching to me to keep out of trouble. I should have jabbed you with that hypodermic needle while I had the notion."

Monk grinned, and I think his grin was what tore it. Monk had promised me, under duress it was true, that he'd cut me in on the excitement, and there was something about the grin that said he was welshing. And happily.

"Come back here!" he yelled.

But I was out now, through the door, and I slammed the door in his homely agitated face. The door had a spring lock, and by the time he found his way around through the back, he would have some looking to do. I wouldn't be there. I ran for the elevators, had good luck and caught an express, and kept my fingers crossed all the way down to the lobby.

The crossed fingers did it. Doc Savage was in the lobby with the Thomas couple and Burroughs. They were arguing, the Thomas pair with pale, emotion-ridden faces, and Doc intent, dominant, obdurate.

Burroughs seemed to be listening, flapping his hands, and scrubbing his face with the white handkerchief. Suddenly he showed spirit. He spoke—I didn't get the words, but it was violent—and then he wheeled and strode to the street. . . . Which was as far, I thought for a moment, as his little blaze of determination was going to take him.

Halting in front of the building, still plainly visible from the lobby, Burroughs displayed a dither. An actor couldn't have done better with indecision. He even did a little teetering dance on his toes. He blotted with the handkerchief again. He threw undecided glances back at Doc, Lucia and Rich Thomas. They were not, or seemed not to be, paying him the least attention.

Burroughs fooled me and didn't come back. He walked away. He was out of sight. Gone. *Doc is making a mistake*, I thought. *That fellow isn't just a friend of the be-destinized Lucia.*

Doc seemed to be winning over Rich and Lucia. He would. They didn't have a chance. Doc Savage in an argument was about as easy to cope with as an earthquake, although he didn't use an earthquake's tactics—very often. There was something mesmeric about Doc's deep-throated, flexible, controlled voice; when he really wanted to talk, he could make a spell, turn black to white with profound convincingness. He was hypnotic. Literally, I mean. As a part of his early training, he had worked under masters of the occult in India, and in Tibet, and although I wasn't inclined to feel the mystics in Tibet were any more mystic than the psychiatrists on Central Park West, Doc Savage had acquired a compelling power from somewhere.

So I kept in the background and watched Rich and Lucia lose the battle of wills. Lucia, actually, was on Doc's side all along, but he didn't need her aid. With words, that wonderful compelling force Doc owned, he laid indecision across Rich's face, then defeat, surrender. And Rich was nodding his head helplessly, just as Doc was also nodding—very much as if hypnotized, I thought. And it could be. I'd seen Doc do unbelievable things with hypnotic suggestion.

Now they turned and went toward the door, arm in arm, like pals. They pushed through the great slabs of glass that were the doors. Lucia had her handbag. She'd taken it from my office upstairs, or her husband had. I couldn't remember which, but anyway she had it, and my little gimmick would be inside. Probably I wouldn't need to use it now. Doc had talked them into telling him what earth-shaking thing destiny had handed to Rich Thomas.

Stepping out confidently now, I came up behind them and said, "I won't break the spell, will I?"

Doc, who normally didn't miss as much as the movement of a fly within fifty feet of him, jumped visibly, wheeled, gave me a look that would have corroded brass.

"I thought Monk—"

"So did he. But the schemes of mice and men gang aft—"

"Pat," he said wearily, "would you do me a favor?"

"Not this time, probably. Not if it's to go away and mind my own business—because, come to think of it, I consider this little mystery my business."

He swung to the Thomas pair, said, "Excuse me a moment, will you," and turned back to me frowning. He gripped my arm.

"Let go my arm, cousin! If you think—"

"No, no," he said impatiently. "Come over here a moment, and I'll tell you why I want you to take your oar out of it."

"Is it some good reason like a young woman should never partake of any excitement?"

"No, it's more to the point than that."

"Okay, then I'll listen."

Unhappily, his attention divided between my intrusiveness, and his imminent success with the Thomas couple, he led me to the curb and along it a few yards, intending to get out of earshot of Rich and Lucia Thomas. . . . And I noticed Mr. Burroughs. He hadn't gone away, not entirely away.

Mr. Burroughs stood about fifty feet distant, facing us, and about him was the air of a man who'd lost his nerve and was returning to have it out.

I pointed, said, "There's Burroughs, Doc. He didn't leave after all—"

I tried to scream. I tried and tried, and got my mouth open, and all the breath crammed against vocal cords that I could, and I would have screamed, only there wasn't time for it. There wasn't the fiftieth of a second that a scream took to get going.

He had come from between two parked cars. A big man, a great oak-fisted man I didn't know, didn't want to know, wished I had never seen. He had what they call a blackjack. A sap, a persuader, a skull-buster. It's against the law to carry them, although they're just a little leather sack containing buckshot.

He didn't hit Doc squarely. But enough. And Doc sank, turning sidewise slowly. Not out. Not kayoed. But not feeling good. The big man hit again, and Doc avoided that one. The man swung four times as if he was fighting bumblebees, and Doc evaded them all. But now there was another man behind

Doc, and he didn't miss. He had a sap too. There were two more men. Three. They came from the air, the sidewalk, out of the sunlight.

Men I didn't know, had never seen. They beat Doc down. He didn't have a chance. Ten men wouldn't have had a chance. And I was in it, trying to help. I got an arm, and I think I broke it, because the man screamed that way.

Flame, unbelievable noise with it came against my face. I was being shot at. He was two feet away. Why he missed, no one can possibly know; it may have been because I was moving hard. And now I moved harder, around and through the men beating Doc—beating, stamping, kicking. I wanted behind them. I wanted the bullets to go into them first.

What was happening to Rich and Lucia Thomas? I got that too. They were receiving attention, and from a pair that were no strangers. From the sparrow, and his witless big shadow. They were being driven into a waiting van.

Mr. Burroughs too, I saw. He was drifting across the sidewalk, his feet traveling about twice as fast as he was, and skidding on the concrete. He was heading for the Thomas limousine, and he went into it, but without opening the door to do so. He went in through a window, headfirst.

This I saw in twisting awry confusion, like the scenes from a motion picture projector where the film had torn and was flipping through crosswise and everywise. Because I was running, twisting and lunging. I was doing a beautiful job of evasive running for the protection of the building lobby. I was doing it without knowing anything about it. Instinct purely. Terror stormed with me, and the street was full of gunsound. I didn't need to push open the fine great plate glass doors. They fell to pieces before me, dissolved into fragments. Bullets had done that. And I went through the brittle, jangling, cascading fangs of glass and dived to the right.

I was safe now. At least death wasn't roaring in my face. But I had for a while yet, seven or eight seconds it may have been, the weird detached feeling, unreal, far-apart, that was so unnatural. I got it—the feeling—off me; I forced it away from me, and the terror that got me then was worse than it had been. For I was certain I was shot. I was sure that was the only thing that would explain the way my physical part had moved without any instructions from my mental part.

But I seemed to be all right. All together. Two arms, two nice legs, all shaking like paint-mixers.

I looked back outside, at the street. It would have been easier to put my head in the mouth of a starving lion.

They were going with Doc Savage already. They had thrown Doc in a car, just heaved him in: I could see Doc's limp arm draped across a door.

They had a second car, and Rich and Lucia Thomas were in that one. The sparrow was with them, and his slow-fire lackey. And two other men who had been in the group who took Doc.

These two cars, one carrying Doc and men, the other Rich and Lucia Thomas and men, were actually in motion when I saw them. Hurried motion. They had poured bullets, noise and excitement into the street, and it was no place to tarry. The two cars were gone in an instant.

And now Burroughs left. He was in the Thomas limousine; a fat mouse in an iron hole was the way he looked with his fear-greyed face sticking barely high enough to see over the cowling. He fled in the long black car, clipping a fender of a parked machine, already traveling forty-five when he took the first corner.

The evening sun now fell in the street, and the air was still, the people in the street were still, and everything stayed quietly suspended until a piece of glass that had been hanging undecided now fell off one of the doors. But that didn't break the silence. It brought on more of it.

Follow them, I thought. *Pat, get going, follow them, you quaking fool. You wanted excitement, you got it, and you can have some more. Just follow them.* So I began telling my legs to take me out on the street and into the first car and follow them. It was not likely I could catch them, less likely that I could trail them, and least probable of all that I could accomplish anything if I did succeed with either of the first two. Those had been rough boys. They were too much for my playhouse. . . .

But the point, the ridiculous point of it, was that my legs wouldn't do anything that I wanted. They had ideas of their own. They were too busy beating together and trying to let me down on the floor.

Then Monk Mayfair was there. Monk, his small eyes bigger than I had ever seen them, his face as if a witch had walked across it. He came galloping from the elevators. He was beside me. He said something that didn't make sense.

He said, "Pat! You're shot!"

I said, "They got Doc! A thing like that never happened before!"

I used a voice I didn't know. A stranger's voice. As calm and clear as a three-heart bid in bridge. It wasn't even related to the family of my terrors.

"You're shot!" Monk said.

"It was my fault!" I said, still in that wonderful voice. "If I hadn't bothered Doc, they wouldn't have taken him by surprise. I know they wouldn't have—so it's my fault. If they kill him, that will be my fault too."

The witch went over Monk's face again, this time with a frightened spell, and he gripped my arm, yelled, "Pat! Stop talking like that!"

"They took Doc away. Men did. They were terrible men. They took Rich and Lucia, and Burroughs ran away—"

"Pat! Oh my God, Pat!" He turned around and bellowed, "Somebody get a doctor, an ambulance!" His small voice was now big the way it was when he got excited. It was a circus calliope. "Get a doctor! This girl's shot and out of her head and—"

I became vaguely interested in a detached far-dreaming way, but there wasn't anything very personal about it. Some girl was injured—I was actually that far from it; I didn't seem much bothered about who the girl was. Just slightly interested, just barely enough to raise a hand and touch my face and notice how sticky it was, then bring the hand far enough from my eyes to focus on it.

The color red was on my hand, and if the color red can get into a scream, it was in mine.

VII

Farrar finished with gauze, tape, and something from a bottle that burned like the devil's tears—a lot of paraphernalia and fuss for no more than they had found wrong with me.

"I'm all together again?"

Farrar said patiently, "On the average of twice a month I give myself a worse wound while shaving."

"You don't need to be sarcastic just because I thought I had been slaughtered."

"I'm not," he said. "I'm profoundly worried."

Monk Mayfair, voluntarily doing something he usually avoided if possible—taking the rap—said sheepishly, "I guess it was my fault. When I saw the blood on her face—after all that shooting—I thought she had been shot." He looked at me. "You're lucky it was only a small cut. But how did you get it?"

"I didn't see any knives being thrown. I guess it was a piece of glass. There was plenty of that."

Monk had been using the telephone, talking with the police, and he handed me the instrument. "They want your description of the outfit that pulled this."

The inadequacy of what I could tell the police made me feel stupidly inadequate. Except for the sparrow and his dull shadow, I couldn't even be sure how many. Seven or eight? Ten? I didn't really know. There could have been ten, and certainly not less than six. The police seemed to think it was a pretty fair description of everyone, considering circumstances, but probably they were accustomed to the vague descriptions most spectators give.

I hung up and gave Monk a look that was undoubtedly as beaten as I felt.

"Monk, I can't get over the feeling it was my fault. If I hadn't bothered Doc—"

He shook his head gloomily. "Nobody bothers Doc enough to get him into trouble, Pat.... Are you sure he didn't *let* them take him? He might have let that happen deliberately so he could get a line on them—"

"No, but I wish I could believe that," I said.

And for a few moments I tried very hard to believe it, to think that Doc Savage had been manipulator rather than victim. But nothing solid would come from the hope. Even though I knew Doc's fantastic way of maneuvering incident to his use—oh, Doc hadn't staked this. He couldn't have.

"Monk, we've got to get hold of Ham, Renny, Johnny and Long Tom," I said grimly. These four were the other members of Doc's group of aides, the men who normally worked with him. "We're going to need help."

Monk's bleak look shocked me. "Renny, Johnny and Long Tom are in London. I cabled them. But they're not going to be able to get here any faster than planes fly."

"What about Ham Brooks?"

"I was coming to that. Ham is on a vacation. He's doing something he never did before—going fishing. You know what a fashion plate and fop with clothes Ham is? You'd think a canoe trip in Quebec would be his idea of purgatory. But that's what he's doing. And God knows where he is. I phoned, sent telegrams, and I've got a Canadian radio station trying to locate him."

"You did all that while Farrar was patching me up?"

"Yes, and damned ineffective it was,"

Monk was a wonderful guy. He was direct and primitive, in spite of the ability as a chemist that had made him known worldwide. You never had to guess what Monk was thinking or feeling. He was discouraged now, and angry at his helplessness. He demonstrated his state of mind by suddenly kicking over a chair.

"By God, if we only knew what to do next!" he yelled.

I went into my gadget museum and brought back a radio direction-finder for the ultra-high-frequencies. It was a good one with a new type of five-element beam antennae—it would spot the signal exactly, with none of that old stuff of not knowing whether the transmitter being nulled upon lay in one of two directions. One direction only, it told you.

"What good will that contraption—"

"I put a continuous-note U.H.F. transmitter in the limousine, or had Colfax do it. Burroughs fled in the machine. . . . Monk, I have a considerable curiosity about that Burroughs. How did he ring to you?"

"He rang," Monk said, "like a cracked bowl. By golly, give me that locator, and I'll go fishing for the guy."

"Be careful."

"You know me," Monk said, and bolted out with the U.H.F. locator.

I knew him. He was never careful. He was as discreet as a foghorn, and his fighting tactics were as well-controlled as a bull on ice. But I had a suspicion Monk's kind of approach would work well with Mr. Burroughs. If Burroughs was a fox in sheep's clothing, Monk was the fellow to shake the wool off him.

I called Miss Colfax.

"Colfax, you know that an armada of thugs have seized Doc Savage, Rich and Lucia Thomas, and they are probably in the worst kind of danger. . . . They were all seized because Rich Thomas has some world-shaking discovery that they're after.

Miss Colfax seemed unusually pale. "Yes. . . . But it is so terribly melodramatic—"

"The world-shaking discovery, you mean? I don't care how it sounds to you, Colfax. I'm sure it's terrific. A gang of men don't shoot up New York streets for peanuts."

"Oh, but I didn't mean—I think I meant it is all so astounding I can hardly credit my senses."

"When we find what the fuss is about, Colfax, I'll bet it's a humdinger. That's why I want to know about Rich Thomas. I want everything that can be dug up on Rich Thomas."

"Rich Thomas? But who is he and—"

"That's the job I'm giving you, Colfax. Get on the telephone and start at it. Your working day is about over, but I'll pay overtime—"

Colfax had been staring at the floor. She looked up rather oddly. "I wouldn't accept overtime for a thing like that."

"Well, you'll get it anyway. This isn't your affair, and I don't expect you to do detective work for nothing."

"You wish me to assemble information on Thomas?"

"Exactly. He's a plant man—I mean plants that grow. A botanist, or whatever the word would be. You can start with that."

"The word," said Colfax, "might be phytotomist, phytobiologist, mycologist, dendrologist—" She stopped the big words, looked away fixedly.

"For heaven's sake, Colfax! Where did you pick up that terminology? . . . Never mind. Rich Thomas is probably well-known in his field. Doc knew him by reputation."

Colfax nodded. "I'll do my best, Pat."

"Thanks, I'm going to the hospital to see if there is any possibility of learning anything from the young fellow Thayer, who walked in here with an ice-pick in his back."

Colfax turned her face toward me, and it was stiff, and her lips hardly moved as she said, "I could do that for you, Pat."

"Go to the hospital to see Thayer? Why should you?"

"It may be dangerous for you to venture on the streets." Colfax said rigidly.

"They won't catch me asleep again, Colfax. I'd almost welcome trouble. It would be an opening in this stone wall we're up against."

Colfax turned away. She had always been a cold, withdrawn and ice-mannered woman, and I had never seen her this upset.

On the way out, I stopped to ask June Davis, the switchboard operator, if she would stay on overtime, and she said she would, gladly. I asked her to carefully list all calls, then brought her a wire recording device and showed her how to use it to get a record of any suspicious voice that might telephone. And I told her to make arrangements with the telephone company to have any call traced quickly, and if the phone people had any objections, to get the police to authorize the tracing.

Twenty minutes later, feeling a little shaky simply because nobody had bothered me enroute, I walked into the hospital. I got good service—not remarkable in itself, since it was funds supplied by Doc Savage which kept the hospital in existence.

But all the service in the world couldn't make young Leo Thayer talk. He was unconscious. There was no way known to surgery to rouse him, even for a few minutes. The coma was certain to last another twelve hours, probably longer. It was stupefying news, and the hospital officials were distraught about it. They'd heard, probably from the police, of Doc Savage's misfortune.

A Doctor Herman Pressman, a tall, tin-faced brain surgeon who was staff chief, stopped me as I turned disconsolately away. "Miss Savage—would you—uh—step into my office," he asked uncertainly.

Sharply curious—the hospital head had something worrying him—I followed him into his glistening office with its antiseptic efficiency, and he closed the door.

He said, "Miss Savage—in view of what has happened to Doc—some information—I'm aware of Doc's disapproval of involving you in danger, but I believe you're the one to know."

"What information is this?"

"The patient—Thayer—data on him which Doc Savage asked us to assemble."

I was startled. Then hope bounded up in me until my face felt hot. "Oh, wonderful, Pressman! Maybe you've got something that will help."

Pressman wasn't, he said—his uncertainty subsided as he talked—sure that it would be of much value, but it was this: Doc Savage had, from the laundry marks on Leo Thayer's clothing, enlisted the aid of the police laundry bureau and located Thayer's home address.

Thayer lived in an apartment in Jackson Heights, a living-room-bedroom combination. He was unmarried, lived alone, was twenty-eight years old, paid his rent regularly, and didn't have to be called down for wild parties. He had a girl friend, a nice person about his age or a little older, dark-haired, pretty in an austere way, who dressed gorgeously. They were engaged, it was understood, but Pressman hadn't been able to learn the girl's name nor anything more about her.

Leo Thayer was a phytotomist. That was one of the words Colfax had used.

"What is that, Pressman?"

"That one got me too, and I looked it up," he said. "It wasn't easy to find, but it's a science dealing with the vegetative substance of plants. A branch of botany, I suppose you would call it. But specialized."

Then Pressman said that Leo Thayer worked for a Mr. Rich Thomas. He was employed by Thomas to work at his profession of phytotomist. I'd known that Thayer worked for Thomas, but not as phytotomist, or plant expert or whatever the word meant.

"What did you find out about Thomas?" I demanded.

Very little, Pressman said. They had tried to contact Thomas to tell him his employee had met with a misfortune, but had failed—naturally, because Thomas and his wife had been out making trouble for Monk and myself—and there was very little more on the book about Thomas, except that he was also a phytotomist.

"That's all," said Pressman. "Except that, really, someone should notify Thayer's employer, Thomas, that the young fellow is in the hospital. I have Thomas' address here—he lives up in Westchester."

"Pressman," I said, "Let's have the Thomas address. You certainly save your climaxes for the last."

VIII

So I drove to Westchester, helped along at eighty miles an hour during the last part of the trip by a pair of cops in a patrol car. They were behind me for a while, but caught me, and we talked it over and they went ahead.

I hoped that the going-over I intended giving the Thomas establishment would help clear up the mystery, particularly as to why there should be so much skull-duggery over something a phytotomist had discovered. And it began to look promising even before I got to the Thomas place.

Stopping at a suburban drugstore, as the country became a winding network of lanes through estates of considerable size, I used the telephone to get my office. Monk surprised me by answering.

"Monk! You're back! Have you got Burroughs?"

"I lost the signal," he said bitterly.

"What! You mean somebody found the transmitter I had Colfax hide in the car?"

"No, I don't think so," Monk explained. "I got a good null on the signal, and a buildup that showed I was getting nearer the transmitter—how much nearer, of course, it's impossible to tell. The locator doesn't do that much for you. . . . But the point is, all of a sudden the signal went out."

"You mean it snapped off? As if the transmitter had been switched off, or smashed?"

"No, a slow die. Or a quick fade. There wasn't any change in the carrier, no click as if power had been cut."

"You know how those U.H.F. tubes behave when the heater voltage fails. Was it like that?"

"No, it took seven or eight seconds to die. Were the batteries fresh?"

"The batteries were perfect."

"I wish we had Long Tom Roberts here," Monk complained. "He's the electrical expert of this gang."

"Check with the police to learn whether the limousine was in a crash—"

"I already did. No dice."

"All right, will you see what you can dig up on Burroughs? Let's know more about the man."

"Will do."

"Good. I'll see you later."

"Hey, wait a minute!" Monk exclaimed. "Where are you? What are you doing? Don't you know there might be trouble floating around looking for you?"

"I have two fine big strong cops for company," I said. "Handsome devils, both of them. I'll be all right."

The policemen liked that, if Monk didn't, and I knew they were going to stick with me. I didn't mind. They weren't particularly handsome, but they seemed to think they were special gifts to the ladies, one of them more than the other.

I asked the druggist behind the prescription counter, figuring a prescription man would know more about the neighbors than the soda clerks, if he could tell me where to find the Rich Thomas home. He said take the left turn at the next corner and follow my pretty nose to an estate with a lot of greenhouses, and added, "Don't tell me you're another one going out there looking for a job?"

I didn't know whether or not to be flattered by his impression that I would be looking for work on a country place.

"Why, aren't the Thomas couple good people to work for?" I asked.

He hesitated, shrugged, said, "I shouldn't be talking about the neighbors but that wife of his gives me a slight pain. A reformer, she is. Know what she did once? Bawled me out for letting kids spike their cokes here. Hell, we don't allow that."

"I've met her," I said. "I wondered if she would be pleasant to work for."

"Oh, she's all right. Probably make you keep bell-hours, get in at nine every night. Husband seems all right, though. Congenial guy, that Rich Thomas. You know what he means from what he says."

"Then they should be fair employers."

He grinned. "Sure, if you bring your own food."

"Bring my own food? What do you mean? Do they put everybody on a diet, or something?"

"That's it."

"What is *it*?"

"Diet," he said dryly. "They insist on feeding their employees out there."

"What's bad about that, in these days of high food costs?"

"It's what they feed them."

"What's that?"

"That's the odd part. Nobody knows—except Rich Thomas, of course. And for some reason or other he won't tell the help what they're being fed. It isn't ordinary stuff—like potatoes and lettuce and fruit. . . . Fellow named Gridley, gardner for them, was telling me about it. Stuff didn't taste bad, he said.

Seemed to agree with him. But he wants to know what he's eating, and he's about to quit." The druggist paused, chuckled, and added, "Seems rumor got around the food wasn't something the help would eat if they knew what it is. You know how quick something like that could play heck with an appetite."

"I can imagine," I said.

The two policemen had been listening, and seemed quite intrigued, whether with me as a woman, or with the mystery as a mystery, or with its connection with Doc Savage, I couldn't tell. But it wasn't important. They went along with me, and contacted headquarters over their radio while they were doing it, to learn that nothing had been heard from Doc Savage.

The Thomas estate, not a flamboyant place, was spread over three or four acres. It was mostly greenhouses which looked well-used, and enclosed in a stone wall to which had been added, quite recently, an extra six feet of steel-mesh factory fence topped by three vicious-looking barbed wires.

"Looks as if they didn't want unannounced visitors," one of the cops remarked, and we went inside and asked for Gridley, the gardener who didn't like the food.

Greenhouses, the glasswork invariably daubed with white-wash to cut down the strength of the sunlight, always look shabby. But some of these were nearly dilapidated. The house, a white frame building, colonial, stood back in a swatch of lawn that was strictly functional.

Gardener Gridley, a flabby, rheumy-eyed man of fifty, was impressed by the policemen. Better still, he either led a blameless life, or had something to conceal by talking willingly—at any rate, he was a fountain of information.

Yes, said Gridley, the food was odd. It was—well, he didn't know how to describe it. You couldn't tell what it was. In appearance, it was—well, you know how custards taste? And cheeses of some types? And some cakes and candies? That was the general idea.

"You think maybe this Thomas was trying to poison you?" one of the policemen asked suspiciously.

"Oh, good Lord, no! Not Mr. Thomas. He's a nice man. And his wife wouldn't let him anyway—she's as straight-laced as a saint."

"Was the stuff you ate highly seasoned?"

"Not specially."

"Did it taste bad?"

"No, it didn't," said Gridley uncomfortably. "It kinda had a good taste, most of it. But different like. . . . Me, I want to know what I'm getting for my grub."

"And Rich Thomas wouldn't tell you?"

"That's right, he wouldn't. Made a big secret of it."

"Big secret?"

"I mean, nobody could get it out of him what we had to eat, and why we had to eat it in the first place."

"You *had* to eat this odd food?"

"Or quit our jobs," said Gridley angrily. "Ain't that a hell of a note!"

I asked, "Anything else odd going on around here lately?"

Gridley shrugged. "Nope. Except the lab has been off-limits for the help."

"The lab?"

He pointed. "That brick building yonder. Mr. Thomas wouldn't even let Mrs. Thomas in there. I heard him telling her to stay out."

We went to look at the laboratory, and there were two peculiar things that met the eye at once: The windows had been bricked up solid recently. The door had been steel-plated.

One of the policeman pointed at the padlock, said, "That wouldn't be an easy thing to open."

"Oh, you couldn't go inside!" gasped Gridley excitedly. "Mr. Thomas has been very secretive about what is inside. He wouldn't like it."

I said, "Suppose you gentlemen take a walk around to the back and see if there is a rear door that might be open."

One of the cops caught on, or anyway took the chance to wink at me, and he and his companion and Gridley wandered around to the rear. Gridley was protesting the back door had been bricked up too.

I tore a flap off the breast-pocket of my jacket, wrapped it around the padlock, found a long twig, moistened the tip with my tongue, applied a bit of what could have passed as lint from another pocket, and touched the fabric on the lock. The result was heat, white and terrific, actually blinding me momentarily before I could turn my eyes away. When I looked again, the lock, all except the staple, was molten liquid dripping to the ground.

Brother, I thought, *I'm not going to wear that stuff as a pocket flap again. Think what would happen if it got touched off accidentally!*

The two officers and Gridley, having seen the flash light up the neighborhood, came running.

"The lock fell off," I explained.

This got a puzzled grin from the one who had winked. He peered at the molten metal, still smoking, and sniffed the air. "Some variety of thermite, if you ask me," he said.

He could go to the head of the class on that. The other officer shoved open the door, drew his gun—probably to impress me, although I would have done the same thing—and stepped inside.

His, "The hell!" boomed out inside. It had an empty sound. He added, "Somebody done a job in here."

He meant a job of destruction. Selective destruction. Certain equipment had been spared, but nothing that would indicate what the laboratory had been used for. There was a large electric furnace of the industrial type, and this had been used to systematically melt down metal and glass parts. There was no way of telling what else had been destroyed by heat.

"Rich Thomas did this," I suggested.

"Could be," said an officer. "Time, patience, and thoroughness went into this job."

I said, "if Rich Thomas was this careful, we're not going to find anything on the place that will help us."

They seemed to think so too.

"Gridley," I said, "do you know a man named Burroughs?"

Gridley nodded eagerly. "Mr. Burroughs, the food products manufacturer," he said. "Yes, Miss. He came here often." He started to say something else, probably that Burroughs came most often to see Mrs. Thomas, and changed it to, "He was a friend of the family, Miss."

"Food products manufacturer?" I asked. "Is that Burroughs' business?"

"Well, yes. Only I don't think he is active in it now. I understood he was retired."

"Know anything else about Burroughs, Gridley?"

He didn't.

We poked around a bit more, accomplished nothing, and took a path that led back to our cars. One of the policeman, the winking one, emitted a grunt, snatched out his gun, and sprang into some bushes that edged the path. There was a scuffle, and the officer came out of the bush with Monk Mayfair.

"Monk!" I gasped. "How did you—I thought you—"

Monk jerked away from the policeman, told the latter who he was, then told me, "When you pulled that stuff about not telling me where you were, it scared me. I checked with the police, and found out where these two officers were escorting you."

Both of the officers looked startled, and one said. "We didn't tell the station where we were going!" But Monk said, "You probably did, and forgot about it." But I knew he was lying.

After he heard what we had found, Monk said, "Let's take a look at what grows in the greenhouses before we go."

We did, and left knowing no more than before. Except that the greenhouses didn't grow any one thing—not flowers alone, nor vines alone. There was a little of almost everything including, carefully cultivated, a lot of common weeds.

Monk decided we should use his car for the trip back, picking up mine later. His reason was obvious, because he was driving one of Doc's cars, and it was armor-plated. The policemen made a way for us back to the city, faster than I really cared to ride.

"You dig up anything on Burroughs, Monk?"

"Some, before you got me excited. . . . He used to have a big job, vice-president, in a corporation that manufactured in the general food line. Got let out a couple of years ago. Retired, he calls it. Fired. His former employers wouldn't say why. Burroughs is unmarried, has a Park Avenue apartment, lives high, and has run through better than a hundred thousand dollars in the two years. He puts up a front. Pretends to be still wealthy, and looking for a new business venture in the foods line. He has less than ten thousand bucks left to his name."

"That's quite a lot on Burroughs."

"It doesn't do us any good," Monk complained. "It doesn't find Doc. I'm getting hell-fired worried about Doc."

"How did you find me at the Thomas place, Monk?"

"Huh? Why, I told you—"

"Try it again, in a way I'll believe."

He grimaced angrily, not particularly out of irritation with me, but because he was bothered about Doc. "Oh, if you must know, Doc has had one of those radio U.H.F transmitter gadgets spotted in your car for months. Just in case you got in a mess, and we had to hunt for you."

"For months, you say? But the batteries on those things run down—"

"Not the new kind—not for about a month. The gadget draws only a few mils of current, and these new batteries hold out suprisingly."

The patrol car left us at Grand Concourse, and after that we had to drive more sanely. I was feeling almost as worried about Doc as Monk looked by the time we reached my business place.

IX

"I think," said Monk, as the elevator carried us up, "that we have the pieces of the puzzle in our hands. If we could only put them together!"

"The same thought is frightening me," I admitted grimly.

We stopped at the phone switchboard to look over the list of calls June Davis had made. Nobody particularly suspicious had called, so she hadn't used the recorder.

Colfax was in the outer office, the client's reception room over which she presided. She was pale, austere, and her voice was as cool as icewater in a glass.

"How did you come out with Thayer, Colfax?"

She lifted her head rigidly and asked, "Is Leo Thayer all right at the hospital? You went there—"

"You were to gather information on Thayer, Colfax. Let's have it."

Her head bent down; her voice was a cool mountain stream flowing over stone. She had everything the hospital had learned about Thayer—he was a plant expert—he worked for Rich Thomas—he lived in Jackson Heights. Then she gave an astonishing, considering how hard it is to make a quick investigation of a man, flood of new data. The town in Iowa where Thayer had been born, his high school, his college—both in Iowa. Three previous jobs Thayer had held before joining Rich Thomas. His good record. Even personal details, where he bought his clothes, names of his friends—she had these latter listed, and handed me the list but there was no one on it who meant anything, except Burroughs—and a lot of other stuff.

"That's wonderful, Colfax."

"Thank you," she said stiffly. "Is Mr. Savage—do you think he's safe?"

"He's certainly not safe, Colfax. We haven't found a trace of him."

In a voice that she drew from some far unpleasant place, Colfax said, "That is quite terrible. . . . And no trace of the Thomas couple, or Burroughs? . . . You tried to trail Burroughs by the little radio transmitter I put in the Thomas limousine, didn't you?"

"We lost it," Monk said. "Lost the signal. It died out."

"Maybe," said Colfax hopelessly, "it faded out. They do, don't they? My radio at home fades. And I've noticed in a car, when you go over a steel bridge, they die out. Couldn't the limousine have gone into a metal building or something? And if it was driven out, you'd hear it again, wouldn't you?"

"The way that radio went out, something happened to it," Monk said.

"Well, I wouldn't know," Colfax said quietly, in a voice she hardly seemed to bring forth.

When we were in my office, Monk remarked, "That Colfax is efficient, isn't she? Dug up everything on Thayer. Too bad none of it helps us much."

Suddenly I was weak at the knees. I went to the desk, walking woodenly, I think, and dropped in a chair there. My face tingled sharply, as if electricity was on it, then it grew abruptly fever-hot. I put my hands on the desk and lying there on the desk they looked silly, inadequate, futile; stupid female hands that had thought they were clever, but really had no competence in them. Belonging, I had to think sickly, to an excitement-chasing girl who had best stick to the beauty business if she couldn't do any better than this.

"It did," I said.

"Huh? Did what?" Monk had his eyes closed now, and he was probably beating at his brain in the hope of flushing an idea out of its usually adept cells.

"Colfax's information did mean something."

Monk's face was erratic—hope, doubt, chased each other—and he demanded, "What do you mean, Pat?"

"Would water—a soaking—stop the thing from transmitting? It would, wouldn't it?"

"The radio in the limousine, you mean? I suppose it would. For a while, anyhow."

"A while—wouldn't it go out permanently?"

"Why, I talked to Long Tom Roberts about that one time. He designed them, you know. He said that the contraption could be dried out if it got wet, and would be as good as new."

"A bomb!"

"Huh?"

"Monk, they—Burroughs or somebody—took the radio out of the car and put it in water. That's what you do with a bomb, isn't it? They thought it was a bomb, That's what happened. The water soaked in slowly, and the little set gradually died out."

"Oh, for crying out loud!" Monk complained. "It's all right to make deductions. But you're jumping at conclusions too wildly."

"Turn on your locator."

"What?" He stared at me. "It won't bring in a thing, I tell you. I lost that transmitter once, and it was smashed or—"

"Want to bet?"

He frowned and scrubbed a hand against the side of his homely face. "You sound strained, as if..." Suddenly he growled, "it won't hurt to try it." And he swung out of the office. I could hear him getting his radio-finder from where he had left it in an anteroom, then he was back. He switched the device into operation. It was fixed in frequency, crystal-controlled, and needed only warming up.... Presently a procession of thin high sounds, like a clock ticking, came from the apparatus.

Monk swung, stupefied, to stare at me. "Pat, how did you—"

"That's it, isn't it? The limousine transmitter?"

He was too stunned to nod. And now he suddenly scooped up the direction receiver, saying violently, "My God, maybe the thing has been back in working order for hours! Why didn't I keep the receiver turned on? What a dope I was!"

He was banging his large feet on the floor in the direction of the door, saying more under his breath that he didn't consider fit for my ears. My, "Monk! What do you think you're doing?" made him swing his head impatiently.

"I'm going to find that limousine. It's the only trail we've got." He shook his head wonderingly. "Pat, that was some deductive job. The transmitter was soaked in water. And it dried out and began working again."

"Wait."

Monk scowled. He hated indecision. He disliked being puzzled. He'd seen a way open for direct action which he did like, and he hated to abandon it. But he did frown, they say, "I don't see where anything that Colfax told you gave you the bomb-in-a-bucket-of-water idea."

"I added some wild guesses."

"Oh, then—"

"Want to see how far a couple more guesses will carry us? It won't take a minute."

He said, impatience in the way he moved his shoulders, and in his voice, "Well—"

"Come on."

Before we reached the room where Colfax would be, I gripped Monk's arm and stopped him. That earlier feeling was back in me now, the feverish futility, the misbehaving of nerves. I didn't like what I was doing, and it was something that I might not like for just a little while, but for a long time.

"Monk, let me handle it," I said stiffly. "I—I've got to know—I'd hate to make a mistake here."

He nodded, none of the puzzlement leaving him, and we went on then, and walked in on Colfax. She was sitting at her desk with an air of pale, brittle intensity.

"Colfax," I said, and my voice wasn't as causal as I wanted by a great lot. "Colfax, you asked me about the condition of young Thayer, and I don't think I answered you. I was excited."

Colfax turned her face to us and smiled, but it was the sort of a smile that is on skulls. She was pale. Colfax was always pale, with an austere china-doll quality, but this was different, and painful to see. She said, very carefully, "I'm sorry. I shouldn't have bothered you with my questions."

"It was all right. He's going to live, Colfax. Barring unforeseen complications. Probably there will be no paralysis."

"Thank you." Again she had nothing but that voice that

seemed to come from an infinite distance, from under a great weight.

"Colfax, that was a good idea you had about the radio. It's on again."

She whitened. Not a little. Quite a lot. She didn't speak.

"We're going to hunt it now," I said.

She had the answer ready. She'd fought it out before, knew what she was going to say. This time the words came freely, but unnaturally, sliding over glassy ice that was strain.

Colfax said, "I'd be careful, Pat. It may be—it could be, you know, a trap. They may not have thought of that at first, then thought of it later—using the little radio to decoy you."

Monk grunted explosively. He hadn't taken time yet to think of that. He started to say something, stopped when I shook my head.

"Colfax," I said. "You knew Thayer's first name."

She wasn't quite as prepared for that. The answer fell out nervously. "But isn't it Leo—"

"Nobody told you—you hadn't heard Thayer's first name—yet you knew it."

She had frozen silence. There was a bluish halo around her lips.

"Colfax," I said. "The cat is crawling out of the bag. Why don't you open up for us?"

Colfax stood up then, and the standing seemed to have no other purpose behind it than a preparation for falling. She dropped. Not successfully, not gracefully. She loosened here and there at the joints, and it was shocking to see an austere, cold-mannered woman like Colfax faint on her feet.

Monk moved quickly and caught her before she was entirely down, and he stared over her shining head at me. "Pat! How did you figure out—"

"I'm not sure. Intuition, maybe. She did know Thayer's first name. She was too concerned about him—but I almost missed that, because Colfax is an inward sort. . . . And I kept wondering why Thayer came here in the first place. That didn't seem logical—for a stabbed man to take an elevator in an office building and find my place. Thayer came here because of Colfax, I imagine."

"The hell! Then Colfax is in it!"

"I think she'll talk when she regains consciousness, Monk."

X

Monk Mayfair drove. Doing it, he was busier than a one-armed juggler—he had the direction-finder to contend with, traffic, the conversation I was holding with Colfax in the rear seat. And on top of that, the not unreasonable chance that we might be waylaid sooner than we expected.

Colfax talked loosely, without animation; the words, facts, were in her like loose marbles in a box that had been opened, and they were being taken out one at a time in a dull, shaken voice. She had not been conscious long.

She had been born in Iowa, the same town as Leo Thayer, she said. And that jolted me vaguely, because I knew what town Thayer had been born in, for it had been on her employment record, but I hadn't noticed the connection.

Leo Thayer had looked her up more than a year ago, she explained, when he had been working for Rich Thomas a few weeks. Thayer fell for Colfax. But Colfax wasn't marrying anyone; she had definite ideas about the desirability of single blessedness as versus blessed events, and the last thing she ever intended to acquire was a husband. . . . This part of her story was important only emphasized a female trait—regardless of her protestations, Colfax was violently in love with young Thayer.

"Did Thayer give you the background of this?" I asked.

He had told her plenty.

I listened. Monk listened also, not giving as much attention as he should have to the green hills, tree-furred, through which we traveled. We had the radio transmitter pretty well located now, and were swinging well to the east through the Long Island countryside, hoping—and our necks might depend on how accurate the hope was—that nobody would expect us to come from this direction. But we hardly noticed the countryside because Colfax's low words, painfully spoken, were more exciting than a string of firecrackers letting off in the car with us.

Leo Thayer had told her what Rich Thomas had discovered. . . . *He had found out how all green growing plants manufacture their organic food by means of the radiant energy absorbed from sunlight.*

Colfax said it like that, her voice underlining the words with a kind of gasping breathlessness. . . . But offhand it didn't mean too much to me. Not something like inventing the electric light, or radio. or how to make flying machines. I glanced up at Monk—just in time to yell at him to straighten up the car and preserve a roadside tree for posterity. Monk was impressed. He was going to need help getting his eyes back in his head.

"Whew!" Monk said, as if someone had shown him eternity.

I debated about exposing my density, then tossed it out for them to see by asking. "Well, so somebody found out how plants grow. I had taken it for granted science knew about that, but given the fact that they didn't, what does it accomplish?"

I should have told them the world was flat. It would have made me seem brighter.

"Great Heavens, Pat!" Monk gasped. "The thing is one of those basic discoveries that can change the whole course of human life!"

"I don't see it."

Colfax said wearily. "She doesn't have the chemical background to comprehend its magnitude, Mr. Mayfair. I wouldn't have either—didn't have, when Leo first told me about it. But—well—it begins to soak into you."

I suggested they use a few facts to open up some cracks in my mind so it could soak into me.

Monk said, "What's the most fundamental human occupation?" He answered that himself. "Farming. . . . What disaster is the most irrepairable of all? Crop disaster. . . . What makes a great nation, more fundamentally than anything else? A strong agricultural economy."

I sat back with a funny feeling. I was beginning to see the light.

"But Rich Thomas would have had to discover how to duplicate the process—"

"He has," said Colfax grimly. "He has—oh, it isn't perfect yet. It may takes months or years of research to put it on a commercial scale." She hesitated, staring off into space, then murmured, "On a laboratory scale, Rich Thomas has been creating food materials just as the plants create it."

"That was the stuff he's been making the hired help eat?"

"Yes."

"They didn't seem happy with the food."

"That was because they were suspicious of it, and Thomas didn't dare tell them the truth. It was palatable. The results were healthy. Experiments were successful."

Monk added his bit: "Pat, all the life on this globe depends on the photosynthetic power of green plants to manufacture food material for themselves.... I remember something that the encyclopedia says about it: Green plants are the alchemists which alone of living things have mastered the secret of converting the sun's rays into food material.... Or something like that."

"The point is," said Colfax, "that the most complex organic substances are created by growing plants. If man can do that, he achieves an independence of nature which will mean so much it's hard to comprehend, because—"

"Let's drop the scientific part for later," I said. "We've got direct troubles ahead of us."

Colfax shuddered. "That is the secret Leo Thayer found some one was trying to steal."

"And Thayer was stabbed because he was investigating the matter?"

"Yes."

"Thayer came to my place because of you, Colfax?"

She nodded, and said, "There is a short story behind that. I had suggested, when Thayer told me of his suspicions, that the thing had enough magnitude to interest Doc Savage. But Thayer said Rich Thomas wouldn't listen to that. Rich Thomas is an individualist. He would have fired Thayer. And Thayer—my poor Thayer—he wanted more than anything to be in on the creation of this great discovery."

"He told you not to let on that you knew him?"

She nodded bitterly. "And I did."

"Why?"

"Because—well—to save Thayer's career."

"But Thayer had come to see me. Wouldn't that have gotten him in bad with Rich Thomas?"

In weariness and confusion, Colfax moved her head from side to side. "Oh, I'm so confused.... The secret was the main thing. Thayer wasn't going to tell that. And if Thayer died, you would know, and investigate.... It was Thayer's way of enlisting Doc Savage's aid."

We crawled through hills now, following an unpaved dusty road. Monk had a road-map on his knees. The dust rose behind us, chalky and sifting over shrubbery that was already chalky from the few other vehicles that had passed before.

It was a lonely and frightening road, made no more soothing by the growing darkness. The sun, dropping into the west some time ago, was pulling dark animal-like shadows behind it. The spirit of terror was embodied in the shadows. That was the way I felt; I knew the others had the same creeping edginess. We might be waylaid. Chances were we would be.

"I wish I had a good aerial map of this country," Monk complained. Later he groaned, "Dammit, I wish I dared radio the police. But that is the first thing those guys will do—tune a short-wave radio in on the police network to keep posted."

"Colfax," I said abruptly. "How did you get that idea about the little radio being on again?"

"I—I think they saw me put it in the limousine," she said uneasily. "A man watched me. He answered the description of one of those who later seized Doc Savage and the Thomas couple."

"Then you just guessed they might use it to trap us?"

"Yes."

Like a steel spring, one tiny spring in the whole complicated tense works, relief loosened in me. I hadn't really realized it until then, but I had been wondering if Colfax hadn't dealt directly with the enemy. But she hadn't. She didn't need to tell me she hadn't. I believed her without that. Colfax was all right.

"The camera, Colfax," I said. "What is on that film in the camera?"

She looked at me blankly, and Monk too. They didn't know about the camera, so I told them. "I gave the film to a shop for fine-grain development, and they promised to rush it. The shop in the building lobby. . . . Then I'm afraid I overlooked it in the excitement."

They didn't know what was on the film. It didn't seem too important now.

I watched the dark frightening tangles of bushes move by, listened to the metallic murmuring of the engine. I stared until fear made my eyes ache, and although I saw literally everything, each insignificant detail of the country we passed through, yet I probably saw nothing at all. We could have turned into a submarine and gone underwater, and I might not have noticed. I was scared.

Even my surprise at finding what the trouble was all about—even that was nothing. I had expected a tangible treasure at stake, something you could take into your hands and spend, like gold or jewels, or a rare mineral. The secret of how plants manufacture food was far different. More valuable, I could see now, than almost anything of the other sort.

"Colfax," I said. "Did Leo Thayer tell you who he suspected?"

Now my voice was also small, littler than Colfax's had been at any time.

Colfax explained, "Other than Leo Thayer and Rich Thomas and Mrs. Thomas, the only person who knows about the discovery is a food manufacturing specialist, whom Mr. Thomas let in on the secret. This man, because of his experience, was supposed to be serving as marketing consultant. Mr. Thomas isn't a business expert, so he hired this man—on a salary, not as a partner, or even a shareholder, to blueprint the marketing set-up for the discovery. I think that man, greedy, knowing he was an employee rather than a partner, planned to—"

"So Burroughs is it," I said.

Colfax stared fixedly ahead.

"Burroughs," she said.

XI

We were going to creep up on the place. We were going to be as cautious as anything. It was a good idea, if it worked, and it didn't.

The place had a feature or two that were not surprising—remoteness, ramshackle looks, a naked dark loneliness—and some others that were not expected, such as the fact that there was no house in the little valley, just a great hulking building in a five-acre scattering of bleak poles. A drab huge buzzard sitting amid its scattered bones.

We pulled to the tip of the last hill, and saw it, and Monk said, "Tobacco-drying barn. Unused. The poles once supported the acres of cloth they grew the tobacco under."

"Why haven't we been waylaid?" I asked thinly. "If it's a trap—"

"Maybe it's not. Maybe—"

Colfax's scream buried his voice as if a cricket had fallen into a hard-blown corner, and she was pointing, indicating a man who had stepped from behind a tree with a rifle. He wanted room for careful aiming.

Monk said, in the shivering echoes of Colfax's screech, "My God, I hope this car is what it's cracked up to be!" He sounded unbelievably sincere. Not too confident, either.

"Get down!" I told Colfax. "I don't trust this bulletproof glass." But she was already on the floor, not shrieking now, just white-faced. She asked, "Haven't you something—a weapon—I can use?" She was all right, Colfax was.

Now the bullet came, the bullet first, before the sound of the rifle. He had shot at Monk, who was driving. He had aimed carefully, and I hadn't been able to quite distinguish what kind of a rifle it was in the semi-darkness, but it was high-powered. A 30-06 caliber, probably, and they put out twenty-nine hundred foot-pounds of muzzle energy, if I recall rightly, and this one hit the glass almost squarely. Monk didn't like what the slug did to the glass, although it didn't come in. I heard his breath go out in a great displeased grunt, startled.

That was why we had come in so brazenly. This car was Doc Savage's, built back in his gadgeteering days when the fantastic was his specialty. It was over-powered, armor-plated, gas-tight, and every niche was crammed with some trinket to handle trouble. It wasn't an army tank, but I preferred it to one.

Monk grabbed at shift levers, jerked the wheel, and we left the road, careened up a slanting bank that would have given a mule pause—four-wheel drive did this—and headed for the rifleman. He shot twice more, then stopped wasting his time. He dodged behind the tree, made for a larger tree, where even this car couldn't follow him.

Monk, more pleased, said, "We've got something for that lad." He jabbed at another button; a hissing joined the troubled sound of the engine.

I lifted up now, looking for the gas, but I couldn't see it. If it was there, it was colorless, and this troubled Monk too, because he swore violently, something he didn't normally do without provocation. . . .

But in a few moments, the dodging man—we hadn't seen him for a bit, because he was keeping out of sight in the brush—got the stuff. We knew that when he reeled blindly into view, running, pawing at his face with a hand, the other hand out in front of him. He went headlong into a tree, evidently breaking his shoulder from the way he began screaming. So it was tear-gas.

"One guard!" Monk yelled happily. "That's fine. Now we'll just drive into that crummy building and have a look."

I said, "I thought Doc had stopped using gadgets?"

He grinned. "He keeps them around. They come in handy."

We were, it developed, going to need everything that would come in handy. Because until now hell had just opened one eye. They were laying for us, and they hadn't expected us to come as sheep—we learned later that an outpost at my building in New York, and another one along the road, had telephoned ahead with the news of us.

They tried grenades now. Not regular fragmentation hand-grenades of the army sort, but ones they had made from dynamite. Dynamite wrapped with wire. Dynamite stuffed in gas pipes. These needed fuses. They threw them like great firecrackers. But, in the darkness, we could see the fuses, the matches flickering.

Monk drove the car hard now. They had expected him to follow the road, and were stationed for that. But he didn't: he cut to the right, in a wide sweep, and none of the grenades—they threw four—landed near enough to more than rock the car.

Monk yelled, "They were really loaded for us!... I'm gonna bust right into that building."

Now we were in the thicket of poles and lattice-work that had once been the covered tobacco yard. The four-wheel drive labored: the car bucked and jumped, reminiscent of the pictures they used to publish when the jeep was first developed.

The men were behind us now. Their bullets weren't. How many ambushers there had been, I didn't know. Enough to let loose plenty of lead; its clanking on the car, like a blacksmith striking hard blows, was a terrifying thing.

Monk, without the proper respect for the poles that supported the lattice of the old tobacco yard, hit one square on. The result piled all of us into the front of the machine.

Colfax said angrily, "Of all the damn driving!" And I looked at her, and she wasn't the cold-mannered Colfax that she'd always been. She was wonderful.

Monk probably didn't hit the barn door more than half as hard as he had intended. A wide door made for trucks; it caved, became a cloud of splinters, if one could call twelve-inch planks splinters. It bothered our car not at all, and our headlights lighted the barn interior.

I think we stopped the car and sat there twenty seconds. It seemed twenty minutes.

Monk rolled down the window and put his head out.

"Hey, hadn't you noticed a little noise?" he asked.

It would be hard to say what I had expected. Bodies. Doc Savage being tortured. Or already dead. The Thomas couple with cigarette burns on their eyes and no fingernails.

What we saw was Doc Savage, looking as disgusted as he would under the circumstances, which was about as disgusted as a fellow who had dropped his cigarette. Doc was not exactly unmarked. The bruises on his head were noticeable, even in that excitement, and they had evidently walked on his face.

Rich and Lucia Thomas were in better condition physically, worse mentally. Rich was pale, shaking, couldn't control his lips. His wife simply stood there flapping her hands in front of her, as if she were taking wrist-relaxing exercises. Her eyes could have been the eyes in a skull.

But what stunned us, they were all free-handed, on foot, and in triumphant possession of one prostrate senseless prisoner—the latter the man whom I thought of as the sparrow.

Monk, bewildered, said, "This is some rescue!"

"It'll pass for one," Doc Savage said. He waited for five or six bullets to come inside, and added, "If we put it off."

Rich Thomas came over, rattled his teeth at us, and said, "We were tied—a man on guard—Mr. Savage had something on his person—he put it on the ropes—they just dissolved." The dashes were put in my more tooth-chattering.

"Gadgets," I said to Doc. "I thought you were off them."

He said, "Don't rub it in." And to Rich Thomas, "Get your wife in the car. Quick!"

"We can't escape in the car!" Thomas wailed. "They'll riddle us!"

Monk assured him that, "Not in this car, they won't!" And he jumped out himself to seize Lucia Thomas himself and toss her into the big sedan. He had, then, a little experience with Lucia Thomas that would have been funny under other conditions. She was afraid of Monk. She had met him before, knew who he was, but she screamed at him as a frightened child would scream at a too-big, too-friendly dog. She kept waving her hands, too, and was still flapping them when he tossed her into the armored machine.

We were loaded in. Doc drove now. We backed out of the old building, and turned around, and the prospects took a dark turn.

A man stepped out from behind a tree with a quart bottle, applied a match to the side of the bottle, to a gasoline-soaked rag wrapped around it, and threw. The bottle fell short, burst, and there was flame on the ground fifteen feet in diameter and twenty feet high.

Monk was among those who didn't like that. "One of those cocktails would finish us! I've seen them do a job on tanks!"

Doc stopped our suddenly dubious fortress. He got a small machine pistol from somewhere and handed it to Monk.

"Do a little shooting. It's loaded with mercy bullets, so try not to hit anybody in the head," Doc said. "What have you used on the car?"

"Just the tear gas," Monk said.

He rolled down a window a crack, picking a window that hadn't been jammed by the rifle bullets knocking against it, and tried out his machine pistol. It's bullfiddle roar deafened us all. I could see where Monk was aiming and I was sure he was, contrary to Doc's instructions, trying to knock a man's head off.

The little gun's big voice slowed the rush toward us from a run to an undecided walk.

"Get going!" Rich Thomas screamed. "We can shoot our way through!"

I thought so, too. It seemed a splendid idea, and the only feasible one. Not too feasible at that. But better than being roasted when they got behind the barn and tossed their flame cocktails at us.

Monk stopped shooting and peered at his weapon. He had completely missed the man he was shooting at.

Doc said, "Get out the trick goggles."

"Huh? Oh!" Monk seemed confused. He dragged out a rather complicated looking headset affair for the eyes.

"Not those," Doc told him. "The ones for use in the smoke."

Then Doc flipped one of the assortment of trinkets on

the dash, with the result that the earth seemed to turn black under us, swell, bloat, rise up and cover us. It was smoke, oddly bluish in color, completely opaque, and spreading as from an oil-tank fire.

The fact that the special car was equipped with smoke wasn't new to me, but the part about the goggles was. Monk had the proper ones now. They weren't quite like the others, but not enough different to be remarkable.

Doc said, "Monk and I will go out now. The smoke will come in. Don't be alarmed. It's harmless." Except for using four very short sentences in a row, he was calm about it.

"Get a pair for me!" I cried.

"We might manage that—in a day or two, for your museum." Doc said. "Come on, Monk. And remember they're likely to do some wild shooting."

Monk said he hoped to make them wilder, and I heard the sedan door open, slam shut.

"Shouldn't we help?" Colfax asked.

"Yes, by sitting tight," I said. "You're now going to witness one of the great spectacles of our time, Doc Savage in action."

"But I can't see a thing," Colfax complained.

The way she said that helped me. I didn't want to sit there either, and the regret in Colfax's voice, the sincere dissatisfaction, as if a fat man had stood up in front of her just as the contender knocked out the champion in a prize-fight, was quite soothing. I was able to sit and be amazed by Colfax.

We listened. There were long bites of silence. Then a commotion yonder. More stillness. Another brief tussle. Like Boy Scouts playing a game of capture-the-flag in the darkness, except that this was deadly.

The wind, I imagined, was carrying the smoke over the enemy. I wasn't in any state of mind of the wind direction, or whether there had been any. But that must be what was happening. And Doc Savage and Monk, able to see in the trick smoke because of their goggles were stalking and striking. Now and then there was random shooting. I heard a gasoline cocktail take off. I could hear its roaring, and it was close enough to cool my blood.

And now Colfax, so help me Colfax began a cool-voiced dissertation on her theory of how the goggles worked. She said, "They're effective on light of wavelengths outside the visible spectrum, ultra-violet or infra-red light or something like that. And the smoke is transparent to the light. You can see with goggles. . . . I remember reading that something of the sort was developed for vision—in darkness, not in smoke—during the last war."

There I was sitting holding my teeth together so hard that my whole head ached. My fingernails biting into my palms. And Colfax was theorizing.

She added, presently, "But they would need a projector for light, wouldn't they? Where are they getting the infra-red light? Did they take a lantern with them?"

I let her wonder. I felt like allowing my teeth join Rich Thomas in a duet.

It was like that until Doc Savage's voice, touched with impatience, asked, "Well, are you all right in there?"

"How is it out there?"

"Come out and see."

I thought that over. True, there hadn't been any shots, screams, or sounds of cracking skulls for a few minutes. But I was doubtful. I wasn't even sure I could recognize Doc's voice, and this might be someone with an imitation.

"Thanks," I said. "We'll like it in here. Until we get a password."

Doc laughed then, and I heard Monk's voice—nobody could imitate Monk's voice—say, "The car filled with smoke when we opened the door to leave. They don't know the moon is shining."

So we got out then, and the breeze had carried the smoke away—that which had been imprisoned in the car drifted away lazily, like a large black cow grazing—and the moon was shining.

The moon shone brightest, I thought, on the fat square porcine face of Mr. Burroughs. I judged, from the soundness with which Burroughs slept, and the new shape that his jaw and nose had both assumed, that Monk was the one who had overtaken Mr. Burroughs.

I went with a flashlight to look over the other victims, and recognized all of them. They were like old acquaintances, and I was a little proud of the descriptions of them that I had given the police.

Coming back, I was in time to hear Rich Thomas saying that he wished, would insist, that Doc Savage take over the administration—presumably he meant the distribution to the world—of the food-creating discovery. But, he reminded, it would need considerably more research. It sounded like something they had discussed previously during the time they were prisoners, and Thomas was sticking by his agreement.

Colfax was rubbing Lucia Thomas' hands. I joined her, and Colfax looked up with shining eyes.

"Wasn't it amazing?" Colfax exclaimed delightedly. "I can see now why you're so fascinated by Doc Savage's adventure!"

Fascinated, I thought. I decided I didn't know what she was talking about. I turned and walked away, wondering if the miracle that Doc had been working for had happened, and I was cured of my liking for adventure, or whether it was just that I was still scared. I didn't feel scared—which was what worried me.

It could be so destined, as Lucia would say.

— THE END

RAYMOND E. FEIST'S EXTRAORDINARY **RIFT WAR SAGA**

Praised as a creation that "invites comparison with Tolkein's LORD OF THE RINGS" (*Best Sellers*), Raymond E. Feist's land of Midkemia is an enchanted realm of elves and dwarves, trolls and darker beings. Filled with high adventure, powerful magics and wondrous imagination, his epic *Rift War Saga* is a new masterpiece of heroic fantasy.

"TOTALLY GRIPPING ... A FANTASY OF EPIC SCOPE, FAST-MOVING ACTION AND VIVID IMAGINATION."
—*The Washington Post Book World*

*A potent dark magic stalks the
island kingdom of Ark,
drawing power from the people and the land.
Ages past, it fueled the War of the Wizards.
Now it rises again.*

THE SERVANTS OF ARK

By Jonathan Wylie

☐ **Volume One: THE FIRST NAMED** (26953-4 •
$3.95/$4.95 in Canada) The powerful wizardess
Amarino has usurped Ark's throne, killing the king
and sending his three sons into hiding. But an
ancient prophecy foretells a great conflict for the
throne against only one prince . . . in a battle that
only a true Servant of Ark could win.

☐ **Volume Two: THE CENTER OF THE CIRCLE**
(On sale in February 1988) • 27056-7 • $3.95/
$4.95 in Canada) A generation after the first
confrontation, Prince Luke faces his father's old
enemy in a new and terrible form.

And coming in July, the final chapter in **THE
SERVANTS OF ARK** trilogy: **THE MAGE-BORN
CHILD.** Don't miss it!

Buy **THE FIRST NAMED** and **THE CENTER OF
THE CIRCLE** on sale wherever Bantam Spectra Books
are sold, or use the handy coupon below for ordering: